"INTRIGUE AND SUSPENSE REIGN SUPREME" (Booklist) IN FIONA BUCKLEY'S ELIZABETHAN MYSTERIES FEATURING URSULA BLANCHARD

"Buckley writes a learned historical mystery. Ursula, too, is a smart lass, one whose degrees must include a B.A. (for bedchamber assignations) and an M.S.W. (for mighty spirited wench)."

—*USA Today*

"Queen Elizabeth maintains a surprisingly vital presence . . . although it is Ursula who best appreciates the beauties—and understands the dangers—of their splendid age."

—*The New York Times Book Review*

"Through the eyes of Ursula, a woman both compassionate and ruthless, Buckley effectively dramatizes the tangled personal and political obligations of the Elizabethan court."

—*Kirkus Reviews*

"Fantastic historical fiction . . . filled with royal intrigue. . . . Fiona Buckley . . . makes the Elizabethan era fun to read about."

—*Midwest Book Review*

Turn the page to read more acclaim for the Elizabethan mysteries from Fiona Buckley . . .

QUEEN OF AMBITION

"Riveting social history in an exciting mystery setting."

—*Booklist*

"Engrossing. . . . Suspenseful."

—*Publishers Weekly*

TO RUIN A QUEEN

"An absorbing page-turner."

—*Booklist*

QUEEN'S RANSOM

"Now is a nice time for Tudor fans to light a flambeau, reach for some sweetmeats, and curl up with *Queen's Ransom*."

—*USA Today*

THE DOUBLET AFFAIR

"Buckley's grasp of period detail and politics, coupled with Ursula's wit and intelligence, make the story doubly satisfying."

—*The Orlando Sentinel (FL)*

"A delectable novel that is must reading."

—*Midwest Book Review*

TO SHIELD THE QUEEN

"Assured storytelling. . . . A terrific tale most accessibly told."

—*The Poisoned Pen*

ALSO BY FIONA BUCKLEY

The Fugitive Queen

A Pawn for a Queen

Queen of Ambition

To Ruin a Queen

Queen's Ransom

The Doublet Affair

To Shield the Queen

The Siren Queen

AN URSULA BLANCHARD MYSTERY AT
QUEEN ELIZABETH I'S COURT

FIONA BUCKLEY

POCKET BOOKS

New York   London   Toronto   Sydney

POCKET BOOKS, a division of Simon & Schuster, Inc.
1230 Avenue of the Americas, New York, NY 10020

ISBN-13: 978-0-7432-3752-9
ISBN-10:   0-7432-3752-8
ISBN-13: 978-0-7434-5749-1 (Pbk)
ISBN-10:   0-7434-5749-8 (Pbk)

First Pocket Books trade paperback edition printing January 2006

10 9 8 7 6 5 4 3 2 1

Library of Congress Cataloging-in-Publication Data

Buckley, Fiona.
    The siren queen: an Ursula Blanchard mystery at Queen Elizabeth I's court/
Fiona Buckley.
    p. cm.
  1. Blanchard, Ursula (Fictitious character)—Fiction. 2. Great Britain—History—
Elizabeth, 1558–1603—Fiction. 3. Elizabeth I, Queen of England, 1533–1603—Fiction.
4. Women detectives—England—Fiction. 5. Courts and courtiers—Fiction.
6. Conspiracies—Fiction. 7. Queens—Fiction. I. Title.

For my good friends
Dolores and Ron

Author's Note

The Ridolfi plot dealt with in this book must have been one of the most confused and complicated ever. The number of people involved looks like the cast list for a Cecil B. DeMille epic. To protect the sanity of both my readers and myself, I have simplified things considerably. This may be hard to believe, but it's true.

As usual, since I am writing fiction, I have blithely invented where it suited me and where the facts I was able to discover didn't actually contradict me. I don't know whether or not Roberto Ridolfi was really married. He is now!

1

The Perils of Passion

There are many dangerous forces in this world of ours, not all of them obvious. The perils of fire, flood, and storm are plain enough, and ambitious men (or women), especially those with armies at their command, are visible menaces too. But there are influences far more subtle and far more charming that can create trouble just as surely.

I wouldn't have got myself caught up in the tangled, deceptive, and frankly nasty events of 1569 but for the perilous nature of love.

More than one kind of love was involved that year. There was the golden-hazy enchantment that Mary Stuart of Scotland was so good at engendering in the male sex, even in men she hadn't actually met. Her magic was so strong that it worked even across distance, through repute alone, and if Thomas Howard, Duke of Norfolk, also saw her as a route to power, that didn't stop him from mislaying his wits in her aureate mist. When that happens to a man, you can't mistake the symptoms. I saw them for myself.

And there was the commonplace but painful love between a girl and an undesirable suitor, and an improbable passion that an aging man suddenly developed for, of all people, my equally ancient and—to me—unprepossessing hanger-on Gladys Morgan. People in their seventies, infertile, rheumaticky, and nearly toothless, can fall in love as thoroughly as any youth or maiden, and that old fellow did.

That wasn't all. There was also a devoted, lifetime love; the total surrender of mind and body that a woman called Mistress Joan Thomson, who lived in Faldene village in Sussex and was a tenant of my uncle Herbert, had for her deceased husband, Will. If any one of those loves had been absent from the amorous chessboard, so much might have been different.

One other kind of love was caught up in the matter, too. Mine—my tenderness and my lifelong sorrow for my mother, who died when I was sixteen. She was Uncle Herbert's sister and she went to court as a young woman, to attend Queen Anne Boleyn, the second wife of King Henry the Eighth. When she came home again, she was with child by a man she wouldn't name.

I, Ursula Faldene, was that child. My mother's parents were outraged but they took her in, and after their deaths, Uncle Herbert and his wife, Aunt Tabitha, though also scandalized, did their duty by us. I even received an education. But life in a constant atmosphere of disapproval wore my mother away. At the age of thirty-six, she died.

I, having the vitality of youth, escaped—by eloping with Gerald Blanchard, the young man who was betrothed to my cousin Mary, the daughter of Uncle Herbert and Aunt Tabitha. I went to Antwerp with Gerald and there our daughter, Meg, was born. As she grew up, she became more like him every day, with her dark hair and her square little chin—and her intelligence. Gerald had worked for an English financier in Spanish-ruled Antwerp, and had helped him to divert a good deal of Spanish treasure into the holds of ships bound for England. For all his lovely smile and his absolute honesty in regard to me, he had been as cunning as a serpent when dealing with the Spanish.

I lost Gerald to the smallpox and came home to England, to serve the queen at court. Later on, I went to France with my second husband, Matthew de la Roche, but while I was on a visit to England, I learned that he had died of plague. At length, I ventured on marriage a third time, with a man much older than myself, calm and reliable, and with Hugh Stannard, I found a tranquility I had never known before.

We had two homes: my own Withysham, only five miles from my family home at Faldene, and Hugh's house, Hawkswood, twenty miles away, over the Surrey border. When we were at Withysham, which was quite often, I always paid at least one visit to my Faldene relatives.

Despite our difficult past (which was very difficult indeed, due to the fact that I had not only stolen my cousin Mary's intended husband but had once been responsible for getting Uncle Herbert arrested), I was now on fairly polite terms with my aunt and uncle. I had eventually canceled out their understandable grudges by trying to help them in a family crisis. I failed, but at least I had tried and they were stiffly grateful. I was also in favor at court, which gave me considerable social standing. Aunt Tabitha appreciated that. Now my visits were courteously received. But my real reason for going there was to visit my mother's grave.

If I hadn't done so on that bright, mild April day in 1569—if, by the time I was thirty-four, I had managed to lay my mother's memory to rest and leave her to the quiet grass and the robins and thrushes that haunted the churchyard—then the events of that year would have been so different.

Yes, indeed. Love is perilous, because it is so powerful. It moves mountains far more easily than faith ever did.

It can kill, too.

There was no special pattern about my visits to Faldene. Usually I went accompanied just by my manservant, Roger Brockley, with my maid, Fran Dale (she was Brockley's wife but I still called her Dale out of habit), perched on his pillion. Now and then, Sybil Jester, the good-humored widow who was my companion and helped me to educate Meg, came along as well.

This time, though, we had been formally invited to dine at Faldene House. The elder son, Francis, had just come home from a diplomatic posting overseas, bringing his wife and two small boys. The dinner was to welcome them back.

So Hugh and Meg had been asked as well, and all of us were arrayed in best clothes and clean ruffs. I was wearing one of the fashionable open ruffs, stiffened with a new kind of starch. Even Gladys had a well-brushed brown dress and a fresh holland ruff. For Gladys Morgan was also in my entourage along with Sybil and the Brockleys. She was on a quiet donkey because she was past managing most horses. I thought it wise to bring her.

Gladys Morgan was an aging Welshwoman who had attached herself to me during a visit I had once made to the Welsh marches. In fact, Brockley and I between us had rescued her from a charge of witchcraft. Unfortunately, the reasons why Gladys had been suspected of witchcraft held good in England just as they had in Wales. She was a skinny, ill-tempered creature whose few remaining teeth were discolored fangs and she had lately developed a deplorable habit of loudly cursing people who annoyed her. Even Brockley, once her gallant defender, had come to detest her. In addition, she was skilled in herbal remedies, which annoyed almost any physician with whom she came into contact.

She had made herself so disliked in Hawkswood that I had moved her permanently to Withysham, but now I feared that when it was time to go back to Hawkswood, Withysham wouldn't be safe for her either.

The week before our visit to Faldene, she had had a particularly unpleasant passage of arms with the Withysham physician. He was a pompous individual who had come to me complaining that Gladys was intruding on his work, by which he meant stealing his patients.

The real root of the trouble was that her potions usually worked better than his. I was secretly convinced that some of his were lethal and that one of his unintentional victims had been my daughter's old nurse, Bridget, who had died of a lung fever the previous winter, probably speeded on her way by his regime of bleeding and purges.

Someone had warned Gladys that he was calling on me, and she had walked in on us and told him to say anything he wanted to say to her face instead of behind her back. He obliged; they quarreled stormily, and finally, she pointed the forefinger and little finger of her left hand at him and in her strong Welsh accent, issued an imaginative curse, expressing the hope, among other things, that his balls would wither and drop off.

I fetched Hugh and he dealt with it in the usual way, with money. He bribed the physician to forget the incident, forbade Gladys to physic the Withysham villagers anymore, and then collapsed onto a settle, literally mopping his brow, while I sent Sybil for mulled wine and reprimanded Gladys so thoroughly that since then, she had behaved herself. I didn't trust her out of my sight, though. If I were going to spend the day at Faldene, so was she.

Gladys was a great trial to me, and yet, in a curious way, I was fond of her. She would always be ugly, but over time, I had insisted that she should wash with reasonable frequency and wear the decent garments I gave her, and she was now no worse-looking than most women of her age. Also, when not in a temper, she had a tough, humorous outlook and a sparkle in her dark Welsh eyes, which had a certain charm, for those who knew her well enough to notice it.

Indeed, if you really took the trouble to look at Gladys, you could see that she hadn't always been ugly. Beyond the nut-cracker nose and chin were the remains of what had once been considerable beauty. Meg was quite attached to her and Gladys sometimes amused my daughter by telling her, in her singsong voice, stories of her youth in the Black Mountains of Wales, where she had often spent nights out on the mountainsides, guarding sheep and marveling at the stars.

Gladys had once, with her potions, saved the life of my dear Fran Dale. Dale, honest Dale, with her prominent blue eyes and the pockmarks left by a long-ago attack of smallpox, had a tendency to take cold and a habit of complaining that she couldn't abide this or that but for all her faults she was the most loyal of servants. For Dale's sake alone, I was prepared to protect and harbor Gladys to the end of her days.

Faldene and Withysham both lay on the northern edge of the Sussex downs. Faldene House was on a hillside, above the village and the church, which was said to date from Saxon times. Aunt

Tabitha's note had asked us to come in good time, "for Francis is full of news and tales of Austria," so we set out as soon as we had broken our fast, and arrived early.

My plan, indeed, was to be so prompt that I could make an unhurried visit to my mother's grave before we rode up to the house. The village people were about when we dismounted at the churchyard gate, but although smoke was rising from the chimney of the vicar's thatched cottage opposite the gate, we saw no sign of the vicar himself. This was a relief, though we knew we would probably find him among the dinner guests at Faldene House.

His name was Dr. Fleet and Hugh and I didn't like him. He was a stiff and rigid individual, recently married to a young wife for whom we felt decidedly sorry. He was the sort who keeps rules for their own sake and, as Hugh put it, "If he doesn't think the existing rules sufficient, he invents a few more. Tiresome man!"

"Just like Aunt Tabitha!" I had said. We were happy to be spared his company now.

There were small trees beside the churchyard, to which we tethered our mounts. Then we went in all together. The place was quiet, or so it seemed at first, until Brockley uttered an exclamation, and pointed.

To the left of the path through the churchyard were a couple of new graves. One, indeed, was not yet occupied. It was freshly dug, with a pile of clods beside it. The other was filled in, but clearly it was recent. For some reason, there seemed to be a pile of furs and blankets on top of it.

Then Meg exclaimed: "Oh! It's a person!" and I saw that the pile contained a human being, and that a face was peering at us from amid the coverings. We stopped to stare, and the person sat up. The wrappings, damp from last night's dew, fell away, revealing a middle-aged woman, clad in a thick woolen dress and shawl and a grimy cap, with wisps of gray hair escaping from it. Her plump face should have been good-natured, but her expression now was one of resentment and alarm. She clutched at her rugs as if for protection and stared mutely back at us. Brockley began to say something reassuring, but Hugh cut him short.

"What in the world is this? Mistress, have you been lying out here on that grave all night long?"

He spoke from concern, I knew, not anger, but he sounded a little sharp and the woman shrank into her damp rugs, her eyes widening, her mouth opening as if to speak, but failing to produce any words.

"The poor soul," said Fran Dale compassionately. "Ma'am, perhaps she's simple?"

People who are in their right senses are usually indignant if anyone suggests otherwise. It worked on this woman, too. "I b'ain't simple!" She had a village woman's accent. "And if I choose to spend my nights out here, where's the harm? I don't hurt nothing!"

"But . . ." I began. I got no further, however. There was a sound of angrily striding feet on the path behind us, and there was Dr. Fleet after all, black gown billowing in the breeze, and a scowl on his otherwise quite fresh-skinned and handsome features.

"What is this? I saw you all from my window, gathered about Will Thomson's grave and I knew at once! So you are here again, woman! Have you no shame, no sense of acceptance of God's will? Have you once again been here *all night?*"

The woman huddled her rugs around her and looked at Dr. Fleet with hatred. "It's my business! It don't harm anyone! I loved my husband and if I want to lie the night on his bed, then you've no right to deny me!"

"I've every right. I'm responsible for the proper upkeep of this churchyard, and for the proper conduct of all in this village of Faldene, and I tell you, woman, that this is a scandal and a disgrace. If it has pleased God to take your husband to Himself, then it's not for you to . . ."

"You don't know what was between Will and me! Thirty years we was wed! If I choose to . . ."

"You will not choose in *my* churchyard!" roared Fleet. "Up, woman, up! Go back to your home. You have a cottage; you have a hearth, a bed, the means to live. You have a son in Westwater, down the valley. What would he say if he could see you now? Up, I say! *Up!*"

"Gently, now," said Brockley.

Hugh glanced at him and suddenly smiled at me. "Brockley's being Sir Galahad again," I whispered.

My manservant was a dignified individual in his fifties. He had sandy hair, graying at the temples, a high forehead dusted with pale freckles, calm gray-blue eyes, and expressionless features. He also had a soothing countryman's voice and as kind a heart as any I have known. He was particularly apt to take the part of beleaguered elderly women. He was eyeing Dr. Fleet with annoyance. "There's no need to shout at the poor soul," he said.

"Isn't there, indeed?" Fleet fumed. "She's been doing this on and off for two months, since we buried Will Thomson. Any time there's a night that's even halfway mild, even in February, she's out here, sleeping on his grave! Why she hasn't died herself of a lung congestion, I can't imagine. But anyway, it's shameful, a lack of the grace of acceptance . . ."

"I loved him," said Mistress Thomson. "If he can't sleep in my bed then I'll sleep on his. You don't understand."

"Do I not? You reveal your mind very clearly, woman. You are obsessed with the flesh, with pleasure that should only be sought for purposes of bringing forth children. It is that which brings you here, that which you call love but is only lust."

"Easy, now. Easy!" Brockley protested, and Meg, troubled by Dr. Fleet's fury, shrank against my side.

"It's true that you really shouldn't do it," said Hugh reasonably to Mistress Thomson. "Or are you trying to kill yourself so that you can be buried with him?"

"Master Stannard is right," said Sybil anxiously, joining in. "You will become ill, if you go on sleeping out."

"She won't listen," said Fleet harshly. "Do you think I haven't said all this, a dozen times over? Do you think her neighbors haven't? I've come in here in the evening and found Mistress Minton that has the cottage next to hers, and the Nutleys, who live opposite, all pleading with her to come home and be sensible, and what did it get them but abuse? You might as well talk to a gravestone! Now, listen to me, Mistress Thomson. If I find you here again, I'll have you doing penance in the church porch every Sunday for a month. You know what is said of women who haunt churchyards in the night. It's said they do it to call up demons and worship the devil. Do you want to be charged with witchcraft?"

I might have known it. Up to now, Gladys, though glowering, had held her peace, standing between Fran Dale and Sybil and glancing from one protagonist to the other, taking the situation in. But Gladys was never one to keep her tongue still for long and Gladys knew from personal experience what it was like to face an accusation of witchcraft. Now she stumped forward, planted herself in front of Dr. Fleet, between him and Mistress Thomson, and looked him in the eye.

"Why don't you leave her alone? What wrong's she done to you or anyone? What's amiss with a woman liking her husband's body?" The words came out clearly and loudly, if in slightly spluttery fashion, due to Gladys's lack of teeth. "Let her be, can't you? She'll come round in her own time and her own way."

"Who is this?" Fleet demanded, turning to me and Hugh. "Your serving woman? Tell her to mind her manners to her betters!"

"Gladys," I said quietly, "come away, now. Come here."

Gladys ignored me.

"There's ain't no such thing as witchcraft, look you. There's just women that aren't happy and women that are a bit odd. *Leave her alone!*"

"That's right," said Mistress Thomson resentfully. "Why can't everyone let me be? If I want to sleep out here . . ."

"I forbid it. For the last time, woman, I forbid it. Must I have you locked in your cottage until you learn sense? Come with me!"

"Leave her be!" yelled Gladys again, but Fleet strode forward, pulled Mistress Thomson's rugs away, and seized her by the arm. Brockley said, "Easy now," once again, and Hugh half moved to intervene, but Gladys's volatile temper had flared and she acted faster than any of them. Stooping, she picked up a clod of earth from the pile beside the empty grave, and hurled it at Fleet. It struck him on the chest and broke, spattering earth all over him, and before either Hugh or I could reach her, Gladys had followed it up with another.

Abandoning Mistress Thomson, Fleet started angrily toward Gladys, who straightened up, dodged behind the pile of clods, and peered malevolently at him around the corner.

"Leave her be, you bully! Leave her be! Cold heart, that's what you've got! You don't know nothing about men and women. Let her alone! If you don't, I'll curse ye!"

"Oh no," I moaned. "Gladys! *Gladys!* Stop that! Come here!"

"I'll get her," said Brockley, and both he and Hugh ran toward her. For a moment, I thought that a most irreverent game of tag was about to begin among the graves. But Gladys, though her walk was something of a hobble, could be surprisingly spry when she wanted to. She evaded them, retreating quickly behind a yew tree. Then, to my horror, she reappeared on the other side of it, pointing at Fleet with the forefinger and little finger of her left hand.

I picked up my skirts and I too ran toward her, shouting: "No, Gladys!" She sidestepped me, however, and then I tripped on the edge of a grave and almost fell. It had a headstone, which I caught at to steady myself, and meanwhile, Gladys, her threatening fingers leveled straight at Dr. Fleet, was well away. "I curse ye!" Her voice cut in eldritch fashion through the spring morning. "A cold curse for a cold heart!"

It struck me that Gladys's way with ill-wishing was improving with practice, if *improving* were the right word. Even when she quarreled with our physician, she hadn't sounded so vicious or so powerful. This was actually frightening. "*I curse ye by a cold hearth and a cold bed . . .*"

"*Gladys!*" I pleaded aloud, but in vain.

"*. . . a cold heart and a cold head, a cold belly and cold breath . . .*"

"Gladys!" wailed Fran Dale and Meg both together.

"*. . . a cold life and a cold death!*"

"For the love of God!" gasped Brockley. He had gone quite pale. Dale ran up and stood close to him as if for comfort. Hugh similarly hastened back to my side and we gazed at each other, appalled. Meg began to cry, and Sybil actually crossed herself, in the old-fashioned way.

Fleet said grimly: "I think there is unquestionably *one* real witch here in this churchyard. Don't you?"

My memory of how we got Gladys away from that churchyard isn't very distinct. I recall that Hugh fetched my uncle Herbert and aunt Tabitha from the house, and while bringing them back to the churchyard, somehow made them believe that Gladys was an old woman who had gone weak in the head, but nothing worse.

Somewhat bemusedly, they added their persuasions to ours and Hugh again resorted to that useful and universal solvent, money—this time in the form of a really large contribution to a fund that Fleet had started in order to put a new stained-glass window in the church.

This conversation took place in the vicarage, in the presence of Fleet's wife. She was a wispy little thing, who seemed very nervous of him, which I could well understand. At one point she did say: "Poor Mistress Thomson! Shouldn't we be kind to her?" but her husband glared at her so savagely that she said no more.

Fortunately, Brockley and Dale had already shown Mistress Thomson the recommended kindness, by persuading her to let them take her home. They rejoined us as we left the vicarage, saying that they had made her some broth and found a neighbor to stay with her. We put aside the visit to my mother's grave and cried off the dinner invitation. Francis would have to be welcomed home without us.

Somehow or other, we got ourselves and Gladys safely back to Withysham. We knew, though, that the news would spread. Dr. Fleet would see that it did. The accusation was serious and no amount of money or talk of weak-minded age could be relied on to stifle it for long. Neither Withysham nor Hawkswood were safe places for Gladys now.

So when a messenger, most opportunely, arrived from a most unexpected quarter, with an invitation to visit London and perhaps consider an early betrothal for my daughter, Meg, we received him with pleasure.

Had it not been for that appalling scene in Faldene church-yard, we might have declined. Meg wouldn't even be fourteen until June. But the proposal was only for a betrothal, with the actual marriage some years away, and there was no harm in look-ing at it.

"We can take Gladys with us and get her away from both Hawkswood and Withysham for a while, until the storm passes," said Hugh. He added dryly: "She's becoming an expen-sive luxury! Yes—I think we'd better all go to London."

2

A Fashion for Marriage

"All the same, we'll have to come home eventually," I said glumly. "I think Gladys is going a little crazy in her old age."

"I doubt it," said Hugh in his dry way. "She's just getting more ill-tempered, if you ask me. All we can do is give people time to forget about her. She can be useful in London. She can help Dale with plain sewing and so on. Tell her to bring along the herbs she uses for the headaches you get sometimes. Meg will like to have her with us. She's fond of Gladys. Meg doesn't believe she's a witch, or crazy, and I fancy the lass is right."

"I wish Meg were older," I said doubtfully. "I don't like these early betrothals."

"There may not be a betrothal," said Hugh easily. "We're just . . . looking at the merchandise, shall we say? We're not bound to enter into any agreement, and even if we do, betrothals aren't as unbreakable as they used to be. We can change our minds if we like and so can Meg. We're not going to force her into anything."

"And it's very kind of the Duke of Norfolk to concern himself with our affairs," I agreed.

Hugh chuckled. "I rather think the word has got round that you are related to the queen. I don't suppose he'd trouble himself otherwise!"

It was true. Few people knew it officially, but these things do slip out. The lover my mother had refused to name, when she came home from court, had been King Henry himself. Queen Elizabeth and I were half sisters. Elizabeth had light red hair while I was dark, and I had hazel eyes whereas hers were golden brown, so we didn't look much alike, but in private, she acknowledged me as her half sister.

We had other links, as well. At one time, I had been one of her Ladies of the Privy Chamber, and for many years, before I married Hugh (and on one occasion, after), I had undertaken secret tasks for her and for Sir William Cecil, her Secretary of State, as an agent, charged with uncovering plots and traitors.

This too had got around, but although Thomas Howard of Norfolk was a member of the royal council and knew of my parentage, I don't think he knew of my work as an agent. If he had, I'm sure he would never have invited me to stay at his London home in 1569, no matter how much he wished to please a relative of the queen, or find a suitable marriage prospect for his young undersecretary Edmund Dean.

The visit meant an upheaval for us. It interrupted the quiet life that Hugh and I both liked so much. At Hawkswood and Withysham alike, Hugh enjoyed his favorite pastimes of growing roses and playing chess, and I, while sharing these pleasant interests, could also attend to Meg's education, work at my embroidery, and go hawking, and forget that in the past I had rejoiced in the heady air of court intrigue and had hazarded my life in it, more than once—and the lives of my good servants Dale and Brockley, too. Going to London to stay with a member of the council no longer had much attraction for me.

The journey also meant problems for Hugh. Like Brockley, my husband was in his fifties, but while Brockley was fit for his age, Hugh suffered from stiff joints. To ride from Withysham to Faldene and back was his limit now and at that we went at a walking pace.

However, Hugh had recently bought a small coach, drawn by two sturdy horses, and hired a coachman—a rubicund, whiskered fellow called John Argent—to drive them and look after them. The track to Faldene was too rough for it, but we could use it on the road to London. Hugh would ride in the coach while the rest of us could go on horseback. We were quite a big party, since in addition to Brockley, we meant to take a couple of other men as escort. As Sybil was a poor horsewoman, she rode pillion with one of them. The other had to take Gladys up behind him. Hugh refused to share his coach with her. "I know you make her wash, my dear Ursula, but to me, she still smells," he said.

Meg herself was intrigued by the idea of a betrothal. Hugh and I assured her that if when she met the young man, she didn't like him, she had only to tell us, and that would be the end of the matter, and that there was in any case no question of marriage for years yet, but she showed no reluctance. In fact, she displayed rather more enthusiasm than I thought desirable in a girl so young.

However, having agreed that she should meet this young man, Edmund Dean, I must make the right preparations. As it chanced, I had lately had some new formal gowns in damask and satin stitched for her, in the clear, vigorous colors—crimson, orange-tawny, apple-green—that suited her dark hair and her intelligent brown eyes. There was a shortage of good fabrics just then and I wasn't altogether satisfied with the quality of the materials, but at least the dresses were new, and in addition, I lent her some of my jewelry.

"But I can take my little silver pendant, can't I?" she said anxiously, revealing that she was still very much a child. The pendant was a simple affair consisting of a very slim chain with a little heart dangling from it. The Hendersons, the people who were looking after her at the time, had had it made for her when she was six and it was her very first piece of jewelry. She was fond of it, though it was not nearly fine enough for a ducal dining chamber.

"Bring it if you like!" Hugh told her, laughing. "You'll find you won't want to wear it in front of the Duke of Norfolk!"

The visit to London would also mean a hiatus in her Latin and Greek studies. "Her tutor can have a holiday, but I can go on with teaching her French," I said to Hugh. "That could be useful if this betrothal idea comes to anything and the young man has a future in diplomacy. If he's in the duke's household, he might well have, even if his immediate background is merchanting."

The duke's letter had described Edmund Dean's background in some detail. He came of a good family with land in Hertfordshire. His father, however, had been a younger son, who had to make his own way in the world and, unusually for a man born into a landed family, had chosen to do so as a merchant. He had done well, and Edmund, though he too was a younger son, had had every hope of setting up in business for himself, with some help from his father until . . .

You will of course be aware of the current trade embargo with Antwerp, the duke's letter had said. *Edmund's father has suffered great damage to his business, as have many such men. Edmund has therefore felt obliged to take employment outside the world of merchanting. However, he hopes that his father's circumstances will recover and that he himself will prosper in my household, and that by the time your daughter reaches the age of, perhaps, seventeen, he will be in a position to wed.*

I certainly knew about the embargo, which was the reason for the shortage of some silken fabrics, not to mention furs, dyestuffs, lamp oil, sugar, and spices, which had hitherto come to England via Antwerp. It all went back to what—I must be honest—had been a piece of frankly sharp financial practice on the part of Queen Elizabeth and her Secretary of State, Sir William Cecil.

They were always anxious to improve England's solvency while doing anything they possibly could to damage that of Philip of Spain and they had combined the two, most successfully, the previous December, when four Spanish ships unwisely took refuge from pirates by scattering and then putting into Plymouth and Southampton. They were carrying between them £85,000 for the Netherlands, where Spanish troops were waiting for their pay. The money had been advanced to Spain by Genoese bankers but still belonged to the Genoese until it reached the Low Countries. Elizabeth and Cecil had had the happy thought of borrowing it instead.

Well, that was one way of putting it. I still maintained an

occasional correspondence with some of the ladies I had known at court as fellow attendants on the queen, or as wives of courtiers. According to one of them, my old friend Mattie Henderson, Guerau de Spes, the new Spanish ambassador, said roundly that she had snatched it, and been put under house arrest as a result.

My husband says that de Spes is an outspoken man, often amusing, for he has a whimsical manner of speech, but he is not much liked, said Mattie's letter. *He is blatant in his Catholic observances and my Rob thinks he sees himself as a kind of crusader, bound by oath to bring poor benighted England back to the one true faith. Rob says it is useless to argue with him—he lives in a world of heroic fancy and all arguments just run off him like water off a duck's plumage.*

I had come across that sort of thing before. My second husband, Matthew, had been a little like that. He, though, had had more tact than this man de Spes had, by the sound of it.

The Genoese agents in London, who didn't care who borrowed their money as long as they could rely on getting it back, said that Elizabeth's credit was better than Philip's and agreed to the deal. The result was that the indignant Spanish administration in the Low Countries closed Antwerp to English vessels and put several English merchants in the Netherlands under arrest. In England, a number of Spanish traders were locked up in retaliation. Relations between Spain and England were now strained, to put it mildly, and many formerly prosperous merchants were suffering lean times or had even gone bankrupt. Master Dean Senior had been among the victims.

"If we do reach an agreement," I said, "I'll be firm about one thing. No marriage until this man *is* in a position to look after Meg properly."

We sent a messenger back ahead of us, accepting the invitation, and were on our way three days after that calamitous visit to Faldene.

We spent a night on the way, dined next day at an inn just outside London, and then went on toward the City, passing Whitehall, where the court was in residence, and traveling along the Strand, with its fine mansions, where a number of ambassadors had their residences and where Cecil also lived.

We were held up in the Strand by a minor procession, going toward Whitehall, which obliged us to move to the side of the road and wait for it to pass. For the most part, it consisted of gentlemen on foot, but in the center of it was a man on a gray horse.

He passed close enough for us to see that his dark velvet cloak and cap had a thick trimming of fur, as though England's spring sunshine hadn't warmth enough for him, and for a moment, I saw his face clearly. It was pale, high in the cheekbone, so that his eyes seemed to look at the world over ramparts, and his mouth was folded into what looked like a permanent and contented smile. It was a curious face, a mixture of cold and warm, wary and self-assured. I didn't like it.

"Who in the world is that?" Hugh wondered aloud, popping his head out of his coach, but he was answered immediately as one of the gentlemen on foot, irritated by some passersby who hadn't got out of the way fast enough, raised his voice in a shout of "Make way for the Spanish ambassador."

"I thought he was under house arrest," said Hugh.

"By the look of it, he's been let out," I said. "And very pleased about it he seems, too!"

We reached the duke's house, which was within the City proper, close to the busy thoroughfare of Bishopsgate, in the afternoon. The last stage of the journey was through crowded, noisy streets where our coachman, John Argent, in accordance with the law, dismounted from his box and led the horses, a wise precaution, for the shouts of the street vendors manning roadside stalls or pushing handcarts through the throng, declaring at the tops of their voices that theirs were the finest gloves, cheeses, hot meat pies, and mousetraps in the land, were an assault on one's hearing. Our horses laid back indignant ears and Argent had to soothe them, in the intervals of exchanging ruderies with devil-may-care coachmen, who were breaking the law and were still driving their charges, clattering along to the peril of anyone who got in their way.

Our animals snorted, too, at the stench from the drainage ditches that ran down the middles or sides of the streets, side-stepping away from them as daintily as the elegant ladies who walked along holding their skirts clear of the dirty cobbles and sniffing at scented pomanders. Argent had his hands full.

The elegant ladies were very elegant indeed. I was realizing how long I had been away from the center of things. Clothes I had thought fashionable were far behind the times. The simple, round French hood had been replaced, apparently, by a hood that dipped above the center of the forehead, into a heart-shape, often edged with pearls or lace, and the latest ruffs were very big indeed. Too big, I thought, for beauty. The new starch had made them possible, but I didn't like them and said so to Hugh, when, at last, we reached the courtyard of Howard House, Norfolk's London residence, and my husband climbed out of the coach.

"You'd better invest in some up-to-date fashions, all the same," he remarked with a chuckle. "Whether you like them or not, or you'll look provincial. His Grace is a widower, so the woman coming down the steps must be his housekeeper, but if that ruff standing out behind her head is under a foot wide, I'm the King of Cathay."

"I'd estimate eight or nine inches but I still think I'd better address you as Your Majesty of Cathay. There's gold thread in that embroidered stomacher and *look* at the pearl edging on her hood. She *can't* be just his housekeeper. He must have got married again."

We smiled at each other in friendly amusement and once again, as so many times before, I was thankful for Hugh. I liked everything about him: his spare body, which always smelled clean; his intelligent blue eyes, his maturity, the peace of our life together. With Gerald life had been happy and exciting, but I only enjoyed it because I was young. I didn't long for it now. With Matthew I had known the wildest passion, but he often made me unhappy, for he was an enemy to the queen I served and had loved even before I knew she was my sister.

By the time I met Hugh, dear Hugh, on whose goodwill and good judgment I had learned to rely, I only wanted serenity and he had given it to me. The Brockleys, who had shaken their heads at first when I said I meant to marry him, had long since agreed that I had chosen wisely.

Even in such matters as the difference between a duchess and a ducal housekeeper, Hugh was right, and the fact that the housekeeper was dressed like royalty was hardly surprising in Thomas Howard's house, which was virtually a small palace full of servants who mostly thought themselves superior in status to anyone else's servants—or even, in some cases, to their employer's guests.

The housekeeper was merely the vanguard of an army. Pages came, maids and grooms, and a terrifyingly dignified butler who stepped in front of them all to bow to us, wish us good afternoon, and snap his fingers at his underlings by way of telling them to see to our horses and luggage. Then he led the way inside. Even Brockley, who usually insisted on making sure that our horses were properly looked after, was overborne by assurances that the ducal stables were an equine paradise and was swept indoors with the rest of us.

Howard House was in the City, but it was a different world from that of the raucous London streets. We were shown to rooms overlooking peaceful gardens, and there provided with every possible comfort: ewers of hot and cold water, basins, soap, warm towels, capacious clothespresses; and for me and Hugh, an immense four-poster bed. Even our two extra men were assured of good pallets in the grooms' dormitory above the stable, while Gladys was given a similar pallet in the maids' quarters on the floor above the guest chambers. Sybil and Meg had a room to themselves with a tester bed in it, and since, in my letter of acceptance, I had asked to have Brockley and Dale accommodated near me, they were given a small chamber adjoining ours.

Later, while they attended to our unpacking and Gladys helped them, Hugh and I, accompanied by Sybil and Meg, were collected by a page, shown downstairs, handed to the care of the butler, and led to a parlor in the style of a small-scale hall, where the walls were adorned by stags' antlers, costly tapestries, and two fine Turkish carpets. Two clerkly individuals were seated at a table, examining some documents, and perched casually on the window seat, reading what I saw from the cover was an English language copy of the Bible, was a man whom I recognized from my days at court as Thomas Howard of Norfolk.

He was little changed, except for being older; in his thirties now, with a few crow's-feet at the corners of his eyes. But otherwise he was as I remembered, small of stature and plain of face. He had pale eyes and a beaky little nose, mousy hair, and exquisite clothes. His mulberry velvet doublet and his ruff were fastidiously clean. He laid his Bible aside as his butler announced us; he slid off the seat and came to us, hands extended.

"I ask your pardon. Thomas Howard at your service! I could not greet you when you first arrived. I was interviewing a lawyer." His smile had a certain charm. "My late wife had two daughters by her first husband, who are the joint heirs to his estate—except that he had other relatives who would like to inherit it instead and are doing their best to seize it. I am beginning legal proceedings on the girls' behalf. At present they're at Kenninghall, my Norfolk home, and I hope that when next I go to Norfolk, I shall have good news for them. Mistress Stannard, I have seen you at court, of course. Some time ago now, but I recognize you all the same. This is your husband? Master Stannard, I am delighted to make your acquaintance. And this must be your daughter, Margaret!"

"Yes, this is Meg," I said. "And may I also present Mistress Sybil Jester, her gentlewoman."

"Enchanting!"

He bowed to Meg and Sybil, who both curtsied in a graceful fashion, which evidently pleased him. Then, with startling abruptness, he took Meg's arm, said, "Come to the light," and led her over to the window, where he stood her in front of him, put a hand on her chin, and turned her face this way and that. I saw her embarrassed expression and felt myself bristle. Beside me, Hugh drew his breath in with a hiss.

Releasing her, the duke instructed my daughter with a gesture to turn right around in front of him. She did so, flushing. He seemed unaware of this, however. "Charming," he said, as he brought her back to us. "Quite charming. Is she really only thirteen?"

"You may speak for yourself, Meg," I said, with steel in my voice.

"I shall be fourteen in June, sir," she told him.

"Marriage ripe?" Norfolk inquired, glancing from her to me. This time I spared her from answering, and said: "Yes, certainly. But we have agreed that Meg shouldn't marry before she is seventeen at the earliest."

"That will hardly be possible, anyway, as I think I explained in my letter to you," said the duke easily. "Well, come this way, all of you. Some modest refreshments have been laid out in the great hall—through that door there. Higford!"

"Sir?" The two clerkly individuals had been carefully minding their own business but both now turned to us and stood up.

"This is my principal secretary, Master Higford," said Norfolk, indicating the elder of the two. "And his chief assistant, Master Barker. . . . But where is Dean, may I ask?"

"Making a fair copy of the draft letter you approved this morning, sir," Higford said.

"Send for him, and ask him to join us in the hall."

The younger man went out obediently. The duke had a peremptory manner with his employees, I thought. I supposed that he hadn't been intentionally rude to Meg. He just took power and privilege for granted. It wouldn't have occurred to him that to treat a young girl like a filly for sale might upset her or her guardians. Well, we would see what Edmund Dean was like.

The Duke of Norfolk's ideas about cuisine were, well, ducal. In the hall, a white cloth had been spread over a long table, on which the modest refreshments awaited us. These, offered in dishes and goblets of silver, included fresh bread rolls, a whole salmon, a platter of cold sliced beef, two steaming tureens of soup, and enough pies, creams, and custards to feed an ordinary family for a week and leave them enough to throw a party at the end of it. Jugs of ale and flagons of wine were provided to wash it all down. Serving maids stood behind the table, ready to fill our plates and goblets for us. I hoped that in the servants' quarters, Brockley and Dale and the rest were being equally well fed.

Norfolk, to whom all this was clearly normal, led us to the table and invited us to partake. He smiled at Meg and added to me: "I am very glad to make your daughter's acquaintance, Mistress Stannard, but nearly as glad to make yours as well, for I believe you can tell me something that I wish to know. Master Dean will be here in a few minutes, but while we await him, perhaps I may question you on this other matter. I believe that you have actually met Mary Stuart of Scotland."

There was a silence.

It didn't last long—perhaps a heartbeat or two—and Norfolk showed no sign of noticing it. Hugh and I were aware of it, though, and Sybil, who was being helped to chicken soup and bread rolls, glanced at us momentarily, as though she too had sensed the moment. I had indeed met Mary Stuart, the deposed Queen of Scotland, currently living in England, in Tutbury Castle in Staffordshire, as a cross between a guest and a prisoner. She had fled from Scotland pursued by the accusation that she had conspired to have her husband, Henry Lord Darnley, blown up with gunpowder, and an inquiry, carried out in England, had petered out, as much as anything because Mary herself had not testified.

I had first met Mary some years ago, when I myself was visiting Scotland. I had been charmed by her. I had met her again the previous year, when, briefly resuming my work as one of Elizabeth's agents, I had carried a secret message to her.

On that second occasion, I had also helped to prevent her from escaping to France, where she might all too easily have raised an army with which to invade Scotland—and then, very possibly, England. In the eyes of Catholics, of whom she was one, Elizabeth's mother, Anne Boleyn, had not been lawfully married to King Henry, and Elizabeth, therefore, was a natural daughter with no right to inherit the crown. Mary believed that it belonged to her. She would have no very pleasant memories of me, and as for me, I would have to remember all my life that I had once let her beguile me, and had thereby let myself be deceived.

"I have met her, yes," I said expressionlessly, after those few heartbeats had gone by.

"Tell me," said Norfolk, and although he was trying to sound offhand, there was an underlying note of eagerness, "is she as lovely and as enchanting as they say?"

I remembered a rumor that Norfolk was interested in marrying her. I looked at him doubtfully, and his plain face broke once more into a smile. "I miss having a wife," he said. "And what a wife she would be, especially if one day she were to return to her throne in Scotland! There have been moves afoot to bring her restoration about—did you know? The Scottish regent, Mary's half brother . . ."

"The Earl of Moray," said Hugh casually, spearing a slice of beef on the end of a silver knife.

"Aye, exactly. Moray is considering the matter. Now, a queen needs a consort—at least, our Elizabeth apparently doesn't, but most queens would—and why should I not become Mary's? This is in confidence, of course." A belated urge toward caution had evidently overtaken him. "It is all very delicate. Mary Stuart is, from all I have heard, a lady of sensibility. I must not think myself acceptable before I am accepted. On the other hand, there has been exchange of letters between us, and she has written calling me her own lord and promising to be a perfect wife to me and to obey me in all things. Well, such a noble lady will have others seeking her hand and may yet change her mind. But if our own sovereign queen will consent to it, then it could come to pass—why not? I am of sufficient rank and it would bind Scotland and England together in friendship. Only I am a romantic," said Norfolk, becoming soulful. "From all I have ever heard of Mary, she is a woman to delight any man . . ."

She was also given to making rash promises. No woman of judgment would ever have made marriage vows to Darnley, or to the Earl of Bothwell, who had probably arranged Darnley's death. After her marriage to Bothwell, public outrage had driven them both out of Scotland. Bothwell was heaven knew where; Mary at Tutbury. The marriage was presumably still in force, although both Mary and Norfolk seemed to have forgotten about it.

Mary, I thought, was of the breed that longs to subject itself to the domination of a man, in which she differed markedly from Elizabeth, who preferred to do her own dominating.

Even the personable Sir Robert Dudley, Earl of Leicester, her Sweet Robin (whom Elizabeth trusted, and sometimes, also, called her Eyes, because he kept her informed of much that would otherwise not have come to her notice), even Dudley, who had once dreamed of marrying her, had never come anywhere near being able to control my royal half sister.

Norfolk was still enthusing about Mary. ". . . such sweet, womanly letters. But I have never yet seen her with my own eyes. So I ask you again: what was your impression of her?"

There was another frozen moment. He was gazing at me like a dog who wants master to throw a stick for him. I wanted to look him in the eye and say: "Unfortunately, she is the kind of woman who might ask her lover to put a barrel of gunpowder under your bed if you offended her," but I couldn't do it. Partly because I was his guest and my daughter was about to be introduced to his protégé with a view to matrimony; partly because it's so hard to disappoint a yearning spaniel.

I had to answer, though. It was necessary to say something. "She has been through hard times," I said, "and her reputation isn't perfect, but you know that, of course."

"Oh yes, but the world is full of jealousy." Norfolk brushed this aside. "Sweet and lovely women are always the target of cruel tongues. I have heard all the stories but they sound to me like no more than a tale of a young woman bewildered and led astray. Mistress Stannard, I am asking, how did she seem to *you*?"

"The hard times haven't destroyed her beauty though perhaps it is a little less than it used to be," I said cautiously. "She does indeed have considerable charm."

"I knew it. I knew it. I have to admit," said the Duke of Norfolk joyfully, "that the reports I have had of her, from people who saw her in Scotland and when she was a young girl in France, have made me fall in love with her already, and it would be no small thing to become the Scottish consort, would it?"

I swallowed. I had no idea what to say next and nor had Hugh, who was regarding me in consternation from beyond

Norfolk's shoulder. The consternation wasn't due to any anxiety over what I *would* say—Hugh trusted my good sense as I trusted his—but to sheer alarm at such a mixture of ambition and simplemindedness.

In an effort to avoid commenting any further on Mary's personality, I finally said: "Are you permitted to correspond with her, sir? I understood that she was kept somewhat cut off from the world."

"Oh, she has her correspondents—John Leslie, Bishop of Ross, and the Spanish ambassador too," said Norfolk easily.

"De Spes?" I said, surprised.

"Why, yes; she is after all a queen and he the representative of a king. They exchange letters with her freely and so do a few others. The Bishop of Ross has smoothed the way for me so that lately, I too have been able to write to Tutbury direct. He will gladly promote a match between us, if Queen Elizabeth can be brought to agree. He desires nothing more than to see Mary restored to her throne and provided with a husband she can trust."

I was most relieved, just at that moment, to hear someone declare that here was Master Edmund Dean, and to see Norfolk turn away at once from the subject of Mary Stuart to something more immediate, although still concerned with marriage, which was evidently in fashion just now. A young man, dressed in a neat black doublet and hose, slashed to show a silvery lining, had entered the room. Norfolk at once beckoned to him and a moment later, he was being introduced to Hugh and myself.

He was presentable enough, that was beyond doubt. He was a little taller than Hugh, and lean, with raven-dark hair, neatly barbered to reveal shapely ears. His bone structure was edged, the straight nose, the long chin, the cheekbones, and eye sockets chiseled so sharply that they seemed about to cut through the pale skin. His eyes were deep-set and blue, not sky blue, but that penetrating shade which I privately call lightning-blue. He smiled, showing excellent teeth.

But the smile didn't reach those remarkable eyes. I wondered what he would look like if he were really amused and realized that unlike the Duke of Norfolk, he completely lacked even the beginnings of crow's-feet at the corners of his eyes. With Edmund Dean, I thought, amusement was a rare event. His eyes would nearly always remain penetrating, and cold.

I wanted my daughter to be happy in her marriage, whenever that came about, and contentment in marriage usually includes a physical attraction between the couple. Edmund Dean certainly wasn't short of sexual magnetism. But that magnetism, like love itself, comes in more than one form. One is the dangerous heat that burns, as perilous as flames are to moths or direct sunlight to one's eyes. There had been something of that in Matthew and it had not, in the end, brought me happiness. There is, too, the glowing warmth that gives both comfort and stimulation. Gerald had had that; so, in a more muted form, had Hugh.

But there is a third kind, which is as cold as the Arctic. Draw close to it and it's like touching a steel blade on a frosty morning. In Edmund Dean, I recognized it instantly.

He was personable, looked healthy, and had been chosen by the Duke of Norfolk, and in my estimation was the kind of man who would marry my daughter only over my dead body.

3

Old Age and a Pomander

"This is the young man I asked you here to meet," Norfolk was saying. "My third secretary at the moment, although it may be only a temporary career. However, he's useful to me, since he speaks flawless Italian and I have dealings with that country from time to time. Come forward, Master Dean, and let me present you to Master and Mistress Stannard . . ."

Dean was bowing to Hugh and offering me his hand. I took it, half expecting it to send a shock up my arm. He turned from me to be introduced to Meg. Meg curtsied, her eyes fixed on his face, which had obviously riveted her attention. Dean smiled at her and spoke a few conventional words of greeting, but then let Hugh steer him aside and engage him in a conversation that I knew would include a polite but searching inquiry into his family, his health, and his past, present, and likely future circumstances. I drew Meg away and encouraged her to take some food. Shyly, she said: "He's very handsome, Mother."

"There are other things to consider," I told her, quite snappily. Behind me, Norfolk was urging Sybil to try the cold beef, and at the same time, I could hear snatches of Hugh's interrogation and Dean's replies.

". . . most unfortunate, the closing of Antwerp. What steps do you propose to take to rebuild your fortunes?"

"My father used to deal with Italy but he reduced that side of the business when he found that he could bring in a wider choice of goods by way of the Low Countries . . . I spent over two years in Italy, however, and once I'm in a position to begin my own business, I intend to build up a trade in the Mediterranean . . ."

A murmur from Hugh and then Dean's voice again. "I certainly expect to recoup within three years . . . as the situation eases, which I'm sure it must, my father will help. I am aware that the landed and merchant communities don't usually mix, but my grandfather, of course, was a landed gentleman. Your daughter—no, stepdaughter, is it not?—will find the life of a merchant's wife not unpleasant. She would be well dressed and would both give and attend gatherings full of interesting people. What languages does she speak, by the way . . . ?"

Hugh moved, turning so that his voice reached me more clearly. "Excellent French but only a little Italian. She is studying Latin and Greek, however."

"Latin? Then her Italian can soon be polished up; the languages are related, after all . . ."

"She is to spend some time at court before there is any question of marriage," said Hugh, a little repressively.

"Admirable." Dean sounded buoyant. "An experience of court life can only be of value to her and to her husband, too. To succeed in any field, one needs good contacts. My lord of Norfolk tells me, from his correspondence with you, that she will have a dowry befitting her station in life . . ."

Hugh moved again and once more said something I couldn't hear. I heard the answer, however.

"I have no entanglements. My father has left it to me to choose my own wife. The maiden is very young as yet, of course, but I can see that she is delightful. I won't pretend that I'm indifferent to her dowry . . ."

"No one is ever indifferent to the question of dowry," Norfolk said, overhearing and turning away from Sybil to speak to me. "But to be charmed by the lady is always an advantage. I am under a lady's spell myself just now and it undoubtedly adds a shine to one's life . . ."

"He likes me," whispered Meg.

I offered her some meat patties and said: "There's a long way to go yet."

"I'd like to talk to him myself."

"I'm sure you will have an opportunity. But do remember that you are only thirteen and that you must be prepared to listen to my advice and that of your stepfather."

"Oh, Mother!" said Meg, with an impish smile that dismissed me as a croaking and joyless old wiseacre. "Here's Brockley!" she added.

Brockley had come into the room unnoticed, and was looking anxiously about him. Catching sight of me, he hurried toward me. "Madam!"

"Yes, Brockley? What is it?"

"I am sorry to intrude, madam. I have a message for His Grace and also, madam, you're needed. Something very unfortunate is happening."

"A message for me?" Norfolk turned to him, frowning. "Can it not wait? I am entertaining guests."

"Well, a messenger has arrived for you, sir. A man named Julius Gale. I understand he has brought a letter from your banker. He is taking refreshment in the kitchen, but he expressly asked that you should be told at once that he was here. And also . . ."

"Yes, Brockley?" I said resignedly. I had sensed disaster.

"It's Gladys, madam. She's causing trouble in the kitchens. I apologize again for intruding, but if possible, could you come?"

Norfolk's kitchens were at the foot of a stone staircase. They were a world of their own, a rambling warren of rooms for every conceivable culinary purpose, threaded by narrow, stone-paved passages with doorways on either side. Mostly these had no doors in them, to make for the easier shifting of sackloads and barrels and carcasses. We passed a dairy where cream was setting and maidservants were slicing cheeses into fancy shapes and then an ale store where Hugh, who had come with us, was nearly tripped up by a barrel. It came rumbling suddenly out of the entrance, propelled by a cheeky-faced lad, who said: "Whoops! Sorry, sir!"

He was promptly pounced on from behind by an older youth who cuffed his colleague around the ear, though not too roughly.

"Watch where you're going, young Walt!"

Cheekiness turned to sullenness. "Oh, leave off! I ain't done no harm. I get paid a pittance and harried for everything."

"Shut your gob!" The older youth eyed us anxiously and Brockley said shortly: "All right. We didn't hear."

"But shutting your gob is good advice, I fancy," said Hugh to the scowling Walt.

"Sorry, sir." He rolled his barrel away ahead of us and the older boy sighed.

"Please excuse him. He's in love and can't afford to wed the girl yet awhile. I tell him, if he works hard and watches his tongue, there's promotion to be had and tips as well and it's a recommendation on its own, to have worked for the duke. A couple of years is nothing at his age. He's but seventeen and the wench not sixteen yet, I hear. But he's the sort that wants everything yesterday."

"We'll forgive him," I said. "This time!"

We hastened on past a butchery, where a couple of brawny individuals in sleeveless jerkins were jointing sheep carcasses with meat cleavers. Next to it was a sinister, ill-lit little room with feathers and bloodstains on the sawdust-strewn floor and unplucked fowl and game birds and a row of deer and bullock carcasses hanging on the walls, ripening for spit or stew pot.

Beyond all this was an archway from which heat rolled out in waves to meet us. Hurrying through, we found ourselves in a huge central kitchen where the spits and pots spluttered and bubbled over the flames in three immense fireplaces. At a table in the middle, perspiring cooks of both sexes were beating eggs, grinding spices, chopping cabbages, pounding dough, and rolling out pastry like so much carpeting.

Brockley didn't stop, however, but led us straight across and into yet another room, which was obviously where the servants ate, for there were food and drink on the table in the middle. Standing beside it, in attitudes of tension, were the dignified butler, the duchess-like housekeeper in her stiff open ruff and her ornamental stomacher, and three others, two men and a woman, who looked like upper servants. The woman was wide-eyed and looked both scared and excited. Another man, whose riding boots suggested that he was the newly arrived messenger, was sitting down, looking worried and slightly apologetic. Finally, also seated, there was Gladys, glowering.

The housekeeper greeted us with relief. "Mistress Stannard! And Master Stannard. So you found them, Master Brockley."

"Gladys belongs to our household," said Hugh briefly. "We hear that there is some kind of trouble which concerns her. Kindly explain."

The housekeeper, the butler, the three other servants, and Gladys all started to talk at once but Hugh shouted: "Stop!" and silence fell again. He pointed at the housekeeper. "You, please. Your name is . . . ?"

"Mistress Dalton, sir. And trouble there most certainly is." She stood there, straight-backed with her hands clasped on her stomacher. I saw that her fingers were folded around an expensive-looking pomander, a ball of pierced silver, no doubt full of perfume. "I was making my rounds and I heard the raised voices from the far side of the kitchen . . ."

"I forgot myself," said the butler fairly. "But I wasn't the only one."

"I think it's my fault," said the messenger placatingly. I looked at him with interest, thinking that even in the presence of such august personages as Mistress Dalton and the butler, he seemed out of place in the kitchen quarters. His voice was too educated, for one thing, and though his brown hose and doublet were slashed only with a muted yellow and had nothing show-off about them (which certainly couldn't be said of the housekeeper's raiment) they were nevertheless cut from excellent cloth.

He was stockily built, with a square, intelligent face, neatly barbered auburn hair, and brown eyes, which were frank and pleasant. In fact, the first thing I thought as I looked at him was that I wished he were Edmund Dean. *This* was the kind of man I would like for Meg.

As if thinking of him had somehow summoned him, Dean himself now swept into the room. "The duke has asked me to see what the matter is." He stood there, surveying us all with a hard blue gaze. "Ah, Master Gale. You have a letter for His Grace? I can take it to him if you wish. Now, what is happening here?"

"The trouble," said Gladys, in her spluttery voice, baring her brown fangs, "is that some folk don't have no manners. There's things you can't help when you get to my age. Things that aren't as easy as they were when you was younger. I can't be changing my linen every minute of the day even if I have had a bit of an accident that no one knows about except me, except that I might pong a bit if you gets up close . . ."

"I sat down beside her," said Gale, "and I was tired. I did sixty miles yesterday and I've come something like forty today. I've ridden from Dover. My employer, Master Roberto Ridolfi, is there at the moment, meeting his wife. She has just arrived from Italy. I . . . well, yes, I moved away because yes, there was an odor, and . . ."

"Yes, you moved away," said Gladys pugnaciously, "wrinkling your nose like I was dirt and I took offense and why not? You wait till you're my age! I told you off!"

"And then," said the butler, "I told her to speak more respectfully and she said that she expected other folk to respect *her* on account of her years, and . . ."

"She does smell," said one of the manservants. "And I said so, backing Master Gale here up, like . . ."

"And I asked her to go and put on something clean, and have a wash," said the housekeeper in a fastidious voice, as though mere discussion of this unsavory subject could worsen the odor, which I could now detect, mixed uneasily with a sweet, cloying scent, probably from Mistress Dalton's pomander.

To which Gladys, it now transpired, strongly objected. "And you got out that great big pomander thing and held it under your nose, you uppish bitch! So I threatened . . ."

"You threatened to curse the whole lot of them!" said Brockley angrily. "I was here. I heard you. You *silly* old woman!"

"I'm not silly, look you. I'm old and I get insulted for things I can't do nought about and I stick up for myself. Otherwise I'd get trodden underfoot like an old doormat!" Gladys spluttered back.

Edmund Dean frowned. "Is this woman," he inquired, "by any chance a witch?"

"No, of course not!" I snapped. "And I should know."

"Quite," said Hugh. "Gladys Morgan is a foolish woman who uses threats such as this simply to make people afraid of her, so that they will treat her with what she calls respect. Gladys, we are ashamed of you."

"And we apologize to all of you for her bad behavior," I added.

"I'm afraid, sir and madam, that that wasn't all," said the butler. Gale shook his head at him and said: "Oh, forget it, Conley. I didn't take it seriously and as I told you a moment ago, I'm sorry for starting this. I'm just tired and I didn't intend to make trouble."

"What happened?" I demanded.

"It was after Master Brockley had gone to fetch you, madam," said the butler to Brockley. "Mistress Dalton ordered Gladys here again to go off and clean herself and then the old woman *did* curse us, all of us."

"She said, *I curse ye all. May calamity fall on the whole bloody lot of you!*" said the wide-eyed woman servant.

Hugh marched forward and seized Gladys's arm. "That's quite enough of that. You come with us now. We're extremely sorry for all this," he added to the company in general. "It won't happen again."

"You really are a fool, Gladys," I said angrily. "Brockley, you'd better take her to her quarters and . . ."

"She's in with me and Magda and we don't want her there no more!" said the woman.

"Then take her to your own quarters, Brockley! Find Dale and get her to fetch Gladys's things and tidy her up." Hugh was nodding his head in agreement. "Go on!" I said. "Get her out of here!"

I was thinking privately that at least it had been a mild curse this time, not the comprehensive and lurid one she had let fly at Dr. Fleet in Faldene churchyard. Even so, Dean looked after her gravely as Brockley, ignoring Gladys's further attempts to justify herself, hustled her away.

"It's all very well, Mistress Stannard, but is it wise to keep such a one about your person?" Dean asked me. "How can one be sure that she is *not* in league with demons?"

"If I were a demon, I'd want to strike up my partnerships with people who could get things done! I'd be after the folk with money and power," remarked Gale. "Just putting the evil eye on a kitchenful of servants doesn't achieve much, does it?"

The kitchenful looked indignant, clearly feeling that he had belittled them. Dean said coldly: "About the letter you've brought?"

"Aye, I've got it here." Gale had a cloth bag slung at his belt. He opened it, took out some folded and sealed missives, examined them, selected one, and handed it to Dean. "The rest I'm carrying north, going by way of Staffordshire. I've orders to wait a day here in case His Grace wishes me to take any letters for him."

"I will inform the duke. I daresay that if he has anything for you, it will be ready tomorrow morning," Dean said. He took the proffered letter and went away. Hugh and I murmured some more apologies and thankfully removed ourselves as well, following Dean back across the kitchen and through the labyrinthine passages.

Wanting to distract Dean from the subject of Gladys, I remarked as we went that Julius Gale was a smart-looking fellow. "I'm surprised he isn't received more formally," I said, "especially if he's carrying letters to and from the duke."

"Gale used to be greeted more formally," said Dean, over his shoulder. "Last time he was here, he was welcomed as usual by the duke in person. Then he set off early the next morning, carrying letters for His Grace, but came back inside an hour, much alarmed, convinced he'd been followed. He stayed another night and was smuggled out disguised as a scullion, the next morning. One of the grooms met him outside the City with a led horse. It was decided that henceforth, he should slip quietly in and out as a visitor to the kitchen quarters. That way, there was less risk of his presence being noted by anyone who might be—well—on the watch."

"His Grace's affairs are so very confidential?" said Hugh.

"His Grace deals with many matters of business," said Dean. "And he has family cares as well. There are always those who envy wealth and influence and wish their possessors harm. Sometimes it is wise for great men such as the duke to be cautious. It is the penalty of greatness."

4

Chicken Stew

"Great man?" I said. "If Norfolk is a great man, I'm the *Queen* of Cathay. No really great man could possibly talk as he does about Mary Stuart!"

"His possessions are great," Hugh pointed out, "and his title. There's no denying that."

We had supped with the duke that evening. The meal was served in a pleasant supper room with linenfold paneling and a view of the grounds, and there were eleven of us at the table. The duke headed it, and his three secretaries were present. So too were Sybil and Meg, and grace was recited by a dark-gowned man who was introduced as Father Luke Mercer, the duke's chaplain. At my request, Brockley and Dale were also with us, seated below the three secretaries but at least partaking of the excellent food. The journey had tired Dale a good deal and I wanted to show her some consideration.

There was conversation but Norfolk did most of the talking, and what he talked about was largely Mary. In fact, supper lasted over an hour and we spent nearly all of it listening to the details he had discovered of Mary Stuart's childhood in France as the dauphin's betrothed.

"One of the Venetian ambassadors said she was a child of exceptional prettiness . . . she had the most tender feelings for her mother; did you know that she fell ill with grief when she heard of her mother's death, even though they had not met for years? . . . She personally nursed her husband, the young French king, when he was dying . . ."

Now, with relief, I was alone with Hugh, who was sitting on the edge of the bed in his linen nightshirt, a loose woolen gown over it for warmth. He was filing his nails by candlelight, while I was already between the sheets, leaning against my pillows, glad that I need no longer make respectful noises in answer to Norfolk's naïve enthusiasms.

"For all his wealth and titles, he seems as besotted with Mary as a plowboy with a milkmaid," I said. "And he hasn't even met her!"

Hugh reached to put the file on a little table and turned to me. "Norfolk's obsession with Mary hardly matters to us. He speaks of it so openly that it can't be unknown to Cecil and the council. It's their worry, not ours. We're here because of Dean. What did you think of him?"

"We've had little chance to weigh him up. Norfolk didn't give us much opportunity at supper! But I didn't take to him, even before he called Norfolk great. He's . . ." It was difficult to put my instinctive aversion to the man into sensible words. "He's cold," I said, finally.

"What I sense," said Hugh, "is something hidden about him, as though he isn't what he appears to be. Well, he's only a secretary for the time being and out of necessity and if he were a thriving merchant, in his own proper world, as it were, he might seem different but . . ."

"I agree. I don't think he's what we want for Meg. She was looking at him," I added, "all the evening. And he was looking at her."

"Yes, I noticed that too, with some concern. So—we are not in favor of going ahead with this betrothal, then?"

"I suppose we must talk further to Dean before we finally decide, but I think not," I said worriedly.

"We shouldn't have come. You were right. She's too young!" Hugh sounded exasperated. "Too young to decide for herself, and too young for us to decide for her. Her nature isn't fully formed yet. And we wouldn't have come, except for Gladys. Ursula, what are we to do about Gladys? I'm beginning to think that after all, she *is* becoming—well, odd, as aged people sometimes do. When we take her home, we may have to keep her under lock and key. Where is she now, by the way?"

"In with Brockley and Dale, on a truckle bed. They don't like it much—they don't like *her* much—but they take my orders. She's been there since Brockley marched her out of the kitchen. She's quietened down. Meg went to see her and asked Gladys to tell her some of her tales of life in Wales."

"We won't have long to wait before Meg really does grow up," Hugh said thoughtfully. "That was very good sense."

"Indeed. And did you know that Meg arranged for a supper tray to be made up for Gladys from the duke's table this evening? She said that the trick with Gladys was to make her feel that people minded about her. I came downstairs before you, if you recall, and I found Meg loading a tray with a slice of game pie, peas with herbs, roast goose cut up small on account of Gladys's teeth, a custard with cinnamon, and a goblet of wine. She took it up to Gladys herself."

"Fine fare to give an old serving woman!" said Hugh, amused.

"Yes, it was. I gather that the servants just had chicken stew, the remains of the salmon, some syllabubs, and small ale. But I think it worked. Before I came to bed, I looked in on Gladys and she seemed quite good-natured."

"All the same, we can't go on like this. Let me think about it. You shouldn't have to shoulder all the responsibility."

"Thank you," I said gratefully. "Hugh . . ."

"What is it, my love?"

"I have the impression that Norfolk is quite serious about proposing marriage to Mary Stuart. From what he said, the queen doesn't know about it. You think the council are sure to know, but do they? He may talk more freely to us than he does at court. I haven't been there lately and he may not think of me—or you—as being part of court circles or having the ear, nowadays, of anyone in a high position. He may know who my father was but I doubt if he knows about my—secret work."

"He's a fool to talk freely to anyone, if he doesn't want the council to find out," said Hugh.

I said: "When I *was* at court, I learned something of his reputation. He is said to be not very clever."

There was a sudden silence. An uncomfortable one.

"Are you saying," said Hugh after a moment, "that before we go home, we ought to make certain at least that Cecil knows?"

He dropped his voice as he spoke, and our eyes met.

"I don't think anyone's hiding behind the tapestries," I said, "but it's odd. One does have an instinct to speak softly. Look, Hugh, what do *you* think we should do?"

Hugh frowned. "We're not here on any kind of assignment. We're just guests. It seems hardly proper to go tattling to Cecil that our host is making plans to marry himself to . . ."

"Quite," I said glumly. "To a queen who is also Elizabeth's rival."

"But he really did speak freely. He calls it confidential but it sounded like an open secret to me."

"The idea of this marriage came up last year," I said slowly. "Cecil knew of it then. But . . ."

"Was it quelled?"

"I'm not sure. I never heard exactly what happened about it." I brightened. "From what Norfolk says, though, he obviously intends to seek the queen's approval before he goes through with it. Perhaps I'm worrying needlessly and . . ." I stopped, interrupted by a sudden hubbub in the distance, of raised voices and running feet. "Whatever's that?"

Hugh slid off the bed and went to look out of the door. Throwing back the covers, I followed him. Our door opened on a wide passage, lit at night with lamps. In one direction, the passage led to the staircase down to the hall and parlor, and in the other, went past the two bedchambers occupied respectively by the Brockleys and by Sybil and Meg, ending at a flight of stone steps. Downward, these led to the kitchen quarters; upward, to the servants' dormitories on the floor above. The noises were coming from above. Somebody was crying noisily and somebody else, by the sound of it, was being appallingly sick. The Brock-

leys, Gladys, Sybil, and Meg now appeared in the other doorways, doing up overgown belts and looking alarmed.

"I'm going to see what's happening," said Hugh. "Brockley!"

"Sir?"

"Come with me. The rest of you stay here."

They were back before long, grim of face.

"About three quarters of the servants have been taken ill.
They've got the gripes and some of them," Hugh said, "are clearing their systems both ends, if you take my meaning. And"—his
eye fell grimly on Gladys, who was still at Dale's side in the bedchamber doorway—"there's a hysterical maidservant or two
talking about witchcraft and being cursed by . . . er . . . Mistress
Morgan that came with the Stannards."

"By that old hag, I s'pose you mean," said Gladys. "You
wouldn't repeat it but that's what they called me, I don't doubt."

"Witchcraft be damned," said Brockley. "I've been down to
the kitchen. There's four more scullions down there—they sleep
there to guard the fire. They're as sick as dogs but they pointed
out a pot of the stew they had at supper. There's some left.
Chicken stew, it is, one of them told me, in between fits of retch-
ing, and I had a sniff at it. That chicken was past its best. I could
smell it. Curses, indeed!"

"And I know what to do for them all, or at least what might
help. Pity there's not much chance they'll ask me!" Gladys
growled.

She would have turned back into the bedchamber, except
that I caught hold of her. "Gladys, what would help? Quick,
tell me!"

"Clear it out of them, what else? Warm salt water. That'll
bring it up. Empty their stomachs right out. Then clean well
water to wash 'em through. I'm going back to bed."

"Come on," I said. "Dale, Meg, Sybil. Let's see what we can
do! Upstairs first!"

"I'll go to the kitchens and help the fellows there," Brockley
said.

The scene in the servants' dormitories upstairs was highly
unpleasant. There was one for the menservants and another for

the women, with a dozen or more occupants in each. In both rooms, someone had managed to light candles, so we could at least see what we were about. Everyone hadn't been stricken and those who were not were trying to help the less fortunate, most of whom were either crouching on chamber pots or leaning over basins. There was a hideous smell of vomit and excreta.

Hugh and I rapped out questions and counted heads and then, with Meg, Sybil, and Dale behind us, we rushed down to the kitchens. As we reached the foot of the steps, we heard more sounds of distress coming from a passageway to the left and we veered along it to investigate. Discovering two doors, opposite to each other, we plunged through one and found ourselves in what looked like the butler Conley's suite. It was empty, however, and we now realized that the noises came from beyond the other doorway. This proved to be the housekeeper's domain. Conley, looking slightly green but not violently ill, was there, holding Mistress Dalton's head as she threw up into an earthenware bowl.

"It was the stew," he said shortly as we came in, and his usual dignified tones had slipped, revealing a down-to-earth London accent and a down-to-earth mind to go with it. "It's happened before, with chickens. The cooks plunge the carcasses into boiling water before they pluck 'em, to make plucking easier . . ."

I nodded. During a secret assignment that had obliged me to work in a pie shop, I had learned a good deal about the art of plucking poultry. After immersion in boiling water, the feathers came out easily if pulled against the grain. But the exposure to heat also meant that the meat didn't keep for long. Chickens treated in such a way had to be cooked promptly.

". . . all the plucking for the day is done in the morning and birds not used for dinner go on one of what I call the supper shelves in the larder. There's dinner shelves, too. Anything that's being kept for tomorrow's dinner is put there, but it shouldn't ever include chicken. We never hang plucked poultry, either. But mistakes can happen, like I said. Some careless lad or lass puts a plucked chicken on the shelf for tomorrow's dinner instead of today's supper, and no one notices because they're always busy and our chief cook always wants everything done yesterday if not last week, and the chicken'll still be there next day, by which time it's started going off, and some not very bright novice cook . . ."

Here, Conley went off at a tangent. "They're never bright when they're novices. Our head cook scares them senseless sometimes; wallops the shit out of them if they do things wrong. Well, the young have got to be trained but you can go too far with these things."

He shook his head and came back to the point. "So some young kitchen hand in a fluster and a hurry, probably being shouted at, takes things off the dinner shelf and puts them on a kitchen table and doesn't think to ask if that chicken ought to be there. Or maybe hasn't yet learned enough to know. And the morning's supply of poultry is being plucked and dumped on the kitchen table too, and before you know where you are, a bad bird's found its way into the stew. I didn't have much stew myself," he added. "There was salmon and I like that better. And I don't want to hear any nonsense about curses, either!"

Mistress Dalton groaned but whether in agreement or otherwise, it was impossible to tell. Gladys would have a supporter in Conley, though. "We'll do what we can, mistress," Hugh said, and rushed us all out again and on to the kitchen.

Here we found the four scullions and Brockley. The fire had been banked but Brockley had livened it up and set water to warm. One of the scullions—in fact, it was young Walt—had recovered enough to stumble about, getting out salt, trays, cups, and jugs, and Brockley was just coming back from the well with a fresh pail of water. We had dosed the remaining three scullions and Mistress Dalton, and Brockley was looking after the scullions while the rest of us were clattering beakers and jugs onto trays to take upstairs, when Edmund Dean arrived, his hair on end and a brocade bedgown tied anyhow round his middle.

"This is appalling! The racket woke the duke and all of us secretaries. I've just been to the servants' rooms. They said you were here, getting remedies together. Julius Gale needs them too—he's ill as well!"

"Badly?" I asked.

"Yes, very badly! I've just been to his room—it's the people who ate supper down here who are ill, and he was among them—and if we don't do something quickly, I think he's so sick, he could die!"

"Is he vomiting?" I asked in practical tones.

"No. He keeps trying but he can't. He's sweating, holding his stomach, and throwing himself about. He's only half conscious! He can't purge himself either."

"Dale and I will see that the servants upstairs are looked after. We know what to do," said Sybil briskly. "Leave it to us, Mistress Stannard. You go and see to Gale."

"Thank you, Sybil. Meg, go and fetch Gladys. She's got the makings of medicines with her. Master Gale may need a purge."

"Not Gladys!" said Dean. "She cursed all the servants and Gale as well and it could be that . . ."

"Nonsense," said Hugh. "They've eaten chicken that's been kept too long, that's all. Gladys is clever at physicking people. Go, Meg!"

Meg sped off. Sybil and Dale each seized a loaded tray and made off up the stairs in her wake. Dean stood glaring at us.

"I don't agree with this!" he said angrily. "That Gladys creature shouldn't go near any of the sick. If harm comes of it, it's on your heads."

"I daresay our heads will survive," snapped Hugh. "Are you ready, Ursula? We'd better hurry."

5

The Significance of a Cipher

Hugh's stiff joints were painful for him on stairs, and Dean took over his tray, which held a goblet of salt water and a basin. Then, however, we had to make what haste we could, to keep up as Dean led the way back to the passageway past our room, on across the head of the main stairs and into another wing with a further wide corridor, where Higford, the senior secretary, now appeared, holding up a branched candlestick with four lit candles in it and looking anxious.

"Thank God you're here. The duke is awake; he knows Gale is ill and he values Gale highly. Come in, quickly!"

We crowded into Gale's room on Higford's heels. There was just one bed; the messenger had been given a small guest chamber to himself. The only light came from Higford's candlestick and a second, similar one on a table, and the glow of a dying fire. Much of the room was in shadow, and the shadows were full of anguish. Master Gale was very sick indeed and his pain was almost palpable.

Hugh went to fetch more light. I put my arm round the patient, placed the basin before him and set about dosing him with the salt water. A few minutes later, Gladys arrived with a nasty-smelling herbal purge. We set about getting that into him, too.

I didn't know how near to death Julius Gale really was. He was a healthy young man, after all. We tended him, though, through the small hours when human vitality is always at its lowest and the whole world feels dead and haunted. Wavering candlelight and distorted shadows make that feeling stronger. If we weren't actually fighting for Gale's life, we felt as though we were. The struggle lasted until dawn and at one point Hugh did say, uncertainly: "Should we send for the chaplain?" However, Gale himself chose to emerge from near unconsciousness just at that moment and said, clearly if weakly: "No, thank you."

By daybreak we had won. The gripes and the nausea, brought on by the salt water and Gladys's potion, had done their work and ceased. We had found some clean sheets in a chest under the window seat and changed the bedding. Once he could answer questions, we learned that being, as I said, a healthy young man, he had an appetite to match, especially after that long ride from Dover, and had eaten not one but three helpings of the wretched stew.

In the morning, by which time we ourselves were utterly exhausted, we handed him over to a couple of servants who, like the butler, had patronized the salmon rather than the stew and were not affected. Dean, who had left us and gone to bed just before dawn, came back and said that he would keep an eye on Gale and his attendants and we retired to our beds. We woke in time for a late dinner with a harassed and apologetic duke, who was so horrified that such a thing could have happened in his kitchens that we found ourselves comforting him as though he were an upset child, with Hugh patting his shoulder while I poured him a glass of wine and made reassuring noises.

Most of the servants were recovering by then, and so, we heard, were three people from outside, who had chanced to eat with them the previous evening.

It seemed that the duke regarded the servants' quarters as an establishment separate from his own and never queried their visitors. Indeed, he was generous enough to give Conley an allowance for kitchen hospitality. If a beggar came to the door, he wasn't chased away at the end of a broom but sent away with food; and if the servants had friends, such friends were welcome—at least as long as the allowance held out—to share their meals.

As a result, strangers apparently wandered freely in and out of Thomas Howard's house. Apart from stray beggars at the back door, tradesmen, town criers, night watchmen, off-duty servants from neighboring houses dropped in regularly. Beside that, the duke himself often had visitors who came accompanied by their own servants, who would also be entertained there. Brockley and Dale, who had eaten with us, had been lucky. Last night's disaster had laid low one night watchman, the assistant butler from a nearby merchant's house, and the aunt of one of Norfolk's maidservants.

Gale, however, was still far from well. During the morning, we heard, he had suffered a renewed bout of nausea and gripes, and in the afternoon, Sybil and I went together to sit with him. We found him feverish, and fretting because his journey north was being delayed.

"You cannot set out until you've recovered," Sybil told him. "How would it help your employers if you were taken ill on the road?"

"I've got letters to deliver from my master, and His Grace, the duke, has given me letters as well and . . ." His eyes widened. "Dear God, where did I put them? I can't remember!" He sat up, swinging his legs over the edge of the bed. "I must make sure they're safe. Both my master and the duke especially charged me to take care of them and . . ."

He stood up, sagged, sat down again with a thud, and grabbed for the basin, which was waiting on a table by the bed. I held it for him while Sybil wrung out a napkin in the warm water that we had ready on the washstand. When he lifted his head, Sybil gently wiped the sweat from his pallid face. "Better out than in," she said encouragingly.

"Maybe, but it's taking the strength out of me. My legs feel like wet string. I can't stand. Will one of you go through my things and try to find those letters? I must know where they are."

"Come. Get back into bed," I said, lifting his ankles, to swing them up. "You need to sleep if you can."

"Yes, but the letters!"

"We'll find them," said Sybil, catching my eye. Her expression said *Better do as he wants otherwise he won't rest.*

We took some time to find them because we began by examining his doublet. I was in the habit of wearing open-fronted overskirts and when I was working as an agent, I stitched pouches inside them, in which I could carry such things as money, confidential documents, a small dagger, and a set of lockpicks. My mind worked in terms of hidden pouches. There were none, however, in Master Gale's garments. We didn't find what we were looking for until Sybil came upon his saddlebags pushed into the corner of a clothespress, and drew them out. The letters were in one of the compartments, three of them, tied together with a silk cord. We carried them to the bed so that Gale could check that they were all there.

With a sigh of relief, he said that they were. He tucked them under his pillow and then, with a hot brick wrapped in flannel pressed against his stomach to comfort his aching abdominal muscles, he slept.

Presently, when we felt fairly sure that he was mending, we handed our watch back to the servants who had looked after him in the morning, and went out. Once outside the door, we exchanged glances. "May I come to your room, with you, Mistress Stannard?" said Sybil.

Sybil and I were good friends. She was a mature woman who had seen trouble in her life and overcome it. She wasn't handsome, since her features had a curious quality, as though they had been compressed between a board under her chin and a heavy weight on top of her head so that her mouth and nostrils were a fraction too wide and her eyebrows swept out too far toward her temples. Yet hers was a face with strength and a surprising amount of attraction. I was very fond of Sybil and trusted her just as I trusted Hugh, or Brockley. She knew about my past adventures. I led the way to Hugh's and my chamber. No one was there save for ourselves. We stood looking at each other. "Sybil?" I said.

"I take it that you noticed too," said Sybil. "Those letters."

"One was addressed to the Earl of Moray, Regent of Scotland," I said. "I take it the seal is that of Gale's employer. He's called Ridolfi. I think he's a banker. Well, a man in Moray's position might well be in touch with a banker. That seems natural enough. The letter with Norfolk's seal on it, addressed to My Lady Mary Stuart, is natural enough as well. He told us he was corresponding with her direct, and Gale mentioned that he meant to travel by way of Staffordshire. But that third one . . ."

"Had a superscription which was nothing but a row of figures. A cipher of some kind, I suppose," said Sybil. "In which case, what's inside is probably in cipher as well."

"The seal was the same as the one on the letter to Moray," I said. "Presumably it was Ridolfi's again. We don't know who it was for, but most probably either Mary or Moray."

"In *cipher,*" repeated Sybil, driving the point home.

People only write letters in cipher in order to hide something. When such a letter is bundled together with missives to people like the Scottish regent and the deposed Scottish queen, in a world where the said queen is ardently scheming to get herself back on to the Scottish throne and also on to that of England, if she can possibly manage it, then the presence of the cipher is a warning signal. Both Sybil and I knew it.

Obliquely, Sybil said: "It would be such . . . such bad manners."

"I know. That's more or less what Hugh said. Last night, we were wondering whether we should report our good host's obsession with Mary. Then the servants started being taken ill and we were interrupted. We had more or less decided that it wasn't necessary, but we didn't know then about that cipher letter."

"We were invited here in good faith," said Sybil.

I nodded unhappily. "And what would I think of a guest who listened to my confidences, saw my correspondence by chance, and then trotted off to Cecil with the news that I was in contact with questionable people? I've investigated and reported on people's private documents in the past, but that was under orders. This is different."

"Is the Earl of Moray really questionable? He's Protestant," said Sybil. "That doesn't make him an enemy to England."

"Mary's questionable enough and Moray is her half brother and he may be interested in getting his sister put back on her throne. If so, then an enemy to England is exactly what he is."

"Are we talking about treason?" asked Sybil.

The word was out that had been nagging silently at our minds ever since we saw that row of incomprehensible numerals.

We were still staring blankly at each other when my husband appeared. I turned to him thankfully. "Hugh! We need your advice!"

I explained. Hugh listened silently and then said: "Let us all sit down. We must think carefully." He took his own advice and moved to the padded window seat. Sybil and I took the settle by the hearth.

"Ursula," said my husband, "tell me all you can remember about what happened when this business of Norfolk and Mary came up before."

"I learned of it last year, when I went north and saw Mary Stuart," I said. "When I came back, I spoke of it to Cecil, but he already knew. He said the matter would go no further, that the queen herself would speak to Norfolk. I was left with the impression that they meant to warn him off but I don't know if they did. It's possible that the idea *wasn't* quelled after all. Perhaps the queen and her council decided on reflection that it might be safer to have Mary married to an English nobleman than to some foreign prince with an army at his back. When she hears that the idea has been revived, Elizabeth may be quite agreeable. Only . . ."

"It's the cipher that disturbs you, isn't it?"

"Yes. I think," I said, "that it's from Gale's employer, who is a banker. It's probably meant for either the regent, or Mary. Perhaps one of them wants money advanced for some purpose or other—but if so . . ."

I stopped and Hugh finished the sentence for me. "It must be very secret, or why put it in code?"

"And in times such as these," I said, "secret purposes tend to be—unlawful."

Hugh's face was growing lined now, with the years, and watching him, I saw the lines deepen with irritation. "Mary Stuart! I think of her as That Woman, you know. Do you know what she reminds me of?"

"No, what?"

"One of those sirens in an Ancient Greek legend, sitting on a rock, singing and combing her hair and luring sailors to destruction. I think she's luring Norfolk! Cecil has eyes and ears in most great houses and he *may* know all about—whatever is going on. But . . ."

"We're not sure," I finished for him. "We've been so long away from court. We're not up-to-date."

"A marriage of this kind . . ." Hugh's voice tailed off, as he thought it out. Then he reached a conclusion. "We all have qualms. I think we're bound to have. But you've been right all along, Ursula. Cecil *ought* to know of this! We must make certain. Damn it," said Hugh. "Dealings with Mary could concern the succession. They mustn't be secret. No, we can *not* just say: Norfolk is our host and so we mustn't report what we've seen. I think . . . I think," said Hugh heavily, "that when we leave for home, we must go by way of Cecil's house."

6

Brown and Muted Yellow

Taking our leave, however, didn't prove to be so easy.

We sought the duke out at once and with great tact, Hugh explained that we fully appreciated his kindness in arranging for us to meet Master Dean, but that we had concluded that Meg, after all, was too young for such plans just yet. "We would rather take her home and give ourselves more time to consider her future."

Thomas Howard, however, urged us to stay a little longer. "You have scarcely given yourselves, or Meg, time to get to know Dean, and his hopes have been raised, you know. He likes the girl very much. Will you not give him a chance to recommend himself to you? Besides, there's Gale. He's still unwell, is he not? And I've been impressed, Mistress Stannard, by the way you and Mistress Jester have nursed him. I wish you'd stay until he's fit again. He's a good, trustworthy fellow and I wouldn't like my friend Ridolfi to think I'd treated his man carelessly."

In the circumstances, we could only agree. Concerned with looking after Gale, I could not very well go out to see Cecil, and although Hugh could have gone, we both felt, in any case, that to go while we were still Norfolk's guests really was in bad taste. However, Gale did recover a good deal during that day and the following morning, he appeared at breakfast.

Breakfast in the duke's house was served in the great hall, but was informal. Food was set out on a sideboard and when people came out of their bedchambers, they strolled in and helped themselves. Gale looked at the food dubiously, but he did take a chop, some bread, and a beaker of milk, while once more lamenting the time he had lost.

"I should leave as soon as I can. I've never fallen ill on a journey before."

"You are still not eating well." Dean was choosing cold chops alongside him. "Don't set off till you're fit. You can make an early start when the time comes."

"I think I must. My lord," he addressed the duke, who, in a gold-embroidered dressing gown, was also pottering at the sideboard, "I will need a fresh horse when I set out. The hireling I arrived on must go back to its home stable and it's a lazy beast, anyway. I'd be glad of a really good horse, to help me make up some of my lost time."

"Oh, by all means, by all means. Borrow Black Baron. Go to the stables, Gale, and ask to look at him. You'll get a fair number of miles out of him at a brisk pace. But Dean is right—you should not start out until you are strong again. Wait until you're sure of your health."

Gale visibly fretted and insisted on inspecting Black Baron at once. Hugh and I went with him and admired the gelding, which was a fine horse, sixteen hands, satiny black with a narrow white blaze, an arrogant head carriage, and the deep chest and long legs that mean speed. But much as I wished to give up my responsibility for his health and go home, I knew Gale was wise when he reluctantly admitted that he wasn't ready to leave yet. The next day was Sunday. He would wait until Monday, he said.

He seemed to be quite recovered by Sunday evening and shortly before supper, declared that yes, he would leave at dawn on the morrow. In our room that night, I said to Hugh: "Could we start out on the morrow as well? I'd like to."

"So would I," said Hugh. "Before Meg becomes any further enamored of Master Dean!"

The last two days had been pleasant enough. We had attended church on the Sunday morning, and each day Norfolk had provided a program of amusements. Henry FitzAlan, the

Earl of Arundel, had come to dine on Sunday. I knew him, for he had been one of Matthew's friends. He was a middle-aged, slightly pompous man with a paunch, but he could be good company and shared some amusing court gossip with us.

He was accompanied by several young men of his household and after dinner, Norfolk organized a tennis match. FitzAlan himself was past the age (and had lost the figure) for tennis, but Norfolk played, along with Arundel's men and Dean and later, the men had a game of bowls, in which Hugh joined. It would all have been very agreeable, but for Meg.

It is in the nature of young girls to be romantic and susceptible to the idea of falling in love. I had hoped, however, that Meg, who had always shown character and common sense, might not be as susceptible as some. By Monday, however, I had begun to fear the worst.

The duke had wanted us all, including Meg, to get to know Dean better and we could hardly refuse. We had to let Meg talk to him. The duke had said that Dean liked her, but since she wasn't yet fourteen, I hoped that he was just amused by a pretty child and wouldn't feel interested in her as a woman. However, he seemed all too willing to stroll with her in Norfolk's well-kept gardens—which, unfortunately, were extensive and provided some lengthy walks.

He did most of the talking. I made a point of staying within earshot and for the most part, he seemed to be telling her about the world of merchanting. That was harmless enough, but once, as we were all sauntering through the topiary garden, where a very ancient gardener, with a brown, gnomelike face, seamed with wrinkles, was trimming the top of a yew hedge into a series of strange geometric shapes, I heard Meg tell Dean earnestly that she thought some commercial ploy that he had been describing to her was truly wonderful and that she admired him greatly. As she spoke, she gazed adoringly up into his face. The sooner Meg was out of his reach, I thought, the better.

"We'd better tell our host that we're going," Hugh said, on Sunday evening, after Arundel had departed. "And we'd better be firm about it."

We did so, explaining that although we had talked to Dean as requested, and let the couple talk to each other, we still felt that Meg was not old enough for a betrothal. Norfolk sighed rather petulantly, but called Dean in and explained our opinion to him. From his expression, Dean's first reaction was annoyance, but he politely agreed that Meg was very young. "Though very charming and I hope that the matter isn't quite closed," he said. "She is at a delightful age. The woman is emerging from the bud of childhood and what a lovely woman she will be."

"And what a lovely dowry she will have," said Hugh cynically, when we were back in our chamber.

"He'll find a better prospect sooner or later, with the duke to help him," I said. "With luck and a little time, he'll just forget about Meg."

And then we had trouble with Meg. "But I *like* him," she told us imploringly. "Mother, Stepfather, can't we be betrothed before we go?"

I tried to explain to her that there was plenty of time, and that the world contained better men than Dean, and that she must remember that once married, she would be completely in his power. "Men sometimes misuse their power. We must make quite sure that whoever you marry isn't of that kind."

"You weren't in the power of Master de la Roche," said Meg acutely. "You came to England to find me when you thought something might have happened to me and he let you go."

"He—allowed me a good deal of latitude," I said.

"It depends on the man, in the end," Hugh said. "We want the right one for you, my lass."

She went on pleading but we wouldn't give way and finally she began to cry. We recommended her to retire to her room and calm herself with a book until supper was served. The next thing that happened was that I looked out of my chamber window, and there was Meg, if you please, chatting among the flower beds not, this time, with Edmund Dean but with that cheeky-faced lad Walt, who had nearly tripped Hugh up with an ale barrel. He was telling her something that had made her giggle.

If Dean wasn't what I wanted for Meg, neither was Walt. I

went down to interrupt them. "Meg, it's time to get ready for supper. Walt, surely you have work to do?"

"Indeed yes, madam," said Walt, sketching a bow that had a trace of irony in it, as though he knew quite well what I was thinking and thought it amusing. He took himself off and I led Meg indoors. We went up to her room and as we entered hers, she looked at me reproachfully.

"Mother, there was no harm in my talking to Walt. We just exchanged a few words, as anyone might do."

"I daresay," I said. "All the same, when a girl reaches your age, she has to be a little careful. It's not fair on lads like Walt, either, to, well, dangle enticements in front of them."

"I wasn't!" Meg was annoyed. "I just went out for some air. It's so warm. I met Walt in the garden. I've spoken with him before."

"Have you, indeed!"

"He's betrothed, Mother. He mostly talks about his Bessie! She's the daughter of a tavern keeper and he wants to persuade her father to take him into the business. There's no son, it seems. He wants to wed as soon as he can. He's not interested in *me*— I'm just someone who will sympathize! He and Bessie are dreadfully in love. I think it's so romantic!"

"Well, don't lead his eyes away from her, then. Oh, there you are, Sybil." Sybil had come into the room, looking mildly anxious, and exclaiming that she had been looking for Meg and couldn't find her. "Has she been here all the time?"

"Not all the time. I went outside and I met the kitchen lad Walt," said Meg. "But Mother thinks I shouldn't have stopped to speak to him."

"No, indeed you shouldn't. You should have stayed in your room as you were told."

Meg let out an unfeminine and dismissive snort, which startled me. She looked so like her father, and yet there were times . . . I had never seen my own father, King Henry. But I had heard him described and he was, of course, her grandfather. At times, I detected in my daughter a confidence, an ability to impose my point of view on others, which was an extraordinary trait in a wench of thirteen. But from what I had heard, it had been very characteristic of King Henry.

"Mother," said Meg, "can I give Walt a present for his betrothed? Wouldn't that be a nice gesture?"

"Well, yes, I suppose it would." It showed a fairly healthy attitude toward Walt and his Bessie, at least. "What would you like to give?"

"Well, there's my old silver pendant. I don't wear it now; Stepfather was right about that. But it seems a waste, and it's pretty and well polished. Might she not like it?"

"Oh, very well," I said, and we made the presentation after supper, though I made sure I was there when Meg handed it to him. He was touched; for a moment, I glimpsed a young man of feeling beneath the cheeky veneer.

"I'll keep it safe and give it to Bessie on our wedding day," he said, as he put it tenderly away in the pocket of his sleeveless working jerkin. "Thank you, Mistress Meg. Thank you, Mistress Stannard."

I hoped that this little incident would at least have distracted Meg from her disappointment over Edmund Dean, but in the morning, she was talking of him and crying all over again, so that we were late for breakfast because we were drying her tears, or I was, at least. Hugh was firmer and told her roundly that her vapors must cease. "If you don't behave, you'll have to travel in the coach with me, because I'm not going to let you make a spectacle of yourself as we go through the streets. We'll use your pony as a packhorse."

Meg loved riding and loved her pony. She wiped her eyes, allowed herself to be dressed for the road, and joined us at the breakfast sideboard. Norfolk was there, but not Dean, for which I was glad. I was then disappointed when he put in an appearance just as we were finishing.

"I have been walking in the grounds, Your Grace," he said to Norfolk. "How old *is* that fellow who's trimming the topiary? Should he still be climbing ladders at his age?"

"Arthur Johnson is the best topiary gardener in London," said Norfolk. "I'd like to have his exclusive services but he prefers to be his own master and hire himself out to whoever he likes. He can look at a yew tree and see what shapes are hidden inside it, and—it's as though he calls the shapes out of the tree. He's a superb craftsman and he hasn't fallen off any ladders yet."

"I beg your pardon, Your Grace."

Higford was present too and I thought I heard him mutter something under his breath at this point. I also thought the something included the word *officious* and referred to Dean, but I couldn't be sure. Most of my attention was on Meg, in case she said or did anything foolish. Fortunately, she had taken Hugh's threat to heart and was behaving herself. She curtsied her farewells to the duke and Dean very demurely and left the room with Hugh and me in a well-mannered fashion.

Julius Gale had left early, as he had planned. "He was off in the half-light, the servants tell me," the duke said. "I told him last night not to be so worried about making up lost time, but he's a conscientious fellow. He'll have taken the north road and be well clear of London by now."

Our horses and Hugh's coach were ready in the courtyard. We had settled privately that Hugh and I and the Brockleys would go to the Strand, where Cecil lived. If he was not there, we would probably find him at the court, in which case, we would leave our horses at a hostelry and hire a boat to carry us to Greenwich Palace, to which we knew—because Norfolk had mentioned it—the court had lately moved.

Meg, Sybil, Gladys, and our escort, however, were to set out at once for Hawkswood. I wanted both Meg and Gladys to leave London as soon as possible.

"Meg has been overexcited and visiting either Cecil or the court won't be good for her," I told Sybil. "Settle her to her studies as soon as you reach home. You know enough Latin to teach her for the time being. As for Gladys, well, we're having to return her to Hawkswood sooner than we wanted to do. Try to get her into the house without too many people noticing, and do your best to keep her away from others. Whatever she says and even if she curses you! Keep her in a chamber on her own until we come. We'll only be a couple of days behind you."

We parted almost at the duke's gate, since those who were bound for Hawkswood were going toward the Thames, to cross London Bridge, while Hugh and I must stay on the London side of the river and travel westward to the Strand. It was a pleasant morning, mild with thinning cloud, which promised sunshine later. The streets were already busy, and once more our coachman had to go afoot and lead his horses.

We had not gone far before he had to guide us aside to avoid a cluster of people peering into a drainage ditch to the left of the road. We took little notice at first. Until I suddenly saw that on the outskirts of this group, someone was holding a fine black horse with a narrow white blaze. I called out to John Argent to stop.

Then, peering over the heads of the gathering, which I could do easily enough from the saddle of my dapple gray mare, Roundel, I saw what was happening at the heart of it.

This part of the street had drainage ditches at the sides. They were narrow but quite deep and were covered over in places, forming short culverts in front of the entrances to the timbered shops and alehouses bordering the road. The crowd had gathered at the end of one such covered stretch. Two men were crouching at the edge of the ditch, reaching down to pull something out from under the culvert. It looked like a pair of legs. As I watched, the rest of the body came into view, sagging limply in their hands. I glimpsed a pale face on a limp neck; and mud-dabbled hair. It was a corpse.

"Hugh," I said, turning toward the coach and leaning down, "I think you should look at this."

He knew from my tone that it mattered. Climbing out, he used his most authoritative voice to make his way through the crowd. I touched Roundel with my spur and urged her closer. When you have looked after someone who is ill, and helped them with very personal services in the process, details of their appearance become printed on your mind. I knew the face of the poor thing that the men had now drawn out into the open and laid beside the ditch. Where it was visible through the mud that caked it, the auburn color of the hair was instantly familiar, too.

And surely, the filthy clothes the man was wearing had been brown originally, and I had seen those muted yellow slashings before.

Hugh was speaking to the men who had pulled the body out. Brockley brought his horse up alongside Roundel. "What is it? What's happening, madam?"

"It's a corpse," I said. "And—well, I think that horse there is Black Baron, the one Julius Gale borrowed. I think—it's his body."

"Julius *Gale*? But, madam, it can't be—he was traveling north. What's he doing here?"

"What's he doing dead?" I answered grimly.

7

Traveling West

There was no question after that of pressing on to the Strand. We were able to identify the dead man and the crowd were willing to defer to Hugh, the gentleman with the coach. Willy-nilly, Hugh found himself in charge. He told Brockley to get a cloak out of our baggage so that the body might be decently covered and sent someone to find a representative of authority.

"A constable of the ward or a justice of the peace; ask him to meet us at the Duke of Norfolk's house. Those of you who got him out of the ditch, kindly follow us. They'll want you to describe how you found him. The poor fellow set out from Howard House, as we did, and we'll take him back there," he said.

Accordingly, Master Gale's limp form was loaded into the coach. Hugh didn't want to ride the black horse, which was snorting and restive, so he took Brockley's cob while Brockley got into Black Baron's saddle. Many of the motley crowd came after us, but they melted away when they saw us seek admittance at the duke's gatehouse. Only those who had found the body came in, most of them nervously, and only because Hugh and Brockley insisted and herded them inside, where they stood in an uneasy huddle in the entrance hall.

Our messages to authority had already borne fruit. As we went through the gatehouse, we heard a crier in the street behind us, proclaiming that murder had been done and declaring a hue and cry after any known footpads who had been seen of late in the neighborhood. Meanwhile, in the entrance hall, the household gathered around. There were exclamations of horror, tears from maidservants and Mistress Dalton, and impromptu prayers from the chaplain for God to defend us against such evildoers. In the midst of it all, Gale was carried to Norfolk's private chapel and laid upon a trestle.

I hadn't seen the chapel before. On Sunday, we had all worshiped at an Anglican church nearby. The chapel was full of Catholic images: an ornate crucifix, several statues and stained-glass representations of various saints, and a very fine statue of the Virgin. I remembered hearing somewhere that Norfolk was only a nominal Protestant, though having seen him reading an English language Bible, I doubted if he were exactly passionate about the old faith either. He was the kind of man who kept a foot on each side of the line, most likely. If he were to live unmolested under Elizabeth's rule and also woo Mary Stuart, he would need to be.

I supposed that Mercer, the chaplain, though he had come with us to church, was Catholic too. No doubt he said Mass here on occasion. Mercer was a sensible fellow, though. It was he who insisted that the body should be immediately stripped, ready for examination as soon as a constable or a justice or their representatives arrived.

I didn't stay for this or listen to the questioning of the men in the vestibule, but Hugh did and afterward came to our chamber to find me, looking irritated.

"The men hadn't much to say," he told me. "One of them saw a foot sticking out of that culvert and called for help from some passersby; that was all. They've been sent away. Then we all went to the chapel. Dean came too and he annoyed me. He tried to say that this was somehow due to Gladys's curse, working again."

"*What?*" I was indignant.

"Some of the sillier maidservants have been saying it, apparently, and Dean is more impressed by the power of curses than an intelligent young man ought to be! Fortunately, Mercer has more sense and so have the officers who came to look at the body—a constable and three officials sent by a local justice; they're still here, discussing it all with Norfolk, who is also showing sense, even if he is a fool about Mary Stuart. He brushed Dean aside and when Gale's body was rolled over so that we could see his back, it was plain what had happened. There's a stab wound, and we found a matching slit in his doublet."

"So it's definitely murder?"

"It was obviously that, from the start," Hugh said. "The horse could have thrown him into the ditch but it would be a clever horse that also pushed him headfirst into the culvert. The wound's small and there's very little blood but from its position; whatever he was stabbed with went straight into his heart. It was done with a very thin blade, and I would say that whoever did it knew exactly where to put the blade in. Either that, or they were remarkably lucky, to kill so neatly with one thrust."

I thought this over. "But—it must have been done in a busy street. London streets come to life at daybreak!"

Hugh shook his head. "He left here in the half-light and he was caught not far from the house. The light would have been poor and the street still fairly quiet. It could have been done by someone who was quick about it. They—he—must have accosted Gale and persuaded him to dismount, or threatened him into it, or simply pulled him out of the saddle, and then, maybe, used the horse as a shield to hide what he was about, while . . . well. Quite feasible, if the killer knew his business."

"How horrible," I said. I was on the settle, with Dale nearby, stitching. Brockley was there too, occupying himself by brushing Hugh's boots. They both looked shocked. "I suppose it was footpads?" I said.

Hugh sank onto the settle at my side. "No. Not footpads," he said.

"What do you mean?"

"His money wasn't taken. It was still there, in a pouch attached to his belt, and he had a good-quality sword and dagger and a gold ring on his right hand. None of those things were touched. But the letters he was carrying, which should have been in his saddlebags, were missing."

"The *letters* were stolen?"

"Yes, and that's not all. What on earth," said Hugh, "was he doing on that road? Remember what you said, Brockley? Gale was traveling west, but why? He should have been going north!"

There was a tap on the door and when we answered, the secretary Higford put his head around it. "His Grace's compliments, and would you join him downstairs? I'll take you to him. There's something new."

Hugh signaled Dale and Brockley to come with us. The duke was waiting in the parlor. He was standing by the table and on it was a small cloth bag with a drawstring. As Higford led us up to him, the duke picked up the bag and drew the contents out.

"Since you brought Gale back, and since Master Stannard was present when the body was examined, I thought as a courtesy that I should tell you what has been found. These are the letters Gale should have been carrying," he said.

"The ones that were missing?" Hugh asked.

Norfolk nodded. "Yes." His small, plain features had a puzzled frown. "He didn't take them with him. Mistress Dalton sent two maids to clean his room and change the bed linen and they found them there."

"They gave them to Mistress Dalton, who brought them to me," Higford said. "I spoke to the maids and asked exactly where the letters were discovered. The wenches said they were in the bag you see there, lying on the floor of the clothespress, in a back corner."

We gazed at the bundle in disbelief. It made no sense at all.

As soon as we could, we withdrew instinctively to our chamber once again: myself, Hugh, and the Brockleys. It was natural for the Brockleys to be called into conference, as it were. They and I had shared many frightening times together before I ever set eyes on Hugh, and he knew it. He was aware of the bond between us and accepted it.

Whether he knew or guessed at the full extent of it, I wasn't sure. I had taken care never to mention the matter, but there had been a time when Brockley and I had come near to being something more than lady and manservant. I had hurt Fran badly, and I was sorry for it. Hugh's arrival in my life was an infinite blessing, for while he was there, the mysterious link between Brockley and me was kept harmless, one of simple, untainted friendship.

I was the first to speak, after a silence. "Letters to Scotland, to Mary Stuart, and one in cipher. All that is suspicious enough even without people getting stabbed and the letters themselves being left behind in a clothespress by their own courier."

"He'd been ill, ma'am," said Dale. "Perhaps it was just a mistake. What if he were still feeling out of sorts—muddleheaded, as it were—and simply forgot them?"

"They were the purpose of his journey, and he was in a great fuss about them while he was ill," I said. "He *could* have left them behind by mistake, but it's very unlikely."

A further silence fell, unexpectedly broken a moment later by a surprising sound from the garden. It would have been commonplace normally but in these circumstances, it came as a shock. It was the sound of someone without a care in the world, whistling a merry tune.

"Who's *that*?" Fran Dale was scandalized. Indignantly, she went to a window, opened it, and leaned out. "For shame! To be whistling blithe love songs when there's a murdered man lying in the chapel and the whole house in disarray! What are you thinking of?"

"Sorry, ma'am." I thought I recognized the voice, and I went to the window to look over Dale's shoulder. I was right. The cheeky-faced youth Walt was walking along on the gravel path just below, carrying a bunch of onions. He looked up at us and grinned.

"The thing is," he said, the grin widening, "I reckon I'm in luck myself and I just can't help it. I want to wed and I thought I'd have to wait years, but I fancy it'll be soon, after all! My Bessie's father says he'll take me on at his tavern as a son-in-law.

I help the butler here with the cellars and I know something of wine and ale. If he does as he says, Bessie and I can marry when we like. I'll be putting this pretty pendant that you and Mistress Meg gave me round Bessie's neck as a wedding gift before many weeks are out!"

He pulled it from his pocket and held it up, sparkling in the sunshine, before once more putting it carefully away. "She'll love it! Life goes on, and that's the way of it!"

He went on his way around the side of the house and a moment later, in the distance, we heard him whistling again.

"He's right, of course," said Hugh, as Dale and I left the window. "Life does go on. There'll be church bells and a crowd of drunken guests to bed the couple in the tavern's best bedchamber, and that insouciant lad will turn from a boy to a man overnight and within a year there'll be a baby kicking in a cradle in the back room, and another one a year later, and I don't suppose Walt will even remember how once a man called Julius Gale left this house at dawn and was lying stabbed in the chapel before midday!"

"I wish I could be half as lighthearted," I said. "I'm thankful that Meg's gone, and Gladys with her, considering what that man Dean has been saying!"

Brockley said slowly: "There's precious little reason in any of this, but I do wonder about that stew. Gale was very ill. Have you thought that somehow or other *that* was an attack on him—someone risked making everyone ill so that it wouldn't be noticeable if one of the victims died, and then made sure that Gale had an extra dose of poison. That would put the guilty person somewhere in this house."

"If the stew was an attempt to murder Gale," I said, "it wasn't very efficient."

"Judging the dose would mean tricky guesswork," Hugh said. "It might be difficult to conduct any experiments in advance! Brockley could be right—though it doesn't prove that the poisoner is in this house. People seem to wander in and out of this building in the most casual manner. I'm always meeting strange faces in the passageways. I wonder sometimes if the duke himself knows who he's employing and who's just drifting through. But I don't think we need to speculate too much. We'll place what we know in the hands of Cecil—that we *must* do— and leave for home at the earliest possible moment, though that won't be until after the inquest, I'm afraid."

"I wish we could go now. I'm afraid to eat or drink anything under this roof," said Dale. "Can't we at least move out to an inn?"

Hugh shook his head. "I'm sure there's no need. The duke is insisting that extra care should be taken with all food served here. It should be safe enough. Besides, if Gale was the intended victim all along—well, the killer has succeeded. Why should there be any more attacks?"

It sounded like common sense. If only it had been.

The rest of the day was confused. I had a sudden wish to go to the chapel and say a prayer for Gale, but when I got there, I found Dean doing the same thing, kneeling by the dead man and too rapt in prayer to notice me. I didn't want to kneel alongside Dean, and went back to Hugh.

Shortly after that, Hugh and I were summoned to answer questions put to us by a justice of the peace, who had by now arrived in person, along with several of the aldermen in whose ward the duke's house stood. When we joined them and Norfolk in the great hall, it seemed to be full of dark velvet gowns with furred edgings, formal ruffs, grave bearded faces, and solemn head shakings over the idea that such a shocking business had touched a man of such eminence as Norfolk.

Norfolk left us, saying that he would wait in the parlor. The questions began. We did our best, but we had little to say beyond describing how we had come upon the crowd around Gale's body. When it was over, we went to find the duke. We found him alone, sitting with his back to the window and gazing at a miniature. He took no notice of us.

Intrigued, I pretended that something in the garden had caught my attention and went to the window, which brought me behind him. Glancing around and peering over his shoulder, I had a glimpse of the miniature and recognized it.

"He was looking at a portrait of Mary Stuart," I told Hugh afterward.

"Ah. I thought so, though I only saw it upside down. Mooning over it, is the phrase I'd use," said Hugh. "The man's really in love."

At the time, Norfolk, apparently realizing at last that we were there, put the miniature away with a sigh and remarked that arrangements must be made for the inquest and that jurymen must be chosen. "And I must send word to Gale's employer, Roberto Ridolfi—he should be back from Dover soon—and make plans for the funeral. So much to do!"

"Can we help?" Hugh asked.

"Yes—send one of my secretaries to me. Any of them. I feel as tired," said Norfolk pettishly, "as though I'd been hunting all day."

The first secretary we came across was Dean, whom we encountered in a passageway. We sent him to the duke. As he was about to go, however, he paused and looked at me seriously. "Mistress Stannard . . ."

"Yes, Master Dean?"

"I'm very sorry that your daughter has left us. I feel I must say it yet again. She is delightful and I still have hopes of her. When you think she is ready, please don't forget me."

He bowed briefly and went off to find the duke, giving neither of us any chance to reply.

"Meg seems to have kindled quite a fire there," said Hugh.

"I know. It makes me uncomfortable. I've every intention of forgetting him!" I said. "If I have anything to do with it, once we're on our way home, he'll never hear of her again."

Dinner that day was late and somewhat haphazard. The duke dined apart with the justice and the aldermen; we were given a smaller meal than usual, served in the parlor. In the evening, however, perhaps to make up for the unsatisfactory dinner, supper was served early. We were there in good time for it, all four of us, since I had by now firmly established that Brockley and Dale should eat with us.

We were the first to arrive, apart from our host. The butler, Conley, was putting wine flagons on the table and apologizing because they hadn't been brought in more promptly.

"I am extremely sorry, Your Grace. I wanted to send the lad Walt, who helps me with the cellars, to draw the wine for me, but he was nowhere to be found and I allowed myself to waste time in searching for him—to have the personal pleasure of clipping his ear," said Conley frankly. "I suspect he's slipped off to see his wench and I shall have an unpleasant surprise awaiting him when he gets back."

And that was the precise moment when, rising up the kitchen stairs, penetrating doors and walls like a cannonball through a house of cards, came a most terrible sound. That was the moment when Mistress Dalton, housekeeper to His Grace Thomas Howard, Duke of Norfolk, began to scream.

8

The Same Hand

I have seen people of rank sit unmoved while what sounds like a war breaks out under their windows and merely nod to their attendants to investigate. This, however, was a disturbance on such a scale that it destroyed all social distinctions. Screams like that fling a noose around mind and body alike. They can drag emperors to their feet and spur tyrants to a gallop. Thomas Howard, Duke of Norfolk, left the supper room headlong, with Conley close behind him. The rest of us raced in pursuit.

The sound certainly came from the kitchens. Rushing to the back stairs and down them into the tangle of little rooms and passageways, we collided with a number of openmouthed and frightened servants, also running toward the cries. All together, we jostled on toward the source of the uproar and found ourselves in the doorway of the shadowy little room where game birds and carcasses were hung before cooking.

Mistress Dalton was standing in the middle of the sawdust-strewn floor. Her elegant headdress was crooked and the opening of her grande-dame ruff gave us a view of taut, vibrating neck sinews. Her hands were clutched over her elaborate stomacher as though to defend her vital organs and her mouth was wide open. She was shrieking at the top of her voice.

It was understandable. Hanging from a hook on the left-hand wall beside a bullock carcass, his head flopping sideways from the rope that encircled his neck, his face distorted in a last, hideous rictus of death and a huge splash of dried blood over his shirt and his sleeveless brown jerkin, was the boy Walt.

He was fully dressed, whereas the bullock had been skinned, but otherwise, he had been treated as just another piece of butcher's meat.

Dale started to scream as well, but Brockley pulled her back into the passageway and somehow got her to choke her cries down. I gagged and caught at the doorpost to steady myself, one hand clapped over my mouth. Conley stepped up to the hysterical housekeeper, caught hold of her shoulders, and shook her hard. She stopped shrieking, pointed at the pathetic thing on the wall, and then collapsed.

Hugh and Conley picked her up. Hugh said to me: "Come with us. Bring Dale. She'll need women with her when she comes to. Conley and I must come back here."

Out in the passage, Dale was clinging to Brockley. The pupils of her protuberant eyes were huge and dark, and her pockmarks stood out as they always did when she was ill or upset. Nevertheless, she pulled herself together at the sight of the unconscious Mistress Dalton and became practical. She came to me when I called to her and between us all we got the housekeeper through the crowd of appalled servants and safely to her suite. Norfolk followed, bringing up the rear. Hugh and Conley laid her on her bed and Conley went for some wine. By the time he was back, Mistress Dalton had come around and was trying to sit up. I took the goblet from Conley and held it while she drank. "That *thing*!" she said, "That . . . that . . . !"

"Drink some more wine," I said firmly.

"Such wickedness!" Outrage was taking over from shock. "Such . . . such contempt! To treat a poor dead lad so! He wasn't a bad lad, for all his pert ways. He worked hard, except that he crept off to see his wench now and then when he shouldn't . . . and the poor lass is there in her father's tavern, still thinking Walt's alive and going to marry her and . . ."

"You just walked in and there he was—like that?" The duke was standing at the foot of the bed. "Can you answer questions, Mistress Dalton? We must know all that you can tell us."

"Conley wanted him," said Mistress Dalton, "but we couldn't find him and Conley had to attend in the parlor. I thought I'd take a few minutes to look for him myself and I went through the passages, in and out of the rooms, and then I went into *that* room and I saw . . . I saw . . . !"

"Have you any idea *when* this could have happened—or who might have done it?"

"No, sir, I haven't; how could I? I've been busy here and there; so much to do, with everything so disturbed; the aldermen and the justice here needing their dinner, and the linen still to be counted after the wash. That poor boy. I never thought to see such a thing in this world. It was like a picture of hell, except that it was real! I'll never forget it till the day I die. Some more wine, Mistress Stannard, *please*!"

"Better get her tipsy," said Norfolk. "It's the kindest thing to do."

When we left Mistress Dalton's room, Norfolk was fastidiously brushing invisible grime off his pale blue doublet and muttering that he was sure it smelt and that in the normal way he never never entered the servants' quarters. Brockley, however, had more serious matters on his mind.

It was indeed Brockley who, with the mixture of perfect deference and perfect determination that was so peculiarly his own, moved the four of us out of Norfolk's house before nightfall and into the Sign of the Green Dragon in the nearby street of Bishopsgate.

"I am sorry to press you, madam," he said, "but Fran is terrified. She has done her best to help you and Mistress Dalton, but if she has to spend tonight under this roof, she will not close her eyes and by tomorrow she will be exhausted and very likely ill. I must ask you and Master Stannard, please, to allow me to take her to a hostelry at once and stay there with her. Master Conley," said Brockley, with unsmiling humor, "has kindly sent one of his *surviving* scullions to make inquiries on my behalf. He reports that the Green Dragon has room for us. I realize that we must all stay in London for the inquests, and if you and Master Stannard feel you should stay in Howard House yourselves, we can return early each morning to carry out our usual duties but . . ."

The four of us had once more foregathered in our chamber. Brockley stood in the middle of the room, impassive as ever, but rocklike, waiting for us to agree.

Dusk was falling now. I thought of the thing we had seen, hanging on the wall of that dreadful little room downstairs. I thought of the duke's fine residence as it was at night: the dark emptiness of the formal rooms, the long passages, some dimly lamplit and some not lit at all, and the cavelike doorways of the kitchen quarters. Candles would only make the shadows blacker, and their flames would flicker and whisper in faint currents of air. The shadows would move and take on shapes. Shapes, perhaps, like the outline of a body suspended against a wall.

"I think we should go," I said to Hugh. "There's just time to put our things together. The duke may not like it but . . . Hugh, *please*!"

"I doubt if we're in any danger," Hugh said. "I suspect that the boy's death is linked to that of Gale. I helped to get Walt down and I had a look at him. It was a messier business this time, and the wound was in front, but it was a similar wound to the one in Gale's back—done by the same sort of weapon; something with a thin, very sharp blade. Maybe he knew something that would have pointed to Gale's murderer, and so the killer silenced him. But the killer, surely, has no need to attack any of us."

"But who, now, can doubt that the killer is in this house?" said Brockley.

Hugh considered. Then he nodded. "Perhaps you're right. Clearly you don't want either your wife or mine to remain here! Very well. I'll speak to the duke now."

Norfolk, to be fair to him, was not offended by our wish to escape from his house. "I'd like to escape from it myself," he said moodily. He even loaned us a couple of servants to help move our luggage, our coach, and our horses. The Green Dragon wasn't luxurious, but I had seen worse inns. Brockley and Dale had to be content with a pallet in an attic, but Hugh and I were given a small but fairly clean chamber, opening onto a gallery above the courtyard, and the landlord offered us a late second supper with a choice of good wines or a beer, which he highly recommended, called Dragons' Brew.

We declined the beer. Brockley said he'd heard of it, and it was notorious for its strength, and also for the strength of the headaches the following day. The landlord, grinning, also asked with interest after events at the duke's house. He had heard of Walt's death already.

"I've noticed before," I said to Hugh, "that innkeepers are always first with the news. Do they have some kind of private signaling system?"

"No. They just have customers in from the houses round-about, and the customers talk in their cups, especially if the cups are full of Dragons' Brew," said Hugh. "I saw one of Norfolk's scullions in here with a tankard when we came in. I daresay he was drinking the stuff! And talking!"

I said: "I hope the inquests are held soon."

Over the matter of the inquests, there was some bad feeling, since the justice who was organizing them first of all thought that Norfolk's own house would be a good venue, offering as it did a big hall and a dignified atmosphere. As we were spending most of our daytimes at Howard House, we were there to witness Thomas Howard's reaction. The Duke of Norfolk, his unre-markable face flushed pink with annoyance above his pristine ruff, and his voice squeaky with passion, expressed to the jus-tice's representatives, and in our hearing, his heartfelt opinion of what he considered an odious suggestion.

"It's plain enough that something very undesirable has been going on in my kitchen quarters but what have I to do with ser-vants' misdeeds? To have the inquests here is as good as announcing that this *scandalous* business is connected with me. It is not. Walt's death and that of Gale may be connected to each other, but they're nothing to do with me. If there are questionable people in my employ, I want them identified and removed but that can be seen to no matter where the inquiry is held. I won't have my reputation compromised like this. The inquests will *not* be held here."

In the event, the two inquests, which took place together, were held in what was apparently a normal venue for such things in that locality, an upper room at another Bishopsgate inn, the Black Bull.

We expected the proceedings to be lengthy but they were not. It took only a short time to establish that Gale had died of a stab wound in the back, made by a thin blade—"but such a blade can kill, if thrust into the heart," said the coroner, who was himself a former soldier. Then the court heard the witnesses who had found Gale's body and established that he had not been robbed of his valuables. The jury quickly concluded that the attack on him had either sprung from a personal feud of some kind or else was an attempt to get hold of confidential letters that he should have been carrying, but which had been left behind in his clothespress in Norfolk's house.

The letters were not produced. Norfolk declared that they were of a highly private nature and had already been sent on their way in the care of one of his own messengers. He added, however, that only one was from himself. Two had been written by Roberto Ridolfi, a banker. All three were addressed to people of eminence and were to do with money. He was not at liberty to say more.

Further details were not requested. I looked at Hugh and he at me. No one had mentioned ciphers and we were both privately convinced that Norfolk's letter at least wasn't concerned with money at all, but with courtship. However, neither of us had actually read any of the letters and we could hardly stand up in the courtroom and declare that we had reason to suspect (though without proof) that our gracious host, the noble Duke of Norfolk, was telling lies.

The three secretaries all bore the duke's testimony out and Edmund Dean didn't mention witchcraft. One of the maidservants, describing how the letters had been found, did start to talk about it but was cut short by the coroner, who as well as being a former soldier, was also a solid and hardheaded man in the middle years and thoroughly experienced in his present post.

"We're talking of dagger wounds and letters concerning financial affairs, young woman. This is not the time or place for beldames' gossip."

It was agreed, by coroner and jury alike, that there was nothing to show whether the letters had been left behind deliberately or in error, by a man who had been ill and perhaps was still not himself. The verdict was murder by a person or persons unknown and further inquiries, said the coroner, must be set afoot.

When the inquest reached Walt, it was quickly decided that he had probably died by the same hand and that he had probably known something dangerous to Gale's killer. This was borne out by one witness whose brief testimony moved my heart. It was the girl Bessie, who had been betrothed to Walt. She was dressed in black, except for her white cap and small ruff, and she was very young. I remembered hearing that she wasn't yet sixteen. I could tell that she found the official atmosphere frightening. Nevertheless, she kept her small square chin raised, and though her voice trembled when she spoke, she made herself heard and she didn't stammer.

Walt had told her, she said, that he had come into some money. On the day of his death he had come to her father's tavern early in the morning and talked with her father, who had agreed that if Walt would put some of his legacy into the tavern, he could become a junior partner in the business, and could marry Bessie whenever the two of them chose.

Her father, following her as a witness, said that Bessie's account was right, and two of Norfolk's menservants agreed that Walt had indeed gone out early that day, and that he had been saying he would be able to marry soon, although he hadn't mentioned any legacy and as far they knew, there was no question of such a thing.

From all of this, the coroner remarked, it seemed a fair guess that Walt was hoping to obtain money from Julius Gale's possible killer, and that he had met whoever it was under Norfolk's roof.

Norfolk's servants were then questioned, and the easygoing habits of the servants' quarters, where visitors came and went unquestioned, and the master of the house, normally, never went at all, emerged very clearly.

Some of the maidservants were distressed by the questioning. Two or three of them cried and said that their characters were being taken away, but no one seriously suspected them of anything. They were all sturdy girls but certainly no one could suppose any of them capable of ambushing a strong and healthy young man like Walt, stabbing him to the heart, putting a cord around his neck, heaving him up to the hook in the meat-hanging room, and then returning to her duties, cap and apron still miraculously straight and clean, to work and no doubt joke and giggle with her colleagues as though nothing untoward had happened.

The menservants were questioned more fiercely, but here sheer chance seemed to have put them beyond suspicion. They all seemed to have been working under someone's eye—each other's for the most part—between the moment when Walt was last seen alive, and the moment when Mistress Dalton discovered him dead.

Again, the verdict was murder by an unknown hand, though probably whoever it was had murdered Julius Gale as well. There was little to show whether the killer belonged to the Norfolk household or came from outside, but the latter (Brockley ground his teeth here, in disagreement) was possible. And that was that.

Once again, inquiries were to continue. Therefore, we couldn't yet leave our inn, in case we were required again. However, the duke was in no mood for arranging entertainments and we saw that, at last, we could visit Cecil without difficulty.

"All the same," I said to Hugh. "Cecil must know of this already. An inquest on a murder in a council member's house! Someone's bound to report it to him. Norfolk himself, very likely."

"I daresay, but will he report all of it?" Hugh said. "Will he admit that his own letter was to Mary Stuart and that one of Ridolfi's was in cipher? Would I, in his place? We must still see Cecil if we can."

Then we discovered that for the time being at least, we couldn't. On the day after the double inquest, Norfolk went to Greenwich to attend a meeting of the royal council. He summoned us to sup with him that evening and told us that his news had been overshadowed by other and mightier storms at the said meeting.

By living quietly in the country, it appeared, we had deprived ourselves of a great deal of interesting information. It seemed that earlier in the year, there had been a particularly stormy council session. Sir Robert Dudley, Earl of Leicester, was a favorite of the queen's but most certainly not a favorite of Cecil's and indeed wasn't popular either with his fellow lords or with the public in general. He had acquired the nickname of the Gypsy because of his dark complexion and it wasn't a term of affection. At this earlier meeting, the Gypsy had loudly declared that the queen had seized the Spanish treasure on Cecil's advice and, therefore, that it was essentially Cecil who had enraged the Spanish and closed Antwerp to our merchants, infuriating and in some cases impoverishing the merchants and, in short, endangering the security of the realm.

The queen, who was present, had spoken up in support of Cecil, wounding her Sweet Robin and causing him to look at Cecil as though he would like to kill him. Others of the council then began to take sides. Old scores had been hauled noisily into the light of day. The trouble had been so serious that it was still reverberating and today's meeting had seen renewed hostilities. The queen was said to be short of temper and sleeping badly. The murder of a courier and a serving lad, however deplorable, hardly warranted the attention of a council that was in a state of schism about far higher matters. People were not only taking sides, but also forming alliances, some of them surprising.

"Some of the council don't care for Cecil," Norfolk told us at supper. "He's a cautious, dried-up stick. He's blocked the ambitions of many and will go on doing so while the queen trusts him and thinks he can do no wrong. She'll even threaten her pet dog Leicester with the Tower if she thinks he's scheming against Cecil—I've heard her do it!

"And now," he said, not altogether without enjoyment, "we've got fellows who normally can't bear the sight of each other strolling side by side and drinking together and talking in corners because whatever they think of one another, they like Cecil even less. He's going to be brought down soon." He now sounded unmistakably pleased. "They're going to discredit him. Even he's afraid of it. He's declared he's seeing no one for the time being—he'll be spending his days in his study, writing full accounts of everything he's done or advised the queen to do, to justify it all. It'll take him a long time," Norfolk added, with his mouth full. He appeared at this point to think he had said enough and contented himself with winking at us and taking more wine.

We hoped he was exaggerating but when, the next day, after breakfast, we left the inn and went to Cecil's house, we were politely turned away. Cecil was engaged with weighty matters and no one was to be admitted. Nonplussed, we went back to Howard House.

Norfolk was awaiting us. "I have an invitation for you. My banker, Roberto Ridolfi, has returned from his errand in Dover— of course, knowing nothing of all these disasters. I sent him a note, explaining what has happened to Gale, but assuring him that his letters are on their way. I gave my own courier an armed escort of three and since none of them have as yet been brought back on a bier, I assume that they've left the City unmolested. He sent me a reply at once, thanking me for all I have done and inviting me to dine at his house tomorrow. He is giving a dinner, with the Spanish ambassador as guest of honor, I understand. He states that I am welcome to bring with me any guests I may have with me. I still regard you as my guests. This dinner is to be quite a sumptuous affair, it seems. Will you come?"

We hesitated and he added: "I understand that the parents of Master Edmund Dean will be present. Signor Ridolfi is acquainted with them. Would it do any harm to meet them?"

I opened my mouth to decline, but Hugh forestalled me.

"We should be delighted," he said suavely.

I had little to say after that. Later, as we were settling for the night, Hugh moved his bedside candle so that the light would shine on my face and said: "You don't look happy. Is that because of this dinner invitation? Ursula, don't you see? While we're waiting to see Cecil, we may as well learn what we can. There may be good reason to look closely at Ridolfi. He's obviously on amiable terms with the Spanish ambassador and that gentleman is no friend to England. Nor is his master, Philip of Spain."

"Am I to understand," I said, "that you think of us as being on an assignment now?"

Hugh considered. "Yes," he said eventually. "I rather believe that I do. Even though no one has commissioned us. We just seem to have stumbled into this. We can't just ignore it."

I sighed. "I wish I were clearer about what it is we can't ignore."

"Two corpses?" suggested Hugh.

"There's no evidence that they're anything to do with Ridolfi, or the Spanish ambassador either."

"Come, now, Ursula. There are connections. A letter in cipher, probably from Ridolfi, probably to Moray or Mary Stuart. The courier passes through Norfolk's house, collecting more correspondence from Norfolk on the way, and then what happens? The courier is murdered. And so is a harmless lad, for no reason that anyone can imagine—except that perhaps he knew something about the murderer. Isn't that enough?"

"Yes. All right." I was unhappy. "I accept that we should go to Ridolfi's house, but . . ."

"What is it? You don't want to meet the Deans—is that it?"

"No. I don't really want to meet them and I don't like the way this business of the betrothal seems to be persisting, but that doesn't matter so very much. It's what was done to Walt!" I burst out. "Mistress Dalton was right; it was an act of contempt. It was *wicked!* It gives me gooseflesh all over. I . . . I can understand how those maidservants felt, the ones who kept on talking about witchcraft. I don't mean Gladys; I'm sure it's nothing to do with Gladys. But to do that to Walt's body was so nasty; like ill-wishing someone even after they were dead. Whoever did it is . . . is *vicious. Awash with spite* . . . ! Hugh, there are inquiries going on into the murders. It's being done! We have no responsibility there—or authority, either. I wish I'd never suggested that we ought to go to Cecil. I know I was the first to say that. But now I just want to run away from all of it!"

Hugh blew out the candle. "Come here," he said.

His body, still firm even though he was far from young, wrapped itself around mine and transmitted warmth to me. He held me close against him. He had lately bestowed a pet name upon me, just as Matthew had once done. Matthew had called me Saltspoon because of my sharp tongue; Hugh, more gently, had observed that my name, Ursula, meant a bear, and had dubbed me Little Bear, like the star constellation which throughout the year swings around the Pole Star.

"Little Bear," he whispered in the darkness of the inn bedchamber. "Something to hug, but something that has teeth and claws as well. Hug me but don't forget your claws. Keep them ready for the enemy. It's a dangerous world and sometimes a wicked one. We have to fight the wickedness, my dear. But not here and now. Here and now, curled up together in this bed, we're safe. My dear little bear . . ."

He never roused quickly; he was past the age for that. But I felt the heat in him, felt desire beginning, and encouraged it. Presently, we came together.

With Hugh, it was not as it had been with those who had gone before him. Hugh did not provide explosions of passion, starbursts and sunbursts, and cries of amazement. With him, it was more like a flower opening to reveal a glow of color; or the warmth of sunshine emerging unexpectedly from cloud. With Hugh, lovemaking was always immensely comforting, leaving me with a sense of safety and peace.

Presently, curled trustfully against him, I slept.

Hugh had done so much for me. Not least, he had freed me from my sorrow for the past, for Gerald and for Matthew.

With Hugh, I could rest.

9

Dubious Topiary

All the same, I woke on the following morning with a blinding headache.

I knew why. I understood Hugh's point of view and even agreed with it, but still I couldn't make myself want to dine at Ridolfi's, least of all in the character of a spy, on the lookout for conspiracies.

There had been a time when I enjoyed such things. I had once told a friend that I loved the call of the wild geese as they flew across wide skies, bound on huge journeys, that their voices were full of sea winds and vast empty spaces, and he had linked that to my liking for adventure. *Will you ever settle for domestic peace? I wonder,* he had said. *Or will the wild geese call to you for the rest of your life?*

But I was younger then. I was approaching my thirty-fifth birthday now and I had chosen domestic peace years ago. I wanted to go home, and my body was very loudly saying so.

Gladys had invented an herbal drink that could relieve these migraine attacks, and she had left a supply of the dried herbs with me. Dale made the infusion and I drank it. The attack wasn't one of the most violent, and the pain receded without nausea.

"I've won my battle," I said to Hugh, when he came to see how I was and found me getting unsteadily out of bed.

"I'm sorry it was so much of a battle," he said gently. Hugh knew, without being told, what had brought this on. "But we're doing the right thing, Ursula."

Roberto Ridolfi had leased a house in the Strand. From Howard House, we went on horseback, except for Hugh, who once more used our coach. It was but a short distance out of the City, through a fine spring morning. Norfolk had six attendants including Higford and Dean ("Barker has little taste for what he calls junketing," said Norfolk) and we had the Brockleys and John Argent.

At the house, Brockley and Argent and two of Norfolk's men went to see the horses cared for, but the rest of us were greeted by a butler as stately as Conley but much larger, carrying a mighty midriff before him as though it were a badge of office. He showed us up a flight of steps into a light, airy vestibule with a mosaic floor in a pattern that had unmistakable echoes of Ancient Rome.

Here we found a short, dark man in a deep green gown of velvet as rich as anything I had ever seen at court, and a shy young lady dressed in russet. She was no more than twenty, with brown eyes and a wave of rich brown hair rolling abundantly from under an elaborate hood.

"Thank you, Greaves," Norfolk said to the butler. "Ah. Roberto." He greeted Ridolfi breezily, as an old friend would. "These are my guests, Master Hugh Stannard and Mistress Stannard. Mistress Stannard has court connections, as I think I told you. My secretaries you already know."

"I am overjoyed once more to meet you, Your Grace." Ridolfi's English was idiomatic, though his accent was marked. "But I was desolated to hear of the sad death of my good Julius Gale—and the other tragedy in your house. A serving boy only, I believe, but we are all equal in God's eyes and if he was not among the faithful, who knows what takes place in the privacy of the mind at the last? Mistress Stannard, I see you are intrigued by the pattern on the floor."

I was looking at it mainly to distract myself from the memory of Walt's insulted corpse. However, I raised my head and said politely that the design was interesting and that I liked the blue and green colors.

Ridolfi smiled. "I had it laid when I arrived. It is a pattern taken from a house I know in Rome, which stands on the site of a Roman villa and still has part of an original floor. My lease here allows me to do such things. I have had more difficulty in other respects," he added. "I didn't examine the grounds carefully enough before signing the lease and I fear I am now the proprietor of a topiary garden which . . . well! I have forbidden it to the maidservants. I blame you, Your Grace. You recommended your topiary gardener—Johnson's his name, is it not?—to my predecessor."

"Arthur Johnson works here too," Norfolk said to us. "The previous tenant of this house encouraged him to give rein to—an unusual sense of humor. However, we are all men and women of the world. You should go and see it. It may amuse you."

Ridolfi at this point recalled that he wasn't welcoming us on his own and turned to the young woman, who was standing quietly half a pace behind him. "Allow me to present my wife, who has just arrived in England. I was in Dover to meet her. Donna speaks little English, but she has the French."

We all exchanged greetings in French with Madame Ridolfi. "At home we call her signora but in England, for some reason, everyone addresses her as madame," Ridolfi said.

"It's of no consequence," Donna said. She had a soft, timid voice, as if she feared that unfriendly ears might be listening, and a very sweet face with a carefully tended olive complexion. Her mouth was small and shapely, her nose prettily turned up at the tip, and her brown eyes were wide and wondering.

Norfolk inquired if Dean's parents had yet arrived. "My friends here are hoping to make their acquaintance."

"Not as yet," Ridolfi said. "But with the sun so warm—or what in England is called warm!—those guests who are already here have roamed into the grounds and my servants have had to follow them with their trays of refreshments. I am, as it were, on duty here until my guest of honor, His Excellency Don Guerau de Spes, the Spanish ambassador, arrives. But if you would care to stroll out as well and enjoy the sunshine, my page will show you the way. Boy!"

At the mention of de Spes, Hugh and I exchanged very small nudges, undetectable by Ridolfi, but we could hardly insist on staying to observe His Excellency's arrival and overhear his conversation. Norfolk could, and did, make it clear that he didn't care to stroll but wished to talk to Ridolfi and His Excellency, whenever the latter should appear, but we had no option other than to follow the page. With the Brockleys behind us, we let ourselves be led through a passage and out of a rear door onto a terrace with a view of the grounds.

These were extensive, stretching to the banks of the Thames. At the left-hand end of the terrace, steps led down to a knot garden. To the right, another flight descended to a gravel path between the terrace and a tall yew hedge. An archway in this gave a glimpse of the topiary which our host and Norfolk had mentioned in such surprising terms.

For the moment, we chose the knot garden instead. More gravel paths threaded this way and that among geometric beds, enclosed by low hedges of lavender. A few flowers were showing: primrose and daffodil, bluebell and heartsease. Some of the beds, however, contained deft arrangements of vegetables and herbs, medicinal and culinary, which made decorative capital out of foliage of different shades and shapes.

There were other guests about, as Ridolfi had said, sauntering in pairs and groups, and being offered refreshments from liveried servants carrying trays. We saw no one whom we recognized, but we accepted wine and sweet cakes for ourselves, and made our way on through the garden to a gate in the low wall beyond. With a squeak of slightly rusted hinges, it let us out onto a slope of scythed turf, going gently down to the river. We strolled to the water's edge. The topiary garden to our right didn't stretch so far but a path emerged from it through another arch of close-clipped yew, leading to a wooden landing stage, where a dinghy and a small barge were moored. Close by was a cluster of alders at the base of a small, flat promontory, not much more than a tongue of grassy land, that jutted into the stream, and at its tip was an untidy heap of vegetation, probably the nest belonging to a pair of swans, which were swimming close by. Soon, no doubt, it would contain this year's eggs.

There was shipping on the river, as usual, but none of it was near at hand. There was a pleasant air of peace and privacy all around.

"He does himself well, this Ridolfi," Hugh said. "These grounds are impressive."

We surveyed this peaceful scene in silence for a few moments, finishing our wine and cakes. We were interrupted, however, by Brockley, who suddenly emerged from the topiary garden and came striding purposefully toward us. I turned to him with a smile, but didn't receive one in return. Brockley's normally calm countenance was, for once, expressing a strong emotion—that of indignation. "Master Stannard! Madam! Fran!"

"What is it, Brockley?" I asked.

"When we'd finished in the stable," said Brockley, "one of Ridolfi's grooms, with a look on his face that I can only call a leer, said that visiting servants would find refreshments in the kitchen but it would be worth my while to peep into the topiary garden first. John Argent preferred the refreshments but I was curious about the topiary. I can only say . . . well, I hardly know *what* to say!"

"Ah, yes," said Hugh. "Norfolk said it might amuse us. Let's take a look."

"Not you, Fran," said Brockley. "I really would rather that you didn't."

"Go off and join Argent, both of you," said Hugh. "And here, take our cups and dishes with you. Come, Ursula. Let's inspect the mysterious horrors among the yew trees."

Abandoning Brockley and Dale, we went through the yew arch, and then stopped short. Hugh started to laugh. "Oh, *really!*" he said.

The topiary was outrageous and it became worse, the more one looked at it. At first sight, the yew trees immediately in front of us seemed to be clipped into nothing more than vaguely conical shapes. Then you looked again and, according to whether you were a very modest person or one with a broad sense of humor, you either recoiled in shock or began to chortle.

"The proportions don't seem quite right, though," said Hugh, between chuckles. "I would say that most men, on average . . ."

"Hugh!" But I was laughing too. My amusement was echoed by a chuckle from somewhere nearby, and looking about me, I saw a ladder leaning against a yew tree, and then, as my gaze traveled upward, I beheld two ancient-looking legs with calf muscles as gnarled as tree roots, a pair of patched and baggy breeches, a bit of grubby shirt, a sleeveless leather jerkin, and finally, the gnomelike face of an elderly man whom I now recognized as the gardener Arthur Johnson, whom I had seen working on Norfolk's topiary. Once more, he was busy with shears, improving, if that is quite the right term, one of the shapes. He had overheard us and grinned down, waving the shears.

"Call myself the best in London for this but even I find that a tree sometimes has a mind of its own. Can't always get *exactly* what you want out of 'em!" he called.

"Oh, I think you've made a fair shot at the target," Hugh told him dryly, causing the old man to emit an evil chuckle. The path led on from the archway, and leaving Johnson behind, we followed it. Farther in, the trees were carved into complete bird and animal shapes in interesting attitudes, and in the very heart of the garden, where another path crossed the first, we found a wooden bench.

"Very thoughtful," said Hugh, sitting down on it. "Somewhere to rest while contemplating all this sculptured vegetation. Johnson's a craftsman. It looks as though that rearing horse is about to come down on the back of the horse next to it, and those geese are superb. If they are geese—they're something of that kind, anyway, whatever they are. I'd say they were geese, wouldn't you? It must have been difficult to get the foliage into those long-necked shapes. They seem to be—er . . ."

"I think they have goslings in mind," I said solemnly. "Ultimately."

We looked at each other and began laughing all over again.

We were echoed by an outbreak of tittering on the far side of the garden. Others besides ourselves were roaming amid the topiary. A movement near at hand caught our attention and as we turned, an elderly gentleman strolled out from behind the romantically inclined geese.

"Ah! A seat. I've been gazing about me, thunderstruck. One could call this place a glimpse of the underside of the human imagination," he remarked gravely, though his eyes were twinkling.

He was surely over seventy, with iron gray hair, thick though tidily trimmed, and an intellectual air. His forehead was high and he had a thoughtful, somewhat furrowed face with heavy brows and a small pointed beard. He was dressed as a scholar might be, in a long, dark robe and he wore no ruff, only a voile collar. He bowed politely.

"Master Harry Scrivener, at your service," he said. "You are also guests of Signor Ridolfi, I take it?"

We introduced ourselves, explaining that we had been generously included in the invitation to Norfolk, though Ridolfi had never met us before and—because we regarded ourselves as here to gather whatever information we could, of any kind—we inquired politely about Master Scrivener's acquaintance with Ridolfi.

We tried not to sound inquisitive, but Scrivener looked as though he could recognize curiosity when he met it. Ours seemed to amuse him, however.

"I met Signor Ridolfi two years ago in Florence, when I traveled there," he said, "accompanying a nephew round Italy. I had just retired from the secretariat of Sir William Cecil and while I was working for him, I made the acquaintance of some Florentines who were visiting London. They offered their hospitality when I went to their country. They knew Ridolfi. I must have made an impression on him. When he came to London, he discovered by chance that I was making a stay in the City, took the trouble to seek me out, and graciously invited me to dine. But let me see—surely . . . ?"

Alert gray eyes, deep-set under heavy eyebrows, were studying me thoughtfully. He then seemed to connect me with an item from some private filing system in his head.

"Mistress Ursula Stannard? Formerly Mistress Blanchard, I believe? Were you not once wed to Gerald Blanchard? I met both of you, I am sure, in Antwerp, ten years ago, in the house of Sir Thomas Gresham, one of Queen Elizabeth's financiers. I was seconded to Gresham for a short time, in 1558. Some of my skills were useful to him."

"We were indeed in Antwerp with Gresham at that time," I agreed. I studied him in return and a memory stirred. An image came into my mind, of Gresham's courtyard, on a summer day. I had been showing three-year-old Meg how to feed the fish in the pool, and Gerald had been in conversation with a man who had the air of a scholar, just as this man had, except that . . .

"I think I recall you," I said. "Though you didn't look quite . . ."

"I probably still had dark hair at the time," said Scrivener, again visibly amused. "Yes. I talked with your husband, Gerald Blanchard, on several occasions. He picked my brains."

I was going to ask him what Gerald had picked his brains about and what the skills were that were so useful to Gresham, but Signor Ridolfi chose that moment to saunter into view along the path from the house. He was with another man, and even before I saw his face, I knew from the richness of his long, fur-trimmed gown who the second man must be. They saw me look at them, and came over to us.

"May I introduce Don Guerau de Spes, the present ambassador from Spain? Your Excellency, this is . . ."

Amid the new flurry of introductions, I forgot about Harry Scrivener for the moment and studied de Spes instead, interested to see at close quarters this man who had quarreled with the queen and had only recently been freed from house arrest. His face was hard to read. His eyes seemed to dance with a secret laughter behind the shelter of the high cheekbones, and I could not tell whether the contented contours of the mouth meant the happiness and confidence proper to a successful man, or whether they were merely complacent.

Hugh and Scrivener were making conventional conversation

with Ridolfi and the ambassador. Hugh remarked that the day was warm. Scrivener said that he hoped the topiary garden had not scandalized His Excellency too much. "It is not Signor Ridolfi's fault."

"He has explained." De Spes spoke good English, in a light, cool voice. "But I am not so easily offended." He waved a casual hand. "I can appreciate a work of imagination, even when it is not—shall we say—of the most virtuous nature. I find this amusing." He turned to me. "Signor Ridolfi has been telling me of my fellow guests. You are Mistress Stannard, but formerly you were Madame de la Roche, were you not? I have heard of you. You come of a Catholic family, I believe. I am sure that if we come to know each other better, we shall be friends."

"Indeed?" said Hugh.

"In the most innocent manner, I promise you, Master Stannard," said de Spes. "I see myself as a knight at arms, fighting in the cause of the true faith wherever I go, and a knight must be pure in heart, must he not?"

"Indeed, he must," said Hugh, in a faintly acid tone, from which I gathered that in my husband's opinion, Ridolfi's topiary garden was an unfortunate place in which to boast of one's pureheartedness. I didn't look at Hugh, but caught Scrivener's glinting eye instead, and realized that he too had noticed the acid, although neither Ridolfi nor de Spes seemed to have done so.

I said: "To fight for the true faith sounds admirable, but it could bring terrible bloodshed. People may not agree on what the true faith is."

De Spes smiled at me. It was the smile of a knowledgeable adult at a simple child. "There is one God, one church, one truth. There can be no disagreement, only willful disobedience. And if that leads to bloodshed—it cannot be helped. That is as God wills. But now, if you will forgive us . . ." He tapped Ridolfi's arm. "Signor, we have things to discuss."

"Yes, indeed. Not that business should disturb a social occasion too much, but perhaps, before the trumpet sounds for dinner, we could have a few private words. Excuse us, please!"

We all assured them that they were excused and watched

them move off along the path leading to the river. Before they were out of sight, they were talking hard, with de Spes, who was taller, leaning his head down toward his companion, as if to make sure that he would be heard clearly without raising his voice.

"Interesting," Scrivener remarked. "I wonder what they're so earnestly discussing?"

"Money, perhaps," I said, "since Ridolfi's a banker."

Hugh, with a snort, said: "Maybe de Spes spent all his substance during his house arrest, sending out for romantic literature!"

A lively fanfare on a trumpet sounded from the house. The three of us left the bench and walked toward the arch at the far end of the garden. As we did so, Hugh embarked on the inquiries I had omitted to make, asking Harry Scrivener what his speciality had been, which had sent him to Antwerp. "You have financial abilities, perhaps?"

"I'd have worked in the Treasury if I had," Scrivener said. "No. My special interest is in codes and ciphers. Sir Thomas Gresham sometimes found it useful to correspond in cipher with his contacts in England. I showed him various ways of doing so and I also did the same for Master Gerald Blanchard, your then-husband, Mistress Stannard. He worked so closely with Gresham."

"I never knew that Gerald understood ciphering!" I said involuntarily.

"Well, he only knew about mine. I created my own. Now that I'm retired, I'm working on it further, refining it. I hope one day to perfect an unbreakable code. It is quite a challenge, but such a thing is sorely needed."

"By whom?" Hugh asked. "Conspirators might find it rather more useful than honest men could wish."

"And honest men might protect themselves from conspirators, if they could communicate in ways that were secure from enemies of the state," said Scrivener. He added: "I have no high opinion of conspirators. They are often very foolish. You have read the book *Utopia*? It was written by an Englishman named Sir Thomas More."

"Yes. About an ideal state," said Hugh.

"There will never be such a thing," said Scrivener with certainty. "A state can only be as perfect as the human beings in it and when were human beings *ever* perfect? But where you have conspirators you are apt to find among them men who believe that the ideal state can be brought into being. That is what I mean by foolishness. It is a kind of innocence. Alas, that doesn't mean that they aren't dangerous. These men are so often ready to do terrible things to make their hopeless dreams come true."

I felt a jab of recognition under my breastbone. I had loved Matthew de la Roche so much, and I had, for a time, let myself be enthralled by Mary Stuart. They both believed that England could be returned to what they called the one true faith, without a bitter civil war; without bloodshed. It was impossible to convince either of them that they were wrong. It suddenly struck me that this was probably the key to de Spes as well. He was of the same kidney. They all had the innocence of which Scrivener was speaking. In Matthew and in Mary Stuart (though not in the Spanish ambassador), the innocence had charm. But Scrivener was right. It also made them dangerous.

"It's my belief," he said, as we passed under the archway out of the topiary garden, "that if a code is hard to break, it may also be hard to use, and innocent dreamers may find such a thing troublesome, and prefer something easier. Such dreamers often don't put the full weight of their minds behind their schemes. They believe that God is on their side and will do the hard work for them. They are mistaken. They may still do great harm, but mercifully, in the end, the advantage usually lies with honest men. Provided they keep their castle walls in good repair, as it were. Can you say they should not improve their defenses in case the enemy steals their ideas? Most inventions can be used for good or ill, alas. Think of gunpowder!"

I thought of Mary Stuart's first husband, Henry Darnley, who had been the victim of a plot that involved planting gunpowder in the cellar of the house where he was sleeping. "True enough," I said, rather grimly.

We joined a stream of people moving into the house and up a curving flight of stairs. There seemed to be a great many guests. At the top of the stairs, we entered the dining chamber and ushers tried to lead Hugh and myself one way and show Scrivener to a seat elsewhere.

Scrivener, however, said he wished to sit with us. "We are in the middle of an interesting conversation," he told the ushers firmly. This caused a certain amount of confusion, but a few minutes later, we had all been seated together.

The dining chamber was lofty and beautiful, with tall leaded windows on two sides, pouring light in on us. Ridolfi appeared, with his wife on his arm and de Spes on the other side of him. They took their places, Ridolfi between Donna and the ambassador, with Norfolk on the other side of de Spes. Ridolfi anounced that grace would said by his chaplain, Father Fernando. When this was over, a procession of servants appeared bearing dishes. In a minstrels' gallery at one end of the room, music began. Norfolk, I saw, was quickly in animated conversation with de Spes.

In a quiet voice, Scrivener remarked: "Signor Ridolfi is well known in court and diplomatic circles in France and Spain as well as in Italy. He has arranged loans for eminent men in all three countries."

"He mixes with the highest, evidently," I said.

"Indeed he does." Servants came to help us to various dishes, and Scrivener for a moment fell silent. I saw him glance at the man on the other side of him, who was, however, deep in talk with the lady who was his farther neighbor. As soon as the servants moved on, Scrivener turned to me. In a low voice he said: "Mistress Stannard, I know a good deal about you. Far more, I fancy, than either Ridolfi or de Spes or even Norfolk. I bear no title and though I have a small manor in Hampshire, I have no town house. I am not among the great. All the same, I did at one time work very closely with Sir William Cecil, who will vouch for me if you ask him. Catholic family or not, you are of the Anglican faith and loyal to the queen. Am I not right?"

"You are right," said Hugh, answering quietly across me.

"I also know that you have undertaken—private work—for the queen, and as far as possible kept it a secret. It is not a total secret, however. I know of it because Cecil himself told me. I admire you greatly. If you are engaged on any such task just now, and I can be of any assistance, I beg you to call on me. I am lodging in Bishopsgate, in the City—in a house with the pretty name of Sweetplum House, from the plum trees that grow in its garden. I expect to be there until September—I am spending the summer in London. The widow Edison, a most respectable woman, is my landlady and you may apply to Sir William Cecil for a character reference. Or, if you wish, to Sir Thomas Gresham, who is currently in England."

In an equally low voice, I said: "Thank you, sir."

10

The Parents of the Groom

". . . and here," said Norfolk, arriving beside us just as the dinner was ending, I bring you Master and Mistress Dean, the parents of my secretary Edmund. My friends, these are the Stannards, whose daughter is being considered as Edmund's future wife, though she is too young for marriage as yet."

"We are overjoyed to meet you," said Master Dean. "We were late in arriving, or we would have greeted you before we all sat down. A matter of business delayed me. These days, no merchant can afford to put off anyone who wishes to see him and might have a useful proposition."

The dinner had gone on for a long time. We and Scrivener had abandoned low-voiced conversation and discussed uncontentious subjects with each other and our respective neighbors. Now, however, the prolonged meal had reached the stage when people began to get up and wander about to talk to friends who were too far away for conversation while all remained seated. The couple on the other side of Hugh had already moved away and now Scrivener, noting that we needed to talk privately to the Deans, murmured that he had glimpsed an old acquaintance and went off to talk to him. The Deans sat down beside us.

"I'll keep Edmund occupied," Norfolk said. "When parents discuss the marriages of their offspring, it is often better if the offspring aren't there. Also, even dukes sometimes find business intruding on pleasure. This morning I dictated a draft letter to a lawyer about this lawsuit over my stepdaughters' property but I think the wording could be improved. I must mention it to Edmund before the new wording slips out of my mind. He is an excellent remembrancer."

"Is the matter of your stepdaughters proving very difficult?" Master Dean asked.

"Extremely. The other party is both wrongheaded and damnably obstinate," said Norfolk and removed himself. Deans and Stannards contemplated each other thoughtfully.

Edmund was his mother's son. It was from her, I thought, that he had inherited that sharp-edged bone structure, and those penetrating eyes. In Mistress Dean, the bones were more delicate, but her eyes had the same blue-lightning quality. Master Dean was slightly plump and his expression slightly harried, possibly on account of business cares, but I felt that anyone who had to live with those eyes was very likely to feel harried.

Meg wasn't going to live with those eyes, not if I could help it, and I resented the way Norfolk had made the introduction; as if the betrothal were still a virtual certainty. Despite our polite noises about Meg's youth, most men would have recognized the courteous code for *no, thank you*. Norfolk was good-hearted in many ways, since he was clearly a conscientious stepfather, but he seemed to have a sadly obtuse streak.

Hugh was already, smoothly, saying the right things. He was inquiring tactfully into the Deans' family history and present circumstances, and simultaneously dropping hints to the effect that we had decided against making definite plans for Meg yet awhile.

". . . the fact is, that until we brought her to London, we hardly realized how young she really is. She is well educated, but in many ways she is still only a child. I am sure that Edmund will improve his position in life; he seems an able young man. But perhaps he would be wiser to establish himself first and then look for a bride."

"His prospects are good," said Edmund's father reassuringly, though his rubicund face remained worried. "I'll be able to help him in due course, I hope. He has told you that, no doubt."

"You have other children besides Edmund, I believe?" I said to Mistress Dean. "His Grace has mentioned that Edmund is a younger son."

"Yes, he has two brothers. The eldest works with his father, and the second boy's in Spain. He has a business there, importing carpets from the Levant. He considered entering a monastery but decided that he had no vocation."

"A monastery? He follows the old faith?" Hugh said.

"We all do," said Mistress Dean. "We pay the fine regularly and thereby buy ourselves out of the need to attend Anglican services. It comes expensive at times, but there, one should be ready to make sacrifices for one's beliefs. The duke has a preference for the old faith himself—which is why he found Edmund so acceptable as an extra secretary. I believe you yourself were brought up in a Catholic family, Mistress Stannard? So the duke told us."

"Yes, that is true," I said. "I was born a Faldene and they are Catholic." I added diplomatically: "But I conform to the law."

"Still, you no doubt have an affinity for the faith of our forefathers. My son will not, of course, interfere with your daughter's choice of worship, though naturally he hopes that in time she will come round to his way of thinking. I wish we could have seen her, for Edmund wrote to us that she was charming and intelligent. I certainly hope . . ."

Will not interfere . . . hopes that in time . . . will come round . . . What happened to that little word *would*? The Deans, like Norfolk, seemed to think the betrothal was assured. I hid my irritation but I was glad of the distraction when Harry Scrivener reappeared beside me.

"If I may intrude for a moment. I am sorry, Mistress Dean. But if I could have a private word with Mistress Stannard . . . ?"

I caught Hugh's eye and he gave me a tiny nod. I rose to my feet. "I will only be a moment." I moved away with Scrivener. "What is it?" I asked softly.

"You'll have to invent a suitable excuse for being called away by a virtual stranger. I shall leave that to you. But I've noticed something which may interest you."

"Yes?"

"I passed close to where Norfolk was talking with one of his secretaries. Edmund Dean, I fancy, the lad who has been suggested as your future son-in-law. He looked remarkably like Mistress Dean, anyway."

"That would be Edmund, yes."

"Our good host came up to them and Edmund handed him a small bag. I think it was a bag of coin—I should say it was quite heavy, anyway. The way it swung . . ."

"Quite. And . . ."

"I heard him say that it was from his father."

I was puzzled. "The return of a loan, perhaps. Master Dean isn't in easy circumstances just now, since the closure of Antwerp. Perhaps he borrowed some money from Ridolfi."

"Maybe," said Scrivener. "But I went on roaming about and keeping my eyes open." The eyes in question had a decided glint of enjoyment in them. "The duke apparently has two secretaries with him—the other's called Higford, I think. I heard him introducing himself to someone. A merchant like Dean Senior, I fancy. One learns to recognize types. The merchant handed over a purse, which Higford then took straight to Ridolfi. Do people usually return bankers' loans to them at private dinners? It seems nearly as odd as Ridolfi and the Spanish ambassador putting their heads together so closely in that very peculiar garden. I was sorry to interrupt your conversation just now, but people come and go at these affairs and you might have taken your leave and vanished before I could speak to you again."

He nodded, turned away, and in a moment was absorbed into another group of people. I went slowly back to Hugh and the Deans. They looked at me inquiringly.

"Just a triviality," I said. "A . . . a message from a mutual friend."

"I have been telling your husband," said Mistress Dean, "that Edmund believes your daughter, Meg—Margaret, as he prefers to call her—has taken a liking to him, just as he has taken a liking to her. That is encouraging—though I admit I set little store by such things. Young people are adaptable and should be prepared to adapt according to their elders' wishes. I did so, and so did my husband."

"Very true. Very true," said Master Dean. I wondered if his wife could hear the mournful note in his voice.

"I married of my own free will, every time," I said. I was tired of playing games with the Deans. "I recommend it, personally. Well. This has been a most interesting meeting. I think we all know much more about each other now. Hugh and I will be on our way home soon, and we shall give careful thought to all we have learned. Shall we not, Hugh?"

"We shall indeed. I think we are all united in wishing both Edmund and Meg the happiest possible futures, whether in each other's company or otherwise. Master Dean, Mistress Dean, it has been a great pleasure to meet you personally. Just by doing so, I think we now know Edmund that much better . . ."

With a gracious exchange of further insincere compliments, we parted from the Deans.

"I wonder," murmured Hugh as we moved out onto the terrace, where no one else could hear us, "what it's like, making love to an icicle?"

"I trust you'll never find out."

"I never have so far, thank God. What was all that about, Ursula? What did that fellow Scrivener really want with you?"

I told him.

"Odd," said Hugh. "*Very* odd. Money being stealthily slipped into Ridolfi's hands . . . has he got all the merchants in London in debt to him somehow?"

"They could be donations," I said slowly. "But if so—for what?"

11

Assignment

"If you were anyone but yourselves," said Sir William Cecil, Secretary of State and a member (just now exceedingly harassed) of Elizabeth's royal council, "I would have had you thrown out by force. I don't usually admit callers who argue with my doorkeeper when he says I'm not seeing visitors, and then sit down in my entrance hall and refuse to move until he agrees to tell me they're here. Not even my fellow councilors would behave like that. They would send in notes, or . . ."

"We're not councilors," said Hugh mildly, "and the doorkeeper refused to take in a note."

"He's new since I was last here," I said. "He didn't recognize me."

"My apologies for that. He was doing what he thought was his duty. Is it true, Ursula, as he says, that when the two of you sat down in my entrance hall and declined to move, *you* sat down *on the floor*?"

"Yes, Sir William. There was only one spare seat, a single stool, and I wanted Hugh to have that, because of his stiff knees. So I sat on the floor. It was difficult," I said in aggrieved tones. "I am wearing a farthingale, as you see, and a large, fashionable open ruff. I felt ridiculous and the farthingale was frankly inconvenient."

A very faint smile creased the Secretary of State's grim lips. "I can imagine. I'm glad I'm not a woman. If you had not been you, my dear Ursula—because I have some confidence in you and when I heard that a Mistress Stannard was sitting on the floor in my entrance hall, I knew you wouldn't behave in such an extra-ordinary way without a good reason—you would have had rough handling. Now, kindly tell me what it's all about."

"It's a long story," said Hugh.

"Then the sooner you begin to tell it, the better. Proceed."

The study that Cecil used in his house in the Strand was smaller than the ones he was usually allocated in Elizabeth's various palaces, and the desk at which he was seated was strewn with so many papers that we literally could not see the surface of it. When his despairing doorkeeper had finally sought and received permission to have us shown in, he had been consulting documents and writing busily with a quill, which, from the way it spluttered and threw ink flecks all over his fingers, badly needed renewing. It looked as though he had no time to trouble with it, or else was too worried to notice.

I felt concerned. From what Norfolk had said, the business of the sequestered Spanish money had brought him under very serious attack from his fellow councilors. He was beleaguered and it showed. In the years I had known him, he had always looked tired. Working for Elizabeth *was* tiring. I knew that too. But I had never seen him look this exhausted.

I was angry with Elizabeth. She ought to be giving him better support. Norfolk had said that she had backed him at first, but if she were still doing so, he wouldn't be in this anxious state. I could guess what was going on in her mind. She had a trick of seizing credit for policies that worked and unloading the blame for failures onto someone else. But she had no right to do that to anyone who had served her as long and as well as Cecil.

"It's complicated," I said. "We can't be sure that the bits and pieces we've come across really are linked. There is a man called Master Harry Scrivener. I met him once in Antwerp and he says he used to work for you . . ."

"Indeed he did," said Cecil. "He's retired now but he was a lawyer and also gifted with ciphers—both at creating and decoding them. He's staying in London at the moment and he visited me a few weeks ago. You've come across him, have you?"

"We met him at the house of an Italian banker called Roberto

Ridolfi. It seems that you've told him about my secret work," I said. "He clearly thinks that something is going on that ought not to be."

"And the fact that he has suspicions too has convinced us that we aren't imagining ours," Hugh said.

"Quite possibly," I said, "what we observed when we dined with the Ridolfis has nothing to do with the deaths concerned with Howard House but . . ."

"The best place to begin, Ursula, is at the beginning. Take things in order and I'll decide for myself what is connected to what."

"I'm sorry. Well, it starts," I said, putting it as succinctly as possible and omitting Gladys's shocking performance in the churchyard at Faldene, "with the Duke of Norfolk taking an interest in one of his young secretaries and writing to us, saying that we might like to consider the fellow, at some point in the future, as a husband for my daughter, Meg . . ."

I told the story as briefly and clearly as I could, with interjections now and then from Hugh, tracing the links in what, as I admitted more than once, was a tenuous chain. The letters Sybil and I had seen during Gale's illness, and the oddity of the cipher. Norfolk's unconcealed interest in Mary Stuart (Cecil's gaze sharpened at this point). The puzzle of Gale's murder and worse, the extremely horrible death of young Walt. The passing of money to Ridolfi after the dinner and his curiously intent—and private—conversation with the Spanish ambassador.

"We apologize for our intrusion here today," said Hugh. "We did it only because we felt that we must tell you what we've observed."

"Yes. Yes, I see." Cecil rose and roamed to the window, his long gown swishing. He came back and sat down again. "And Scrivener has scented a mystery too, has he? He was always a shrewd man. He comes of an interesting family. His grandfather, as a young man, back in the days of the wars between York and Lancaster, was the younger son of a fairly prosperous Hampshire yeoman farmer. He was a bright lad, and his family had him educated in an abbey, from the age of about ten, with the idea that he might become a monk. He never took vows, though, because at the age of nineteen, he was thrown out for wenching."

As was his way, Cecil said this in a solemn voice, signaling that it was not a laughing matter, but there was a spark of laughter in his eyes, all the same. "According to Harry," he said, "his grandfather was caught slipping back over the wall after an assignation in the nearby village. Well, he had to find a way of supporting himself out in the world and since the monks had taught him to read and write, he decided to make a living at it. He copied manuscripts, wrote letters on behalf of people who couldn't write their own, and so on. He did well. That's how the family acquired their surname—Scrivener. He married, and his son followed in his footsteps, and so did his grandson—Harry. Harry's father could afford a really good education for him and thus he was able to qualify as a lawyer and get himself into my employment. He's a good man, trustworthy and talented. I found his skills with ciphers very useful at times."

"You trusted him to the point of telling him about me," I said.

"Oh yes. I had occasion, now and then, to mention you in memoranda to the queen. He was one of the chosen few who made copies of confidential documents for me. He is completely reliable."

"He seemed to think," I said, "that I might actually be on an assignment. He offered to help me if necessary."

"He would. Well, well. Now, I did know that Norfolk was still interested in marrying Mary. I take it you're aware that de Spes was under house arrest for a while. Did you wonder why that didn't last longer?"

"Well, yes," I said.

"The queen and I decided that we might learn more of his activities by letting him loose—or seeming to do so. He was freed, but he has been watched and his correspondence has been opened. In his letters to Philip of Spain, he has mentioned Norfolk's interest in Mary. Norfolk's housekeeper, Mistress Dalton," Cecil added, "is in my pay. One of my clerks is her nephew. His parents are dead and his kind aunt visits him when Norfolk's household is in London, and writes to him when it's elsewhere. She reports on Norfolk's affairs through him. She confirms what we have learned from de Spes."

"No wonder she can afford to dress like a duchess," I said, marveling, not for the first time, at Cecil's information network.

Though it now transpired that even so, there were limitations.

"We've never found out how Norfolk and Mary hope to get over the fact that she's still married to Bothwell. I suppose she'll try to get it annulled. She'll plead duress, I daresay." His lip curled. "I think the scheme is to put Mary back on the Scottish throne, with Norfolk as her consort, and then try to have her made heir to Elizabeth. In which case Norfolk might one day be king consort here. Efforts would be made to turn her into an Anglican, of course."

"Isn't Norfolk Catholic, more or less?" I asked, though doubtfully, remembering that English Bible. "He has Popish images in his chapel."

"Norfolk will attach himself to whatever faith promises the best rewards," said Cecil sourly. "Mary's half brother, the Earl of Moray, the Scottish regent, was in England early this year and Norfolk discussed Mary's restoration with him. There was a plot among the northern earls—they're mostly Catholic—to assassinate him on his way home, to leave the way clearer for Mary's return."

"*Was* there?" This was new to Hugh as well as to me.

"Yes, but Norfolk stopped it. He gave Moray armed protection, in return for a promise that Moray would support Mary's restoration. Given, of course, that Elizabeth consents. As yet, no one has ventured to ask her! I suspect that a number of the council members rather like the scheme, mainly because they know I don't! If they can convince Elizabeth that Mary should be restored and that her marriage to Norfolk is a good idea . . ."

"But surely, the queen would *never* agree to such a marriage!" I said. "Norfolk would be aiming at the throne, or as good as."

"Elizabeth feels, on principle, that princes should not be ejected from their thrones. If it can happen to one, it could happen to another. And at least Norfolk isn't a foreign, Catholic prince with an army behind him! That was the argument in favor of Mary's marriage to Darnley, if you remember. It's possible that the queen *might* be brought to consent. Whereas I would not. In all honesty I could never recommend it." He looked at us and once more we saw that grim smile. "You have been staying with Norfolk. What is your opinion of him as a future king—of either Scotland or England?"

We thought of Thomas Howard, of his pale eyes and beaky nose, his overfastidiousness, his occasional petulance, his good heart and his sentimentality. His too visible ambition. His obtuse streak. Our silence was answer enough.

"Quite," said Cecil. "And most of my fellow council members must feel the same, but some of them are so eager to lever me and Her Majesty apart that they are simply indifferent to his drawbacks. But if she once loses confidence in me . . ."

He looked at me. There was no laughter now in his tired blue eyes. I had never seen them so weary and so unhappy. It was wrong, I thought, very wrong indeed that a man so conscientious should be made to look like that.

"Who will guide and steady her if I'm not there?" Cecil said. "We have worked in partnership for years. In giving her my advice, I have always—*always*—put England's interests, and Elizabeth's interests, which I regard as the same thing, first. I promised her I would, at the time of her accession. And she *told* me that she expected such advice from me. She asked me always to speak according to my conscience and my judgment, and not simply to please her. But time brings changes. A young, untried princess, new to power, is one thing. A woman in her thirties, who has been queen for a decade is another. If she were to turn or be turned against me, and look for advice to someone who was more self-seeking . . ."

"Robert Dudley, Earl of Leicester," said Hugh.

"Quite," said Cecil wearily. "She loves him, though not as the world understands that word when applied to a man and a woman. But he is not the man to guide England safely. I am afraid, for myself, for her, for England. And now, we have these killings: Gale and the boy."

"Did you already know about them?" Hugh asked.

"Oh yes. Via Mistress Dalton at first. In fact, I sent for a copy of the inquest records, and I've read them. Later, though, Norfolk himself told me about the business. Despite our dispute earlier this year, we are still on speaking terms. There are matters on which he wants my advice. He puts his own interpretation on it all. Julius Gale was no doubt killed by some private enemy of his own. The letters he was carrying were found in his room, perfectly safe, and probably had nothing to do with the matter. The boy Walt perhaps knew something dangerous to the killer and was therefore disposed of as well. So many people have secrets in their lives, Norfolk says, questionable acquaintances or interests which they conceal from their employers and their more respectable friends."

I said doubtfully: "Well, that could be so, I suppose."

Cecil snorted. "I believe there are certain kinds of fish which, when startled, give out an inky substance that hides them while they make their escape. Norfolk's theories were very like a cloud of ink. I wondered what was going on behind them. Now, you tell me that this man Ridolfi, who has dealings with Norfolk, and, apparently a secret correspondence with either Mary Stuart or Moray, is also having confidential conversations with de Spes, a man that I neither like nor trust. Nor does the queen," he added. "She and I are in accord about the Spanish ambassador, at least! She said to me once that de Spes is two men in one body: a whimsical dreamer and a cold fanatic."

I thought of de Spes's romantic style of talking, of the secretive smile and the embattled, watchful eyes, and realized that Elizabeth, acute as ever, had interpreted them aright. I said: "I think that sums him up perfectly. Do you have any observers in Roberto Ridolfi's house?"

"Not at the moment." Cecil paused and then said: "Master Stannard, you have in the past graciously allowed your wife to serve her queen even though it meant being separated from her for a time. Would you consent to that again?"

I wanted to protest but then I saw Hugh's expression. I knew what he was going to say. He was an unusual man. He would say that my duty to the queen came before my duty to him. He would remind me too that she and I were half sisters. He had done so before.

"I would raise no objection," Hugh said quietly. "But I don't wish my wife to be put in danger."

"There is no need for that," Cecil said. "Not if you are circumspect, Ursula. There have been times in the past when you weren't, but no one ordered you to risk getting your throat cut. You rushed headlong into danger all by yourself. I certainly never told you to do so! I don't like using you, a married woman with a child, in this way at all. But I think that without risk to yourself, you could easily fill this need."

"How?" I asked. I had the feeling that my back was against a wall. My only chance of escape, as far as I could see, lay in the fact that I couldn't imagine how I could be introduced into Ridolfi's household.

Cecil had the answer, of course. I might have known.

"I mentioned that Norfolk has been seeking my advice," he said. "Are you aware that he's entangled in a lawsuit over lands which are, or should be, his stepdaughters' inheritance?"

"Yes," I told him.

"I think I can help him. Customary law is on his side, for one thing. In the absence of a son, it has always been normal for inheritances such as this to be split between the daughters. I do happen to be Master of the Wards, which means that, given I have adequate points of law to work with, I can make recommendations when such cases come to court. My recommendations," he added, "are usually heeded."

Involuntarily, I smiled. It was such a charming way of saying: *I order and they jump.*

"Norfolk became quite amiable after our discussion of the matter," he said. "Almost gossipy. He mentioned that lately, Ridolfi's wife has come to England and it seems that Ridolfi wants a gentlewoman companion for her. Madame Ridolfi speaks little English and needs a lady who speaks either French or Italian, who can assist her in learning English, help her to shop for gowns and household goods, show her the way about London, and so on."

Remembering Ridolfi's gentle, brown-eyed wife, I said reluctantly: "Yes, she'll need someone of that kind. I've met her, you know. She'll need someone to help her with the household servants, too."

"Norfolk mentioned that as well. Some of the servants came with the family from Italy, so she has no difficulty there. But there are quite a few English ones as well and she would like to be able to talk to them directly." He laughed. "It seems that the English servants all address her as Madame, as though she were a Frenchwoman, though she doesn't mind, and says that if it's easier, she's prepared to be known as Madame while she's in England. They call her husband Master Ridolfi. English servants don't seem able to get their tongues round Signor and Signora, and I daresay the same will be true of half the people she meets in society as well. The English are an insular nation. Even I, for all my high position, can speak no tongue but my own."

I said nothing, and he studied my face. "It would be a temporary arrangement, for three months or so. When you met—I'll call her Madame Ridolfi as well—did you like her?"

"Well—yes. At least, I didn't have much conversation with her, but what I saw, I liked."

I had lost the contest already. I knew it.

"I may be able to persuade Norfolk into smoothing the way for you," Cecil said. "We could say that your husband has business at home, but that you wish to stay in London to buy new fashions for yourself and your daughter. I could suggest that the two ladies would be company for each other. That way, we might arrange for you to join Madame Ridolfi as a friend, not in any sense as a servant."

I longed to say *no*. Then I thought of Julius Gale, being hauled out of a roadside culvert by his feet. I thought of Walt, insulted even in death, hung like a carcass alongside game birds and bullocks.

Cecil was right. Something had to be done.

12

The House by the River

"I realize that your family is Catholic," I said, plowing determinedly on, standing in the middle of Norfolk's parlor and gazing resolutely into Edmund Dean's unfriendly blue eyes. They were so intense that they had almost physical force. "I was myself reared in a Catholic household," I said. "The reason why we have decided against this betrothal is the one we have given already. My daughter is too young."

I didn't want bad blood between myself and Dean, for I would probably come into contact with him again in the near future. Norfolk and Ridolfi, I had gathered, saw a good deal of each other when they were both in London, and I would be spending at least the next three months with the Ridolfis. They had taken the bait as easily as ponies take apples. I was to become Donna Ridolfi's gentlewoman companion.

I wished Hugh could have been there to support me but Hugh had already left for Hawkswood. Chance had lent color to the excuse that he was too busy to stay in London with me, though we wished it hadn't. He had gone because of a worrying letter from Sybil.

Sybil, being both educated and ladylike, had worded the letter in dignified fashion but her alarm came through all too clearly.

. . . Meg has been downhearted. It seems that she wanted to be betrothed to Master Dean and has even said that she thinks of herself as

betrothed to him because, apparently, she told him so one day when they were walking together. I do my best to distract her but I fear she is lovesick. She does not attend to her studies as she should and even rides out and goes hawking as though it were a duty rather than a joy.

As regards Gladys Morgan, I did all I could to follow your instructions, but it is not possible to keep her confined in the house, she being most offended by this notion. She caused so much ado when she found her chamber door locked that it seemed best to allow her some freedom. I bade her to be circumspect in all she said and did, and at first all went well, but then she offered to make a medicine for an ailing maidservant and went out into the fields to find herbs and there met the Hawkswood vicar. He asked her what she was about and when she told him, he said she was acting presumptuously, pretending to be a physician, which is an art to be practiced only by men, and that he feared her purpose was witchcraft. Whereupon she cursed him in some fashion and, alas, some dwellers in a nearby cottage heard them disputing and came out and were not pleased to see Gladys, whom they knew and distrusted. This caused her to turn on them and curse them too.

I now have her under lock and key again and have promised the vicar and the villagers (who sent a deputation to me) that she will not annoy them again. I repeated that she was a foolish old woman with a bitter tongue but no unnatural powers. The vicar said, however, that if any harm befell him or the cottagers, charges will be brought.

No such harm has yet come but what if it occurs by chance? I most earnestly seek your advice and your presence too, if possible . . .

All of which, reduced to its gist and invested with the full force of the emotion behind it, meant: *Meg is in love with Master Dean and thinks she is promised to him and I don't know what to do about it, while Gladys is impossible and will get herself hanged if she isn't careful. Coping with either of them is beyond me. I call for help!*

So, Hugh had gone to Hawkswood to do what he could, but before he left, we agreed that I should put the ambiguities of tact aside and make a final end of the betrothal question.

"Otherwise it may drag on and there may be further approaches," I said. "The way we were introduced to his parents was a warning. They might even pay a visit to Hawkswood and disturb Meg further."

"I agree. It's time to be definite," Hugh said.

This was proving difficult. Dean didn't seem at all disposed to take no for an answer.

"Mistress Stannard, if my adherence to the old faith is not a difficulty, then why is Margaret's youth such a barrier? Time will mend that! I have already said there can be no question of marriage until my circumstances are better and the wench is older. That was always understood. Early betrothals often work out well. The young people concerned know that their future is settled. Your girl is dutiful and obedient to you, I am sure."

I was much less sure of that, though I could scarcely tell him that my daughter's independent spirit was more likely to be ranged on his side than on mine.

Patiently, I tried again. "We came in good faith. But soon after we came here and, as it were, saw Meg in the position of a girl being presented as a marriage prospect, we realized that we had made a grave error. We were sorry, as we felt that we had led both the duke and yourself on to believe—to have hopes—to . . ."

I was dithering. That frosty stare was unnerving me. "Master Dean," I said, sounding harsh out of sheer desperation. "Please! We have changed our minds. We shall not consider any betrothal for Meg until she is at least seventeen and has spent at least a year at court. By then, if all goes as you expect, you will have made your way and found another wife. There is no point in continuing these . . . negotiations."

"I see. You will not take into account that I—and perhaps your daughter too—may have fallen in love?"

"Meg is too young to fall in love, just as she is too young to be betrothed. And you, I'm sure, won't pledge your whole life to a dream."

"Very well. I wish your Meg—though I like her full name of Margaret much better—a happy life and a happy marriage, if not to me. I am sorry, for believe me, she has enchanted me and I will not forget her. I understand you are to visit Madame Ridolfi soon? I wish you a pleasant time with her. I am sure she will find you a great support as she learns her way about an unfamiliar city. Good day, Mistress Stannard."

He bowed, turned on his heel, and went out. He had said all the right things. No one could fault his words. But if he had at last accepted his rejection, it wasn't in any amiable spirit. There had been such a flash of fury in his eyes that, as he left the room, I found that I was trembling.

I was also sure that I had done the right thing. This was not the man for Meg.

I went to take my leave of Norfolk. "You and Master Stannard have really decided against Dean?" he said regretfully. "I must admit I'd hoped . . . it would have been doing him a kindness."

"I know. I'm sorry. But"—since Hugh was not there to be questioned, I unloaded the responsibility onto his shoulders—"my husband was very firm about the matter."

"I understand. Well, if you are to be with the Ridolfis for a while, we shall no doubt meet again. That will be a pleasure."

"Indeed it will," I said, conventionally.

I had come on foot from the Green Dragon, attended by the Brockleys, who were waiting for me in the entrance hall. Brockley raised inquiring brows as I joined them, and I nodded. "It's done. He wasn't pleased," I added in a low voice, since we were still on Norfolk's premises and Dean probably close by. "But it's over now and finished."

"I think you're quite right, ma'am," said Dale. "We both do."

"We must go back to the inn and pack," I said. "The Ridolfis expect us later today." The Brockleys were to accompany me. The Ridolfis saw me as an equal, and entitled to have my own servants.

We returned to the inn through the warm spring weather, threading our way amid the crowds. In the innyard, the first thing I saw was Hugh's coach, with its shafts in the air, and one of our sturdy brown coach horses tethered to a stable door while John Argent wisped its coat to a shine with a handful of hay.

"Hugh's back!" I said. I sped at once up the outside staircase to the gallery that ran in front of the bedchambers and pushed our door open. "Are you there, Hugh? I've just been to Howard House . . ."

I stopped short. Hugh was on the window seat reading. He

looked up as I spoke, his expression uncharacteristically hang-dog.

On a stool close by, mumbling to herself over the work, sat Gladys Morgan, mending one of his shirts.

The Brockleys, who had followed me, now caught up. I heard Dale whisper: "Oh dear!" and as for Brockley . . .

Brockley hardly ever swore in the presence of women. He considered it impolite. This time, however, he forgot himself. "I can hardly believe it," said Brockley's voice in my ear, low but shaking with outrage. "It's that bloody old hag again!"

"Hugh, I can't take her to the Ridolfi house. I just can't."

"It's the only way. I'm sorry, Ursula, but I can think of nothing else to do with her. I got Sybil to make sure she was decently washed and dressed and provided with good spare clothing before we left. I *had* to bring her away. The feeling against her is running so high in Hawkswood that we daren't keep her there and Withysham is just as bad."

"But, Hugh, *how* can I take her with me to the Ridolfis?"

"There's no prejudice against her there and . . ."

"She'll soon create some! Besides, she made a few enemies in Norfolk's house and the two households see a lot of each other. Their servants meet and talk."

"It still won't be nearly as bad as in Hawkswood or Withysham and there ought to be ways of making sure it doesn't get worse. You can tell Madame Ridolfi that Gladys is not quite in her right senses and that nothing she says should be taken seriously any more than the tantrums of a child—and you can ask the Brockleys to watch her. I doubt if Roger Brockley will have much work to do; being Gladys's keeper can be an occupation for him."

"He won't be pleased! He felt kindly enough toward her when she was a persecuted old woman on the Welsh border, but since he's had to live in the same household, he's much less tolerant!"

"You pay him to do what you want, not what he wants,"

Hugh pointed out. Hugh always won. He never insisted on being obeyed but by force of personality and a knack of producing reasonable arguments, he usually was.

We had stepped out to the gallery to hold our conversation in private, after leaving the Brockleys with Gladys. We now went back. Dale had begun to pack my clothes while Brockley held pannier lids open for her. He was shooting unfriendly glances at Gladys, who was where we had left her, on her stool, sewing. I saw that she was indeed clean and neatly dressed in a dark red gown with a small white ruff. At first sight, Gladys seemed like an ordinary, quite dignified, elderly serving woman. If only, I thought, she could be relied on to behave like one!

But there was nothing to be done. "How is Meg?" I asked. Meg, after all, mattered more to me than Gladys or even an assignment for the Secretary of State.

"Lovesick, as Sybil told us," Hugh said, "but she is young. She'll recover. She sings love songs when she thinks no one's listening, and roams in the garden at Hawkswood, sighing romantically. Sybil found the name *Edmund* carved into the stem of one of my rose trees! I told Sybil to arrange a routine, with regular hours for studying and riding, music and stitchery, and keep to it, and I myself gave Meg a Latin translation to do and told her that I expected to see it finished by the time I came back. She'll be all right."

"Oh, my dear, of course I have no objection!" said Donna Ridolfi in French. It was late in the afternoon of the same day. Hugh had stayed at the inn and would leave next morning to return to Hawkswood. I and my entourage (which now included Gladys), had arrived at the Ridolfi house after dinner. We had been shown our quarters and I was at present in a downstairs parlor with Donna, who was plying me with wine and confectionery. Both were oversweet for my taste but I supposed I would have to adjust myself.

"Difficult old servants are a problem everyone has!" Donna said. "My husband wishes he were not saddled with that terrible topiary gardener, Arthur Johnson. Not that Johnson's wits have anything amiss with them but, well, when you came to our dinner, did you see the yew garden that he made?"

"Yes, I did." Brockley had been grumbling because if we were all to live in the Ridolfi house, Dale would be sure to see it too.

"I need hardly say more," said my hostess sadly. "Have another sweetmeat, my dear. I eat too many, I know." She looked down with regret at her ornate brocade dress. "My husband is amused by the topiary garden, but he still considers Johnson a foul old man. He ogles the maidservants and says things that embarrass some of the shyer ones. Roberto has spoken to him but Johnson pretended he couldn't understand my husband's accent."

"I will try to help. That's why I'm here, after all," I said, seeing a way to make myself useful, though it was a moot point whether Johnson would take any notice of me, either.

"You are very kind, my dear. We'll leave it a day or two, while you settle in . . . oh, yes, Master Hillman?"

"Excuse me," said the young man who had just come along the terrace and stepped in through the garden door of the parlor. He had a cloth-wrapped package under his arm and an air of looking for someone. At the sight of us, he politely removed his hat.

"The windows are open," he said, "and I accidentally overheard you, Madame Ridolfi. I wonder if you would let me take a hand in this matter of Arthur Johnson." His French was fluent but the English accent was unmistakable. He smiled at me. "You must be Mistress Stannard. My name is George Hillman. But Madame Ridolfi should do the introducing, of course. I am just a new employee. I am sorry, Madame."

"This is my husband's new secretary and courier," said Madame Ridolfi. "He has come to replace that poor fellow Gale, who was murdered. Master Hillman, if you can curb Johnson's tongue for us, we would be only too grateful. Can you?"

"I can speak to him, saying that I have your authority, if you so wish. A man might have more influence over him and he won't be able to pretend he doesn't understand *me*. I have heard him making suggestive remarks to the maidservants and I agree that he should be checked."

"Please try!" said Donna. "I'm sure Mistress Stannard doesn't really want the task."

"No, I don't," I said.

I was looking carefully at Master Hillman. He was in many ways very like Julius Gale—less stocky and taller by a couple of inches, but similar in his red-brown coloring, in the square shape of his good-looking face, and in the frankness of his expression. He sounded educated and his clothes were good, as though he came from a well-to-do family. His hat was a mildly dashing brown velvet affair with an amethyst brooch in it. The brooch looked costly. I wondered what his background was.

A movement outside caught our attention, and we all turned to see Johnson going into the topiary garden with his shears. He was not alone. At his side was a small, slightly bent female figure in a dark red dress.

"Who is that with him?" Hillman asked.

"One of my servants," I said. "Gladys Morgan. She's a trifle . . ." I tapped my forehead. "She does plain sewing and little jobs like that. My other servants are supposed to keep an eye on her—she sleeps on a truckle bed in their room, in fact—but she's obviously eluded them. So she's making friends with Arthur Johnson! They'll make quite a pair. Nothing he says is likely to embarrass *her*."

"It isn't the moment, perhaps, to pursue Johnson with strictures on his behavior," said Hillman. "Indeed, I have another errand, which must come first. Madame, where is your husband? This package has arrived for him, from a City merchant. A messenger delivered it just now."

"You'll find him in his study," said Madame Ridolfi.

Master Hillman withdrew. He passed close to me as he did so, and I had a brief but close look at the cloth-wrapped package. Whatever was inside the cloth had sharp corners and was probably a box.

I did more than just look at it. I heard it. Faintly, but definitely, it clinked. More money was being passed to Ridolfi, and privately, not at his business premises.

Interesting.

13

Where the Swans Are

It wasn't the first time I had entered a stranger's household in order—to put it crudely but honestly—to spy on the people there. I had once entered a respectable manor house allegedly to teach the daughters embroidery, while poking into their father's private correspondence; another time, I had worked in a pie shop, gutting poultry, rolling pastry, serving customers, and trying to discover whether my employer was plotting against the life of the queen. I had learned how to go about the spying business.

Above all, to avoid suspicion, one must perform the duties for which one is ostensibly there. I actually did improve the embroidery of the Mason girls, and I had sweated through hot summer days in that pie shop, doing the work for which I was being paid, albeit inadequately.

In the Ridolfi household, therefore, I tried to be genuinely useful to Donna, which wasn't difficult, for she was a delightful young woman. It was no lie that I wanted new gowns for myself and Meg, and Donna wanted new clothes too. Also she was interested in the details of her household. She liked sometimes to buy supplies in person, rather than leave it to her servants. She was serious for her age, which was indeed only twenty, and though she was so shy, she was still very aware of her position as mistress of the house. The portly butler, Greaves, respected her and fortunately they could converse because Greaves's previous employer had taken him to France, where he had acquired some French ("and my round belly," Greaves admitted to me. "The French cook so well!").

I took Donna to markets and merchants, interpreting for her, but also encouraging her to try out her English and speak for herself. Under my guidance, she learned the English names of materials and garments, foodstuffs and household goods; soon she was able to ask for cuts of meat and specify spices and could order candles or lamp oil. She learned to request weights or quantities and arrange for their delivery.

I walked in the grounds with her, discussing the plants in the knot garden and telling her their English names, and I established a daily hour of formal English instruction for her. She was a quick learner and I was used to teaching, having helped Meg with her studies. Before I left the Ridolfi household, I decided, Donna would be at home in London.

She seemed to like me, which was helpful in one way, though it created a difficulty in another because it was hard for me to get away from her. Her husband was out, attending to business, for most of the day and she depended on me for company. If we were not shopping, or supervising in the kitchen or garden, or studying English, she wanted me to sit with her, to talk and sew, or to practice music. She could play both spinet and lute and when she found that I could do the same, was eager to try out duets with me. If she had a fault, it was a tendency to cling. If I asked for time to myself, she did not refuse it, but she would pout, just a little.

In addition, she expected me to attend the Mass that their chaplain, Father Fernando, said each morning in the upstairs parlor, and also to come to the same parlor before supper, to listen while Fernando read passages from devotional works. Ridolfi was usually present on both occasions and I would watch him covertly. I could tell, by the ardor with which he prayed and listened, how intensely he believed. It could have been touching, but in a man who could be sending cipher letters to Mary Stuart, it was alarming.

Ridolfi, in fact, displayed more ardor in his religious observances than his chaplain did. Fernando was elderly, a pink-faced little man with a white tonsure who, I think, just wished for a quiet life. I rather liked him, but these regular sacred observances were horribly in my way, for they were just one more obstacle to snooping.

However, this too was something I had learned to overcome. Once you know a household's routine, you also know the chinks, the gaps during which stealthy investigation can take place. The middle of the day was always busy, with dinner to be served both in the dining room and, as a rule, in Ridolfi's study. He usually came home for the meal but ate it at his desk, before hurrying back to the City. But when he returned home in the evening, he and Donna generally spent an hour or so in private, in their chamber or in one of the parlors, and then I was free.

I had to be wary of the servants, of course, but at that time of day, the cleaning work of the house was finished, and the servants would usually be in their own part of the house unless summoned by their employers to bring refreshments or carry messages. With caution, it was possible to do a good deal of prowling then, looking in closets and presses, and even into locked document boxes. I had once more taken to wearing divided overgowns with pouches stitched inside the opening, and in those pouches, I carried my old lockpicks.

But I found nothing of note. The month of May came and went. At Hawkswood, Meg's fourteenth birthday was drawing near and I sent her a crimson damask gown and a gold necklace. June arrived. I knew that investigations had continued into the deaths of Gale and Walt, and when I or the Brockleys encountered anyone from Norfolk's household, we asked about them, but so far, it seemed, the mysteries remained unsolved.

I could do nothing toward solving them myself. I stayed where I was, wrote harmless letters to Hugh and to Meg, missed them both to an extreme degree, and got nowhere. If Ridolfi were up to any mischief, he was keeping it well concealed.

When he was at home, I did my best to watch his movements and take note of his visitors, but I didn't see any more money change hands. I felt I was plowing a very stony field, but I kept at it. In my experience, if there were anything at all to find, traces would ultimately appear, probably when one least expected them.

"How foolish of me," Donna murmured. "I have left my lute music downstairs. I was playing for my husband after supper yesterday. He is fond of music, you know, Ursula."

"Yes." I looked around from arranging my own music at the spinet in the upstairs parlor. "I remember how good the music was that was played when I dined here, with my husband and the Duke of Norfolk."

"Indeed, yes. Roberto is so cultured." One of Donna's charms was her obvious admiration for Ridolfi, who, in her eyes, was a prince who could do no wrong. I hoped I wouldn't one day shatter her trust in him.

Dinner was over and Donna wanted to spend the afternoon practicing her music. Fran Dale was with us, quietly stitching, but Donna's maid was not there. Brockley had gone out to buy physic for an ailing horse and Gladys was in the garden, talking to Arthur Johnson as she often did. Hillman had duly spoken to him and Johnson had behaved better since. I worried far more about Gladys upsetting him than the other way about, and I had told him that she was a little odd at times, but harmless. He chuckled and assured me that he wouldn't take her amiss. They seemed to get on together and while she was with him, I didn't think she would get into trouble.

Donna, meanwhile, was asking permission to send Dale in search of her music. I smiled and shook my head. "I'll go," I said, getting up from the spinet. "I know where it is, I think. You were in the downstairs parlor yesterday evening, were you not? I will be quicker, and Dale has already run dozens of errands for me today."

Dale caught my eye and smiled. She had run hardly any errands that day but she knew that every time I had a chance to move about the house, I seized it, just in case I came on something of interest.

I left the room, crossed the dining chamber, and went down the wide stairs. A few moments ago, I thought I had heard someone knock at the front door and be admitted. Ridolfi had dined in his study as usual and had not yet left to go back to the City. The caller might be with him now.

The wide stairs led down to a vestibule at the back of the house, equivalent in size to the reception hall at the front. This rear hall had dark paneling, and was as shadowy as the other was light. Doors led off to various ground floor rooms, one of them the parlor where the music had been left. Another was Ridolfi's study. As I reached the vestibule, I heard voices from behind the study door.

No one was about. I was wearing soft slippers, a considered choice. On silent feet, I stepped up to the door and put my ear against it.

I had done this kind of thing before, as well. It was distasteful but often necessary and if it made me feel like a prying maidservant, it couldn't be helped. It was nerve-racking, too, just as searching other people's papers always was, because of the risk of being caught. When I had one ear to a door, the other was always alert for approaching steps.

In the Ridolfi house, I had nearly been caught twice already and all for nothing, since I never heard anything more interesting than Ridolfi commissioning a miniature painting of Donna or warning someone away from a foolish investment. I didn't expect anything better this time. I simply tried my luck.

One of the voices belonged to Ridolfi. He was speaking English, though, and whoever was with him sounded like a London man. I thought his voice was faintly familiar but I couldn't put a name to him. Listening intently, I thought his tone was strained, uncertain.

". . . expect to have it ready tomorrow morning, and I can bring it when you like . . ."

"I am most grateful, though I knew I could rely on you."

"I hope I'm doing right. The scheme should placate the Spanish administration and that can only benefit merchants like myself, who have let too much of our trade become dependent on Antwerp, but this is the first time I have been involved in politics and I'm not sure . . ."

"A modest contribution to a respectable cause can't be called getting involved in politics, my friend. Some more wine? It really is a respectable cause, you know. Mary Stuart is the rightful queen of Scotland and there is nothing wrong in wanting to see her wisely married and restored to her place in the world. Even if it does mean buying support here and there. Men are so venal," said Ridolfi regretfully.

"There will be opposition. Unless she is willing to become an Anglican . . ."

"That will never be, nor should it!" There was unmistakable passion in Ridolfi's voice. "She would lose my support at once and my support counts for something, believe me!"

"Ah, well. I have no strong feelings on the matter myself . . ."

"I am sorry to hear it. You English are so . . . so phlegmatic in these matters. It troubles me. Your immortal souls are in peril and you seem unconcerned!"

"I . . . er . . . don't think we altogether agree there," said the visitor's voice mildly.

"Well, well, we will not argue about it. You said earlier that you didn't wish to bring the money to the house . . ."

They were moving away, turning their backs on the door. I pressed my ear harder against the paneling. I heard the other man say something about discretion, and then Ridolfi laughed.

"You mean that if something went wrong, it wouldn't do if you were known to have visited me more than once. You'd rather not have come here at all. Ah well, you're not the only one who's timid!" Ridolfi's voice was resonant. I could still hear him, at least. ". . . for those who wish to be discreet, I can make other arrangements. Your house is on the river, like mine, is it not? Some way from here, but still, if you wish to visit me secretly, come by water! I can arrange for us to meet out of sight of the house, just after nightfall. I often do so, for people who have no real excuse for visiting me. Tomorrow evening would be convenient. See now—come over to the window. You can see from here that . . ."

Annoyingly, Ridolfi too moved out of earshot. However, he must have turned back a moment later, for then I heard him say: ". . . de Spes has met me there once or twice. In his whimsical way, he calls it *where the swans are.* He refers to it thus because he says, if we should be overheard, no one will know what it means. He is always afraid of listening ears. The government is so suspicious, he says!"

"He clearly has a poetic mind," said the other voice, dryly this time. Whoever owned it wasn't a nonentity, I thought, and wished I could fit a face to it.

"De Spes is ever poetic," said Ridolfi. "He can hardly see a tree without indulging in flights of fancy about dryads. Until tomorrow, then . . ."

I retreated, tiptoeing rapidly away from the study door and into the parlor. I found the sheets of music and picked them up. I stood for a moment thinking and then made my way quickly out of a door on the far side of the parlor, through a short passage and out to the stable yard. I looked for a groom and presently found two of them in the harness room, polishing saddles.

"When Roger Brockley comes back, will you tell him that Mistress Stannard wishes to see him at once?"

Incuriously, they assured me that they would. I made my way back indoors and upstairs to where Donna was waiting. I heard and saw nothing of Ridolfi or his guest on the way. Donna was strumming the spinet, somewhat restively.

"I was about to send Dale to find you," she said. "You were so long!"

"I went to see if Brockley had come back yet," I said. "He wasn't there, so I left a message that I wanted to see him when he returned. I want to ask about the ailing horse. I'm so sorry to have kept you waiting. Let's begin without delay!"

Word was brought about an hour later that Brockley was back. Donna excused me, though with a trace of a pout, as usual. I went straight down to the stable yard and found him insisting that the horse—it was the packhorse that had brought my belongings—should be separated from the rest because it was coughing and the other horses might catch it. There was an overflow stable block for use when the Ridolfis had a crowd of visitors, but at the moment it was empty. "It would be best to put the packhorse there," Brockley was saying.

"If you'll put some bedding down for him, I'll lead him across," I said to Brockley. In a low voice, I added: "I want to talk to you . . ."

14

Skulking in the Alders

"This is like old times," I said the following evening, as Brockley and I made our way toward the river, by way of the topiary garden, to avoid being seen from the windows. "Do you remember how we set out in the dark to investigate a document box in that castle on the Welsh border?"

Brockley said: "I remember it well, madam. You found a dead man lying on a study floor and we spent the rest of the night in a dungeon."

The topiary garden was itself a little menacing at dusk. As we hurried through its shadowy paths, I wished I hadn't reminded us of Vetch Castle. We had been in grave danger then.

Danger of more than one kind, too. That was the time when Brockley and I had come closer to each other than was proper for a lady and her manservant. The most perilous moment in our friendship had taken place in that castle dungeon.

I think Brockley was remembering the same things. Smoothly changing the subject, he now said: "How did you account to Madame Ridolfi for leaving her this evening?"

"It was difficult. That's why I'm later than I meant to be. Master Ridolfi shut himself in his study after supper and then Madame wanted me with her while the chaplain read to us again. In the end I pretended I had a headache and asked to go to my room. I waited there long enough to let Father Fernando get under way with his reading, and then slipped downstairs and into the garden and found you among the yew trees."

"I was wondering whether you would manage to come at all," Brockley said. We reached the far end of the yew garden and emerged by the river. "Well," he remarked inquiringly, "what next?"

It was chilly. June, the midsummer month, had this year brought cold winds and overcast skies. We both had stout cloaks but even so, we hardly felt warm. "From what I overheard," I said, "Ridolfi's tryst should be soon and it's 'where the swans are.' Well, there they are, swimming by the bank. I thought," I said doubtfully, "that we could hide in those alders. I looked at them earlier and there's a little clearing in the middle."

"There's nowhere else to hide," Brockley agreed. "If they meet on that miniature headland, we just might be able to hear what's said, though it's windy, and that won't help. But we should be able to see who Ridolfi meets—that's something. Hush!" He stiffened. "There's a boat coming. I can hear the oars and there's a lantern on board. Look!"

"We'd better hide ourselves now," I whispered. "And hope for the best."

We pushed our way into the clump of alders. There was indeed a clear space in the center and we could peer out between the heart-shaped leaves and watch the lantern light move slowly toward us across the water. Meanwhile, we could still talk, in whispers.

To reminisce was mischievous but once again, I was tempted. "Do you remember," I whispered, "the time we had to hide in a cupboard—at Lockhill Manor. In 1561, it must have been. I thought we'd be caught, that time. It was a very near thing."

"I've always hoped," Brockley muttered, "that the frights you've had would one day cure you of plunging into danger. I sometimes fear, madam, that your quiet domestic life bores you a little."

That bordered on impertinence but I had invited it. After a pause, I said: "I like my everyday life. I like being married to

Hugh. It's just that sometimes . . . I still hear the call of the wild geese. Do you know what I mean? Did you know that Mattie's husband, Rob Henderson, once said that of me?"

"Yes, madam. I overheard when he said it." My excellent manservant heaved a sigh. "I pray, madam, that for all our sakes, you will one day cease to hear it! I most truly wish . . ."

He stopped, and his hand closed on my forearm, gripping it hard and dispassionately. "The boat's almost here," he whispered.

We fell silent. The sound of the oars was close at hand now. There was a light scrape as a dinghy came to rest alongside the stage. I squinted through the foliage, and in the twilight, mingled with the gleam of the lantern, I saw a hand toss a loop of rope over a mooring bollard.

Someone climbed out of the boat. Brockley moved to see better, but drew back sharply, rubbing his nose, having scraped it on a branch. "I can't make out who it is!" he breathed.

"He's got his back to us," I whispered back. "Wait. He's turning round to moor the boat properly. He's picking up the lamp. Oh!"

"What is it?"

"I know him!" I muttered it into Brockley's ear. "Well, more or less. I thought I'd heard his voice before somewhere. He's a merchant. His name's Paige—he deals in tapestries and fine fabrics. I took Madame Ridolfi to his warehouse to buy taffeta from him only two days ago."

"Indeed? Where's he going now?"

Carefully, trying not to rustle the leaves, we moved to see better. The fabric merchant was walking off the standing stage. He paused on the bank, looking about him, holding up the lamp, which showed him clearly. He was a big man with an auburn beard and beneath the heavy cloak which had protected him from the cold river winds, I glimpsed tawny velvet and a gold chain. Paige was the kind of man who normally went about with several attendants to brush the crowd out of the way. Furtiveness didn't suit him.

His pause lasted several moments, during which Brockley

and I froze. Master Paige, however, seemed satisfied. He gave a small nod, as if telling himself that all was well, and walked forward again. Brockley shifted position once more, found another gap to peer through, and gave an irritated grunt.

"What is it? Where's he gone?" I muttered. "I thought he'd come this way."

"No, he's gone into the topiary garden. Do we follow?"

Ridolfi must have given Paige some extra instructions which I hadn't heard. The topiary garden was a surprise, and an awkward one. "It's risky," I said doubtfully. "We could come upon him and Ridolfi straightaway. It still isn't quite dark. I wish I'd heard more through the study door. He could be waiting for Ridolfi just inside."

"We could go as far as the arch and listen. Once they meet, they'll begin to talk. We'd hear that if they were nearby."

Cautiously, we left our shelter and stole toward the arch, pausing just outside. We did hear voices, faintly, some way within the garden by the sound of them. Warily, we moved in, one at a time, edging sideways and keeping close to the sides of the arch, afraid of showing ourselves against the faint light that still lingered over the river.

We were glad of our caution, for almost at once, the faint voices increased in volume. Ridolfi's was raised in tones of indignation, and then we realized that he and Paige were coming back toward us. We could not retreat through the arch. Just in time, we hid behind the nearest yew tree.

Ridolfi, speaking English and obviously furious, was holding forth. ". . . you gave me an undertaking . . . contributions are essential and in time, you would have been rewarded . . . Queen Mary pays her debts . . ."

"I told you before and I tell you again, I have never liked being caught up in political matters and this very day, my son, who went with the merchant fleet that sailed to Hamburg, came home bringing a consignment of fine Flemish tapestries. If we can trade through Hamburg, the whole situation is different." The two of them had halted in the archway, only feet away from us, which was both alarming and convenient. "My business is back on an even keel and I feel no need to become tangled up in any schemes to placate the Spaniards. Give me credit that at least I came in person to tell you of my decision and assure you that I will not reveal your dealings to any other person."

"Yes, for that I must be grateful, I suppose. I should be very careful, Master Paige, that you do *not* reveal my dealings. I would make sure that you regretted it."

"Keep your threats, Master Ridolfi. You might find that I am able to protect myself better than you think. I am a man of position!" retorted Paige. He swung round, cloak swishing, and strode away. Ridolfi stood there, hands on hips, outlined in the archway. Under his breath he muttered what sounded like an oath. Farther away, we heard Paige get into his boat and grunt as he pushed off. Ridolfi turned away and walked off through the topiary garden once more, presumably making for the house.

"Well, I suppose we've learned something," I whispered. "From what I heard at the study door, Paige was bringing money. Now he's changed his mind. I must say I'm relieved about that, for his sake."

"He's a merchant, you said, madam?" Brockley asked.

"Yes. I know him. I usually buy from him when I come to London. You've been with me, sometimes. Didn't you recognize him?"

"I couldn't see well enough." I sensed rather than saw that Brockley was frowning. "But if that's Paige, he sells to Cecil! I would have said he was a completely respectable man!"

"That's just the point. The Antwerp business has hit trade so badly that some of the merchants have become desperate, Paige included, I presume. But I think I have heard some gossip at Ridolfi's table, about a merchant fleet sailing for Hamburg, with warships to guard it. Our merchants are finding ways to trade without Antwerp. Paige is getting himself out of whatever's going on, and a good thing too. I daresay he wasn't the only one drawn in. I hope they all back out!"

I hoped it very much. There were images in my mind of small craft being sucked into a deadly vortex; of spiders crouching in the middle of scarcely visible webs, waiting for unwary flies to glide in to their doom. It sounded as though big bearded Master Paige had decided, in time, not to be among the flies. I could but pray for the rest.

We waited awhile for safety's sake, but Ridolfi didn't return. It was late when we finally emerged from hiding and made our way back to the house going circumspectly by way of the knot garden.

The cloudy sky had cleared somewhat, however, and as we reached the terrace, a nearly full moon came out, lighting up the back of the house. We were disconcerted to see, at one end of the terrace, a ladder propped against the wall and a figure stealthily climbing it toward a candlelit window above. I caught at Brockley's elbow and pointed.

We ran along the terrace. The figure couldn't be Paige, who was out on the river and whose bulky form was ill-adapted for climbing ladders, anyway, and it surely wouldn't turn out to be Ridolfi. "Who on earth . . . ?" I said, as we came to the foot of the ladder. "Isn't that the window of Hillman's room?"

"No. His is the one below. I think that one's . . ."

We were near enough now for a clear view at least of the ladder-climber's legs. I would have known those knotted calf muscles anywhere. "Arthur Johnson!" I said.

"And that window, madam, if I'm not mistaken, is that of the maidservants' dormitory. What the devil are you about, Johnson?"

At that moment, from somewhere above, there came an angry shriek. This was followed by a mingling of female squeals and laughter and suddenly the casement just above the top of the ladder was flung open and the contents of a bowlful of liquid were hurled out. Arthur Johnson, however, with an air of expertise, as though this had happened before, leaned sideways and most of the arc of liquid missed him. We ourselves jumped out of the way just in time and even so, Brockley's cloak was splashed. He took a damp fold between finger and thumb and sniffed at it. "It isn't water," he said with distaste.

The window banged shut, to the accompaniment of what sounded like a few insulting remarks in a feminine voice, and the elderly gardener came backward down the ladder. His seamed face was grinning.

"That's the maidservants' room!" said Brockley furiously. "It's late," he added to me. "They're probably undressing now." He grabbed Johnson as the gardener stepped off the ladder. "What were you at, climbing up there to peer at the young wenches, you dirty-minded fellow!"

"I don't mean no harm. They're a pretty sight. Warms my old heart, it does, when I get a glimpse. I wouldn't hurt any of them," said Johnson. His grin was positively evil. "Just a bit of fun. I've got sense, I have. If I get wed again, I'll do the proper thing and find myself a good old woman that can cook for a man as don't have many teeth, and 'members the same bygone years that I do. Got my eye on that old woman of yours, Mistress Stannard, as matter of fact. She knows how to make physic for my aching old bones, too. I could do worse."

"Gladys?" I said, so astonished that I forgot to be disapproving. "I did tell you, you know, that Gladys is . . . a little strange at times."

"Oh, aye, all that witchy nonsense. She only does it to scare people and stop them brushing her aside because she's old," said Johnson shrewdly. "Gets up her nose, that does. She don't act like that with me, cos I give her some attention." He leered. "All the ladies want a man paying heed to them. I tell her she's a fine old girl and take her walkin' round the garden—my, my, there's nothing she don't know about herbs—and she's sweet as an angel. Oh yes, I got my eye on her. But looking at young wenches—what man doesn't want a bit of that? Even if you can't digest rich food no more, you can still feast off the smell of it."

"You're a disgrace!" I said. "I thought you'd listened when Master Hillman spoke to you, but evidently you paid him no heed at all!"

"Quite so!" Brockley snapped. "I've a good mind to speak to Signor Ridolfi. And why are you still here at this time of night, anyway?"

"I often sleep over when I've work not finished. The wenches have talked to the master already. He values my work so he just told them to do what they did just now. It's a sort of game. They don't mind."

"Oh, get on your way!" shouted Brockley, and attempted to help Johnson's departure with his boot, except that the gardener neatly evaded him, before leering at us both again, observing that he'd much like to know what *we'd* been doing, a-walking in the garden in the dark; nice goings-on for a lady and a manservant, in his opinion, and with that, he took himself off with remarkable speed before Brockley could get at him.

15

Herbal Concoctions

At the house, Brockley went off to the kitchen, to put his spattered cloak to soak and find a drink of ale to counter the smell of the maidservants' parting gift to Johnson. I would have gone straight to my chamber, except that suddenly I heard voices in the downstairs parlor, speaking French. One of the voices was that of Ridolfi.

Though it was late, there were people about. The maidservants had gone to bed but I could hear Greaves reminding someone to prepare a spiced wine for the nightcap that Master Hillman liked each evening, and a couple of kitchen boys passed me, bringing in a supply of firewood. I couldn't put an ear to the door this time. Instead, I went boldly in to join the company.

I found both Ridolfis there, along with the little pink-faced chaplain, Father Fernando, and George Hillman. Signor Ridolfi was sitting in a relaxed fashion beside his wife and not looking at all as though he had just come from a clandestine meeting. Donna was clearly surprised to see me, since I was supposed to have gone to bed with a headache.

I had prepared for this, just in case. "I decided that I needed fresh air more than anything. Instead of going to bed, I went into the knot garden for a while. I feel better for it."

"I am glad," said Donna. "Come and have a seat."

I did so, remarking that I hoped I wasn't intruding and

adding that in the knot garden, I had noticed some of the herbs that my woman Gladys used to cure my headaches. After all, I thought privately, I did have genuine headaches sometimes. "Will it be in order," I asked Donna, "if Gladys picks some and dries them?"

"By all means. And of course you are not intruding. We were only talking of a journey that Hillman must soon undertake. He's going to Scotland. Oh, such a cold, barbarous country, from all I've heard. I find England chilly enough!"

"I believe that Mistress Stannard has visited Scotland," Ridolfi said, "and met Mary Stuart there. Norfolk tells me, Mistress Stannard, that you used to live in France with your previous husband and that he was Matthew de la Roche, one of Queen Mary's most ardent supporters."

"That is so," I assured him gravely and added that I had met Mary Stuart several times and found her charming.

After our last encounter, Mary wouldn't say the same of me, and I hoped that Ridolfi would never ask her to give me a character reference but there was no point in worrying about matters I couldn't control.

"I am sure that Queen Mary found it a pleasure to converse with Mistress Stannard. She speaks such excellent French," Father Fernando observed. He himself spoke it well, though I now knew that he was Spanish.

"Indeed, yes," Hillman remarked. "With the true accent of Paris."

"When I lived in France," I said, "my home was in the Loire Valley. Matthew had a château there."

"Indeed? My mother greatly loved that district," Hillman observed. "An aunt of hers married a Frenchman who lived there. As a girl, my mother visited them several times."

"You must miss your mother," Ridolfi said sympathetically. "She died only a year ago," he explained to me. "I know the Hillman family a little. George's father also died, some years ago, but perhaps ten years since, he came to Italy on business and brought his wife and his sons. I met them socially—a delightful family. You were about sixteen then, Hillman. Recently, when I needed a new secretary and found that young George was in London, grown to manhood and looking for a post, I took him on at once. I was sorry to learn of his mother's death. Antonia was a truly gracious lady."

"Yes, she was," said Hillman sadly. "And most beautiful."

"Your mother was called Antonia, Master Hillman?" I asked him. "That's an unusual name—classical, surely? That's the second classical name I've come across lately. Your predecessor in your post here was called Julius. It's quite a coincidence."

"Oh, it's no coincidence. Julius was my cousin. My mother was one of two sisters, daughters of a scholar who taught Latin and Greek. He gave his daughters Roman names—Antonia and Julia. Julia was Julius's mother. She persuaded her husband to give their son a Roman name as well. My own father disliked the notion, though, and insisted that his children must have good plain names, which is how I came to be baptized George. My elder brother is called William."

"I knew of the relationship, of course," said Ridolfi easily. "It was another reason for being glad to take Hillman on. But I fear I have upset you, Hillman, reminding you of your mother. I am sorry. Father Fernando, would you say a Mass tomorrow for the repose of Antonia's soul?"

"Of course!" said Fernando. "The poor English! Deprived of the comfort of the Mass; they spend their lives without consolation. It is greatly to be hoped that soon, we can lead them home to the fold."

I remembered Ridolfi saying something roughly similar to Paige, in the study, and as the thought went through my mind, Ridolfi himself said a solemn *amen*.

Hillman said nothing. I considered him thoughtfully. Like Julius Gale, he was a very attractive young fellow. Yet he served a suspect man and was about to carry letters to a suspect destination. What part had Julius Gale played in whatever mysterious drama was unfolding by such uneasy stages and was his cousin a player in that drama too?

Ridolfi rose. "Hillman, I shall spend much of tomorrow preparing the letters you are to take to Scotland. It will be a busy day and I may not be ready to sign them until after supper, but I'll certainly do it then because you must leave the following morning. I wish you to make the best speed you can, without foundering your horses. You can change horses as often as you need to do. Don't worry about the cost."

"Very well, sir."

I pretended indifference, while absorbing this information. This evening, skulking in the alders with Brockley, I had learned little. But here, suddenly tossed to me by fate, was something worth investigating. Letters! I thought hungrily. Bound for Scotland, and in some degree of haste. Before Hillman left the house, I wanted to see those letters.

The prospect was in some ways depressing, though.

"If there's any part of my curious career that I've really loathed," I said to the Brockleys, "it's peering into other people's correspondence. Mainly because it's nearly always dangerous!"

"I certainly can't see how we're to do it this time, madam," Brockley said. "I doubt if Master Hillman will oblige us by eating a bad chicken stew and asking you to make sure his letters are safe!"

"And Ridolfi said he doubted if he'd be able to sign the letters till after supper," I added. "I fancy that Hillman will just take them to his room when he goes to bed. Oh, damn."

As so often before, we were gathered in my chamber: the Brockleys and myself and this time, Gladys. The rest of the household was in bed. I was, as it were, holding a council of war by candlelight. There was a small fire, because of the unseasonable cold, and Gladys was using it to make hot drinks for us. Her infusions contained extraordinary mixtures of herbs and usually needed sweetening with honey, but they were reasonably palatable.

I was pleased with Gladys these days. Since we'd come to the Ridolfi house, she had given no trouble and although Dale and I had to remind her regularly about washing and changing her clothes, our efforts were worthwhile. Gladys looked ordinary enough and so far, her behavior had matched her appearance. She was now sitting on a stool by the hearth, steadily stirring. She looked around.

"Slip him some of that poppy stuff you always keep by you. He'll sleep sound an' you can tiptoe in when he's snoring, make sure he's got his curtains drawn round him, and then take a quick look round his room."

"That wouldn't be right." Dale was shocked. "It's . . . like poisoning someone."

"It won't poison him," said Gladys, dipping her spoon, lifting it out, and letting its contents pour back into the pot, while she gazed critically at its color. "It ain't poison! It's just a draft for sleep."

It was true. I had used it myself. I had learned of it in Scotland and later I had found a London apothecary who knew the drug and could supply it. Don't use it often, the apothecary had said. In emergencies, though, it was valuable.

"How can we give it to him without him knowing?" I said.

"That's easy," said Gladys. "He has wine mulled with honey and spices every night. Collects it from the kitchen, he does, and takes it up with him."

"Yes," I said. "I heard Greaves, this evening, telling someone to get it ready. But it wouldn't be easy to doctor it without being noticed! There's always someone in the kitchen."

"All you got to do," said Gladys patiently, as though I were a stupid child, "is get at it once it's in his room. As soon as he takes it in there, bang on his door and call him away for a minute or two, while I slip in and put the dose in the wine. I've been in the kitchen when it's being mixed. He has it that thick with the spices and honey; it's enough to drown the taste of anything and that stuff don't have much taste anyhow. He won't know. He'll just sleep like a little baby, and wake up feeling fresh and ready to travel to the moon, if need be."

We thought of several schemes for getting Hillman out of his room after he had retired for the night. Finally, I adopted a somewhat unkind ruse, but it worked very well. I had in my jewel box an amethyst brooch very like the one that Hillman sometimes put in his hat, and as it chanced, I hadn't worn it since I came to the Ridolfi household. At the end of the next day, after everyone had retired, Dale hovered in the kitchens, gossiping, while Brockley hovered near the stairs, and between them they made certain of the moment when Hillman took his goblet upstairs. Brockley then went at once to knock on his door and ask him to come down again, to the parlor. I was waiting there, with the brooch on the table before me, in a pool of candlelight. Pointing to it as Hillman came in, I asked him sternly if it were his.

Hillman was still dressed, having had no time to be anything else. He looked tired, however, and he was understandably irritated.

"Was it necessary to call me down because you've found a piece of jewelry that could be mine? I've a long ride tomorrow and I could do with my sleep." He picked the brooch up and examined it. "Surely Brockley could just have brought it to me! It isn't mine, as a matter of fact. I have one not unlike it, but mine is upstairs, in my hat."

"It was found," I said severely, "on the floor in the chamber used by Master Brockley here and his wife. If it were yours, I would have asked you to explain what you were doing there. It is not the sort of question to ask casually in a doorway."

Hillman's expression was a mixture of the exasperated and the amused. "Am I supposed to have had a liaison with Fran Brockley while her husband was elsewhere?"

"Not exactly. But if this belonged to you, I would ask for an explanation. However, if it isn't yours . . ."

"It isn't. I can produce mine, if you like."

We went through with the pretense and Brockley went with him to fetch his own brooch. Gladys had had plenty of time to slip into Hillman's room with her sleeping draft. "I hope she did it. There was no sign of her," Brockley said afterward. The brooch was brought to me for comparison; I apologized to Hillman for my suspicions and for disturbing him, and let him go crossly back to his room.

"I won't ever be able to wear that brooch in this house," I said regretfully. "Now. We've got to give time for the drug to work. It's quick as a rule but it lasts well. We'll wait an hour. It will let everyone else settle down, too. We'd better go to my chamber."

My room was lit by two branched candelabra. Gladys was there, on a settle with Dale, waiting for us. I raised my eyebrows at her as we came in and she nodded. "Aye, it's done. He'd taken a sip, I reckon, but not more. There was plenty left."

We all seated ourselves. "Brockley," I said, "when you fetched Hillman, and when you went with him to find the brooch, did you have a chance of looking round his room? And does he bolt his door? If he does, we're defeated before we start."

"He didn't need to draw any bolts when I went up the first time to fetch him and tapped on his door," Brockley said. "I think we can get in. Yes, I did have a chance to look round. His saddlebags were on the floor by the bed. Most likely, the letters will be in them. Best try there first. If not, we'll have to try his doublets, and they'll be in the clothespress. That stands by the right-hand wall as you go in. But the betting is on the saddlebags."

"I'll go in alone," I said. "No need for you to be involved any further, Brockley."

Brockley regarded me gravely. "I shall accompany you, madam. I can't allow you to do this on your own."

"That's good of you, Brockley, but . . ."

I wanted him with me but there had been a protective note in his voice. Too protective. I had felt the jerk in Dale's mind.

"Master Stannard would expect me to go with you," said Brockley firmly.

Very very faintly, I heard Dale's sigh as she relaxed, reminded that I had a husband. Hugh was a tolerant man, but he wasn't one to extend that tolerance to rivals.

We waited for the hour I had prescribed, all of us taut with nerves. I possessed a little hourglass, which I set on the small table by the bed, to keep track of the time. I also made sure that my writing set was ready on the table as well, with spare candles handy. "If we do get hold of the letters, I hope they're short and we don't have to take all night over copying them!" I said.

★ ★ ★

The hour dragged. When it was finally over, Brockley and I went quietly out. We both wore soft shoes and Brockley had a hooded candlestick. I had found it in my room, where it had evidently been put for me to use if I wished. It was made of silver, and the polished hood which sheltered the flame from one side not only enhanced the light but also reduced the flickering and, of course, shed the light only in one direction. If I kept the mouth of the hood turned away from Hillman's bed, it wouldn't easily disturb him, but it would illumine my task all the better.

Like shadows we moved through the house, through the passages to the room where Hillman slept. His door was closed, but when I tried it, it was unbolted, as Brockley had anticipated. It opened noiselessly.

The room within was dark. Softly, taking the candle from Brockley, I edged the door a little wider and we crept in. Hillman had drawn his bed curtains only partially, but he was in a deep sleep. We could hear his even breathing and a faint, rhythmic snore. Brockley touched my arm and then pointed. I made out the saddlebags beside the bed.

Brockley stayed near the door, in shadow. I stole to the saddlebags, set my light down on the floor, turned to cast its light on the bags, and very very carefully, began to undo the buckled straps of the nearest compartment.

I was trembling and I could hear my heart pounding in my chest. To my utter relief, I struck treasure at the first attempt. My fingers found a velvet bag with, surely, papers inside. Slowly I drew it out, loosed the drawstring, and removed the contents. Yes. Letters, two of them, apparently, rolled into cylinders and sealed.

Noiselessly, I picked up the candlestick, rose, and tiptoed out of the room. Brockley came with me. A moment later we were outside and had closed the door after us; within five more minutes we were in my bedchamber again, where Dale and Gladys awaited us. In the candlelight, their eyes were enormous.

"I think we've got them," I said. "We'll have to return them presently—but first, let's have a look."

I had been prepared, albeit nervously, to cope as best I could with seals. With the aid of a sharp knife heated in a candle flame, a seal can be cut free if one is deft enough, and even replaced afterward, using a little more melted wax. It's a delicate business, though. I was thankful to discover that although the letters in Hillman's care had wax seals on them, Ridolfi, this time, had decided to keep his authorship secret. He hadn't stamped his device into the wax. The seals could be removed and replaced very easily.

When we had opened our booty, we found that although there seemed to be only two letters, one was rather thick, and when we unrolled it, there were three missives inside, folded together. We spread all four letters out. Then we came to a halt. There was nothing that we could read. The text in every case consisted of an incomprehensible jumble of figures. All the writing was in cipher.

"We meant to copy them," said Brockley. "Do we copy these?"

"Yes," I said.

It was difficult work. The accurate copying of meaningless lines of figures, or even letters, is far more difficult than copying words that make sense, and candlelight doesn't help. Mercifully, none of the messages were long. Brockley, who had had some education as a boy and wrote a neat hand, did two and I did two, working slowly and checking each line as we went, for avoiding mistakes was vital. Errors might make it impossible ever to break the cipher.

When at last the work was done, I rubbed my sore eyes and folded the copies away in one of my hidden pouches. I rolled the originals up as before, putting on fresh seals. "Now," I said. "I'll get them back."

"No, madam," said Brockley. "I will. Tell me how to make sure they go back into the right compartments of the saddle-bags."

"The one I took them from is the nearest when you crouch where I did, and I left it unbuckled," I said. "The other buckles are all still done up—I never touched them. But . . ."

"No, madam! I'll take the risk this time. I shouldn't have let you do it the first time. I died a thousand deaths, waiting there for you. This time, you stay here."

"But if you're caught . . ."

"I've been paid by Cecil, but you know nothing about it. Leave this to me," said Brockley.

He took the letters and the hooded candle and went out. I waited with my heart now thudding so anxiously that it was a wonder it didn't shake the walls and bring people running to find out what that strange, dull thumping could be. But in only a few minutes, he was sliding back into the room, with his rare smile glinting. "It's done. He's still fast asleep."

I passed a hand over my brows, where a very real pulse of pain had begun. "Thank you, Brockley. *Thank* you."

Gladys cleared her throat. "You're getting one of your bad heads, mistress. I can see it coming on. I've got some of the herbs here that I use to put you right, and some fresh chamomile and feverfew that I got from the herb garden here only today. Fresh-picked is always best if you can get it. I'll make you a tisane afore you go to your bed."

"Gladys, you must need rest yourself."

"Not till I've done this for you, mistress," said Gladys with determination.

I was glad of her medicine, because by the time it was ready, the pain was growing ominous. It eased, however, when I finally lay down and when I woke in the morning, though I was still short of sleep, my head was clear and such sleep as I had enjoyed had been sound and peaceful.

The same, however, could not be said of George Hillman.

16

A Friend in Need

"You are ready for your journey? You slept well, I trust?" said Ridolfi casually to Hillman over our breakfast chops.

Or perhaps not so casually, because Hillman looked odd; he kept rubbing his eyes and shaking his head as if to clear his vision, and he had a puzzled expression.

"I *slept*," said Hillman with emphasis on the second word, "but I had the maddest dreams. It was like being delirious. I was setting out on my journey and riding my horse through the sky, and there were red and purple clouds all round me; then I thought I was in my bed and awake, but there were elfin lights bobbing about as though a league of fairies were wandering through my room; then I was plunging out of the window and soaring up to go head over heels among the stars. When I woke this morning I thought I must have started a fever in the night, but I don't feel ill and my skin's cool enough. Extraordinary."

Fran Dale, who was breakfasting at the same time, glanced anxiously first at Hillman and then at me. I cleared my throat and remarked that everyone had a bad night or a few wild dreams sometimes.

"I daresay, but these . . . !" Hillman sounded aggrieved, as though his strange night had been a personal affront. *I don't believe in goblins and I've had to spend the whole night with them,* said his tone. He was a very normal young man.

I hoped that my face didn't reflect the way my stomach had turned over when Hillman mentioned lights near his bed. He must, I thought in horror, have come half awake at some point when either I or Brockley was in his room, groping in his saddle-bags!

"You are sure you are in good health now?" Ridolfi said to Hillman. "If not . . ."

"In perfect health, I thank you, sir. I have already asked that my horse be saddled and brought round for me as soon as I finish breaking my fast."

His appetite was clearly undamaged, but he finished eating before anyone else, and left the room in haste. Madame Ridolfi was as usual taking a tray in her bedchamber. I murmured to Dale that she was to summon Brockley and Gladys to my room and very soon, I and my coconspirators were once more gathered together, and I was telling those who hadn't heard, what Hillman had said about his strange experiences last night. "How much did you give him?" I said to Gladys.

"Enough, look you," said Gladys sulkily. "I only *just* give him enough from the sound of it. I reckon he almost woke up!"

"Yes, I think he did," I said with feeling. Dale eyed me with concern. "You're upset, ma'am," she said. "I can see it."

"I think we were on the edge of disaster last night," I said. "And now I'm tired but somehow, I've got to get away from Madame Ridolfi today and take those transcripts to Cecil. He has codebreakers on his staff. I'm very anxious to get the transcripts out of my hands and into his. I won't feel safe until that's done."

"Safe, madam?" Brockley asked.

I sat down on the edge of my bed and nodded. As I did so, a fresh shaft of pain went through my left temple. A migraine attack might be looming after all, it seemed. "Do you forget what happened to Gale?" I said. "And Walt . . . I'll never forget poor Walt, as long as I live. We're dealing with people who not only do murder, Brockley, but who do it in hatred."

"Ma'am . . ." Dale's blue eyes were bulging and her pock-marks were suddenly very noticeable. As always, when she was frightened.

"I know, Dale. You want to get out of this tangle. So do I, for all our sakes and our safety, as well. If once I get those letters to Cecil, I think he'll agree that I can discover that I'm urgently wanted at home. Then we'll be off as quick as we can."

"I can take the letters to Cecil, madam," Brockley said.

"Thank you, Brockley, but . . ." I looked at the little hearth, which someone had raked out while we were at breakfast, and where kindling was laid for a new fire. "Gladys, will you light that fire, please, and make me another potion against headaches. Dale, please tell Madame Ridolfi that again I am not well, and intend to rest this morning until I feel better and may then walk a little in the open air. I know she wishes to shop, but she can do that now without my help! When she's left the house, I'll go to Cecil. I'd rather not ask you to go, Brockley. No one knows we have those transcripts, but they're still dangerous things to be carrying."

"Fran and I will accompany you, madam. That at least, I insist upon."

"Very well," I said.

Gladys made the potion and it was effective. The migraine abandoned its attempts to return. I was still tired though, and was glad enough to stay on my bed until Madame Ridolfi had visited me, expressed her concern, been reassured, and agreed to go out without me. I waited until I was sure that both the Ridolfis had left the house, Roberto on his way to the City, Donna in quest of damask and brocade. Then I got up, ignoring my weariness. "Let us hurry," I said.

June was at last behaving like summer. Indeed, I wished it could be cooler. Today, the sun was very hot and the Strand was dusty. However, we hadn't far to go. There was no hindrance at Cecil's house this time. I was admitted at once and we were led straight to Cecil's study. The man behind the desk rose politely to his feet as I entered. I said: "But . . . er . . ."

The man now occupying the Secretary of State's private study wasn't Cecil. This individual was a good deal younger, though his grave expression was worthy of the most venerable archbishop and his black hair had already begun to recede from his temples. He was very dark altogether, hair, beard, and eyes. Even his skin had a swarthy tone.

"Mistress Stannard! Welcome. Please come in and be seated. Tom"—he was addressing the page who had brought us—"take Mistress Stannard's people downstairs and offer them refreshment while they wait. I am most happy . . ."

"One moment," I said. "I understood . . . I mean, I came to see Sir William Cecil and I don't know . . ."

"Forgive me." He had an archbishop's formal manners, too. "I am forgetting. We haven't met before and evidently Sir William has had no occasion to mention me to you. I am Sir Francis Walsingham, one of the juniors of his department."

"I see," I said, not seeing at all, since this was not only Cecil's private office but was in his private house.

Walsingham seemed to pick my puzzled questions out of the air. "On Sir William's instructions, I have come to finish some outstanding work of his while he attends a preliminary hearing of the Norfolk case. You know of that, I believe? Thomas Howard is an honest and admirable stepfather, it seems, and Sir William is anxious to help as much as he can in the matter of the stepdaughters' inheritance."

"Oh. Yes . . . yes, I knew about the lawsuit," I said.

"Quite. And now, what can I do for you? You may trust me as you would have trusted Sir William, I promise you. I know what kind of tasks you have carried out for him in the past."

In my concealed pouch, the transcripts crackled. I longed to be rid of them, but something was putting this impulse in check.

The something, oddly enough, was the memory of the merchant Paige, a perfectly honest merchant whose customer I had been, on and off, for years. Paige was probably out of Mary Stuart's web now, but he had been in it, very lately. Norfolk was caught in it too, and so were great men in Scotland and even here on the English royal council; Ridolfi himself was perhaps as much prey as spider. The same might even be said of de Spes. The arch spider, assuredly, was Mary.

I didn't know, couldn't possibly know, how many other flies she had caught, or who they were. What it came to was that I didn't know enough about Walsingham to trust him.

Later, I wished I had. If I'd handed over those letters, then and there, collected my people, and made off home without delay, I might yet have averted the disasters in which the business ended. That matters could have been even worse than they were, is some comfort, but all the same, they will haunt me all my days. I still see it sometimes in my dreams. I was doing my best, but I hadn't the knowledge I needed to judge aright.

"Sir Francis," I said gently, "the matter is deeply confidential and I hope you will pardon me, but I can discuss it only with Sir William Cecil. May I know when it will be possible to see him?"

"Not today, for sure," said Walsingham. "And not tomorrow either. The following day, perhaps. But, Mistress Stannard, I assure you that I have his full confidence and that you need not fear to talk to me."

"I'm sure I need not," I said. "But nevertheless, I must observe perfect discretion in this. I am happy to have met you, Sir Francis. For the moment, however, I must say adieu."

"Now what do we do, madam?" Brockley asked, as soon as we were back in the street, in a disappointed group at the side of the Strand thoroughfare.

I longed for rest but instead, I said: "We go to Bishopsgate, to Sweetplum House, where the widow Edison lets lodgings. I need someone I can call a friend, someone reliable who knows about codes. Master Harry Scrivener has just retired from Cecil's service and Cecil vouches for his honesty. I met him at the Ridolfi house, but if he were in their toils, I doubt if he'd have encouraged my suspicions as he did; nor can I see how they could use him, since he's no longer privy to Cecil's secrets. I think I can rely on Master Scrivener. He just might be the answer."

17

Capricious Fortune

That wayward lady, Fortune, has a way of requiring the virtue of patience. Harry Scrivener wasn't at home.

We hired a boat to take us to London Bridge, the nearest point on the Thames, walked to Bishopsgate, and found Sweet-plum House easily enough. It was a tall black-and-white building, fashionably timbered, with windows overhanging the street. The widow Edison was there, wielding a broom and shouting loudly but amiably at a maidservant. She was an impressive figure, beefy of build and exuding a kind of ferocious good humor. She exuded speech, too, in torrential quantities.

Yes, that was right, Master Scrivener was one of her lodgers, though she called him Mr. because she was all for making life simple and she liked being called Mrs. in the modern way, rather than the old-fashioned mistress, which she always reckoned was for gentry anyhow. Mr. Scrivener had the big front room on the first floor. He was no trouble; she'd be sorry to lose him when he went home. But no, he wasn't in. Who would be on such a fine day? He was in London to see old friends and maybe buy this and that for there were things to be got in London, and well she knew it, that couldn't be matched anywhere else and she should know, being widow to a cloth merchant. But he'd said he'd be home for his dinner, if we'd care to wait. There'd be a bite to spare if we wanted it and didn't mind her charging for it, since this was her living, and what her husband had left her was put by safe against her old age, she being childless.

Here she did actually pause to draw breath but before any of us had time to speak, she was off again.

Lamb steaks grilled on a spit, with peas and beans, that's what she'd planned for dinner—half after twelve, she'd be serving it—and she could send the girl out for more steaks, and there'd be rice with honey and almonds to follow . . . only, if we were going off again till dinnertime, she'd want to be paid in advance, for if we changed our minds, there she'd be with a lot of lamb steaks that wouldn't keep in this weather . . .

Getting a few words in at last, I agreed to pay in advance for three dinners, did so, and then went off with the Brockleys to roam restlessly across London Bridge, looking at the shops and stalls upon it and the shipping that passed beneath, until noon, when we made our way back to Sweetplum. There, at last, in the big main room of the house, we found Scrivener, cool in shirt-sleeves, his doublet over his arm, learning from Mrs. Edison that he was likely to have company at the meal.

"Mistress Stannard! I thought from the description that it might be you. But Mrs. Edison could not recall your name."

Mrs. Edison hadn't asked it and had rolled over me like a flood tide when I tried to tell her. However, I smiled, introduced Brockley and Dale, and in a quiet voice, I said: "When we met at the Ridolfi dinner, you offered help should I ever need it. I need it now." Mrs. Edison, having brought us inside, had gone to the kitchen and was probably out of earshot, but this matter was very private. I was cautious.

Scrivener's thick iron-gray eyebrows rose, a wordless signal that he understood. "After dinner," he said obliquely. "Upstairs."

We ate in the big room, which was a communal chamber. Other lodgers came in to partake as well. But once we were fed (the meal was excellent; I would have recommended Mrs. Edison's cooking to royalty) Scrivener led us up a narrow flight of stairs to his first-floor sanctum.

"I'm lucky," he said, throwing the door open and going at once to pull stools out from under a writing table and plump the cushions on the window seat. "It's a large room and sunny. There's noise from Bishopsgate down below but it falls quiet at dusk and what of it, anyway? I like the City. I'm visiting it for pleasure this summer. I thought of taking a house, but then said to myself: what a bother. I shall have to hire servants and why trouble myself for a matter of a few months? A decent lodging where I can have privacy if I want it; that will do very well and be much cheaper. Now, what can I do to help you?"

"It's very confidential," I said. "But honest. I promise."

"I accept that, Mistress Stannard. So—what exactly is *it*?"

I produced the transcripts of the enciphered letters. "Cecil told me I could trust you. I want to decode these. Can it be done?"

Serious as this business was, it was amusing to see how Scrivener's face lit up when I handed him the copies of Ridolfi's letters. It was plain that such ciphers were the delight of his life.

"But this is enchanting." He spread the sheets out on his table, pushing a writing set and a pile of unused paper out of the way. "Tell me—if I may ask—where did this cipher come from? It's rare to find one that makes use of numerals rather than letters or symbols but numeric ciphers are my own speciality. I'm even wondering if it's one of mine."

Despite Cecil's assurances, I hesitated. I *had* met Scrivener at the Ridolfi house and even though he was retired, he no doubt still had contact with former colleagues; he might be in a position to help Ridolfi in one way or another: by passing messages, by persuasive talk, even, simply, by helping Ridolfi write and decode cipher messages. Perhaps I had been wrong to come here.

As though he had read my mind, Scrivener said: "We met in the house of Signor Ridolfi, did we not? Mistress Stannard, Cecil was kind enough to tell you that you could trust me, but although I have lately been his guest, I can't in all conscience say the same of Ridolfi. We have not discussed ciphers recently, but when I met him the first time, two years ago in Florence, well—on that occasion, we did. In fact, I showed him how a cipher I had then just created would work. Therefore, I ask you once more, does Signor Ridolfi have anything to do with these?"

Still, I hesitated, and Scrivener glanced at the Brockleys. "My companions are altogether reliable," I said quickly. "They helped me to obtain the documents you hold in your hand." I hesitated once more and then made up my mind. "I think I must be open with you. Cecil did vouch for you. God help us all if I'm making a mistake. You are right. Ridolfi wrote these letters."

"Better men than Cecil have been deceived," said Scrivener seriously. "But not by me. You needn't fear to be frank with me. However, tell me only what I need to know. I won't ask precisely how you came by these. They are not the originals, I take it?"

"No. They're copies that we made. We were careful over accuracy."

"I'm glad to hear it! Well . . ." Scrivener laid the letters down and drew his writing set and a sheet of blank paper toward him. "We can but test a few possibilities. What do you know, already, of ciphers?"

"Very little. I have come across one, but that was something that a couple of brothers had invented privately and it wasn't like this. It didn't substitute letters or numbers for other letters—it used words for letters. This is quite strange to me."

"I'd like to hear about the one you encountered. It sounds intriguing. However, as a start, let me show you what, in all innocence, two years ago, I showed Signor Ridolfi. The point is that in the most usual ciphers, the letters in the clear, ordinary text are replaced by code letters, numbers, or symbols. The cipher is harder to break if the system lets the replacement letters—or numbers or symbols—vary. I mean, you could have a code in which the letter A was always replaced by, say, W. But it would be better if A was sometimes represented by W and sometimes by some other letter. Perhaps by more than one other letter. Or numeral. That was what I had in mind when I invented this. Look."

He began to write. I pulled a stool up close and watched. "First of all," he said, "I put the alphabet across the page, like this . . ."

a b c d e f g h i j k l m n o p q r s t u v w x y z

". . . and then, beneath it, I write numbers, 1 to 26, since the alphabet has 26 letters in it. Like this, making sure that each number is neatly placed under the letter to which it refers. Thus . . ."

a	b	c	d	e	f	g	h	i	j	k	l	m
1	2	3	4	5	6	7	8	9	10	11	12	13

n	o	p	q	r	s	t	u	v	w	x	y	z
14	15	16	17	18	19	20	21	22	23	24	25	26

"That's the first stage," he said. "It doesn't stop there because if it did, it would be too easy to break—even if we complicated things a trifle by, say, moving all the figures along one or two places like this . . ."

He wrote again, showing us what he meant. The result was:

a	b	c	d	e	f	g	h	i	j	k	l	m
3	4	5	6	7	8	9	10	11	12	13	14	15

n	o	p	q	r	s	t	u	v	w	x	y	z
16	17	18	19	20	21	22	23	24	25	26	1	2

"You could use any sequence of figures," I said, interested. "I mean, you could start at—say—32, and go on from there, 32, 33, 34 . . . or begin at 105 . . ."

"You could indeed," said Scrivener, regarding me with approval, as a Latin master might consider a pupil who had grasped the ablative absolute at the first attempt. "But I didn't complicate matters so much when I talked to Ridolfi. In fact, I just showed him how to work the code using 1 for A, and going on to 26. Now, on that basis, suppose we wanted to encipher, oh, shall we say your name? Ursula. That comes out as 21, 18, 19, 21, 12, 1. Any halfway competent clerk could break that, probably inside ten minutes, but, aha!"

He beamed at me. "Now we go on to stage two. We have turned your name into figures. On each of them, we perform a little arithmetical calculation, but not the same one every time.

The system I showed Ridolfi was that the first figure—in this case, 21—is multiplied by 3, the second by 4, the third by 5, the fourth by 6, and then you start again, multiplying the fifth figure—that's 12—by 3—and so on. Are you accustomed to figurework at all? And can you use an abacus?"

"Yes. I used to help my uncle Herbert with his accounts," I said.

Scrivener went to a chest, opened it, and brought out a box, from which he took a small abacus. It was a pretty thing, with wooden beads painted in brilliant colors. He handed it to me along with his quill pen. "Can you do it for your name? You multiply 21 by 3 . . ."

I tackled the task, arriving after a while at 63, 72, 95, 126, 36, 4. "The letter U occurs twice in my name," I said. "When we did the first stage of the code, U came out as 21. But now that we've done a calculation on each figure, the letter U has worked out to 63 and 126. Quite different."

"Yes. The more different calculations you have, the less chance there is of a repetition. I found that four was the minimum if you really want to avoid that. If we'd only used three calculations, your letter U would have been 63 both times."

I worked this out and found that he was right. The Brockleys had come to lean over the table as well. Brockley said: "It's difficult to keep track of where you are."

"In the sequence of calculations, you mean?" I said. "Yes, it is."

Scrivener looked slightly pained. The pupil who had done so well with the ablative absolute had taken a severe toss at the gerund. "When you write out your first stage of numerals," he said, taking his quill back from me, "you first of all write out the numbers you're going to multiply them by—like this." He wrote quickly.

3 4 5 6

"Then," he said, "you put the enciphered numbers, produced by your first stage, beneath them in columns. I'll go on using Ursula as an example—see? Like this."

3	4	5	6
21	18	19	21
12	1		

"I don't see . . ." I began.

"Each figure is multiplied by the number at the head of its column," said Scrivener patiently.

I looked again and understood. I nodded.

"You'd have to destroy all your workings out afterward," he said, "but this way, you wouldn't easily go wrong."

"Let's try something longer," I said. "I want to understand this properly. I may not be able to decipher these letters—after all, there seem to be so many possible variations—but all this is interesting. I want to grasp the idea behind it properly. Let me see . . ."

Scrivener chuckled. "Who shall we involve in this sorry conspiracy, you mean? The queen's Sweet Robin, her Eyes, as I believe she variously calls him; shall we have him? He is not widely popular. Let us encipher the words *My Lord of Leicester.* We write it out—so—and then, under each letter, goes its first-stage number—still using the simple system where A equals 1."

M Y L O R D O F L E I C E S T E R
13 25 12 15 18 4 15 6 12 5 9 3 5 19 20 5 18

"Then," he said, "you sort it all out into its four columns, so."

3	4	5	6
13	25	12	15
18	4	15	6
12	5	9	3
5	19	20	5
18			

We all studied this with interest and I picked up the abacus again. "Let me see."

It was something of a struggle. My tongue came out between my teeth, as though I were a small child wrestling with a first attempt to learn the alphabet. Finally, though, I sat back in triumph. After much muttering and clicking, because I was out of practice, I had arrived at 39, 100, 60, 90, 54, 16, 75, 36, 36, 20, 45, 18, 15, 76, 100, 30, 54.

I considered this with my head on one side. "There are some repeated figures. Thirty-six, for instance."

"Yes, but those two thirty-sixes represent different letters. The first one is the F of OF and the second is the L of LORD."

"But the R in LORD and at the end of LEICESTER both work out to 54."

"It does happen," Scrivener agreed. "But not too often."

"My head's spinning," said Dale, making us all laugh.

And then it was Dale, who, leaning forward and pointing excitedly at the top sheet on the pile of coded documents, said: "But this one starts with just those figures! Look! 39, 100, 60, 90 . . ."

We all stared at each other, excitement silently rising. "Can you test it, madam?" Brockley asked.

"The last letter in LEICESTER is R," I said. "In stage one, that's 18, and it comes under column one, so it's multiplied by 3 and that's"—I once more checked on the abacus—"54. Yes, there's no doubt about that. So . . . so . . ."

"The next figure to be deciphered has to be *divided* by 4," said Scrivener. "Go on."

"The next figure *is* 4," I said. "So that would be 1! The letter A, presumably, at least if this is just being done by the most straightforward system. Then what? The next figure is 95. I've got to divide that by . . . yes, I see, by 5. That's . . . that's . . ." The abacus clicked furiously. "That's 19," I said triumphantly. "That's S. Then comes 36, which has to be divided by 6—which *is* 6. That's F. Then . . ."

A few minutes later, I had the sequence 1, 19, 6, 1, 18, 1, and 19 and had written out their alphabetic equivalents.

"*As far as!*" Brockley almost shouted.

I turned to Scrivener, and he reached out and folded the letters I had brought over quietly, so that he could no longer see their contents.

"We've cracked the code," he said. "Ridolfi has simply used the basic version which I showed him in Florence. Now, you have said that this business is confidential. Then keep it so. I don't want to know! You have the key." He held the folded sheets out to me. "Take these away and interpret them in private. There is a lot of material here," he added. "Don't try to do it all at once. Take pauses for rest and thus avoid errors. You'll need the abacus. Do you have one of your own?"

"No, not here," I said. "There's one at home in Hawkswood."

"You'd better borrow mine. Here—put it in its box. Then no one will see it and wonder what you want it for. Keep it if you like; I have another. Good luck. I will help again if you need me. I will be here tomorrow morning until the hour of ten."

"I don't like the idea of working by candlelight again," I said. "I'm much too tired. But the evenings are light. I'll make an excuse, take supper tonight in my chamber, and deal with these letters then."

"I think I must leave it to you," Brockley said. "I never learned to handle an abacus. I can write to your dictation if you wish."

"I'd be glad," I said. "It would help. It's going to take time, you know. I think I shall have to be ill again!"

Well, that wouldn't be difficult, I thought. My lack of sleep the previous night was still making itself felt. I would have no trouble in looking convincingly wan. The plan should work.

I might have known. That capricious lady, Fortune, wasn't going to let me get away with anything as well organized as that.

18

Long-Necked Birds

The moment we were back in the Ridolfi house, it was clear that something was wrong. The maidservant who let us in had a flustered air and in the distance, I could hear angry shouts and somebody crying. Then Signor Ridolfi himself appeared from the direction of his study. He rushed straight to me, seized me by the arm, and burst into voluble speech.

"Mistress Stannard! I am most glad to see you, most glad! I returned home to dine today and what do I find? My wife is out; you are out also, and my dinner is all in confusion."

"I'm so sorry," I said inadequately. I had been trying to think of a tale to tell Madame Ridolfi, to explain my own long absence when I was supposed to be unwell, and I was glad she was still out. However, I was bewildered by Signor Ridolfi's problems with his dinner. His meals weren't my responsibility.

Then the situation clarified. "Your servant, Mistress Stannard, your *elderly* servant—Gladys, that is her name, is it not?— she has quarreled with the topiary gardener and set all my kitchen by the ears. I must ask you to control her."

"*Gladys!* We might have known," said Brockley, under his breath, and Dale echoed him, sighing: "Gladys. Oh, of course."

The faraway disturbance was continuing and the maidservant had scurried away, apparently to join it. I could hear what sounded like a man—though it wasn't Father Fernando—

reciting prayers. I sighed, in my turn. "Just what has happened?" I asked.

"I was halfway through my dinner," said Ridolfi. "In my study as usual. But the second half wasn't served when it should have been. I came out of my study and shouted to know why no one had brought it, and then Greaves came to tell me that that old serving woman of yours was wrangling with Arthur Johnson, in the kitchen, where my servants were gathering to start their dinner when I had finished mine. Greaves said that my servants don't like either of them much but they're used to Johnson and laugh at him, while your Gladys Morgan frightens them. They took Johnson's side and your woman turned on them and said things that upset them and all work in the kitchen came to a stop."

Behind me, Brockley muttered a heartfelt, "Strewth!" and I felt my heart sink, like a stone thrown into deep water. ". . . er . . . just what did she say?" I asked, dreading to hear that she had cursed them.

"Greaves said she told them all they were a pack of fools," said Ridolfi. "And then, I am sorry to tell you, it seems she looked at the ceiling and asked the powers in the heavens what else could be expected in a Papist household! I did not know she was not of our faith! Nor did I know she held us in such contempt! Did *you*?"

". . . er . . . no. Gladys rarely speaks of such matters," I told him.

"Well, she spoke of them today. Then, it seems that one of the maidservants had heard something about Gladys from some servant of Norfolk's, who came with him once to this house. She blurted out that according to Thomas Howard's man, everyone in Howard House believes Gladys is a witch because she'd cursed them, whereupon they all fell ill. Then, my cook, instead of serving up my next course, took to reciting paternosters and crossing himself, and this Gladys stuck out the forefinger and little finger of her left hand . . ."

"Oh no!" I said involuntarily.

". . . and said she'd let them off this time but they'd better be careful, and with that she burst out laughing, or cackling, Greaves said, and walked out of the kitchen. Johnson went after her. They started shouting at each other out on the terrace and most of my servants rushed out to listen except for my cook, who's still praying aloud. Greaves said he'd fetch the rest of my meal but he hasn't done so. Mistress Stannard, the woman is *your* responsibility. I must ask you to deal with her!"

Still grasping my arm, he fairly marched me through to the back of the house. On the way, we passed the door to the kitchen quarters, where the cook was still praying, but we didn't stop there and I realized that most of the noise came from somewhere else. We reached the terrace and there, with many of the servants gathered interestedly around, were Johnson and Gladys Morgan, still in furious face-to-face confrontation.

". . . and don't you call me a silly old fool again! That ain't no way for a decent woman to talk to an honest man! Been at my work, I have, man and boy, for sixty years come next Michaelmas and folk as have eyes in their heads and a bit of sense there as well, can see for theirselves what I've clipped my yew trees into!"

"Silly old fool I said and so you are!" screeched Gladys. "All this fuss over nothing that matters a straw, look you! How many more times do I need to say it afore you see sense? I tell you again, they're just long-necked birds! And all green—they're not even white. They could be anything, bloody herons as like as not! And what's more . . ."

"*Herons?* First it's geese, then it's herons! I clipped them yew trees into swans, *swans,* and if you 'ad the sense just to look at the shape of them, you'd know! Swans ain't the same shape as geese or herons!"

"Bah!"

"Bah yourself!"

"Oh, really!" I said. "How old are they? They sound as if they're in a nursery!"

Ridolfi thrust me forward. "*Do* something!" he growled in my ear. "I can't. I don't want her cursing me," he added, candidly if cravenly. "And I think Greaves is frightened of her, too."

". . . I'm telling you, you old hag . . ."

"Who're you calling a hag?"

I started forward, but stopped short as Johnson's retort reached me.

". . . it's as well you said no to me this morning, acos if you hadn't, I'd be backing out of the marriage now! I wouldn't have you as a wife for a hundred sovereigns!"

"You wouldn't get me for a hundred sovereigns! My price is above rubies, so it is!" bawled Gladys.

"Has he proposed to her?" I asked blankly, turning back to Ridolfi.

"By the sound of it, yes," said Ridolfi. "But I want this racket stopped. Go *on*!"

I advanced on the couple. "Gladys! *Gladys!* And Johnson! What are you about, shouting like that so that all the world can hear?"

Engrossed with each other, face-to-face like two cats on a wall and ready to spit or scratch at any moment, the pair ignored me. At this point Greaves caused a diversion by appearing from the house, catching sight of his employer and at once shouting busily that all the servants should get back inside and that the rest of Signor Ridolfi's dinner was now awaiting him in the study.

"And Madame Ridolfi's coach is back and she wants her sewing maids—make haste, Eliza! Phoebe, that means you as well! Come along!"

Brockley and Dale, who had followed me to the terrace, now decided to take a hand themselves. Brockley grabbed Gladys and pulled her away from the angry gardener, while Dale glared at the hovering servants and declared that coming out to stare was just encouraging the uproar and she couldn't abide such shocking scenes! The shocking scene, however, was far from over. Brockley dragged Gladys over to me, and Mistress Morgan now condescended to notice my existence.

"He's a daft old man, he is!" she informed me, pointing rudely at Johnson. "First of all he wants me to marry him—at his age! Ought to have his grimy mind on higher things, he ought!—and then . . ."

"My mind ain't grimy, you horrible old witch!" yelled Johnson. You're the one that's grimy! Carrying on as if I was beneath you and not worth considering! Can't even be gracious to a fellow that's offerin' you his hand and heart, you can't. And you as foul as a midden your own self! You allus smell, you do."

"He didn't say that when he was sweet-talking me this morning!" Gladys spluttered, addressing me. "It was all compliments then! First of all, he wants me to wed him; now he's calling me grimy!"

"An' so you are!"

"He's a good one to talk—him that peeps in at windows if he thinks the maids are in there undressing! He's going woodwild, mistress, all because I thought them there birds he's carved out of the yew bushes in that garden there were geese and they're swans."

"I thought they were geese myself," I said, causing Johnson to scowl at me as ferociously as though I had questioned his paternity. I glared back at him. "It all seems to be a great to-do over nothing much and as for you, Gladys, you've made yourself unpopular among Signor Ridolfi's servants now! Weren't Hawkswood, Withysham, the vicar of Faldene, and Howard House enough for you? You've no more sense than a child of five and that's just what you sounded like just now!"

"Nothing much!" bawled Johnson. "She insults my work and you call it nothing much!"

"And you're as bad! It's not for me to give you orders but I think Signor Ridolfi would like you to return to your work, or, if you have finished for the day, to go away. Gladys, come with me! And don't try cursing me; I shan't be impressed. Come along at once! Signor Ridolfi, I am *extremely* sorry. Please go and finish your dinner. I'll see to this."

Somehow or other, Brockley, Dale, and I hustled Gladys indoors. "We'll take her to our chamber," Brockley said. She muttered and grumbled and was inclined to resist but we bundled her up the stairs somehow, pushed her into the Brockleys' room, and turned the key on her.

★ ★ ★

Coping with Gladys had been an exhausting nuisance. "I wanted to settle down at once and start on the deciphering," I said, as the three of us retreated breathlessly into my chamber. "I feel almost too tired now to breathe! I hope Madame Ridolfi doesn't want me this afternoon. We'll have to say that I felt better and went out, but that now I've been badly upset by this business of Gladys and have gone to lie down again. I think ⌐ . ."

I stopped, struck by a revelation out of nowhere. They looked at me curiously. "Madam?" said Brockley.

"I've just realized!" I said. I sank down on the side of the bed. "I've just *seen*! Gladys and Johnson showed me. I ought to be grateful to them. Where the swans are . . . we were watching the wrong swans the other night! Ridolfi didn't mean the real ones, he meant the topiary ones! That's where Paige went. *That's* where we should have hidden. That's where Signor Ridolfi meets his contacts! Of course! Why, one of the seats is beside one of those swan-shaped bushes! It's an obvious meeting place. I've let myself be distracted from this business of his secret meetings, and I shouldn't have. When he was making the arrangement with Paige, he implied that he'd made similar arrangements before. I daresay he'll make them again! We ought to be on watch."

I rubbed my forehead and they eyed me concernedly.

"We can't go prowling in the topiary tonight," said Brockley. "You need some rest, madam. And there's still the deciphering."

"Yes, of course. You're right. Well," I said. "The cipher is the first thing. Let's begin on that, while we can."

I had the letters in my concealed pouch. It was as well that I was only just reaching for them when the tap on the door came and Donna's voice outside said: "Mistress Stannard?" I quickly withdrew my hand, empty, kicked off my shoes, swung my feet onto the bed, threw myself into a lying position, and nodded to Dale to let Donna in. She swept into the room in a swirl of brocade skirts and a stream of French in her soft, pretty voice.

"Mistress Stannard! I heard you were better and had risen and been out! Do please come and see what fine materials I have bought! Enough for five new gowns, and I did all the haggling myself; I am so proud of that! One of the gowns shall be for you, *ma chère amie,* and one shall be for your young daughter . . . !"

"My daughter?" I queried.

"Oh yes, indeed. I have such a surprise for you! I thought you must be sad, separated for so long from your sweet girl and indeed from your husband. I wrote to Master Stannard at your Hawkswood house, and asked if your daughter at least could come to us. He has sent word that he agrees. Your sweet Meg will be here tomorrow!"

"Oh," I said blankly.

"And now," exclaimed Madame Ridolfi, "do come and see what I have bought!"

It seemed wiser not to resist her, to do nothing that might seem odd or suspicious. For the rest of the afternoon I wearily examined materials and patterns, trying to appear interested and animated, while time went by and the unread letters crackled now and then in my pouch. Evening and suppertime came and, after my show of lively interest in the gowns Donna was planning, it was difficult to claim that I was suddenly unwell, though I was by now so tired that it was true. I arranged for Gladys to be given food in the Brockleys' quarters, but I supped in the dining room and not, as I had intended, in my chamber.

The meal was ending when Donna, yawning, said that the long, busy day had made her sleepy and said she would have an early night. This would leave me free to go to my room and begin work. I was relieved, for all of thirty seconds, until Ridolfi answered his wife.

"I will join you later," he said casually. "I intend to take a stroll in the garden at dusk. There is a nightingale," he added romantically. "It begins to sing at that time and I like to hear it at close quarters."

A massive depression descended on me. Was a good night's sleep only a wild dream? I had hoped to do some deciphering before midnight, but if Ridolfi were really going to wander into the grounds to listen to nightingales, I was, in Hugh's words, the

King of Cathay. I would have wagered my much-loved Withysham itself and a bag of sovereigns that he had an assignation by the long-necked topiary birds.

I would have to work late into the night on the letters, and yet, somehow, I must be awake enough tomorrow to meet its demands. To welcome Meg . . .

Meg! I loved Meg. I wanted to be with her. But I did not want her here, in this hotbed of plots and murder. Hugh had probably thought I knew of Madame Ridolfi's invitation and therefore agreed with it. If only she had spoken to me first! How would I ever find the energy to pretend gratitude to Madame Ridolfi, to greet my daughter as I ought to greet her, to deal with any aftermath of Gladys's appalling behavior today—and to get to Cecil with whatever I learned during the long night that now stretched ahead of me?

Nor was it just that I was tired. The depression that had attacked me was more than mere downheartedness. With it had come a terrible sense of dread, a further heavy weight pressing down on top of my weariness, which was leaden enough on its own.

If only, oh if only, I had left that cipher in the hands of Walsingham, packed us all up, and left the Ridolfi house at once.

If only.

19

"When Mary Is on the Throne"

"Madam," Brockley whispered, "you're shivering. Are you well? It isn't cold."

True enough. The summer evening was warm and there really was a nightingale. Brockley had insisted on coming with me, on the grounds that Master Stannard would wish it, madam, and we had slipped out of the house, this time taking the risk of being seen going through the knot garden so that we could enter the topiary garden at the river end and be certain that at least we hadn't been seen entering that.

I had reconnoitered in advance and found a hiding place close to the bench where the paths crossed, and close, too, to the bushes that had been clipped into what we now knew were meant to be swans.

Unlike Gladys or even ourselves, de Spes had not confused Johnson's long-necked topiary birds with geese or herons, but had identified them as swans, and used them to pinpoint his trysting place. *Where the swans are,* he had said, but he could equally well have said *where the horses are.* Of the four angles made by the paths, two were occupied by swans, and the other two by the horses on which Hugh had commented.

These were exceptionally complex examples of the topiary art and more successful than the swans. Each pair of horses was clipped from a single bush and each consisted of a smaller animal, tossing its head—the manes were masterpieces—and a bigger one, rearing above its companion. In each case, on the side nearest the path, the rearing stallion's swirling tail, carved in relief, as it were, filled the gap between its hind legs and those of what was undoubtedly meant to be the mare. But on the sides away from the path, there were hollows, little caves of yew, perfect places of concealment and one was near enough to the bench for eavesdropping. It was a fair guess that if Ridolfi met anyone here, they would sit on the bench.

There was room for us both. However, as we fitted ourselves into our dark green niche, Brockley seemed anxious. He had a knack of sensing my moods, my fears, without being told of them. He was quite right. I was shivering but not with cold.

"It's fear," I said candidly. "I'm sure now that this business is connected to Gale and Walt and that's bad enough, but it's not just that I'm afraid of being caught. I have a sense of foreboding that I can't shake off. I wish Meg weren't coming here. I wish Madame Ridolfi hadn't meddled. I don't want Meg anywhere near this place!"

"This is not like you, madam. You are not as a rule superstitious."

"I know. But that's what I feel."

Brockley shook his head in puzzlement. We fell silent. I could feel his warmth and his nearness, but where once this would have been disturbing, it was no longer so. All that had passed long ago. We were simply partners in a dangerous mission, keeping vigil together and taking strength from one another.

Presently, I felt him tauten. "I hear footsteps," he whispered.

We froze into complete immobility. The shadows were deepening now, and we had our dark cloaks on. We would be invisible as long as we stayed still.

The footsteps came along the path from the house. They passed us and stopped. Peering very cautiously around a frond of yew, I saw a figure beside the nearest pair of swans. It moved, restlessly, and we heard what sounded like a grunt of impatience. Then the figure subsided onto the wooden bench. Silence fell anew.

"It's Ridolfi," Brockley breathed.

Time went by. Ridolfi got up once or twice, walked restlessly to the river entrance to look out of it, and then came back. Once or twice we heard him mutter to himself in an irritated way.

Then, at last, just as the light was about to go entirely, we saw the gleam of a lantern in the arch. Someone came quickly along the path and there was a murmured exchange of greetings. Once more, I risked peering around the edge of our hiding place and was rewarded by a glimpse of the newcomer's face in the lantern light. I recognized the high cheekbones and the self-satisfied smile at once.

Edging back, I mouthed: "That's the Spanish ambassador," into Brockley's ear.

Both of them sat down on the bench. They began to talk. Brockley and I strained to hear.

In the course of the Ridolfi business, I think I pressed my ears to more doors, lurked in more twilight gardens, than on any other assignment in my whole life. Eavesdropping on other people's conversations was like a recurring theme in a piece of music. It was also tiresome because one never managed to overhear a conversation properly. The speakers moved about, turned this way and that. Their voices came and went like sounds carried on a capricious wind.

This time, we couldn't hear at all well. Ridolfi and de Spes kept their voices down and there was a good thickness of yew-tree horse between ourselves and them. One's ears do adjust, though. Presently, I began to make out words here and there. To my surprise, they were speaking English, presumably because it was a tongue they had in common, and they seemed to be talking about money.

". . . have you warned him to set nothing moving until we have ten thousand marks at least in hand?" That was de Spes.

". . . he has already been in touch with . . ." That was Ridolfi, sounding apologetic.

". . . too soon. The man is overexcitable. He behaves like a rustic swain in love . . ." De Spes was contemptuous of somebody or other.

". . . at least he is still with us, not like . . . offered five hundred marks but changed his mind . . . from my own resources . . ."

At that moment, they both rose and began, though slowly, to move away from the bench, as people do who are ending a conversation but haven't quite finished. For a few moments, it brought them closer to us and several sentences did actually reach us clearly.

"I regret," de Spes said, "that we had to meet in this clandestine manner but by stealing through my garden and taking a dinghy all alone, I think I have avoided surveillance. My letters are still being read and some of my servants say they have been followed. It is insulting. The English! A nation damned until Holy Church rescues them. Your generosity won't be forgotten, when Mary Stuart is on the throne of England."

Ridolfi said something less distinct but the words "war is costly" were lucid enough, and the ambassador's reply came to us complete.

"On that, we must *not* embark without aid from my master. I repeat what I said when I came here as your dinner guest. Philip will not move until the English Catholics are ready to take up arms."

"And behind that, there must be at least ten thousand marks," said Ridolfi with some bitterness.

Then they were past and walking out of earshot toward the river. But there had been no mistaking the words we had heard. I felt myself go rigid and Brockley closed his hand fiercely on my arm as if afraid that I would leap from hiding and confront the two of them. I didn't stir, however, and his grip relaxed. Ridolfi and de Spes disappeared through the archway. We stayed where we were for some time, but Ridolfi must have gone back to the house by way of the knot garden. He did not return through the topiary.

As we made our cautious way back to the house, Brockley remarked: "If I were going to engage in a conversation like that, madam, I'd do it in the middle of a field, or on a boat on the river, where people couldn't hide nearby with ears all agog. Those two men are fools."

"That may be the most encouraging thing about this whole affair," I said. "It makes it less likely to succeed. But it's dangerous enough, all the same. Let us hurry."

In my chamber, Dale was anxiously awaiting us. "Did you learn anything useful, ma'am?" she asked.

"More than I liked," I said grimly. I pulled the coded letters, now somewhat crumpled, out of my pouch and spread them on the table. "And it's more vital than ever that I translate these, so that I can carry the fullest possible news to Cecil. Light some more candles, will you, Dale? Where's Gladys? I hope she hasn't caused any more trouble."

"No, ma'am. She's on her truckle bed in our chamber, asleep."

"Good. What we learned, Dale . . . well, tell her, Brockley."

Brockley slowly quoted: *"When Mary Stuart is on the throne of England . . ."*

Dale's eyes widened. "Did . . . someone . . . say *that*?"

"The Spanish ambassador," I told her. I pushed my weariness resolutely away. I had no time for it now. "These letters!"

20

One Single Sentence

When at last I got into bed that night, I did sleep, out of sheer exhaustion. But when I woke in the morning, only half-rested, I turned onto my face and wept, trying to empty what felt to me like a bottomless well, until I felt a hand on my shoulder and looked around to find Dale at my side.

"Ma'am . . . Mistress Stannard . . . oh, my dear."

"Dale!"

I reached out to her and she turned back the covers and cast herself down beside me, taking me in her arms. Her face was tired, for she and Brockley had stayed with me until last night's work was done. "Ma'am . . . I am so sorry. I am so very, very sorry."

"Is it true? I didn't dream it? It was really there, in that last letter?"

"Yes, ma'am. You left the letters and transcripts by your bed. When we had settled you and you were asleep, Roger saw them there and took them to our room for safety. We looked at them again this morning."

"What?" I sat up, horrified. "I left the letters on my table? Thank God Brockley removed them! I think I was half crazed last night," I whispered.

"And no wonder, ma'am. Roger and I have scarcely slept, for talking it over and wondering what you'll do. What *will* you do?"

"See Sir William Cecil," I said. "Even if I have to chase him up and down the Thames from one palace to another, or ride to the Scottish border to catch him!"

"Ma'am, the other things in the letters . . ."

"Oh yes. He must see all the transcripts, anyway. Getting them to him is my duty as an English subject," I said. "What I may feel about Cecil himself. Or even," I added, "about my royal sister the queen."

"Should Gladys and I make up a potion for you, ma'am? In case this brings on one of your migraines?"

"It won't," I said, suddenly sure of it. "It's too damned important for that. Don't worry. I'll dress now. I'll have the strength of ten today."

At breakfast, Donna asked me to spend the morning with her, preparing some embroidery to trim the new gowns she was planning. "Until Meg arrives, anyway," she said.

"I'm sorry," I said brusquely. "I have a private matter to attend to this morning. I must take Brockley and Dale and go out."

Donna and Ridolfi both gazed at me in amazement, astonished, I think, as much by my harsh tone as by the unheralded advent of urgent and apparently secret errands.

"And," I said, "I must be on my way at once. I am sorry that I can't explain. Please look after Meg if she arrives before I come back."

Before we left, Dale said: "I took some food up to Gladys, ma'am. She's still in our room. Do we lock her in, or what?"

"Let her be," I said distractedly. "I told her yesterday she was to stay in your room until she had permission to leave it. I don't want to waste time now. I want to be on my way."

At Cecil's house, his butler, I think, read something in my face that disturbed him. He said anxiously that his master wasn't available but asked if Lady Cecil could help. I agreed to this and he ushered the three of us into the presence of Mildred, Lady Cecil, the Secretary of State's wife. She and I knew each other well. It had been mostly Mildred, years ago, who had found foster parents for Meg while I was at court, attending the queen.

She was a woman of great intellect and dignity and the moment we were shown into her parlor and I was face-to-face with her, I felt steadier. She rose to greet us and stood quietly, her hands linked over her stomacher. Her very style of dress, with its modest farthingale and small ruff, was a statement of good sense and moderation. Her intelligent eyes studied me and she too recognized the signs of grave distress.

"What is it, Ursula? You need to see my husband?"

"It's urgent. At Sir William's behest, I have been staying in the house of the banker Roberto Ridolfi. There are things which I must report to Sir William without delay. I *must*."

"He is in the house but he's in conference with Francis Walsingham. I believe you met Walsingham briefly the other day?"

"Yes. I wanted to hand the letters over to be deciphered by Sir William's own clerks. I wish to God I had. I wish I'd never read them. I wish I didn't know . . ."

I stopped, choking.

Mildred stepped to a doorway and called. Someone came at once and she said briefly: "Fetch wine for four, and immediately." Coming back, she said: "All three of you look exhausted and you, Ursula, have obviously had a very bad shock." She sat down on a settle and signaled for me to do the same. "Can you tell me what happened?"

"I'd like to." My own voice sounded strangled. "But I must see Sir William first. I must . . ."

She glanced at the Brockleys, who were standing by. Brockley said: "We know, my lady. Yes. But we can say nothing until Mistress Stannard gives permission."

"Since my husband sent you to the Ridolfi household, he will, I think, be willing to see you. But take some wine first, and compose yourself. Meanwhile, I will tell him you're here and that it's important. You wouldn't make a mistake there, Ursula; that I know."

The wine came, and the message, couched in properly urgent terms, was dispatched by the page who had brought in the tray. As I sipped at my glass, I asked: "Who is Walsingham? Is he trustworthy?"

"He's a rising star in my husband's service. He has already brought in valuable information, following a stay in France, and I believe," said Mildred, her fine eyes crinkling with humor, "that some of the less reverent spirits at court are laying bets on whether he will one day follow Sir William as the next Secretary of State. There has been talk of promoting my husband to some still greater position. Ah." The page had reappeared. "Yes?"

"Sir William will see Mistress Stannard at once, my lady."

"Thank you, Tom. I'll bring her myself. Please wait, and when they've finished their wine, take Mistress Stannard's people downstairs and see that they have any refreshment they need. Come, Ursula."

I had hoped to see Cecil alone but when I was shown into his study, I found the grave, dark Walsingham with him. However, it seemed that Cecil and his wife both trusted him. He was no doubt reliable, just as Harry Scrivener had proved to be reliable. I had been a fool. I had withheld trust from men who were entitled to it and given trust where I should not. It was Cecil, Cecil himself, who had betrayed me.

Cecil, as perceptive as his butler and his wife, looked at me and wasted no time. "Ursula? I gather that this is serious. Seat yourself, and explain. What have you discovered?"

I brought out the papers I was carrying in my hidden pouch and laid them in front of him, on his desk. "Brockley and I have overheard an interesting conversation between our host Signor Ridolfi and the Spanish ambassador, and also, I have these. They're copies of cipher messages that Roberto Ridolfi recently sent to various people. I have been able to interpret them and here are the deciphered versions. I have written out details of the cipher, so that your own clerks can verify my work. I consulted Harry Scrivener for advice. He helped me to break the cipher but he hasn't seen the contents of the letters."

"Go on."

"There are four letters here altogether. One is to John Leslie, Bishop of Ross. Two others were enclosed with it—one to Mary Stuart and one to Sir Robert Dudley, Earl of Leicester. The fourth, which was separate, is to the Scottish regent, Moray. The messenger, apparently, was to deliver the packet of three to the bishop here in London and then ride for Scotland with the regent's letter.

"It happened," I said carefully, "that in order to accustom myself to the work of deciphering, I left the longest letter until last. That is the one to the Bishop of Ross. There is one sentence in it which has a peculiar significance to me. I have underlined it."

Cecil looked me in the face and I looked straight back at him. In that exchange of glances, there was accusation on my side and on his, the recognition of it. His brows rose inquiringly. Walsingham, standing beside the desk, watched us with his dark eyes narrowed, as if trying to interpret the unspoken messages between us.

Then Cecil picked up the letters.

There was a long silence, while he studied what I had given him. Walsingham looked over his shoulder, reading along with him. At length, they both raised their heads and gazed at me.

I said: "I must now speak of what Brockley and I overheard. He is my witness to this, for he was with me. Last night, de Spes, the Spanish ambassador, made a clandestine visit to Ridolfi. We heard de Spes say that his master would not move unless he knew that the English Catholics were ready to rise. Ridolfi remarked that war was costly. They appear to be collecting money for that purpose. And we heard de Spes say the words *'when Mary is on the throne of England.'*"

Neither Cecil nor Walsingham moved, but I sensed the shock that ran through them.

Then Cecil said: "So that's it." His voice was quiet, shaken, as though he were suddenly short of breath for talking.

"You half-guessed, sir," Walsingham said. "You said only yesterday that you believed that Mary had her eye on more than just the Scottish throne."

"Since restoring her would make her Elizabeth's natural heir, I was bound to think so." Cecil's tone was still hushed. "However, I still supposed that Mary and her adherents looked on her accession in England only as something that might one day happen in the way of nature. I've been so blind. They intend to *make* it happen! We're seeing the first moves in an assassination plot. Dear God! I've behaved like an innocent. I'm old enough to know better!"

There was a silence. Then he picked one of the letters up. "Let me clarify what these letters say. This, to Mary Stuart, assures her that efforts are continuing to persuade the Scots— especially her brother Moray, the regent—that she should be reinstated as queen in Scotland. It also assures her that the Duke of Norfolk continues interest in marrying her, and expresses the further hope that if Queen Elizabeth can be induced to approve the marriage and the restoration, this may drive a wedge between Elizabeth and myself, as Ridolfi is quite sure that nothing in the world will induce *me* to approve them. He mentions a number of council members, including Leicester and Norfolk, who know of the marriage negotiations, and are encouraging them. Most of these gentlemen are those who would like to see my influence destroyed. I have my enemies. As well I know!"

He paused, and then resumed, his tone grim. "The letter also says that Norfolk is in touch with the northern earls. It doesn't say what he is in touch with them for, but the final comment, that the Spanish administration in the Netherlands has been alerted, is a useful pointer. It tallies with the remarks you overheard last night!"

"We also heard Ridolfi say that a man whose name we didn't catch has already been in touch with someone—again we don't know who—but it sounded as though de Spes thought this was happening too soon," I said. "It *could* have meant Norfolk and the northern earls."

"Very likely," said Cecil. He picked up a second letter. "This is the one to Moray in Scotland, expressing anxiety because he is so lukewarm regarding Mary's restoration. It is a relief to know that someone in this sorry muddle still has a little sense in his head! Mary was a fool. When she first came to Scotland, Moray was ready to be a good brother to her, but when he warned her against Darnley, they fell out, and when he suspected her of being involved in Darnley's murder, they fell out further than ever. They hate each other now.

"Here, Ridolfi points out that if Mary is married to Norfolk, she will have a mature male partner to help and advise her. I wonder if Moray will find that a persuasive argument! He's probably got a taste for power now. He may think that Mary with a mature male partner at her side is a more depressing prospect than Mary wild and willful."

He put the second letter down and Walsingham handed him the next. "This is the one to the Earl of Leicester, sir."

"Ah. Yes. The Gypsy. Well, he would be involved in any scheme to get rid of me," Cecil said. "I could have expected that. This doesn't say much. The prospects for the Norfolk marriage are encouraging but Regent Moray is being unhelpful. There's nothing of great importance there. Leicester can't possibly want Mary as queen of England. I greatly doubt that he has the remotest idea what his coconspirators are up to. But now . . ." He took up the missive to the Bishop of Ross, handling it with great distaste, between finger and thumb. ". . . now we come to this."

Once again, his eyes met mine but this time impersonally. "It really is a muddle, isn't it?"

I was wounded and angry but I had been shaken, too, by the far-reaching extent of the plot that we had uncovered. "This whole business is so huge," I said. "It seems to bring in so many people . . . so many different kinds of people. The queen's councilors, the Bishop of Ross, Moray, Mary, Ridolfi, Spain . . ."

"And some of those involved," said Cecil, "such as Leicester, assuredly don't know that they're joining hands with people whose intentions are quite other than their own. And who are sniggering at the simpletons they've trapped into helping them. I congratulate you on your work, Ursula."

I said, "Thank you," in a stiff voice.

Cecil nodded, but returned at once to his exposition of the letters. "According to this one to Ross, Ridolfi fears that Moray has begun to suspect the ultimate purpose and that this is one reason why he is dragging his feet. Ah. Yes. I missed this at my first glance through. He adds that it is vital that the Earl of Leicester shouldn't suspect. He is very worried in case Leicester *does* sense something amiss. He remarks that one of the queen's pet names for Leicester is her Eyes, which means that she relies on him to notice what is happening out of her sight.

"The letter then goes on to repeat much of what is in the other letters but adds that the process of gathering funds is not yet complete and *must* be complete before the scheme can go ahead, for it will surely result in bloodshed. Money is needed to recruit and pay soldiers and arm them. Ridolfi himself is providing personal money and a bank loan, and a number of other individuals have been drawn in. These include merchants who realize that Mary's restoration will please Spain, and may therefore induce the administration in the Netherlands to reopen Antwerp."

He paused. "It would seem," he said after a moment, "that Mary's marriage to Norfolk and her restoration in Scotland represent the first step in this ugly conspiracy. The second will be to foment a Catholic rising in England and put Mary on Elizabeth's throne. Nothing is actually said of the plans for Elizabeth, though we can all guess what they are. And also . . ."

For the third time, our eyes locked.

"I am sorry, Ursula. In the last paragraph of this letter, Ridolfi says that although Spain and France are traditional rivals, there are supporters of the scheme in France, who have been gathering money for it. The Seigneur Matthew de la Roche of Blanchepierre has acted as the assembly point and in April he forwarded two thousand marks to Ridolfi. You have underlined the words <u>Matthew de la Roche of Blanchepierre</u>."

"Yes," I said. "Unless it's a relative of the same name. But as far as I know, none of his relatives were called Matthew."

"So you know," said Cecil, and his voice was genuinely regretful. "You know that your second husband, De la Roche, did not die in an outbreak of plague as you believed, but is still alive in France."

"And my marriage to Hugh is void," I said bitterly. "And I have been lied to and betrayed. By whom?"

★ ★ ★

At the end of another very long silence, Cecil said: "Your marriage to Hugh Stannard is lawful. You were married to De la Roche in a secret ceremony conducted by a Catholic priest who was not entitled, in the eyes of Queen Elizabeth, to perform such a ceremony in this country, and you were also married under duress. The queen, as head of both church and state in England, has annuled your marriage to De la Roche. I can show you the document. That annulment was in force before you ever met Master Stannard. You need have no fears."

I said, "There were letters. From Matthew's people in Blanchepierre, his home in France. They told me . . ."

"That he had died in the plague. Do you remember, Ursula, some years ago, unmasking a gifted forger who had created with his own hands some documents which he thought might injure her majesty?"

"Yes. Very clearly."

"He really was—and is—gifted," said Cecil. "Such men can be useful. It was part of the deal we did with him. His neck would be spared and he would not be imprisoned, but his gifts henceforth were to be used in the queen's service."

"Were there letters for Matthew as well? Does he believe . . . what does he believe?"

"That you are dead. That the plague broke out here, as well."

"You have known all along. You, and the queen. You *planned* all this? Arranged it?"

"Yes, Ursula. You were too valuable to lose; nor was it in your best interests to return to a marriage which was all too likely, in the end, to place you in an intolerable position. You loved De la Roche, but he is an enemy of this realm. What, in the end, would that have done to you?"

"It was my business," I said. "I would have dealt with it in my own way. No one had the right to interfere."

"You are also," said Cecil steadily, watching me, "the queen's half sister. It's all right." He glanced sidelong at Walsingham. "Sir Francis here knows about it. You are not of dynastic significance, since you are not legitimate, but you are of emotional importance to Her Majesty. If the facts of your paternity had leaked out in France, you could have become a very useful hostage. I should perhaps tell you, by the way, that Matthew has remarried and has a son."

"Have you any idea," I asked him bitterly, "any idea at all, what you have done? What it was *like,* seeing his name in that letter?"

It had been a moment for which I can scarcely find words, even now, when I am old, my passions turned to cold ashes, and the men I once loved nothing but memories. Matthew's name had emerged from the welter of the cipher by stages. 52 5 120 60 32 25 138 12 20 60 6 54 60 15 48 15. Those had been the numerals, and I began dividing them—the 52 was in the column for division by 4—quite unsuspecting, and very tired. The candles were burning low and my eyes felt hot and heavy. It was deep in the night, and I ached for sleep.

I was almost in a trance as the name *Matthew* came off the end of my quill, and even then I only thought of it as a name. My second husband had been called Matthew but so were many men. It meant nothing, beyond a slight reminder of days gone by.

Then *de la* also emerged but this too was a commonplace in France. It still meant nothing . . . until I began on the last five numerals, 54 60 15 48 15, and watched the word *Roche,* incredibly, come to light.

Even then, I had thought: it is another man of the same name. Perhaps it is a relation of Matthew's. But I had known the names of his family members. There hadn't been that many of them: an uncle and some cousins. There was no one called Matthew among them. And then I went on transcribing and there was no more doubt. *Of Blanchepierre.* That was how the next few numerals came out.

Even *then,* it made no sense. Matthew had been dead for nearly five years. I had laid his memory to rest. But the words were there, and there was only one man to whom they could refer.

Dale and Brockley had been in the room. They saw me pause, and stare, and they came to my side to see what I had found. Brockley said: "Good God! It can't be!" Dale said: "Ma'am! Does it really say . . . ?"

"Yes," I told them. "And when the news came to me in England, I wasn't allowed to go to France, to Blanchepierre, to weep beside his grave. Cecil and the queen forbade it. I wonder how much they know."

If he was alive, I thought feverishly, then he was still, surely, my husband. And with that, things I thought I had forgotten came surging back. All that had been between us. Quarrels and tears and laughter and . . .

Lovemaking. The fiercest and stormiest lovemaking I had ever known and the most exultant. Not the vigorous but steady and warm unions I had known with my first husband, Gerald; not the friendly unions I experienced with Hugh. And certainly not . . .

There had been one other, which had had something in it of Matthew's stormy quality, but which I had, for very good reasons, detested. I would never say that about Matthew's lovemaking.

His stood alone in my memory. I thought I had put it in the past. I didn't expect that at the realization that he still lived, the old desire for him would overtake me again like a flood of molten gold.

And then the flood passed, to be replaced by another, which was nothing at all like molten gold; more like a cascade of ice water. I had made a new life. If Matthew were to walk into my bedchamber now, this moment, there would be one moment of ecstasy in which I would run into his arms and after that . . .

After that, a great deal of difficulty, anxiety, and inconvenience. As I sat there in the guttering candlelight, I found the tears running down my face. I had made a new life. I had been happy. I *liked* Hugh. I liked our quiet interests; our domestic occupations. I liked having a husband who didn't plot against the queen I loved and served, seeking to destroy the peace of my homeland and lay it open to the Inquisition that terrorized Spain and which we had tasted, in a fashion, under Mary Tudor.

My body, which was still young and could not forget, cried out for Matthew, but my mind said no, please, no, leave things as they are. I don't want to go back. I *can't* go back. I can't leave Hugh, or my life here and I won't, I *won't* take Meg to France to be taught doctrines that I reject.

Another memory slid into my mind. A hot, airless, fetid room and a state of pain and fear that were also unforgettable. The day I had given birth to Matthew's stillborn son, and nearly lost my own life in the process. I didn't want to risk another pregnancy. With Hugh, childless despite two previous wives and several mistresses, I felt safe from it.

"I must finish this," I had said wearily to the Brockleys. "And then I must sleep. Tomorrow . . . tomorrow I must report what I've found."

Now I had done so. I had reported it all. Cecil's quiet blue eyes, so very different from Edmund Dean's, regarded me steadily. I couldn't tell what he was thinking.

"You can't know what you've done," I said. "It is a dreadful thing, to lose—to think you have lost—someone, and to mourn and then to accept and to begin again, with someone else; to undo the past, knot by knot—and then find that it's still there! That he's still there . . . !"

Words abandoned me. I could say nothing more. I tried to keep my head up, not to give way before Cecil and the unsmiling, brooding Walsingham. Cecil said something to Walsingham, sharply, in a low voice, and Sir Francis left the room.

"He will fetch my wife," Cecil said. "And your woman, Dale. Cry if you want to, Ursula. I won't look."

He got to his feet and went to gaze out of the window. I put my head down on his desk and surrendered. Presently, Mildred and Dale came to me and took me away. "I'm all right," I told them, still sobbing, but they led me to a bedchamber and I was made to lie down while a warm posset was made for me, and then they sat with me while I drank it.

"You should rest," Mildred said. "Sleep if you can."

"I can't," I said, as I drained the cup. "I mustn't linger. I must go back to the Ridolfis. My daughter, Meg, is arriving today—at Madame Ridolfi's invitation—and I must be there to take charge of her as soon as I can."

"But do you feel well enough to . . . ?"

"I must! Meg will feel lost if I'm not there." I put my empty cup aside and swung my feet off the bed. Exhaustion at once poured over me and my head and throat throbbed with my tears, but for Meg, I could and would ignore them all. "I would like to go at once!"

"We are both sorry for what has happened," said Mildred. "There were . . . reasons."

Yes, there were reasons, I thought bitterly. I knew what they were. I even understood them. Always the loyal servant of Elizabeth and Cecil, that was me, that was Ursula. No matter what they did to me, because they represented England, because they were the guardians of England, and England had no others.

Somehow I got myself out of the Cecils' house and went back to the Ridolfis with Dale and Brockley. The first thing I saw as I arrived were men in the livery of Norfolk, leading horses toward the stable yard. And the first person I met as I came into the entrance hall was Donna.

"Oh, Ursula, there you are! Have you finished your so-secret errand? Your daughter is here. How charming she is! The Duke of Norfolk is here too, to visit my husband, and he has his young secretary Master Dean with him. I believe there has been talk of Dean as a suitor for your girl, has there not? He and Meg were very pleased to see each other. He has taken her into the garden. I'm afraid," said Donna, sadly, but with regrettably sparkling eyes, "that he is showing her the topiary . . ."

21

A Way of Escape

In that moment, I forgot Matthew as completely as though he had never existed. I also forgot the perfidy of Cecil and the queen, and forgot to go on puzzling over the confused and alarming conspiracy that my host Robert Ridolfi seemed to be fomenting. I forgot the confusion of being an ex-widow and a semi-wife; I forgot to be a secret agent. I became on the instant a protective mother, whose innocent daughter's heart was under siege by a man I instinctively disliked, in a garden full of erotic images.

"Excuse *me!*" I said to Donna and swept past her, along the corridor, out across the terrace, and hotfoot into the midst of the topiary.

I found them on the seat beside the swans and horses. Edmund Dean's arm was around my daughter and in his other hand he had a book, from which he was reading aloud to her. He had a good speaking voice, measured and clear. As I came within earshot, I caught a phrase or two.

"*. . . and wilt thou leave me thus, that has given thee my heart never for to depart, neither for pain nor smart? And wilt thou leave me thus? Say nay! Say nay! . . .*"

I knew the poem and I knew who its author was. Sir Thomas Wyatt was a favorite poet of mine and I had lately bought a new edition of his collected works. He had been a courtier in the days of Henry the Eighth and he had almost certainly been in love with Queen Anne Boleyn. He had been narrowly acquitted of being her lover in the physical sense. He was as persuasive and ardent a poet as ever set quill to paper and a suitor armed with his verses was well equipped to beguile older and wiser women than my little Meg.

I bore down on the pair of them, a female Jove, prepared to hurl thunderbolts. "Meg! What are you doing here? Master Dean, I do not recall giving you leave to take my daughter walking anywhere and least of all *here!*"

"I beg your pardon, mistress!"

Dean rose, bowing, full of contrition—outwardly, at least. But as he straightened up and looked me in the face, his intense stare told me that he was not really disconcerted. He had decided to woo Meg, it seemed, and he took it for granted that his wishes would prevail over mine.

Brockley had followed me into the topiary, though not Dale. During our stay at the Ridolfis she had seen the place more than once, but he still preferred her not to enter it. "Brockley," I said over my shoulder, "take Meg indoors. She must wash her face and hands before dinner."

"Mother, Edmund was reading a poem to me . . ."

"I have a copy in my chamber. You can read the rest for yourself whenever you like. Go with Brockley, please."

"But, Mother . . ."

"Come, Meg, do as your mother says!" Brockley stepped smartly forward, took Meg's arm and virtually lifted her off the bench. She tried to protest but I snapped: *"Meg! Go!"* so fiercely that she ceased to resist and went, drooping. I gazed after her, my fury giving way to despondency. Just how far in love was my hitherto amenable and delightful daughter?

I turned to Dean. "Was it not made clear to you, sir, that we did not wish to pursue this matter of Meg's betrothal?"

"But only, madam, on account of her youth, which time will amend, all too soon, and—she is so lovely. I am sorry to have displeased you." He was trying his beguilements on me now. In a confiding voice that went very ill with those penetrating eyes, he said: "I admit it; I want her to leave a little of her heart with me, so that three or four years hence, she may say to you: What of Master Dean? And perhaps the matter can be reopened then?"

This was what came of trying to withdraw from the marriage negotiations with tact. All the same, I made one last attempt to be tactful. "I cannot understand," I said, "why a girl as young as Meg attracts you so much. You're a grown man."

"But, Mistress Stannard, it *is* her youth that I like. Far more than her dowry, if the truth be told. Being young, she will be compliant. She can be molded into my ideal of a wife. Then I shall be pleased, and she will be happy. Do you not see?"

Yes, I saw.

To hell with tact.

"Master Dean," I said, "I think I should tell you that Master Stannard and I realized that something of the sort was in your mind and although we didn't say so then, that is another reason why we have definitely decided against any marriage between you and Meg. My daughter is . . ."

The granddaughter of King Henry the Eighth, and the half niece of Queen Elizabeth, and not, therefore, in the least likely to be the piece of pliable clay that Dean evidently imagined.

". . . my daughter is not to be molded, but to be valued. She is not a white page for you to write on. Her character and intelligence have written their own signatures there already. The Duke of Norfolk meant well when he made the introduction, but our considered decision is—no. Never again attempt to walk or talk with her alone. Good day to you."

He had gone white. He said nothing, but bowed once more, and turning away from him, I walked quickly back toward the house. It was then made plain to me that there was something, or rather, someone, else whom I had forgotten in my race to rescue Meg. The discovery of Matthew's name in that letter had driven Gladys Morgan completely out of my head. I had a vague memory of Dale saying she had taken Gladys some breakfast that morning, in the Brockleys' room, and, yes, Dale had asked what we were to do about Gladys, and I had said let her be. She knew she was supposed to stay in the Brockleys' quarters and I was in a hurry to be off to the Cecils' house.

I had vaguely—stupidly—assumed that Gladys would obey orders. She had not. As I came to the archway in front of the terrace, I found my way barred by her and by Arthur Johnson. They were quarreling again, not loudly, but angrily all the same. Johnson was gesticulating with a pair of clippers. As I approached, Gladys burst into an eldritch cackle, swung away from Johnson, and scuttled off ahead of me toward the house.

"*Now* what's the matter with you two?" I said irritably to Johnson.

"She's laughing at me, that's what," said the old man sullenly. "Once again, I give her a chance. Again, I offer my hand and my heart and this time she don't just say no thanks, she *laughs* at me. Old besom!"

"I shouldn't ask her again. And you're well out of it. She's got a shocking temper."

Johnson made a noise that sounded like "Aaaaah!" with a piglike snort at the end of it, and strode off, holding his clippers like a dagger. I stood still in order to let him go, but then, afraid that Edmund Dean would follow me and catch up with me, I hurried on, wanting to avoid him.

I noticed then that the sense of foreboding that had descended on me the previous day was still with me. Whatever it presaged had not yet come to pass, it seemed. It was still there, looming and threatening.

Threatening whom?

As I reached the terrace and lifted my hem clear of the step, I heard the now-familiar squeak of the gate between the knot garden and the river. I stopped again and turned. There was no sign of Dean, but a dignified lady, and an entourage of two gentleman and three more ladies behind her, were all coming through the knot garden, presumably from the landing stage. Even at a distance, I recognized Lady Cecil. I made my way off the terrace to meet her.

"Lady Cecil!"

"My dear Ursula. You left more quickly than my husband expected. He has sent me after you. May we talk?"

"Madame Ridolfi is just coming," I said.

Donna and Greaves were both hastening from the house to greet the unexpected guest. Mildred moved deftly to deal with them. "Madame Ridolfi? Forgive this unexpected visit. We haven't met before but I am the wife of Sir William Cecil, the Secretary of State. We are old friends of Mistress Stannard here."

Donna, anxiously curtsying, started to exclaim that Lady Cecil was most welcome, and would she and her companions like to dine, but Mildred firmly dismissed the invitation.

"No, no. Your cook need not be troubled with us. We will all return home for dinner. The truth is, I have an errand to Ursula. If you could arrange for us to talk in privacy? Some wine for my companions, perhaps? I see you have an attractive terrace where they could sit."

Five minutes later, Mildred's entourage had been seated on the terrace, while she and I were alone together in the downstairs parlor with the windows closed. I felt uncertain. I liked and trusted Mildred but I was wary of any messages from Cecil. I did not know what to say.

Mildred, however, was older than I, and self-possessed in a way that I would never be. She knew how to manage the situation.

"I'm not here to plead Sir William's cause, Ursula. I myself did not know that your husband was still alive, not till Sir Francis told me, when he fetched me to the study to help you. But you left us so precipitately that Sir William had no chance to talk to you further, and he wished so to do. Also, whether you believe it or not, he is very concerned for you. So am I."

"What things does Sir William want to talk to me about?"

"To begin with, he wants to thank you again, formally, for the valuable information you brought him this morning. We know you must be very very angry about the deception practiced on you, but the conspiracy you have helped to reveal still interests you, does it not?"

"I am aware," I said, "that the safety of England and the safety of the queen are the same thing, and that my marital affairs are very small ale by comparison."

"You can be as astounding sometimes as Elizabeth herself.

Well, it's not so surprising. You are both cubs of the same lion. Oh yes. I am privy to the secret."

"I think Norfolk is, too," I said. "How do these things get out?"

"Very easily. A few words overheard by the wrong person— or a Spanish spy who is as clever at reading other people's documents as you are, my dear Ursula. The truth about your parentage was kept hidden for years because no one ever spoke of it. But once the queen and Sir William began to think they should tell you, they had to mention it between themselves and I believe they exchanged memoranda. Your parentage was one of the reasons for the deception that kept you in England."

"I daresay," I said stiffly.

"Well, we needn't talk about that now. I said I wasn't here to justify the deception. Sir William says that the news you brought him this morning has filled the gaps in his knowledge. He can see the whole pattern now. After you left," said Mildred, "I went to find him and discovered him pacing his study and muttering. Walsingham was there and William was tossing remarks out to him every now and then. He said that he believes he can see how the trouble can be stopped before it starts, without a huge scandal and the deaths of men he once called friends. He is helping Norfolk with a lawsuit—you know about that?"

"Yes."

"If the verdict goes in Norfolk's favor, and my husband thinks it will—he has a good deal of say in the matter—then Norfolk will, he feels, be inclined to listen to advice. If warned that causing trouble in the north might cost him his head—well, he might be induced to back away."

Curiosity got the better of me. "What were Sir William's other sources of information, besides me? I know he had them."

"There has been talk. Fragments of conversation, overheard in the anterooms of the court. Half the council are privy to the scheme for reinstating Mary, I fear—the half that resent my husband's influence over the queen and wish to drive them apart. But his main informant is dead. It was Julius Gale. That was one of the things that William wanted to tell you."

"*Gale!*"

"Yes. When he was killed, he was on his way to our house, to bring my husband the letters he was carrying, to be opened and copied before he rode on to deliver them."

"So that's why he was found traveling west instead of north! But the letters weren't on him!"

"No, and that's a puzzle. We are sure he meant to bring them. Gale had already done us good service. He was recruited by Walsingham, who has quite a gift for finding useful people."

I blinked. "Gale was replaced in Ridolfi's service by a kinsman, George Hillman. Hillman's taken the originals of those letters to the Bishop of Ross and to Moray. Is he one of Walsingham's men as well?"

"Not yet, but Walsingham intends to approach him, when he returns. As far as is known, Hillman is quite unaware of the nature of the correspondence he carries. He's a respectable young man and a Protestant. With luck, we'll soon have him as an agent in this house. But now I come to the chief reason why William sent me after you. He doesn't think that you and Meg should stay here, even for another day. You have taken grave risks already. If by any chance you should be suspected . . ."

"I know. Julius Gale. And Walt."

"I am charged," said Mildred, "to bring you away with me now. I will make your excuses. I will say that Sir William insists that you come to stay with us. We are old friends of yours, wanting to borrow a little of your company. We are people of some eminence," said Mildred, smiling, "and can afford to be a trifle high-handed. I have come to fetch you, and how can you possibly say no to the Secretary of State and his wife?"

"I have to say no! After this morning, after finding out about Matthew, I couldn't possibly agree . . ."

"Yes, you can. To get Meg away from here if for no other reason."

"I certainly want to do that." I thought grimly of Meg on that seat with Dean's arm around her. "You know that we brought her to London in the first place to consider betrothing her to one of Norfolk's secretaries?"

"Yes. Sir William told me."

"We didn't like him, so we sent Meg home. Unfortunately, she was impressed with him and even more unfortunately, Madame Ridolfi invited her back to London, to join me here, thinking she was doing me a kindness thereby. Meg arrived today, before I came back, and when I did so . . ."

I explained, with some bitterness, how I had found the two of them together. "And that's not all," I said. "I have an elderly servant, Gladys Morgan, who is worrying the life out of me. I think she's not quite right in the head but she's not so far gone that she can't give the come-hither to Ridolfi's topiary gardener, who is about her age, and . . ."

I explained that too, whereupon Mildred threw back her handsome head and burst out laughing. "It's not funny!" I protested.

"No, I suppose it isn't. Oh, my dear." Mildred wiped her eyes. "Ursula, why are we standing in the middle of the room like this when there are perfectly good stools and settles all around us. Let us sit. I'm sorry, but the idea of that gnome of a gardener—I know Johnson; we have him, too!—and your aged crone . . . !"

"You've never seen *her*!"

"Yes, I have. Once. Sir William and I visited you at Hawkswood two years ago—remember?"

"She'll be a nuisance, wherever she is, but . . . you are right. I want to get both her and Meg away from here as soon as I can. Only . . ."

"Not to our house? But we're offering a way of escape, immediate escape. Ursula, we're truly afraid for you."

I said: "If only it hadn't been such an elaborate deception. Forged lies about death! I mourned for Matthew! I grieved and wept and I was unhappy because I was not even allowed to see his grave, and all the time, in France, he was grieving for me! What am I to tell Hugh?"

"You need not tell him anything, unless you wish. Ursula, listen. Matthew de la Roche, from the time you first knew him, has been Mary Stuart's man. He has plotted against Elizabeth. He is still plotting. One day, you would have had to choose between Elizabeth and Matthew, finally and forever. One day, if you had stayed with him, he would have broken your heart. Do you not realize that?"

"I always hoped . . . I always hoped . . ."

"What? That he would change? Or that somehow, you might hold the balance between his beliefs and yours and keep your center steady, keep the small, safe, closed-in place that husband and wife share together somehow free of contamination? Could you have done that for a lifetime?" She searched my face. "Ursula, is there something you want to say? There is trouble in your eyes."

"What I want to say is so terrible."

"What is it? That in the last resort you would have chosen him above Elizabeth?"

"No. I might not have had to choose because I might not have lived long enough. I nearly died when I had Meg. And I nearly died trying to have Matthew's son. I . . ."

I stopped. I couldn't get the words out. I couldn't possibly say *Sir William Cecil lied to me and deceived me for his own convenience and that of the queen and in so doing may well have saved my life.*

Mildred, however, merely nodded. "It's all right, Ursula. Don't tear yourself to pieces. You are not being asked to forgive Sir William, let alone to thank him. Only to let the two of us protect you for a short time."

"Lady Cecil, I promise that I'll leave here and go home to Hawkswood tomorrow. I must go anyway because I *must* tell Hugh about Matthew. We have no secrets from each other. Dean has pursued Meg here—I shall say to the Ridolfis that I don't like that and that I'm sorry to disoblige Madame Ridolfi, but I'm taking my daughter home. It's a little late to pack everything up and leave today, but . . ."

"Er . . ." said Mildred.

I raised my eyebrows. "You don't want me to go home?"

Mildred said: "There was one more thing that Sir William wanted to talk to you about. Even though you are angry with him, he wants your help and hopes you will give it."

"Does he, indeed?"

"Not as a favor to him. Only for . . . the realm."

I sighed. "What is it?"

"It isn't dangerous."

"Yes, but what is it?"

"He wants you," said Mildred Cecil, "to pay a private visit to the Earl of Leicester."

22

The Queen's Sweet Robin

Mildred removed us from the Ridolfi house, as she herself had said she would, by sheer high-handedness. No, no, she could not dine; she had so many calls on her time. But having heard that her dear Ursula was in London, she begged Donna's indulgence, but she must carry Ursula and her family off forthwith. The tone of voice meant that she would carry us off anyway, with or without anyone's indulgence. Whether or not I would be returning wasn't mentioned.

Within the hour, we were on our way. I found Meg, Brockley, Dale, and Gladys all together in my chamber and of the four of them, only Meg looked downhearted about leaving the Ridolfis. The others were frankly relieved. "Glad to be away from that daft old man Johnson," Gladys said. "Keeps staring at me, he do. He's moon-mad. Says he's fallen for me—at my age, look you!—and then starts gibberin' all because I mistook his swans for geese!"

Almost everyone in the house came to the entrance hall to bid us farewell, including the visitors—the Duke of Norfolk and Edmund Dean. Norfolk asked me to give his compliments to Sir William and to inquire what the prospects now were for his lawsuit. Meg managed to kiss Edmund Dean good-bye and he whispered something into her ear that made her giggle. I shepherded her away, bidding Dean a cool farewell and refusing to be impressed by the arctic coldness of his manner to me. Meg made the journey to the Cecils' house in silence, but she didn't try to argue, for which I was thankful.

We traveled by water, except for Brockley, who with the help of one of Ridolfi's grooms, brought our horses along by road. As soon as we arrived, Mildred led me apart, into a small, tapestried reception room, placed me in a window seat with soft cushions and a view of the garden through the leaded panes behind me, and disappeared. Almost as soon as she had gone, Sir William Cecil came in. As I had expected.

Cecil suffered on occasion from gout and I noticed that he was limping now. In silence, I watched as he pulled a stool near me and sat thankfully down on it.

"Well, Ursula. My wife tells me that you are willing to pay a visit to my lord of Leicester."

I did not want to be here but I had nevertheless come of my own free will. Furthermore, if I had not agreed in so many words to carry out his errand, whatever it was, to Robin Dudley of Leicester, I hadn't refused, either. There was no point in being mulish.

"I don't understand quite what I am to say to him. Where is he, by the way? Is he at court?" I could probably arrange to be lodged at court. It might be a way of getting smoothly out of the Cecil household.

"The court has moved to Richmond. Leicester, however, is still close by. He has taken over Paget Place, at the eastern end of the Strand. It used to be occupied by de Spes," Cecil said. A slight smile lightened his grave features. "De Spes has been obliged to move his ambassador's residence to Southwark, south of the river and well away from the Strand with its useful social contacts and chances both of hearing useful things and finding receptive ears for that persuasive voice of his. The lease on Paget Place ran out and Leicester outbid the Spanish ambassador's budget for renewing it. I think he did it on purpose, to make life more difficult for de Spes."

"That's interesting."

"It's suggestive. I think that Robin Dudley isn't privy to de

Spes's more dubious schemes but that he does suspect their existence. I fancy he's becoming uncomfortable about his own dealings with Mary Stuart. You need only go to the end of the Strand to see him."

"And I am to say—what?"

"Warn him, Ursula. Confirm his suspicions. He and I are not friends and never have been. He has become entangled in this . . . this octopus of a plot . . . because he sees it as a chance to injure me. He will not take advice from me but he knows you well and he knows of the work you have done. To you, he may listen."

"He started me on my secret work," I said. "It began when he wanted someone to watch over his wife. I failed then. She died anyway."

"But you went on to give worthwhile service to the queen and you found out what really happened to Amy Dudley. He respects you."

"Is he another who knows of my parentage?"

"I don't know, but probably. The queen has few secrets from him. Tell me, Ursula, does Meg know?" Cecil asked suddenly.

"Not yet," I said stiffly. It was so very difficult to talk to Cecil in a normal manner. Every time I looked at him, the memory of Matthew's name emerging from that cipher came surging back. "One day, perhaps," I said.

"I think you must, eventually, or someone else will. She's nearly grown up, you know. However, to return to the matter in hand; getting Leicester to withdraw his support for Norfolk's marriage and Mary's reinstatement really is important. I don't like him any more than he likes me, but to the queen, he is Sweet Robin, her Eyes. While he . . . I think he long since gave up hope of marrying her, but oddly enough, I think that he loves her now more than he did when he saw her as a way to power."

"A good deal of power still goes with being her friend and one of her favorites," I remarked distantly.

"Oh yes, that's true. Probably Dudley himself doesn't know where love ends and self-interest begins. That," said Cecil, "is mainly why I don't like the man. He isn't honest with himself.

But the queen will be bitterly hurt if she thinks he has betrayed her, and if he gets any deeper into this business, that is what could happen. He's acting behind Elizabeth's back. I want to get him out of it."

"You want to avoid arresting him?"

"Or anyone. Oh, Walsingham would like me to have all the known conspirators—Norfolk, Leicester, Ridolfi, and de Spes as well—seized and thrown into the Tower, but I have said no. I will *not* tear the whole structure of the council apart, not if I can avoid it. I would rather make these wretched schemes just wither away. I think I can deal with Norfolk. I mean to see that that lawsuit of his goes in his favor. He'll be grateful. He may even pay heed to my advice. That," said Cecil, "will scupper the marriage. It still leaves the possibility of Mary's reinstatement, but if Leicester then backs out as well, the first step in this horrible scheme will lack two vital supporters."

"And the rest may then lose heart?"

"With luck, yes. So there is your task. Show the truth to Elizabeth's Eyes. Try to convince him that the price of damaging me could be too high."

"I see. When shall I go?"

"Tomorrow, if you will. Today, I have no doubt, you are tired and upset and need rest. Ursula . . ."

"Sir William?"

"We have not mentioned the matter that caused you to quarrel with me this morning. But untreated wounds can fester. When Mildred fetched you, did she mention Matthew de la Roche?"

I looked away from him, through the square leaded window-panes at the garden below. There were beds of rich color: phlox and lupin, hollyhock, gillyflower, and rose. But the misery of the deception that Cecil and the queen had practiced on me was between that fair garden and myself, a more effective barrier than any panes of glass.

Cecil was waiting for an answer. I turned back to him. "Yes. She pointed out—that there were reasons."

"I asked her to do that. There is something, though, that I wish to say to you before we let the matter fall into silence. You were married to Matthew virtually by force. You were in love with him, but force was needed because you knew he was our queen's enemy. Later, you left him and lived apart from him for a long time, because of that. Is that not true?"

"Yes. It is true."

"I have just criticized Robin Dudley of Leicester because he is not honest with himself. I will do you the honor, Ursula, of believing that you won't make that mistake."

"You are trying to tell me that I may be better off without Matthew de la Roche."

"I think you should ask yourself that. There's no need to discuss it with me. Your father, Ursula—your royal father . . ."

"Yes?"

"It has always seemed to me," said Cecil, "that he was given to self-deception, even more than Dudley is. I was not yet twenty when Queen Anne Boleyn was executed; and no more than a boy throughout the years when King Henry was trying to rid himself of his first queen, Katherine of Aragon, in order to marry Anne. But I did learn the facts, some of them then and some later, when I entered into court life, and it has long seemed to me that although he swore that he wished to divorce Queen Katherine only because God had denied them a son, and he thought that perhaps their marriage was flawed because she had once been married to his brother Arthur, and perhaps he even convinced himself that that was true—well, the root and heart of the matter was that he desired Anne, and she wouldn't give in to him, not until he could offer her marriage.

"It was when I first began to realize that, that I also began to understand how much harm self-deception can do. The queen knows, as well. She deceives others often enough . . ."

"I know," I said bitterly.

"Quite. But not," said Cecil in a gentle voice, "herself. That, I have never known her to do. I beg you not to deceive *yourself*, either. What you tell Hugh Stannard is of course your own business. And now, let the subject be closed between us. Perhaps you would like to dine with Mildred. I shall not be there. A tray in the study will do for Walsingham and me. We have work to do."

"There's something I'd like to ask," I said. "Has anything further been discovered about the deaths of Julius Gale and the boy Walt? Is anything further even being done?"

"It certainly is. Norfolk's household have been questioned again. But asking questions is one thing. Getting answers is another. So far," said Cecil, "there have been no answers. No one saw anything. No one knows anything. The mysteries remain unsolved."

Over dinner, Mildred said to me: "Your marriage to Hugh really is legal, you know. It's a good deal more legal than any marriage between Mary and Norfolk would be! She hasn't had the wedding to Bothwell annuled yet. What are you going to tell Hugh about—Matthew?"

"The truth," I said. "What else?"

Paget Place was very much a nobleman's house. De Spes must have been furious at having to leave it. Four splendid gables gave elegance to the roof and there was a tower, with battlements, as though the owner of the house were prepared to resist attack if necessary. I and the Brockleys did the dignified thing and arrived on horseback, with Dale on her husband's pillion. We were received graciously at the gatehouse, where my name was recognized, but when I said that I had urgent business with my lord of Leicester, the butler into whose care the gatekeeper handed us asked if I would mind following him to the stableyard.

"A consignment of young horses from the west country has been sent here for his inspection, and the stableyard is where we shall find him. If you are willing to wait, Mistress Stannard, I will show you into the great hall and I'm sure that his lordship will join you as soon as he has finished but you say your business is urgent. When callers come with important business, he prefers them to be brought to him at once. It's not unusual, with him."

Leicester was still the Master of the Queen's Horse and he was obviously at work. I had undertaken this task because it was my duty; but I didn't like it. I had slept badly because of worrying about it. It meant broaching a subject so delicate that I could hardly see how to mention it without virtually accusing the man of something very near to treason. I wanted my errand to be over as soon as possible.

"I will speak to my lord of Leicester wherever he may be," I said. "If he truly has no objection."

The butler led the way, with Dale and myself behind him, and Brockley leading the horses after us. The stableyard was beautiful, the stone-built stable block and tack room in good repair, the cobbles swept, with not a single dandelion or blade of grass showing between them. The yard had a well and a pump of its own, protected by a low wooden screen to avoid accidents, if a horse became excited.

At present, two very good-looking animals, a blue roan and a chestnut, were tethered to a rail on the stable wall, while a bay gelding with black points and a coat that glistened with grooming was being trotted around the yard by a young groom. By the look of him, the gelding was also young and he was very full of himself. Seeing our horses, he whinnied excitedly at the prospect of new friends and half-reared, almost lifting the lad off his feet. Another groom hurried out of the tack room and beckoned Brockley and his charges into the stable and out of sight.

Watching it all from the middle of the yard, in his shirt-sleeves, feet astride and his arms akimbo, was the queen's Sweet Robin, the swarthy Earl of Leicester. He raised his brows at me and Dale, looking slightly put out by our arrival, but neverthe-less, he signed to us to join him, which we did, keeping out of the way of the lively youngster. "Mistress Stannard! What brings you here?" he said as I reached him. Then, without waiting for an answer, he nodded at the colt. "What do you think of him?"

"He's a trifle spirited," I said, as the bay decided that the screen around the water supply assuredly concealed a crouching lion, and skittered sideways across the yard, dragging the unfor-tunate young groom with him. "He needs schooling. And fewer oats, I should think."

"I meant his conformation. The need for schooling's obvious!"

"He's a beauty," I said sincerely, looking with admiration at the rounded quarters, the jaunty carriage of head and tail, and the smoothly sloping shoulders. "I can hardly see a flaw."

"Neither can I. I won't let Her Majesty even glimpse him until I've worked some of the ginger out of him, or she'll want to try him out herself! Catherine de' Medici," he added, "has much to answer for."

I laughed aloud. I did not like Leicester. I knew too much about him, and for some odd reason, which I never did quite fathom, I was unmoved by his unquestionable good looks. He was just as unmoved by any attractions that I might possess. No one can explain these things, but there are times when they do simplify life. Because of our mutual indifference, Leicester and I, on the rare occasions when we had dealings with each other, could negotiate calmly. If he said something amusing, I was free to laugh, and it was not an answer to a sexual gambit.

"You mean the sidesaddle she invented?" I said.

"I do. There was a time when ladies sat quietly sideways in saddles shaped like boxes while someone else led the horse. If they *had* to ride fast, they rode astride, and that was in emergencies only. But then the Queen of France went and designed a side saddle which gave a woman a stirrup and a pommel to grip and let her look ahead, between the horse's ears, and since then, you've all gone mad. The queen rides headlong, like a cavalryman in a charge and so, my dear Ursula, do you. I've seen you."

Dale dodged behind me as the excitable colt plunged again. "I think the boy isn't heavy enough to manage him," I said.

"I agree. *Hobson!*" He pitched his voice with skill, so that it carried, and yet it wasn't a shout. It wouldn't frighten any nervous animals. The groom who had taken charge of Brockley emerged from the stable again and in the same well-modulated tone, Leicester ordered him to take over the colt. "He's sweating. Walk him up and down at the end there till he cools off and don't let him prance about. Tell Jack to trot Blue Taunton round the yard instead."

A few moments later, as we watched Hobson show the paces of the blue roan, which was better behaved than the bay, Leicester said: "So, what *has* brought you here, Ursula? It must be important."

"It's very important, my lord of Leicester . . ."

"You've known me long enough to call me Robin."

"I'm here on an errand that's so vital that formality seems somehow right. It's also so vital that I let the butler bring me here instead of waiting in formal fashion in the house. A paradox, as it were. My lord, you won't be pleased with what I have to say, but I can only beg you to listen, and believe that I come in friendship, with your best interests, and those of the queen, in mind."

Leicester was a tall man. He looked thoughtfully down at me. "How ominous it all sounds! It concerns the queen?"

"Yes, it does."

"Then you may be sure I'll listen." Again, he gave his voice that carrying yet unalarming pitch. "Hobson, Jack, take the horses back into the stable. I'll see Sorrel Taunton's paces later." Again he looked down at me. "But I think we ought to talk in more suitable surroundings. Come."

It was a warm day. We went through the great hall, a splendid place with an astonishing array of Turkish carpets in it, hanging on the walls, covering the table, and even spread on the floor for people to trample on, but we didn't stop there. Instead, we went out onto a terrace, not unlike the Ridolfis' terrace, but wider and longer, overlooking stretches of turf and well-kept knot gardens, extending down to the river. Tables and benches were set on the terrace and we sat down, Dudley and I opposite each other, at a table, and Dale on a seat a little way off. The butler appeared immediately with wine and two glasses, and Dudley promptly sent him to fetch a third.

"I know you, Ursula. You treat your servants as if they were your brother and sister. I had better give Dale some wine as well or you'll look at me as though you thought me a skinflint."

"I wouldn't be so discourteous, my lord, and I know that you're no miser. But yes, I would like Dale to have a glass of wine," I said.

Then, when the third glass had come and we had all been served, I looked at him directly and answered the question in his face. "I fear you may well think me discourteous—but I can only repeat that I'm here in friendship. I had better be frank and straightforward and hope you will accept that I'm doing my best. Sir William Cecil sent me here . . ."

"Did he, now?" Leicester's tone was acid. He crossed an ankle over a knee and his foot twitched ominously.

"But not," I said, "*not,* as a messenger from an enemy. Far from it. My lord of Leicester, we are all three servants of the queen. I know that you have . . . have been encouraging the scheme to make a match between Mary Stuart and the Duke of Norfolk, and to return her to power in Scotland. Believe me, it's not in the queen's best interests. There are others who are working to encourage the plan as well, but they see it only as a first step toward a much more sinister objective."

His face darkened, as I had known it would. Since he was so swarthy to begin with, the result was thunderous. "How do you know all this? You admit you are Cecil's mouthpiece? I suppose he sent you in the hope that I might be too much of a gentleman to order a lady like yourself out of my house? And might even let you finish your—message?"

"Being a lady," I said, "is a drawback, if anything. It's more difficult to be taken seriously. I don't want you to give me the courtesy of a hearing only because I'm a light or slight person. I'm neither."

"Are you quoting my own words at me?"

"Yes, my lord."

I was indeed. When his wife had died in a mysterious accident, nine or so years before, he had sent instructions for the inquest, insisting that the jury must be made up of discreet and substantial men, and no light or slight persons. Leicester's dark eyes glinted in acknowledgment of a hit. He was a good sportsman.

"I know you well enough not to discount you, Ursula! Very well. I'll hear the rest." He leaned back in his settle and his foot stopped twitching. "Go on."

I chose my words carefully. Steady and factual, that was the approach which would best succeed with Leicester. "The sinister objective of which I spoke," I said, "begins with establishing Mary as Elizabeth's accredited heir. Some of those involved hope to convert her to the Anglican faith first . . ."

"Of course. What else?" said Leicester irritably.

". . . but there are others whose hopes are different. *They* hope that eventually, through Mary, the old faith will be brought back to England. Very likely, with the Inquisition. They are even prepared to foment a Catholic rebellion in order to bring it about."

"How have you and Cecil learned all this?" His tone was still aggressive but the threatening thunder was a little farther away.

"Cecil has ways of keeping himself informed," I said. "I am one of them. A man called Julius Gale was another. I was staying at Norfolk's house when . . ."

I began to explain. He only interrupted once, near the start of my account, remarking that he had known of the two deaths, of course—Gale and the boy. "There have been investigations, I believe, but no one has been apprehended."

"There is every reason to believe that the murders were linked," I said, "and also linked to the conspiracy we are discussing. The conspiracy is much bigger than it seemed at first. My lord, if you knew it all, you would never let yourself become involved in anything to do with Mary Stuart. Please let me continue."

He fell silent and I finished my explanation. Then he said: "A rebellion, you say. There is talk of raising the Catholic north, money is being gathered for the purpose, and Philip of Spain is prepared to send help once he knows that the north is ready to rise and the money is available? I have it right? *That* is what you are saying?"

"Yes."

"So what are you—and Cecil—asking me to do?"

"Cecil wants the whole business to dissolve before it has begun. He wants the crazy dreams of these conspirators to remain just dreams. He doesn't want uproar and heads on blocks. Free yourself, my lord. For your own sake and the queen's. She needs both you and Cecil. And you don't want to find yourself in the Tower, do you?"

"I've been in the Tower," said Leicester shortly. "When I was young, before Her Majesty acceded."

I knew he had. Also, his father had been executed for treachery. My reminder had been deliberate.

"What does Cecil propose to do about Norfolk?" he inquired.

"He hopes to persuade Norfolk to back out. We trust that you will back out, too. You will know how best to do it. I wouldn't presume to advise you on the detail."

Leicester got up and moved restlessly about on the terrace and back. "I agree," he said, "that I've had uneasy moments. To put so much power within reach of such a vain, sentimental weathercock as Norfolk—or that siren of a Scottish queen . . . I have thought to myself: is this wise?

"I was once offered to her as a husband; I imagine you have heard about that? I never did find out how serious the queen was when she did that. But despite all the reports I have heard of Mary's beauty and charm, I was never in the least drawn toward her. Later on, when I heard about Kirk o' Field, I felt very glad that I wasn't! Norfolk was horrified by that story to start with, you know."

He sat down again, this time without crossing ankle on knee. "When the idea was first mooted that he might be a future husband for her, he said he'd rather sleep on a safe pillow. But now, it seems that the prospect of a crown matrimonial and a few ingratiating letters from a famous charmer have turned his head."

"You may well be right."

"And you would say to me: Make sure you don't lose *your* head. Is that it?"

"More or less."

"Thank you, Ursula. I will think over all that you have told me, with the utmost care. It took courage to come to me like this."

"You weren't likely to do me any actual harm," I pointed out. "At worst, you would have called the butler to show me out. But I'm glad you listened. I have your safety, and the queen's, at heart."

"The queen's *safety*!" It was as though a mist had lifted from his mind, showing him a frightful vista, hitherto concealed from him. "Yes. I see. You think that . . . ?"

"Isn't it obvious?" I said. "Before Mary can hope to sit on the throne, Elizabeth would have to be in her grave."

I had done my best. With the Brockleys, I rode back to Cecil's house, looking forward to saying: *I have done what you asked of me, Sir William. Now, may I pack and go home?*

Only one thing disturbed my mood and that was the curious sense of foreboding that was still with me, like the flicker of lightning on a dark horizon. It had not lessened.

At Cecil's house, as usual, Brockley took the horses away and Dale accompanied me indoors. We were crossing the paneled entrance hall when Cecil and Mildred came somberly to meet us.

"Ursula, my dear, I am so sorry . . ."

"We are both sorry," said Cecil gravely. "This is hard for you."

"Sorry? About what?" I stopped short. "What is it? Is it Hugh? Meg?" The sense of imminent disaster loomed over me, a storm cloud about to break. "Is one of them ill? Or . . . ?" I couldn't say the word *dead*.

"It's nothing to do with either Hugh or Meg," said Mildred. "It's your woman Gladys Morgan."

"I did protest," said Cecil, "but there was nothing to be done. The arresting officers had a proper warrant signed by a justice of the peace. As a man of the law, I could not forbid them . . ."

"What couldn't you forbid them?"

"Gladys Morgan," said Cecil, "has been arrested and taken away, on a charge of encompassing death by witchcraft."

23

Stab in the Back

Gladys. It was Gladys who was in mortal danger; Gladys whose peril I had sensed without understanding it. My sense of foreboding surged anew at the sound of her name, and every protective instinct in me came alert.

"But who's bringing the charge?" I shouted. "Whose death is Gladys supposed to have encompassed?" They had brought me into the little room where Cecil had talked to me the day before. Dale was hovering, almost clucking, at my side.

Cecil placed a steadying hand on my shoulder. "You'll find this hard to believe, but the man she is accused of killing is Julius Gale."

I broke away from him and threw myself onto a settle. "Am I going out of my mind? Did I hear you aright? How can it be Gale! He was attacked in the street and stabbed in the back!"

"It's a complicated tale," said Mildred gently. "Let William tell it, in order, as it happened. He went with Gladys and the arresting officers and he knows all the details."

"But who . . . ?"

"It starts," said Cecil, "with Arthur Johnson, the topiary gardener. He laid the first complaint . . ."

I interrupted him again, unable to help it. "*Johnson?* But that's just spite! She laughed at him when he proposed to her and she mistook his topiary swans for geese!"

"Perhaps," said Cecil. "Johnson didn't accuse her of murder, not at first. But he went to Ridolfi and said he'd seen Gladys picking herbs in the knot garden, and that he looked through a window that night . . ."

"Oh, *did* he? Peeping at the maids again, I take it. I wonder he had the nerve to admit it."

"He says he was clearing a blocked drain."

"If this situation weren't so serious," I said furiously, "that would make me laugh. Clearing a drain, indeed!"

"Whatever he was doing," Cecil said, "he claims that through a window, he saw Gladys put something in the nightcap which George Hillman was going to drink."

"She did, at my orders, as I told you. Why didn't Johnson mention it at the time?"

"He didn't think it was important—that she was just topping it up. Gladys says she was adding spices; that she'd met Hillman coming to the kitchen to ask for them and said she'd fetch them. She's being loyal to you, I think. She also says that Madame Ridolfi gave her permission to pick herbs for headache medicine for you. Madame Ridolfi confirms this, but Johnson said that once Gladys was free to take herbs at all, she could have taken whichever ones she wanted. He said that the morning after he saw Gladys put something in Hillman's drink, Hillman complained of having had wild dreams. Johnson heard about it—servants' talk—and thought it over . . ."

"She had made him angry, so he decided that here was a chance to get his revenge! But where does Gale come into it?"

"It seems that when Johnson took his complaint to Ridolfi, Norfolk and his secretary Edmund Dean were in the house, as they often are, and they were within hearing. Dean joined in and declared that Gladys had cursed people at Howard House and that those she cursed had fallen ill. . ."

"They had bad chicken in a stew," I said wearily.

"Dean said that one of the victims, Julius Gale, after apparently recovering from the illness, then died mysteriously in the street. He said that he saw the body and that the wound which was supposed to be the cause of death was just a tiny slit and maybe wasn't a stab wound at all. It could have been a simple cut, accidentally come by and not fatal . . ."

"That's complete nonsense!"

"Oh, I agree with you," said Cecil. "So does Walsingham. But nonetheless, with the consent of Ridolfi and Norfolk, off went Dean and Johnson to lay information against Gladys, and now she is charged with procuring Gale's death, and also of attempting to kill Hillman. The accusation there has crystalized, as it were. She is being accused of using poisonous herbs backed up by black arts. On those two counts, she has been arrested."

"Oh my God," I said. I was shaking now.

"If she is found guilty on either count," said Cecil, "she'll hang."

Concernedly, Mildred said: "Ursula, we will help Gladys if we can. But meanwhile, however frightened and angry you are, your own health must be considered. We are about to dine . . ."

"I can't eat!"

"Perhaps not in the dining chamber, but would you take something if it's served in your room? Meg's there. She and Gladys were there together when the arresting officers came and Meg just stayed in the room. She's very upset but she didn't want anyone to sit with her. She said she'd wait for you. She ought to have some food, as well."

I knew she was right. "Very well," I said tremulously. "Meg and I will both eat in my chamber. And so will Dale and Brockley, if you would be so kind. Dale, fetch Brockley. I'll go up now."

Aware that the Cecils' anxious gaze was following me, I went up to my chamber, where I found Meg lying on my bed, crying.

"Mother, they took Gladys away. She was so frightened. I know she says foolish things sometimes, but she's just old and gets muddled, and she was *terrified* . . . !"

"I know, darling."

"But what are we going to *do*? Even Sir William couldn't stop them from taking her! He went with her and tried to argue for her but they wouldn't let her go! I saw him come back, looking so sad!"

"We'll eat first," I said. I was fighting back tears of my own. "They're bringing us something here. While we eat, I'll think."

The Brockleys joined us. Dale had told Brockley what had happened and the first thing he said was: "If there's anything we can do, just tell us." The food arrived and although it tasted to me like sawdust, I made myself take a few mouthfuls and coaxed Meg to swallow something too. The Brockleys ate quietly, saying little but watching me with worried eyes.

My mind was working furiously. When we had all finished, I said to Meg: "I'm going to do what I can for Gladys but meanwhile, you're not to stay here all alone crying your eyes out. Come. We'll find Lady Cecil and ask if you can sit with her."

I saw Meg settled with Lady Mildred and then went back to the Brockleys. We're going out. The tide's right. We're going to hire a boat and go in search of Edmund Dean. I want to talk to him."

There was no guarantee that I would find him. He was Norfolk's employee; he went where his master did and Norfolk could easily have gone to the court or set off on a visit. If so, his secretaries would go with him. I must just hope for the best, I thought desperately.

It was one of those times when there wasn't a boat in sight for hire, and when one did come into view, it was already full of passengers. The next one was empty but failed to see our signals. A good twenty minutes passed before we finally got ourselves embarked and then I sat there fuming while the banks slid by with painful slowness, because we seemed to have hired the laziest ferryman on the Thames. If he'd put some energy into it, he could have made good use of the ebb tide but he rowed at leisure and I knew his type all too well. It's never any use asking them, even politely, to go faster. They dawdle worse than ever, just to show their independence. Brockley knew that as well, and held his peace though I could see that he too was seething.

All the same, I took my impatience out on Brockley when he said: "But, madam, what do you hope to do if we find Dean and talk to him?"

"Bang his head on the nearest wall until he promises to drop this silly charge, of course! Then I'll find Johnson and do the same to him."

"You don't really mean that, madam. Do you think . . ." Brockley hesitated, meeting my angry eyes, but I had never really been able to intimidate Roger Brockley. "Do you think that either of them will listen to you? Especially Dean. I didn't hear all of your last conversation with him, but did you part on friendly terms?"

"No. Very unfriendly."

"So—what if he simply says no?"

Yes, indeed! What?

When we disembarked, I set such a pace on the walk to Norfolk's house that Dale developed a stitch and Brockley had to insist that we slow down. He was no doubt wise, for we did at least arrive at the gate in orderly fashion, rather than red in the face and out of breath. Conley came majestically to receive us. "I am here on a matter of great urgency," I told him. "Is Edmund Dean within?"

"He is on an errand to the Ridolfi house, madam. But if your business is so very urgent, perhaps my lord can help. He is with his tailor just now but if you would wait for a little, he may be willing to see you."

I wanted to swear because of Dean's absence but then, in a moment of unpleasant realization, I saw that Brockley was right again. Any attempt on my part to intercede for Gladys with Dean would probably fail. Dean's resentment against me might well be behind this idiotic charge. It was Norfolk's authority I needed. He was Dean's employer and ought to be able to exert some control over him. And—yes, Norfolk was vulnerable.

"The matter is very serious," I told Conley fiercely. "The duke may be able to help. Please tell him I am here. At once!"

He led us inside, and as soon as he did so, I heard Norfolk's voice. He wasn't upstairs, it seemed, but in one of the ground-floor rooms.

What I did next, I did—I know now—under the influence of something very like hysteria. It had been gathering all the time we were in that boat, watching that lackadaisical oarsman. I was so afraid for Gladys.

I knew her so well. She was short-tempered, volatile, and in many ways, ignorant, and she couldn't guard her tongue. Furthermore, I was now certain that as the years went on, her mind really had begun to falter. She had come to the point of half-believing in her own pretense of occult powers. I also knew that when she was confronted by armed men with a warrant for her arrest, she would suddenly have seen reality. It had happened before. She would see the pit in front of her and too late, she would see herself as she was: old, frail, powerless, and afraid of death. She would be terror-stricken, shaking and dribbling with fear.

So, when Conley tried to usher us into the antlered parlor, where I had first met Norfolk, saying in unhurried fashion that he would inform his lordship of my presence, I found his dignified calm just too much to bear. Something inside me snapped. Brushing past Conley, ignoring his protests, I made toward the Duke of Norfolk's voice, sweeping through an anteroom and straight toward the source, a closed door on the right.

"Madam, you can't . . . !"

Conley had rushed after me and was trying to get in my way. Once more I dodged him, knocked vigorously on the door, and called Norfolk's name. I heard him answer, and I think I really did believe he had called an invitation to enter, but in truth I was too wrought up to listen properly. I threw the door open and marched in, and Norfolk, clad in a loose shirt and no doublet, beaky-nosed and hopping on one leg like an outsize sparrow as he tried to get his hose back on, just turned away in time to avoid considerable embarrassment.

The new hose he had been trying on—an elaborate puffed and slashed outfit, all violet and silver and ostentation—was having pinned adjustments checked over by the tailor, a short, bearded man, who looked at me in outrage. His dignity was the equal of Conley's and somehow he managed not to lose any of it even though his mouth was full of pins.

"Oh, I'm so sorry!" I said, taken aback and turning scarlet, and behind me, Conley indignantly shooed the Brockleys out of the way. He then strode into the room, slamming the door in their faces.

"I couldn't stop her, sir. I am extremely sorry, but she went past me like a mad thing. Mistress Stannard, please come away now and . . ."

Norfolk cut him short. "Never mind, Conley. Let Mistress Stannard explain herself. Mistress Stannard, do you always burst unannounced into gentlemen's private rooms? Did you not hear me call to you to wait? Surely you can see that I am in no fit state to receive a visit from a lady?"

"My lord!" I said. "I am sorry to come upon you like this but it's an emergency. Something terrible has happened!"

I then did the best thing I could possibly have done in the circumstances, probably the only thing which would have cooled Norfolk's entirely reasonable wrath and called forth sympathy instead.

I broke down in tears.

"Now," said Norfolk, when he had resumed his doublet as well as his hose and somehow or other had got the two of us ensconced in the parlor. He had also made the scandalized Conley bring a flagon of strong red wine and had watched me gulp some of it down, "now, please, Mistress Stannard, tell me what the matter is and why you think I can help. All right, Conley, you can go away. I accept that you couldn't stop her and perhaps there is a good reason behind all this."

"There is. And I'm truly sorry. I was wrong to rush in on you like that. But I am nearly out of my mind. Are the Brockleys being looked after?" I added, as an afterthought.

"By good Mistress Dalton, in the servants' quarters," said Conley in chilly tones, and withdrew.

I looked at Norfolk. "You're the only person I can think of who might be able to help, and every hour of delay means more fear and suffering for someone who can't defend herself. Please listen."

"You can see I am willing to do so. Go on."

"My woman, Gladys Morgan . . ."

"That terrible old crone who caused such a furore when you were staying here?"

"She is just old and a little silly. Yes, it's Gladys. She has been arrested on a charge of witchcraft, and your third secretary, Edmund Dean, has apparently laid information that she cursed the messenger Julius Gale and that his death was due to that, to witchcraft, and not to being accosted and stabbed. And you know," I said with passion, "that it isn't true. You *know* that Gale was stabbed. You saw the wound, did you not?"

"It was just a slit. Even then, it seemed strange to me that such a small thing could cause a man's death. I know the coroner said that it could, but there is another possibility, which Dean has also raised. Perhaps the hand that used the blade was under the influence of dark forces. Mistress Stannard, why should anyone want to kill Gale except for pure mischief and joy in evildoing?" Norfolk was all righteous innocence. "He was only a courier. He wasn't robbed. Even the letters he was carrying weren't stolen, as we thought at first. They were here all the time."

"I don't believe in those dark forces, my lord, and surely you don't either. I am asking you to speak to Dean, to insist that he must accept that there *was* a stab wound and that there is no evidence that any . . . any occult power had anything to do with Gale's death. Get Dean to withdraw his evidence! *Please,* order him to admit the truth. I'm afraid for Gladys! She's old, foolish, and frightened out of her wits. I can't bear to think of her . . . I can't bear it . . ."

Norfolk hurriedly poured me another glass of wine, before I could dissolve into tears again. "But *why* should anyone murder Gale?" he said again, wonderingly.

"Why should Gladys?" I countered.

My frenzy was passing now, once more enabling me to think. Norfolk was balking; very well, I would apply pressure. "Gale was not on the road to the north, as he should have been," I said. "Did you not think that strange?"

"I did, of course, but perhaps he had some private errand—some friend for whom he had a message which he wished to deliver before leaving London . . ."

Quietly, I said: "How the letters came to be found in his room, I don't know. But I think he *meant* to take them to the house of Sir William Cecil, to be copied before he took them on to their destinations. The correspondence you and Signor Ridolfi have been having with Mary Stuart, the Bishop of Ross, and Regent Moray, has been under scrutiny."

"What?" Norfolk was in the act of pouring wine for himself. He nearly dropped the flagon. His expression of horror was almost comical. He looked as though I had hit him with a brick.

"My lord," I said, "I have been staying in the house of Sir William Cecil. He was my informant. I assure you that he has no animus against you. But you're involved in a very dangerous business."

He gulped at his wine and then attempted to smile kindly, as a sophisticated man might smile at a child who was pretending to worldly knowledge it couldn't possibly possess. "What are you talking about? Come, come! I have been considering marriage with a charming woman who would bring me many worldly advantages . . ."

I just looked at him, without speaking. I had no need to speak. Norfolk's own conscience and Norfolk's own fears were doing it for me. I watched his eyes widen and saw him turn pale. After a moment, I said mildly: "You have been in touch, I think, with the Catholic earls in the north—Derby, Westmorland, Northumberland?"

"I . . ." He stopped, nonplussed.

"Cecil wishes you well and fears you are running a grave risk. He would like to be your friend. He is helping you with a lawsuit, I know; surely that's evidence of his goodwill. What he would like to see you do," I said, "is step back from these schemes and plans. Dissociate yourself."

"Does he know you're here? Did he send you?"

"No. He has no idea where I've gone. My daughter, Meg, is still in his house, though, and she knows where I am." I let the note of warning sound in my voice and Norfolk produced a feeble kind of indignation.

"My dear Mistress Stannard! You are in no danger in my house!"

"Indeed, I hope not. But do you not see that you need Cecil's friendship? He tried to prevent Gladys's arrest. He would be grateful if you would help to destroy the charge which has been laid against her."

"I see. What *exactly* do you wish me to do?"

I thought I'd made it clear already, but I obliged him by repeating it. "I want you, sir, to bring Edmund Dean to heel. To bear witness yourself that Gale died by stabbing. My lord, you are the Duke of Norfolk!" I resorted to flattery. "Dean will obey you and the justice who issued the warrant for Gladys's arrest will surely listen to you!"

He refilled his glass again and I saw that his hand was not quite steady. "I wish I knew who really killed Gale. I wish I knew why!"

"To stop him from going to Cecil."

"But they had only to warn Signor Ridolfi and get Gale dismissed from his service. There was no need to murder him."

"Those particular letters might have amounted to some sort of emergency. Whoever killed him must have thought he had them on him. Who knows? Will you try to save Gladys?"

Norfolk drew himself up. "What if I say no? I have a sense of loyalty to my inferiors. I would have to make Dean look foolish and he is, after all, my secretary and has served me well. I am sure he is sincere . . ."

I said: "I repeat. My daughter knows I have come here. And if you will not help Gladys, I will ask Cecil to go to the queen and tell her everything he has learned concerning your marriage plans and your dealings with the north and if he doesn't wish to, then I'll do it myself."

He sat staring at me and I saw his lower lip wobble. "All I ask is that you tell the truth and make Dean tell it as well!" I said. "Please!"

"Naturally, if I am called as a witness, I shall say what I saw when Gale's body was carried into my house. What else would I do?"

He was a muddlehead. He had just, more or less, threatened to lie about it because he valued Edmund Dean's feelings more highly than justice for poor Gladys. I didn't remind him.

"Thank you," I said. "I'll be grateful, always. So will Gladys."

Norfolk didn't answer for a moment. His gaze shifted from

my face to look past me, so intently that I turned to look, thinking that someone else must have entered the room. No one was there, however. What he was seeing was a vision born from his own mind. Then he said: "If I must give up my hopes, my dreams, I shall lose her."

"Her?" For a moment I was puzzled and then I understood. "You mean—Mary Stuart?"

"Yes. My Mary." His glance returned to me. Insignificant little man though he was, he had in that moment a curious stature. "You probably can't understand, but I love her."

I said nothing. As on the day when I first arrived at Howard House, I found it impossible to remind him that his adored Mary might well have the violent demise of her husband Darnley on her conscience.

It seemed, in fact, the right moment to rise, make my curtsy and go. Norfolk called Conley to show me out. "Conley," I said, as we went through the vestibule, "is Arthur Johnson here today?"

"No, Mistress Stannard. He is working at the Ridolfi house at present, I believe."

"Thank you. Please fetch my servants."

He gave me an unfriendly look but did as I asked. I led my companions back to the river. We were in luck, for the tide was turning and getting a boat back the way we had come would not be difficult.

"What happened?" Brockley asked.

"I think he'll testify to the existence of that stab wound and make Dean admit it as well. That should put an end to the charge of encompassing Gale's death."

"That's a mercy."

"Are we going back to Sir William's house?" Dale asked.

"No," I said. "We're going to Signor Ridolfi. There's still a charge against Gladys connected with Hillman. I don't particularly want to have to stand up in court and explain that she put a sleeping draft in his nighttime drink on my instructions! There are two people at the Ridolfi house that I want to see. One's Edmund Dean. I may as well speak to him if I can. The other one is Johnson."

24

Checkmate by a Gnome

The boatman put us down at the Ridolfi landing stage. People could not arrive at the landing stage unobserved; there was always someone on the watch and Greaves met us as we walked through the knot garden.

"Mistress Stannard! Madame sent me out to meet you. She will be glad to see you. Come this way."

Perforce, we followed him to the terrace where we found Donna and her maid, a pretty Italian girl, industriously stitching, seated on either side of a worktable. Donna jumped up when she saw me. "But how delightful! Have you come to see how I am getting on without you? I miss you so much! But I have profited from your company! Look!" She held up the work she was doing; a half-finished sleeve of silvery damask with buttons to secure it at the shoulder. "I bought this material from Master Paige—and I beat him down to twenty-six shillings a yard!"

The average price for such a material *was* twenty-six shillings a yard. Paige had probably asked thirty shillings and then let himself be hammered down to the price he had meant to charge all along. I smiled at her, admired the damask, and complimented her on her stitchwork, but when Donna invited me to join her, I shook my head. "This isn't just a social visit, Madame Ridolfi. Something has happened. It concerns my woman, Gladys Morgan."

Briefly, I explained. Donna's maid interrupted me once, exclaiming in bad French that she had been afraid of Gladys and that she was not surprised that the old woman had been taken up for witchcraft, but Donna, quite sharply, told her to keep her place and not interfere. "Naturally, Mistress Stannard will do what she can for her servants! Would I not do the same for you?" The maid subsided and I said, "I must speak to Edmund Dean, if I can. I heard that he was here."

"Dean? Not that I know. However . . ." She picked up a little silver bell from the worktable and rang it. Greaves appeared very quickly. "Madam?"

"Has Edmund Dean been here today, Greaves?"

"Yes, madam. He came on foot, bringing a letter from his master. Signor Ridolfi was out, though expected shortly, and Dean wasn't sure whether to wait for an answer or not. Then a message reached him here and he said he was going off somewhere by river. I didn't see the messenger and can't say whether the message was from Howard House or not."

"I see," I said. Well, the Duke of Norfolk would deal with Edmund Dean, or so I hoped. Johnson was now more important. "Is Arthur Johnson here?" I asked. "I must talk to him too, if possible."

"Yes, madam," Greaves said. "He's working on the topiary. Everything grows so fast at this time of year."

"Then if you will excuse me . . . ?"

"Yes, of course," said Donna, her nice brown eyes full of regret that I hadn't come for the sake of her company.

As we went into the topiary garden, Brockley said, "Madam, will you let me start the talking?"

I looked at him gratefully. He had done this before—taken over when I had a problem difficult for a woman to solve. Johnson might well turn out to be such a problem. "I wish you would," I said.

We found Johnson up a ladder, clipping the mane of a rearing horse. "Can't come down," he said when we halted below and Brockley called to him. "Too busy." His brown gnome's face peered down at us. "This here mane's grown out of shape in a week. In summer, I don't know how I keep up. You want to talk to me; you just do it while I keep on clippin'."

"This is important," said Brockley. "We can't talk to you properly while you're up there. You must come down."

"You tell me what it's about and maybe I will and maybe I won't."

"Gladys Morgan," said Brockley.

"What about 'er? Rotten old besom, and a witch, to boot."

"Come *down!*" said Brockley. "Or I'll make you." He seized the ladder and shook it in a threatening manner, and Johnson descended, backward, stepped off the last rung and stood there glaring at us.

"What about old Gladys, then? Her and her curses!"

"She's been arrested," I said, unable after all, to leave it to Brockley. "As well you know! But you also know very well that she's not a witch! Witchy nonsense, you called it once. You said it to me!"

"Oh, I did, did I?"

"Yes, you did. I heard you," Brockley told him roughly. "You only laid information because she turned you down and didn't appreciate your topiary work enough!"

"Turned me down? Yes, so she did! A decent man offers her his hand and heart an' all she can do is laugh at them! Wounded me, she did!"

For a moment, the feeling in his voice changed from malice to pain and I realized that the pain was real. Gladys really had hurt him. But the malice returned fast enough. His bright old eyes sparkled with it.

"But it weren't long afore I were thinkin' I'm better off without the likes of her because I saw her, I did, putting summat in Master Hillman's drink, the night afore he said he'd had wild dreams and so forth, *and* I'd seen her a-pickin' summat in the herb garden that same evening!" His voice was triumphant now, as though he thought he had checkmated us.

"I'll enjoy coming to the trial and hearing you explain what you were doing up a ladder, peering in at windows," Brockley said. "The window just above is that of the maidservants. I take it you were peeping at them again, for all you claim you were clearing a drain!"

"So I were. You try and prove I weren't."

"Gladys," I said boldly, deciding to go for half the truth, at least, "was adding extra spices. Master Hillman had sipped his drink and found that he wanted more flavorings. Gladys and I met him when he came out of his room in search of them. He mentioned where he was going and Gladys said she would see to it for him."

Hillman would come back from Scotland in due course and might quarrel with this, but I would worry about that later. If necessary, I would tell him what Gladys and I had really done and why. Cecil would surely back me up. Hillman was Gale's kinsman and Walsingham hoped he would be Gale's replacement. He would very likely understand.

"Then what were that old hag a-doin' in the herb garden?" demanded Johnson truculently.

"You will not call Mistress Morgan a hag," said Brockley coldly. Now that Gladys was in grave trouble, all his gallantry toward her had returned.

"She was picking herbs for a potion against sick headaches," I said, truthfully. "My headaches, to be precise. That's all."

"You see," said Brockley, "your evidence amounts to nothing. We may as well tell you that Edmund Dean is likely to withdraw his evidence as well. You'll be on your own and we'll refute you."

"What does that mean—refute?"

"It means we'll make it clear that what you saw wasn't what you thought," said Dale, joining in, shrill in her support for me and Brockley.

"All right," said the gnome, showing his gap teeth—so very like Gladys's own fangs—in a far from genial smile. "So what I say don't count for nothing. But them as Gladys cursed at Howard House, *they'll* likely speak up. I know all about that, from them. I work there, same as I do here. They'll say how she cursed 'em and they all fell sick . . ."

"They ate stew with bad chicken in it!"

"So *you* say." The crafty old eyes smiled unpleasantly at me. "But it ain't only them. There's more."

"More?" I said.

Again, that fanged grin, that cunning leer. "Gladys told me this an' that as well, in the days when it were sweet talk atween us. Like how she cursed folk at those places where you lot live as a rule. Somewhere called Hawks something or other, and somewhere called Withysham, and there were a third . . . Faldene or some such."

I felt myself become very still.

"Makes sense to you, do it?" The sly old eyes were watching me. "Went fer the vicar there, she did, over how he was treatin' some other crazy old soul. She cursed folk at all three places, she told me, and she laughed at how they looked when she let fly at 'em, and how she made the physicians wild, makin' potions that were better than what theirs were."

"Oh, God," I said.

"You may well call on God. So may she. Justice'll be sendin' to all them places, to the physicians there and that vicar. They'll be called to witness, too. Goin' to go and bully them, are you? Think they'll listen? More likely to have you up as well, I reckon!"

We said nothing. There would be no silencing any of the physicians, while Dr. Fleet, the vicar of Faldene, would be the most lethal of all and would probably call on his fellow vicars at Hawkswood and Withysham to back him up. They would, too. Any misfortune that had befallen anyone at whom Gladys had aimed a curse would be put down to it. And life is full of misfortunes. Had anything gone amiss with Dr. Fleet . . . I remembered, shivering, the curse Gladys had leveled at him.

I curse ye by a cold hearth and a cold bed, a cold heart and a cold head, a cold belly and cold breath, a cold life and a cold death!

The words had stuck in my head.

It was because Gladys had uttered that curse that we had set out for Howard House at all. Now it might well destroy her. In those few words she had very likely started something which she could not stop.

If she had hurt Johnson's feelings, he looked like getting his revenge. The gnome had checkmated us, it seemed.

* * *

"I hate him," I said passionately, as the three of us marched out of the garden. For once, Brockley hadn't even noticed that Dale had been exposed to the scandalous topiary. "I *hate* him. He's disgusting!"

"I've seen things very like him in stagnant ponds," Brockley agreed, straight-faced as ever when he was joking.

I snorted, a noise between rage and bitter laughter. We returned to Donna to make our farewells. She asked if Johnson had been helpful and was clearly sorry when I said no, but said sadly that she had no influence over him and could not help. I kissed her good-bye and then the three of us walked dejectedly back along the Strand to Cecil's house.

And once more, there in the entrance hall, were the Cecils, with anxious faces. It was weird, as though time had slipped backward. Feeling suddenly almost too tired to stand, I said: "What is it now?"

"Dear Ursula, thank goodness you're back!" They said it in unison. "We've been looking out for you," Mildred added.

"What's happened?"

"You must come upstairs," said Cecil. "It's Meg."

"*Meg!*" I couldn't bear this. I had enough to endure. The thought of what might happen to Gladys sickened me, and though my guts twisted at the very thought of telling Hugh that Matthew was still alive, I knew I must soon brace myself to do so. I couldn't endure another calamity, least of all one involving my daughter. "What's wrong with her?"

Mildred caught at my arm as I was about to plunge past them on the way to the stairs. "It's all right. She's here, quite safe. But she did give us the slip earlier. She was supposed to have stayed with me. I asked her to read to me while I did some embroidery, but she seemed very distracted—and after a while, I was called to deal with some household matter and when I returned, she had gone! One of our maids saw her going out but didn't stop her, assuming that she had permission . . ."

"But she's back, you say? In that case, what . . ."

"She came back some time ago," said Cecil. "But she is in

tears. She won't stop crying. She keeps asking for you, and she won't tell anyone else what the matter is."

"Where *is* she?" I demanded, once more making for the stairs.

"In your chamber!" Mildred called.

I was already halfway there, going up the stairs two at a time. I rushed straight to my room and there, indeed, was Meg, lying on my bed, her cap awry and her dark hair soaked at the temples with sweat and tears. She was huddled, with her knees close to her chest, and her nose turned into the pillow but she looked around as I came in, and then, with a wail, she threw herself off the bed and into my arms. I held her tightly.

"Meg! Meg, sweetheart. It's all right. I'm here. I'm here." I saw Dale hovering at the door. "Mulled wine!" I said. It is a sovereign answer to shock and hysteria. Dale disappeared and I sat down on the bed, holding Meg as close as I could and crooning to her.

"What is it, darling? You can tell me!"

"I went to see Edmund Dean."

"You—*what*? I've been looking for him, too, though I didn't find him. I'll tell you all about that later. Why did you go alone? Did he do something to you?" Horrible visions of assault, of rape, rushed through my mind.

Meg, though, was shaking her head furiously. "Not that. Not what you're thinking. But it's just as bad."

"*Just as bad?* It can't be. Meg, what are you talking about? And *why* did you go?"

"Because of Gladys. I thought, if I asked him, he wouldn't give evidence against Gladys. He might even be able to stop the whole thing, get her set free. If he would say that Master Gale really was stabbed, and if he pooh-poohed the servants at Howard House who might talk about her curses, well, a jury might listen to him. But he wouldn't. He wouldn't. He said he couldn't even though he was in love with me, and then, to prove he was in love with me, he gave me a present. He gave me this."

She pulled something from under her pillow, and held it out to me on her palm. It was a slim, coiled silver chain, with a small silver heart strung on it. A simple pendant. The pendant she had given to Walt, as a gift for Bessie, his future wife. The pendant we had last seen being slipped into the pocket of his sleeveless jerkin.

"I knew it at once. There are markings on the back that I recognized. How did it come to *Edmund*?" whispered Meg.

I said: "Tell me exactly what happened. Everything."

25

The Voice of Meg

This part of the story rightly belongs to Meg. I will let her speak for herself, telling the tale as she told it to me. Now that I was with her, she was able to dry her tears, and although she held my hand tightly while she talked, once she had begun, she spoke with surprising calm and coherence. I had never loved her more.

Mother, I know it was wrong (said Meg). I know I shouldn't have gone out to find Master Dean on my own, but it was for Gladys. You weren't here when the men took her away. You didn't see. She couldn't believe it. I think they asked to see Sir William first of all—at least, he was with them when they came to fetch her. He looked so anxious. She and I were here, because I was embroidering and your window seat has a better light than the one in my room. She was telling me one of her stories about Wales, about how she left home when she was only twelve, and earned her living tending sheep . . .

I'm sorry. I'm getting off the point. These men came into the room and straightaway, I didn't like them. They were so big and . . . and quiet in a threatening sort of way and they didn't look as if they'd ever smiled in their lives. One of them said: *I arrest you, Mistress Morgan, on a charge of having unlawful dealings with demons, and encompassing death by witchcraft* and Gladys . . .

Gladys stared at them and she *changed*. She shrank and started to shiver and she cried out that her curses never meant anything; that they were just a way of making people respect her, and they—she meant the two men—ought to try being old and ugly and see what it did to them . . .

Sir William tried to explain to us. He said the gardener, Arthur Johnson, had lodged the first complaint, but that Edmund Dean had made another, which was more serious because he said Gladys had something to do with Master Gale's death. I knew about Master Gale because although we were already on our way home when his body was found, you wrote about it to Mistress Jester at Hawkswood. From what your letter said, it was obvious that Gladys wasn't responsible. That's just *silly*. Master Gale was stabbed, wasn't he?

Sir William said he would go with her and that she must be calm but she struggled when the men took hold of her. She screamed and bit one of them and she fought as they dragged her out, and on the way down the stairs she started to cry, and to shout out that she'd done nothing, she was just a poor old woman. And she *is;* that's the truth of it. She *is*.

I thought that if I went to talk to Master Dean, perhaps he'd listen to me. I knew you wouldn't like me to go but it was for *Gladys*.

Mother, when you and Stepfather brought me to Howard House in the first place, it was to meet Master Dean, perhaps to become betrothed to him. I thought that you wanted me to like him. Well, when I met him—I don't think I liked him exactly, but the moment I saw him, well, after that I couldn't get him out of my mind. I kept thinking about him! It was exciting. His *eyes* . . .

Later on, you changed your minds and you weren't pleased when he took me for walks in the gardens of Howard House. I thought you weren't being fair. First I was supposed to like him, and then I was supposed not to, just to start and stop to order, as though I were a pony with a rider, but I couldn't.

I know I've only just reached fourteen, but I do know what it means to like someone and that didn't seem to be what I felt for Master Dean. It was more as though I were a moth, being drawn toward a flame. He didn't touch me often, but he did take my hand now and then, or put an arm about me; once I remember he pushed back my cap and stroked my hair, and once he kissed me. Whenever he did that I felt . . . I can't explain. I wanted more, and yet I was afraid of it, too. I couldn't leave off thinking about him but when I thought about marrying him, being left alone with him, being in his power forever, I felt scared. I wanted it to happen, and yet I didn't want it to happen or not for a long time, maybe not ever.

But I *did* keep thinking about him, even after you sent me home. I dreamed of him at night. I carved his name on the stem of a rose tree. When Stepfather said he'd got to take Gladys back to London, I cried because he wouldn't take me as well. When Madame Ridolfi sent for me to come and join you, I was thrilled! Stepfather let me go because he thought that you knew of the invitation and wanted me with you.

When I arrived at the Ridolfi house, you weren't there, but Master Dean was. A little later, you came back and found us in the topiary garden. I didn't like that garden, Mother; it's embarrassing. But Edmund took me there and tried to get me to laugh at some of the . . . the shapes, and then we sat down and he said something that frightened me very much. I'd asked him just what had happened to Master Gale. I said: "You were at Howard House at the time. Was he really killed in the street, in broad daylight?"

"Not quite. It was around dawn," he said. "He'd made an early start." I said, what a dreadful thing. Then he said: "Don't waste your sympathy on Gale, Margaret. I follow the old, true religion, which I hope will one day hold sway again in England. I can tell you this—that Gale was no friend to it. He deserved what he got."

I hated hearing him say that. He sounded so cold, not quite human. But then he put his arm around me and told me that I was growing beautiful and that he loved me and hoped one day to make me his wife and then he brought out a book of poetry and began reading. I was horrified when the men came for Gladys and I heard that it was partly because of him that Gladys was taken away.

I was still thinking about it when you came back from visiting the Earl of Leicester. When you heard what had happened, you went off again, I didn't know where. I thought probably to the justice who'd issued the warrant. I didn't think of *you* going to find Dean, or Johnson either. You'd told me to stay with Lady Cecil and I did for a while, but she was called away and suddenly I couldn't, any longer, sit there fretting and not *do* anything. I thought, Surely, if Edmund loves me, he'll stop all this if I ask it of him. So I went out and along the Strand to the Ridolfi house . . .

"How did you know Edmund might be there?"

He told me yesterday, in the topiary garden, that the Duke of Norfolk is doing business of some kind with Ridolfi, raising money for something, I think, and is very often with the Ridolfis, and that Edmund frequently goes with him, or takes messages there. I thought I'd try there first and he *was* there. The minute I was let in, I saw him crossing the vestibule. He saw me and came to me, and I said: "Please, Master Dean, I must speak to you privately. It's very important. Please."

He was nice, then. He put his head around a door and told someone that he'd been called away by a messenger, and was leaving by river—could he borrow the Ridolfi dinghy for a short time? Someone answered yes, and then he came back to me and said that now we could be completely private and free from interruption. He led me straight through the house and the garden, and untied the dinghy from the landing stage. "We don't want a boatman listening," he said. "We'll be quite alone out on the river."

And that's what we did. He rowed us out and then let us drift, and he said to me: "Now, what's it all about?"

Well, I told him. How Gladys had been arrested and how frightened she was, and how Sir William had said that Edmund himself was a witness against her and was accusing her of killing Julius Gale through her curses. I said I'd known Gladys for years, and she was only a harmless old woman if a little foolish, and her curses nothing but empty words. And I said that my mother had written to my gentlewoman at Hawkswood, telling her how Master Gale had been murdered by stabbing. Curses had nothing to do with it. But he said . . .

He said: "Do you think, dear little Margaret, that the devil cannot use human hands to do his work? Once the door is opened to him, as it can be opened by those who practice the black arts, he will use what tools are available. A knife *may* have been thrust into Julius Gale, though I myself am not sure of that. But even if it's true, how was the killer inspired to use it? Who is to say the devil wasn't whispering in his ear? The devil having been summoned by, as you say, a foolish old woman. It is very foolish to have commerce with the forces of evil but that doesn't excuse it. It is still a mortal sin."

I pleaded, I implored. I promised anything, anything . . . I even said I'd run away with him and marry him in secret, if only he would help Gladys. He just shook his head and said no. He said that he was not yet ready to marry. He said he loved me truly, but that I was still little more than a child and I did not understand such things as the wiles of the devil.

I was in tears by then. He laughed and said he couldn't comfort me properly in a boat; that perhaps the boat had been a mistake! "Quite useless for courtship!" he said. And then he said: "But I have a little gift that I bought for you. I meant to give it to you when I was reading to you in the topiary garden, but we were interrupted. Here it is."

Then he put his hand in his belt pouch and brought out that silver pendant. He leaned forward and gave me a kiss and showed me the pendant. Then he put it round my neck. He was treating me like a little girl whose troubles can be put right by a sweetmeat, and all of a sudden I wasn't fascinated by him anymore. I could see myself through his eyes: a piece of soft clay that he thought he could mold into anything he wanted, train to think in any way he chose. I *hated* him. But that wasn't all.

He can't have bought that pendant. It's *my* pendant, which I gave to Walt! I *know* those markings; they're the device of the jeweler who made it. How did it get into Edmund's hands? Walt wouldn't have given it to him! Why should he? What had Dean to do with Walt? Mother, suppose, just suppose, it was Dean who murdered Walt and . . . and, well, just came upon the pendant at the same time and thought, ah, here's a pretty trinket for silly little Margaret?

I suppose Walt could have sold it or lost it and Edmund could have bought it or picked it up, but we only gave it to Walt the day before he was killed! And he was so pleased with it, so touched! I'm sure he wouldn't have sold it or been careless with it. Edmund said that Master Gale deserved all he got. Suppose he was the one who killed Gale, and Walt found out? All of a sudden, he was saying he'd be able to marry Bessie after all, wasn't he? I wondered if he'd asked Edmund to give him money for his silence. And what if Edmund is using Gladys to carry the blame for Gale's death, and divert attention well and truly away from him?

It all went through my head in a flash. It wasn't clear at first. Just a muddle—but I did know that now I hated Edmund and that I was also frightened to death of him. I thanked him for the pendant. I stopped crying. I asked to go home. He rowed me along the bank to the landing place here and put me ashore. By the time I'd got back to my room, my head had cleared. I knew what I believed he had done. Oh, Mother—it's so *horrible*. Poor, poor Gladys!

I looked in astonishment at my daughter. When we set out for Norfolk's house originally, she had been still a child. Now I saw that although she had only just passed her fourteenth birthday, she had moved, suddenly, into womanhood. Intelligent womanhood. She inherited that, I thought, from both sides of her family. Her father, Gerald Blanchard, had certainly had brains, but I too was sharp-minded, and her half aunt, Queen Elizabeth, had a formidable intellect.

How many young girls of Meg's age could have understood, so quickly, what that pendant meant? I looked at her with new eyes, knowing that she was unique and that I was proud of her, and that I must safeguard her future as though she were a rare and precious gem.

I looked at the pendant. That too was surely unique. It had originally been made for her, and probably there were no others quite like it. In which case, Dean had lied about the way he came by it.

"Walt still had the pendant on the day he was killed," I said. "Dale and I spoke to him that morning. He said he would be giving it to Bessie as a wedding gift before many weeks were out. He was dead within hours of saying that. My darling Meg," I said. "We need to talk to Sir William. Will you tell this story to Sir William Cecil? Now?"

"Yes, Mother. Yes, of course. Mother . . ."

"Yes, sweetheart?"

"Will it save Gladys? If Edmund withdraws his charges, or it's proved that he was the one who killed Master Gale, for reasons of his own—nothing to do with witchcraft!—will Gladys be released?"

I put my arms around her and held her tightly. I was thinking of the physicians and vicars of Hawkswood and Withysham; and of Dr. Fleet, the vicar of Faldene, and of the chances of life and the things that could have happened to people in those places since I was last there.

"I don't know, my love," I said. "I don't know."

26

The Lutestring

Cecil hadn't gone to Richmond with the court, preferring, when necessary, to travel from his house in the Strand to Richmond by river, despite the sinuousness of the Thames. As he admitted, relations between him and Elizabeth were not too cordial. She had indeed seized the Spanish treasure on his advice, and though the English merchants were now trading through Hamburg and trade was recovering, she still chose to blame him for the debacle over Antwerp.

I stayed on in the Cecil household, not gladly, but because Sir William requested it, in a way that was first cousin to an order, and because I understood that serious matters were in hand. I had myself said to Mildred that my marital affairs were small ale by comparison. For one reason, I was glad to be still in London because Master Harry Scrivener called on Cecil, to bid his old friend farewell before leaving the City and going back to his house in Hampshire. I had the opportunity to thank Master Scrivener for the help he had given me, assure him that my efforts at deciphering had been a success, and wish him a good journey home.

I didn't mention the shock that had emerged from the jumble of figures—the appalling, unbelievable, sight of Matthew's name. But that day I asked Cecil to send for Hugh. I had tried several times to put the news into a letter, but somehow it felt wrong to tell it that way. I needed to do it face-to-face. If I could not go to Hugh, then please, I said, let him come to me.

Cecil did not move against Edmund Dean at once. He reminded me of a stalking cat, waiting to pounce. "If it's true that Dean was responsible for killing Gale and Walt," he said, "then those are details in a much larger pattern. As I said, I don't want to tear the council to pieces. Bring Dean in too soon, and the whole plot may be shown up while it's still active, which would destroy too many people who are better *not* destroyed. If this nasty scheme doesn't exist anymore when we arrest Dean, he won't be able to do nearly so much damage."

He had called me to his study to talk to me. He was at his desk; I was restlessly pacing. "But murder can't be hushed up," I protested.

"I know, but the threat of being executed for treason instead of merely homicide could stop Dean from talking too freely in court. It's the eighth of July now. The verdict on Norfolk's lawsuit will be known in two days' time," said Cecil. "You've worked on Norfolk too—you were out of order there, but the result may be good. He's looking worried, while Leicester's going about with a permanent frown. I think your interview with him is working too, like yeast in bread dough. We'll let it mature. Meanwhile, I've sent for Hugh as you asked, and I shall have George Hillman and whatever correspondence he is carrying intercepted when he gets back to London. Then we'll know where Moray stands in the matter.

"My eyes and ears in Scotland," he added, "have reported to me that Moray's feet are getting very cold indeed. He's shuffling them. He doesn't think the other Scottish lords will agree to Mary's restoration. We shall see," said Cecil, as his light blue eyes lit with a grim smile.

I said: "Gladys . . ."

Cecil sighed. "I have made inquiries. Statements have been taken from the physicians and vicars of your two homes and from the Reverend Fleet at Faldene. She cursed Dr. Fleet, did she not?"

"Yes." I looked at him fearfully.

"Dr. Fleet has lost his young wife, to an ague of a kind more common in winter than in summer. He attributes her death to Gladys's curse. She may, as it were, replace Julius as the person whose death Gladys encompassed by witchcraft. There have also been a couple of unexpected deaths among the villagers at Hawkswood and apparently, they were people that Gladys had favored with her—ill-wishing."

"No. Oh *no!*"

"I'm sorry. We'll do our best but don't hope too much."

"I've seen her. I visited her. I was allowed to take her some comforts: blankets and food. She's . . ."

I couldn't go on. I had seen prison cells in the Tower, but this dank, smelly dungeon in Marshalsea Prison was worse. I found Gladys shut in with a crowd of others, all filthy, the pitiful and the genuinely evil herded together, witches and pickpockets, street women and murderers. I hardly recognized the shriveled, pining thing that Gladys had become. She clutched at me with hands like claws, begging me to give her hope, to promise her that the worst wouldn't happen, that she would soon be free, swearing desperately that she would never pretend to curse anyone again. On my return to Cecil's house, I locked myself in my room, all alone, and cried for hours. After that I had had to decide what to tell my daughter.

"I wish," I said with passion, "that I could send Meg back to Hawkswood and the care of Mistress Jester."

"She may be needed when Dean is finally arrested. What have you told her about Gladys?"

"I lied a little, about my visit. I said that Gladys seemed well and that I thought she didn't fully understand her danger. But I can't deny to Meg that Gladys *is* in danger. I've warned her. She wept," I said. "But . . ."

"Natural enough, but you were right to prepare her. False hope is rarely a good idea. She'll come through, you know. Even if Gladys doesn't."

"I know. Sometime during this last summer," I said, "she ceased to be a child. I only realized it after the change had taken place."

"The time comes," Cecil said. "It's always a surprise. But sometimes it's brought on by circumstances, sooner than nature intended."

"I know," I said. I added: "Thank you for sending for Hugh. I badly want to talk to him."

"You have really decided to tell him about Matthew?"

"There was never any doubt of that," I said.

The verdict on Norfolk's lawsuit went in Norfolk's favor and he came to see Cecil, full of earnest gratitude. Then, at last, George Hillman came back from Scotland. On the same day, Hugh arrived.

"I have things to tell you," I said to Hugh as soon as we were alone in our chamber.

"Cecil's told me how you uncovered the real extent of the danger. I congratulate you. Meg appears to be taking after you."

"Meg has astounded me. Thank you for bringing Sybil, by the way. She's healthy company for Meg. They're reading Latin together now. But there's something else, Hugh. Something that is very difficult for me to tell you."

"And that is?"

I swallowed. "I found this out, as well, when I was deciphering those letters. Cecil has left it to me to tell you or not. I felt I must. But it's all right, Hugh. Apparently it's been made all right. We really are man and wife, according to the law."

Hugh's brows rose. "We really are . . . ? Ursula, what on earth are you talking about?"

I had lain awake at night, choosing the words with which to break this news. Broken it must be; between me and Hugh there could be no lies, no secrets. He had to know, even if putting it into words felt as though grappling hooks were dragging at my entrails. But the words . . .

The plainest, the simplest, seemed best. "My second husband, Matthew de la Roche, is still alive," I said.

"What?" Hugh looked as though he thought his hearing was faulty.

"Matthew's still alive," I repeated. "He didn't die of the plague. The letters that said he had were forgeries. Forgeries were sent to him, as well. He thinks that *I'm* dead. But our marriage is sound, so Cecil tells me. The queen has annuled my union with Matthew. She is head of the Anglican Church in England and she did it on the grounds that I wasn't married to Matthew by the Anglican rite but by a priest who had no business to conduct such a ceremony in this country, and because I was forced into it. She has declared our marriage lawful."

He said nothing for a moment. I sat quiet, waiting and afraid. Then he turned to me again and he was smiling. "My very dear Ursula. It doesn't come as a surprise."

"You mean you . . . you *knew*?"

Hugh shook his head. "No, though I was very startled just now to realize that you did! I suspected, that's all. You are valuable to the queen and to Cecil and then there's your kinship to Elizabeth. Once they got you out of France and back to England, they must have been tempted to think of a way to keep you here. De la Roche's death was so very convenient, was it not? However, since we now know for certain . . ."

We had been in the window seat. Abruptly, he stood up and roamed about. Then he came back and stood beside me, looking out of the window. Without turning to me to me, he said: "What will you do now, Ursula? When all this is over, I mean. When you have done your duty by Cecil, borne witness as I suppose you may have to do, and seen Gladys through to whatever the outcome of this horrible business may be. Will you stay with me, or will you repudiate the annulment and go back to De la Roche. I know you loved him. Do you still?"

He spoke very calmly, very reasonably, but between us, there was an invisible thread like an overtaut lutestring. Every word we spoke made it quiver, giving off a sound too high for the physical ear to hear, but heard, felt, all the same, by the senses of the mind, which are not limited as are those of the body.

With equal calm, I said: "I believe he has remarried, and has a son."

"That doesn't answer the question."

"It does in a way. If I went back to him, I would wreck that marriage as well as our own. I've had time to think about it. I don't believe I could go back. It's true I loved him . . ."

For a dreadful moment, much as when his name first

emerged from the cipher, Matthew's memory rushed in on me. It was as though he were there. I could see his dark, diamond-shaped eyes under their dramatic brows—his wide shoulders and long chin; I could see his smile, feel his body against mine. I remembered the smell of him; a sharp, spicy mixture of leather and sweat and cinnamon, from an exotic soap that he liked to use. The room spun, giddily.

Hugh turned at last and looked at me. I thought he was reading my mind. The dizziness faded, and with it, so did Matthew's troublesome phantom.

"I really did love him," I said, and if my voice shook, it was only a little. "And perhaps," I said steadily, "I still do, but I wasn't truly happy with him. I left him once, as you know. I never had any *peace* with Matthew. I was never happy in France, and I don't want Meg to be brought up there. She wouldn't want to go, anyway; I know she wouldn't. She's best off with you and me. And besides all that . . ."

I didn't wish to talk of that confinement that had nearly killed me and which my son had not survived. But there was no need. There were other things to say.

"I have had both peace and happiness with you," I said. "I'd like to keep them and I don't think one can go back, in any case. If I did, I would pine to be back with you! Matthew is . . ." The words *yesterday's stale bread* came, shockingly, into my mind. They were too brutal to utter aloud. I acknowledged the truth of them in silence. Then I said: "I choose to stay with you. If you want me."

Hugh said: "Since I did have suspicions about De la Roche's death, I took precautions. In my will, Ursula, I have left everything to you but I have not named you as my wife. My will calls you *The lady known as Mistress Ursula Stannard, formerly known as Madame de la Roche, formerly known as Ursula Blanchard.* I have made you safe for life, my little bear. The will is valid even if our marriage is not."

"But it is!"

And this time my voice didn't shake, but was warm and steady, and I was in his arms when the page came, with the summons from Sir William Cecil.

27

Jeweler's Mark

The page led us to Cecil's study, where we found Cecil, Walsingham, and George Hillman all awaiting us. It was some time since I had seen Hillman, and now it struck me all over again, what a pleasant young man he was. His face was anxious, though. He was sunburnt from his traveling, but beneath the brown skin, he was pale, and as we came in, he was saying, in desperately earnest tones, that he could only swear that he had had no idea, no idea at all, of what he was carrying, and that Signor Ridolfi hadn't dictated the letters to him, only given them to him sealed, and told him where to take them.

The transcriptions of the letters were laid out on the desk, crowding it somewhat, since it was already laden with Cecil's handsome silver and ebony writing set, a pile of writing paper, a stack of document boxes, several massive books, and a small, pretty silver box, which looked somewhat out of place amid so much gravitas.

Hillman was now explaining that his cousin Julius had worked for Ridolfi. "I never thought there was any harm in taking his post over. My family are loyal subjects of Queen Elizabeth. I never dreamed . . ."

"I repeat—no one thinks you did," Cecil said soothingly, obviously reiterating part of a conversation that had taken place before we arrived. "Please calm yourself. Ah. Master Stannard, and Mistress Stannard. Enter, and be seated."

Cecil was at his desk, Hillman and Walsingham were standing. I noticed however, that cushions had been placed on the window seat and that there were extra stools in the study, as though more people were expected. Hugh and I took upholstered stools close to the desk. Walsingham was now doing the talking.

"Your cousin," he said to Hillman, "was more than a loyal subject; he was secretly a useful servant to the crown. We believe he was killed when he was bringing—or was believed to be bringing—letters to us, which he considered to be treasonous. You have now taken on his work as secretary and courier to Ridolfi and we have been considering whether we should ask you to don your kinsman's other mantle as well, and serve us as an informant, as Julius did."

Hillman looked horrified. "Sir Francis! I couldn't do it! I'm a plain man. I can't dissemble. I would be suspected, caught out . . ."

"Once more, calm yourself," said Cecil. "No one is going to force you against your will. You have answered our questions and your answers have satisfied us. We're keeping you here for quite another reason. Ah. Here is Mistress Meg."

The page, who had gone out, now reappeared, escorting Meg and Sybil. Sybil was visibly puzzled and Meg looked shy. I glanced at Cecil in surprise. "Why has Meg been summoned?"

"We may need her," said Cecil quietly. He nodded to the page. "Your third errand," he said. "Fetch him now."

"Fetch whom?" Hugh inquired.

"Edmund Dean," said Cecil.

Meg went red and then white. Unconsciously, she moved closer to Sybil. I indicated that the two of them should take the window seat. I did this instinctively, because it was well away from the door, and when Dean came in, he wouldn't be close to Meg. "Has Dean been arrested?" I asked.

"Not yet," said Cecil. "He has had a courteous invitation to visit me at my home, as he may be able to do me a service. The invitation didn't enlarge further. I didn't want him brought here under armed escort, just in case we have it wrong. That would embarrass us both."

"Is the armed escort available if wanted?" Hugh asked acutely.

Cecil's gave his grim smile. "Oh yes."

Dean came in briskly, very much the efficient young secretary with a career ahead of him, and a determination to prove himself fit for it.

"Sir William Cecil. Sir Francis Walsingham. And the Stannards and their charming daughter, Margaret. And Mistress Jester." His bows were perfect. "I received your invitation, Sir William. Or was it a summons of some kind? I confess it surprised me—I can't think of any way in which I can be of service to you. However, if I can, I am of course more than willing. His Grace of Norfolk has been kind enough to give me the afternoon free to attend upon you."

"That was gracious of him," said Cecil expressionlessly. "Master Dean, I believe that you and your parents, although you conform outwardly to the laws regarding religion in this land, at heart believe in the old faith of our fathers."

"That is so, but we make no show of it." Dean was not disconcerted. "His Grace of Norfolk has a similar attitude, as have other members of the royal council, I believe. None of us have ever been censured for it, and none of us have caused trouble, as far as I'm aware."

"You are privy to much of your master's business and correspondence, however, as indeed his other secretaries, Higford and Barker, are?"

"Yes. Naturally. But, Sir William, I cannot discuss His Grace's private business. It would be a breach of confidence. You would need to take such matters up with him."

"If necessary, we will do so. We only want to clarify certain things. Now." Cecil reached out for the little silver box and opened it. "Have you ever seen this before?" he asked, as he tipped its contents into his hand and held it out to Dean. I saw Meg crane forward and heard her soft, indrawn breath.

Nestling in Cecil's palm was the silver pendant, the slim

chain, and the little heart. Dean looked down at it and then turned to Meg. Once more, she turned crimson. Sybil took her hand reassuringly.

"Margaret?" His voice was sorrowful, a little reproving. He stared at her, making me want to jump up and put myself between them, to block that intent gaze from her. I knew it would pierce her through and through.

As it was, I sat still but caught Meg's eye and smiled at her. With Sybil's fingers gripping hers, and my smile to encourage her, she raised her chin, turned to Dean, met his eyes squarely, and said: "You gave it to me as a present, the last time we met. You said you had bought it for me."

"So I did. From a jeweler in the City! What *is* all this?"

But he was shaken. We could all sense it. Probably he hadn't realized he was doing it, but the moment he saw the pendant, he had looked swiftly around the room as if to assess the chances of escape. It was the natural response of the cornered animal. I recognized it and if I had done so, then surely Hugh had as well, and Cecil, and Walsingham.

"Call the page," said Cecil to Walsingham, who went at once to the door. The boy must have been waiting just outside, for he came in at once. "Fetch Master Wright," said Cecil.

"Who on earth," said Hugh, leaning over to speak into my ear, "is Master Wright? Do you know, Ursula?"

"No. I've never heard of him."

Cecil had caught our exchange, whispered though it was. He gave us something very like a conspiratorial grin. "Wait and see," he said, and Walsingham also offered us a grin, a saturnine affair, since his stern, dark face wasn't designed to express humor.

Master Wright turned out to be a small, thin man with a pointed white beard and short, neatly combed gray hair. He wore a dark brown suit of good but not showy cut. A couple of moderately valuable rings, one of plain gold and one of gold and turquoise, adorned clean, sinewy fingers.

He seemed interested in his surroundings, but not overawed by them, and had evidently had speech with Cecil and Walsingham already, since he greeted them by name. He didn't seem overawed by them, either. His manner combined a willingness to oblige with just a trace of impatience.

He was a type familiar to Hugh and to me. He was a craftsman of some kind, probably with a small but well-established business of his own. Such men are usually respected members of their guild and consider themselves the equal of any man alive, regardless of lands, wealth, titles, or fame. Dean, who was of a different kidney, to whom such things were of great importance, regarded him with mild contempt, which disturbed Master Wright not one whit.

"I am sorry to have called you here from your work," Cecil said to him. "However, it seemed necessary. First, let everyone in this room hear you confirm your name and your occupation. You are Master Jonas Wright, jeweler, of Hampton, beside the Thames?"

"I am, Sir William."

"And you have been in Hampton, working at your craft, since what year?"

"I've been a jeweler in that village these twenty-two years, sir. I opened my shop there in 1547."

"You make jewelry to order?"

"I do, sir."

"And most of your pieces are individual? Made for one customer only?"

"In the general way, sir. I have certain patterns that I repeat if asked. I charge less for those since there's no design work to do." Master Wright already knew what kind of questions he would be asked, I thought, and was ready for them. His answers were all prompt and clear.

"Do you mark your work in any way?" Cecil asked.

"Always, sir, whether the piece is unique or not. But unique items are marked a little differently from a repeated design."

"So you could identify an item you had made and you could tell for sure whether it was unique or not?"

"Yes, certainly I could."

Cecil held out the pendant. "Can you identify this?"

Master Wright took it across to the window and Meg slid off

the seat to let him examine it close to the daylight. He did so with interest. There was a silence. Master Wright fished in a pocket and brought out a small eyeglass, with which he studied the pendant even more closely.

"Yes," he said at length. "My mark is here. I make it unobtrusive but the eyeglass shows it clearly." Returning to the desk, he handed both glass and pendant to Cecil again. "You may see for yourself. The mark consists of my initials, J and W, intertwined. It's engraved on the back of the little heart, and the fact that the letters are intertwined proves that there is no other piece like this. For repeated designs, I simply put the letters side by side. I even believe I remember this little pendant, though it was a number of years ago. It was for a little girl, I think."

Cecil, having inspected the mark, passed pendant and glass on to Walsingham, who also inspected it, before handing the eyeglass back to Master Wright, who pocketed it.

"Now I've had time to think," he remarked, "I can put a name to the people who ordered this. They've bought other things from me through the years. Master and Mistress Henderson, of Thamesbank House."

"That's right!" Meg broke in. "I was only six, then. I was living at Thamesbank as their ward. They had that pendant made for my sixth birthday. And I knew it by your mark as well!"

"I have been to Thamesbank and spoken to them," Cecil said. "They remembered ordering the gift although they could not be sure that after so many years, they would recognize it for certain. However, Master Wright's identification seems definite. This pendant is unique, and it formerly belonged to Mistress Meg here. Thank you, Master Wright. If you wish, you may leave now."

"What is all this *about*?" said Edmund Dean exasperatedly.

Master Wright, displaying little curiosity, and no reluctance at all to leave the scene without further explanation, made his farewell bows and took himself off, with the air of a man who has many calls on his time and can't waste any more of it hobnobbing with a mere Secretary of State.

Cecil said to Meg: "It seems clear that this silver heart and chain were given to you when you were small. How did they leave your possession and then return to you? Come and stand by my desk. No, don't look at Master Dean, or worry about him. Everything is all right. Just tell everyone in this room all about it and don't be nervous."

"Go on, Meg," I said. "Do as Sir William asks."

"I loved it," Meg said. "It was my first piece of jewelry. But when I came to London, this year, with Mother and Stepfather, and we stayed at Howard House, it didn't seem quite the right thing to wear, not for the guest of a duke. Mother loaned me some better jewelry, and although I'd brought the pendant with me . . ."

Her voice trailed off, and Walsingham, with a new gentleness that showed a different side of him, a man who however hard in his professional life might well be the kindest of souls at home, said: "We understand. So what happened next?"

"I gave it away. On the spur of the moment. There was a young lad at Howard House, employed about the kitchen and cellar. His name was Walt and he was betrothed, but he couldn't yet marry because he needed to put some money together first."

I was watching Dean. I saw his jaw muscles tighten. It wouldn't have been noticeable if I hadn't had my eye on him. Apart from that, he was motionless.

"Anyway," Meg said, "I thought of giving the pendant to him to give to her, as a sort of wedding gift, when the time came. I thought that she would probably wear it, whereas I had stopped using it . . ."

"Go on," said Walsingham.

"That's all. I did give it to Walt. Mother agreed. She came with me and we gave it to him together. Mother!"

"Yes. I confirm it," I said. "I also confirm that Walt had it in his possession on the morning of the day he died. He showed it to me then. He said he had had some luck and would be able to marry his Bessie sooner than he thought."

"And when did you see this pendant again?" Cecil asked Meg.

"The last time I spoke with Master Dean, only a few days

ago. He gave it to *me* as a present. He said he'd bought it. But if so, then Walt must have sold it and I don't believe he would have done. He was so pleased with it and he said Bessie would like it so much, and besides, Mother says he hadn't time."

Very calmly, Dean said: "I don't understand what all this means. Am I being accused of something?"

"Possibly," said Cecil. "Would you like to explain once more how you came by that pendant?"

"I have explained. I told Margaret. I bought it. Young Walt must have slipped out and sold it after all. Perhaps he had some unexpected need for money. Who knows what these boys get up to? Serving boys, apprentices, they have a world of their own. That's the only explanation."

Cecil addressed me directly. "What time was it when you spoke to Walt and saw that he had the pendant still?"

"In the morning, an hour or so before dinner," I said.

"I called at Howard House this morning," said Walsingham. "I spoke to Conley, the butler. He remembers that day very well. Finding one of the servants hung up on a hook among the veal and venison carcasses tends to fix the surrounding events in the memory, he said to me. Walt did go out that day, but quite early in the morning. When he came back, he said he had been to see the father of the girl he hoped to marry—a tavern-keeper, I understand. After that, he didn't leave the house again. The place was busy. People were coming and going because of the death of Julius Gale. The justice and the aldermen dined with the duke. Extra casks had to be brought out of the cellar and extra flagons drawn; some special dishes had to be prepared. According to Conley, after returning from seeing his Bessie's father, Walt only went out of doors once, to the kitchen garden to pull some onions."

"He was carrying onions when I spoke to him," I said.

"Now," said Cecil. "Once again, Master Dean. How did you come by this pretty little silver chain and heart?"

"I keep telling you!"

"You are not," said Sir Francis, who had now moved behind the desk and was standing beside Cecil's chair, leaning down to take notes, "telling the truth."

"Are you suggesting that I stole it?"

Hugh cleared his throat. "Or looted it," he said mildly.

"Just a minute." We all turned. Hillman's expression was bewildered. "I don't understand this. All this can't be to do with a stolen pendant! Sir William! Sir Francis! Are you suggesting that this man here, Edmund Dean, murdered Walt?"

"It has to be a possibility," said Cecil.

"But—Walt was a serving lad. Sir William—you're the Secretary of State, and all these people have been called here . . . I know we are all equal in the sight of God but all the same . . ."

"It's madness. I think the Secretary of State has been sleeping out in a full moon!" Dean was white, I thought, with both fear and anger. "Why would I kill a servant boy and steal a pendant from him? What do you take me for? A footpad—except that I committed my crime in a house instead of in the street!"

"The boy Walt had apparently come into some money, rather unexpectedly," said Walsingham. "We have also sent officers to interview his prospective father-in-law. He says that Walt offered him quite a respectable sum as a contribution to the tavern business. He had the coins in a bag and he said that there might be more coming soon. He said he had received a legacy, though Conley insists that Walt never mentioned such a thing to any of his fellow servants."

"I believe," said Cecil to Dean, "that you told Mistress Meg that Julius Gale was an enemy to your faith and deserved what he got. We are in fact suggesting that he got it from you. That you knew that he was carrying letters of a treasonous nature, and that he meant to show them to us, and that you did indeed go out like a footpad, waylay and kill him, and that Walt, somehow, knew of your guilt and demanded money for his silence. You paid him to keep him quiet, but later that day, you found, or made, an opportunity to . . ."

"Please!" Hillman spoke again and now his sunburnt face had suffused with angry blood. "Am I to understand that this man, in all probability, *killed my cousin*?"

I saw Cecil open his mouth, presumably to answer, but Hillman didn't wait for him. He sprang at Dean, and in an instant, the dignified if impromptu inquiry in Cecil's office turned into a scrimmage. Hugh got up quickly, seized Meg's arm, pushed me behind him, and backed the three of us into a corner, as far out of harm's way as possible. Sybil, alarmed, drew her feet up onto the window seat as Dean and Hillman, locked together and swearing, swayed back and forth across the room.

Walsingham rushed around the desk and tried to intervene but was sent staggering by a blow from Dean's fist. He reeled back against the desk, which rocked, sending the document boxes in a cascade to the floor, where the struggling pair fell over them. Hillman, flat on his back, was trying to get his hands around Dean's throat. Then Dean, twisting eel-like, freed one hand and went for his dagger. The blade flashed in the air. Hillman abandoned his attack on his adversary's throat and seized his wrist instead, holding the steel away. I remember seeing the sequence quite clearly, as though it were happening in slow motion, although in fact it took only a few seconds. At the end of those few seconds, Cecil still seated unmoving at his desk, raised his voice. *"Guard!"*

The armed men he had said were at hand were in the room before the word was well out. They seized the combatants, dragging them apart and holding them firmly. One of them wrenched Dean's dagger from his hand and threw it clattering onto the desk. Hillman's nose was bleeding. "I'b sorry," he said nasally to Cecil. "I'b very sorry. But if he killed Julius . . ."

"You may release him," Cecil said to the men holding Hillman. "His behavior was natural if deplorable. Sit him down and do something about his nose; I don't want blood all over my study. Behave yourself from now on, Master Hillman. As for you . . ."

He turned to Dean. Dean stared back at him. His dark hair was tangled and his doublet half off, and if I didn't know that the eyes of human beings can't actually shoot sparks, I would say that his were doing so. Blue sparks, lightning color. Hot and cold both at once. Sparks of hatred.

"You stand accused of the murders both of Julius Gale and the boy Walt," said Cecil. "Of Gale because he was working for us and making us privy to the correspondence that Norfolk and

Ridolfi were having—with a view to reestablishing Mary Stuart on the Scottish throne and one day, perhaps, installing her on the English throne and destroying our reformed religion. Of Walt because he discovered your guilt and tried to make you pay. Have you anything to say in your defense?"

"Nothing whatsoever," said Dean, astoundingly. His chin came up. "I killed them both. I'm *proud* of it. I'd do it again."

28

The Cold Curse

There was a stunned silence. At my side, I felt Meg trembling. I took her hand.

"Be careful what you say," said Walsingham. "Witnesses are present, who are likely to repeat what they hear when you come to trial."

"It's *when,* is it? Not *if*? I am to be arrested, that's clear. Well, so be it. What I did, I did for the one true faith. I'd do it again! If I must lose my life, I give it gladly. Gale was an enemy. He was trying to betray a noble cause and it was right that he should die!"

"How did you know he was bringing letters for us to see?" Walsingham asked with interest.

"He'd picked up letters from Howard House before. Once when he had to wait a day for a letter to be ready, I came upon him reading an English Bible. It belonged to Norfolk, more shame to him. But if Gale were reading it—and he was doing so with attention, not with disapproval—then I knew that he was not to be relied on. And then, as it chanced, I was returning from an errand just as he finally set out and I saw him take the wrong road. I thought about that English Bible and I wondered what he was doing, so I followed him. I followed him *here*. Then I knew. So, the next time he passed through Howard House, with letters from Ridolfi and from Norfolk, I followed him again, only that time he knew that someone was on his heels and he turned back.

The duke saw to it that he got away safely, though at least he never managed to reach this house, Master Cecil. The time after that, he tried to come here again but on that occasion, I was cleverer. I went out ahead of him, waylaid him, killed him, and took the letters back to his room. That's why they weren't found on him but in his clothespress!"

His voice was ringing out, his pride in what he had done so great that it had overwhelmed his fear of the doom he was bringing on himself.

"Why did you take the letters back?" Walsingham asked him.

"To keep them safe, of course! Oh, people would wonder why he wasn't carrying them but he had been ill. He could have left them behind by accident. But that damned boy was about the house and he saw me go into Gale's room, and the cheeky, inquisitive wretch peeped in at the door and saw me put the letters in the press. Later on, when Gale's body was brought back and people were saying his letters were missing, the boy understood what he had seen. Then he came to me and demanded money! Well, he's burning in hell now, and I am glad of it!"

"And you left him among the hanging carcasses," I said.

"It was there that I killed him."

"And stole the pendant from him?" asked Walsingham sourly.

"No," said Dean disdainfully. "He fought back. I was a trifle clumsy." He sounded as though he were apologizing for a minor inefficiency. "I had one hand round his mouth, trying to make sure he didn't cry out, while I used my knife with the other, but he twisted like a snake and that sleeveless jerkin he always wore was flapping about and getting tangled round my knife-arm. I did see a glint as something slid out of the pocket, but I thought nothing of it until afterward, when I went to change my doublet. It was a black doublet and it didn't show bloodstains much but it was wise to change it—and there was the pendant, with its chain caught up in a bit of pulled embroidery on the right sleeve."

"So you kept it," I said.

"Was I likely to go back and return it to him?" retorted Dean.

"But to hang Walt like that," I said. "On a meathook . . ."

"It was a measure of the scorn I felt for him." The contempt in Dean's voice brought the gooseflesh out on my skin. Meg was now clinging to me with both hands.

"Was Gale's illness real?" I asked suddenly. "Or did you cause it, regardless of the other victims, in an attempt to kill him before he left Howard House?"

Dean looked at me, with nearly as much disdain as he apparently felt for Walt. "Do women question men upon such matters? Are you Secretary of State, mistress? Or one of his minions?"

"Mistress Stannard is one of my minions, as you put it," said Cecil. "And one of the queen's minions. She is welcome to question you."

"Was that illness," I said, "really bad chicken or something else?"

"Answer her," said Cecil.

"Oh, it was bad chicken at first. Norfolk's kitchen is sometimes as chaotic as his thinking and you must have noticed what a muddled mind he has. I fetched you to help Gale—remember? I hoped he'd die but I had to pretend to do my best for him! It was an opportunity, though—oh yes, you're right there. I slipped something in one of the possets that were made for him and prayed it would make an end of him, but he was too strong. So it had to be my thin-bladed knife and an attack along the road."

"And an attempt to blame poor Gladys; to pretend she caused it all by witchcraft!" Meg shrieked. "How could I ever have thought I liked you!" She stared at him with loathing and then hid her face against me.

"I can't see why you had to kill Gale," Walsingham remarked. "You had only to tell his master Ridolfi that he wasn't trustworthy and get him dismissed."

"He betrayed our cause! Was he to escape with nothing but dismissal? He betrayed our faith and our noble Lady Mary, who is our hope for the future! When she is on the thrones of Scotland and England, then she will bring the light of truth back to those poor lost lands . . ."

"The siren queen has claimed another victim," muttered

Hugh. "Where is she now? Tutbury Castle, isn't it? She ought to be sitting on a rock and combing her hair to entice foolish sailors."

"When I saw her last year, it hadn't grown again properly after she cut it before she fled from Scotland," I muttered back. "I've heard she's taken to wearing wigs."

This mundane exchange steadied me. It also steadied Meg, who let out a little snort that was at least half a giggle and turned her face up to me. "Just put Dean out of your mind," I whispered. "One day we'll do better for you. You've been very brave. Keep it up."

"This land," Cecil was saying, "and Scotland too, in my opinion, will do very well without your help, Master Dean. Take him away!"

"One moment!" As the guards started to pull Dean toward the door, he resisted. His eyes were on me and on Meg. The men paused.

"Mistress Margaret. I am sorry that our acquaintance was so short and sorry that I have caused you pain. I will always remember you. Perhaps you will remember me too, as the first man to give you his heart—though it was of silver, not gold, as hearts are supposed to be."

"I have one more question," I said. I stared at him, hard, meeting that piercing glance and refusing to be browbeaten by it. "One of the letters Gale was carrying," I said, "was in cipher. Have you any idea what was in it? I think Signor Ridolfi wrote it."

"You need not try to shield Ridolfi," Walsingham put in. "He will be arrested later today. We already have evidence against him."

"Indeed? Then I am proud to say that yes, I have talked to Signor Ridolfi and he was open with me. That letter was a plea to Queen Mary never to yield to persuasions to abandon her religion, for on her rest the dreams of all who are faithful to the true faith. And an assurance that His Holiness, the Pope, would give his blessing to anything done in the cause of bringing the true faith back to England."

"Ridolfi has had a lucrative career on English soil," Walsingham remarked. "The extent of his gratitude amazes me."

"Signor Ridolfi longs for Queen Mary's release from captivity." Dean rolled out the fine phrases proudly, exaltedly. "Like me, like many others, he longs for her triumphant coronation as Queen of England and Scotland both. And for the destruction of her enemies, and all who nurture evil in her lands."

"Such as poor Gladys, I suppose," I said bitterly.

"Very likely," said Cecil. "And I think that just now, we had better not inquire into the full meaning of that word *anything*— which the Pope has undertaken to bless. Take him away."

"Poor Gladys," Dean said mockingly over his shoulder, as he was pulled toward the door. "A wicked woman if ever there was one. I've spoken with Johnson. He was at Howard House today. No one now, alas, can claim that Gale died by witchcraft, but the testimony of Norfolk's kitchen staff, and of respected men from the places where she has lived with you and your husband, will be enough, I think. She has ill-wished people and two Hawkswood villagers died this summer—and did she not fling a curse of cold-ness at the Reverend Fleet of Faldene?"

"People do die, now and then, and the cold curse was just a nonsense!" I snapped.

"But it seems," said Dean, "that shortly before that day, he had married a young wife. He will testify that after Gladys Morgan ill-wished him, his wife became cold to him . . ."

"Perhaps she didn't like the way he treated one of his parish-ioners. Neither did Gladys. That was why she uttered that absurd curse! I already know that Fleet's wife has died and it was nothing to do with Gladys!"

Dean ignored the interruption. "His wife's manner to him distressed him so much," he said, "that he could no longer play the husband to her, and now he is widowed, because his wife took cold not long ago and died of a lung congestion, which peo-ple do more often in midwinter than in summer."

"These things happen," said Cecil impatiently. "They are the natural misfortunes of life. They occur without any ill-wishing."

"Indeed? Well, Mistress Stannard. You are fond of that old woman, Gladys Morgan, perhaps. I think that when she suffers her well-earned fate, you will suffer too. I rejoice at it."

"Take him *out!*" barked Cecil. "*Now!*"

"I shall be proud," said Dean, clutching at the doorpost so as to speak a final word, "*proud,* do you hear? Proud to die as a martyr for my faith!"

"*You* talk of ill-wishing?" I said savagely to Dean. I turned to Hugh. "Do you remember what I said once before? *But to do that to Walt's body was so nasty; like ill-wishing someone even after they were dead. Whoever did it is . . . is vicious. Awash with spite!* He killed Gale out of sheer spite and those last words of his, just now, they were spite as well and yet he dares pretend to be righteous about Gladys! I wonder what it's like to be as full of malice as he is?"

"Saints and martyrs," remarked Cecil, as Dean was at last removed and Walsingham began to pick up his fallen papers and boxes, "are the greatest nuisances in society. Pickpockets are far less trouble!"

Meg had given way. She wasn't making a noise but the tears were streaming down her face. "I'm not crying about him," she whispered defensively, through them. "It's Gladys. Oh, *Gladys!* I loved her stories and she isn't a witch, she *isn't* . . ."

Sybil, very pale but as ever, in command of herself, left the window seat and came to us, trying to help me soothe her. Meg looked wildly from one of us to the other. "Will Gladys really be . . . ? But it isn't true; she didn't; she couldn't! I'll speak up if she comes to trial! Oh, *Mother!*"

Hillman's nosebleed had been stopped. He still looked disheveled, and there were bloodstains on his clothes. But his face was kind as he came forward. Clearly he wished to speak to Hugh and to me, and we turned to him inquiringly.

"When I was fetched here today," he said, "I learned that Johnson tried to involve me in this business of Gladys Morgan—and I was also told that when I had all those violent dreams, the night before I left for Scotland, it was because you had—er—given me something, Mistress Stannard . . ."

"Yes. I did. I'm sorry, but . . ."

"I wish I'd known what was behind it. I would have loaned the letters to you if I'd known. I am not on Edmund Dean's side."

"That's obvious!" said Hugh, looking at the bloodstains.

"And, Mistress Meg—please don't cry. It's brave of you to say you'll speak up for Gladys but be careful. You are young and it will be easy for vicars and physicians to say she has bewitched you; even that you're a witch yourself." He looked at me. "You must take care of her. If nothing more can be done for Gladys— at least protect this young girl."

Meg looked at him, her tears subsiding a little, and he smiled at her. "You're too courageous and too pretty to put at risk," he told her.

I looked at Cecil. "I want to take Meg home. It will be permitted?"

"Meg may go home now; Dean has confessed and we won't need either of you at his trial. But for Gladys's sake, I think you should remain."

"I can take her," Sybil said. "If Mistress Stannard can't yet leave London, Meg and I will go back to Hawkswood, as we did before."

"Yes," said Cecil. Meg began to exclaim that she couldn't abandon Gladys, that she must speak at the trial, but over her bent head, Hugh and I exchanged glances and came to a decision.

"No, Meg," I said. "No, my darling. Sybil will take you home."

29

Above the Law

"I want to see the queen," I said to Cecil, "as soon as possible."

Cecil nodded. "It's time Her Majesty became aware of what has been going on, but I would prefer not to tell her formally. I'm still out of her favor," he said, and sighed. I regarded him with sympathy. I knew very well how distressed he always was on the occasions when Elizabeth turned against him.

"Formality," he said, "would oblige her to take action. Perhaps to do things she does not wish to do, or that I don't wish her to do! God knows, she has had trouble enough this year. My wife talks with her ladies. The queen has had sleepless nights, many of them, over the trouble in her council."

I nodded. I knew of Elizabeth's tendency to insomnia.

"You," said Cecil, "can be—shall we say, cautious. Keep Leicester's name out of it if you can, but warn her—informally—about Norfolk. Don't mention Ridolfi's—er—religious agenda, please. We intend to make sure that Dean doesn't mention it either, when he comes to trial. By the way, you will not appear at the trial. Ridolfi is not to know that you had any part to play in this. As far as he's concerned, you were his wife's companion and a friend of the Cecils, but nothing more. Your secret career will always remain a secret, as far as possible."

"Dean may talk proudly of being a martyr for his faith but he hasn't yet had a traitor's death fully described to him," Walsingham said. "When he has, I think he will be willing to be told what he should and should not say in court. He murdered Gale for betraying Norfolk's marriage schemes, nothing more. That will be the official story and Dean won't contradict it, I promise you!"

I wondered who would do the describing. Walsingham looked to me more than capable of the task. He was the kind who would find words for lurid details in a completely dispassionate tone of voice, coolly watching his words find their mark as he spoke. Walsingham was as loyal a man as ever entered Elizabeth's service, and I learned later that I had guessed right about his private life, for he was a good and well-loved husband and father. But I never liked him, while I always did like Cecil, despite his meddling in my life.

"Norfolk isn't actually guilty of treason yet," Cecil said. "He has no right to enter into a powerful marriage without the queen's consent, but unless he actually ties the knot without permission, he has not committed a crime."

"He's sounded the northern lords to see if they'll support him in arms in case of a Catholic rising," I said doubtfully. "Isn't that a crime?"

"They haven't given him much response. It may all die away into nothingness. If not, the queen will have to be fully informed and we can take action quickly, but that's for later and very much a matter of *if*. I don't *want* Norfolk brought to the block. Your warnings and mine are bearing fruit, Ursula. Mistress Dalton pulled herself together valiantly after finding Walt's body, though I understand that she collapsed at the time, and she's been turning in reports as usual. She has seen a draft of a letter from Norfolk, asking the northern lords *not* to rise, after all. She doesn't know whether he's sent it, but he's prepared it. Ursula, whispers must eventually reach the queen but I want to control what is said. Will you do it? Alert the queen quietly to, shall we say, a limited exposition?"

"Yes. I want to ask her to intercede for Gladys too."

"I wish you luck," said Cecil somberly.

* * *

I loved Richmond Palace. There was something magical in its structure, in its slim turrets and elegant windows, as though it belonged to a pretty legend. This was no stern fortress like the Tower of London or Windsor Castle; nor did it hold the unhappy memories that haunted the galleries of Hampton Court.

Such a pity that the conversation Hugh and I had with Queen Elizabeth three hours after our arrival was so painful, so out of tune with the enchanting surroundings.

She was not, these days, as mercurial as she had been. Once, Elizabeth had been giving to lightning changes of mood, from imperious ruler to playful kitten, to spitting cat, to vulnerable maiden, and had been known to run through them all in the course of half an hour. At times she had nearly driven Cecil out of his mind with such behavior.

She was an experienced ruler now, and far more mature. She had borne the crown for a decade and acquired a deeper, stronger dignity. Her clothes were of a greater sumptuousness; even her voice was lower in register. The crimped waves of pale red hair in front of her pearl-edged caps were a little, just a little, faded and her golden brown eyes were effortlessly commanding.

But something of the mercurial Elizabeth still existed, even though, nowadays, the kitten had grown into a lioness. She was less accessible than she had been and to come into her presence we had to pass through three sets of guards and finally be escorted to her by two of her gentlemen pensioners, as she called the men in red and gold livery, who waited on her personally and ran her more important errands. She received us in one of her private rooms, but three of her ladies were with her. However, when I said that the news we had for her, though informal, was confidential, she sent the gentlemen and ladies away. When we had cautiously explained that Cecil felt she should know that Norfolk was once more playing with the notion of marrying Mary Stuart and even appeared to have fallen in love with her at a distance, she took to striding around the chamber in a fury, damask skirts swishing like a lioness's tail, while that beautiful voice expressed a powerful wish to have the Duke of Norfolk seized forthwith, conveyed to the Tower, and beheaded.

Hugh, who had never witnessed anything like this before, stood bemused. I hoped that the storm would pass. I put a reassuring hand on his arm and we both stood still, out of her path, and waited. At length, Elizabeth sank onto a settle. Her tawny eyes were flashing. "I suppose Cecil claims that Norfolk has not committed any actual crime!"

"We understood that that was so, ma'am," said Hugh cautiously. "Of course, we are not experts on the law."

"No, but Cecil is! You admit that he has sent you here. Is there more to this—are there other ramifications that I don't yet know?"

I was ready for that. "I don't know for sure, ma'am. It is possible, but Cecil thinks they are vague—glints in the eyes of dreamers, as it were."

"If they're dreaming of reinstating Mary Stuart on the throne of Scotland, they'll dream in vain. Never, if I can help it," said Elizabeth savagely. "Not even if she's married to a real Protestant and Norfolk's not a real anything. I know him! That man would trim his sails to any convenient wind. I know about the Popish images in his chapel! He'd toss the whole lot into the Thames if it suited him; only if he marries Mary, it wouldn't suit *her.* Hah! I fancy he's among the dreamers and maybe one of his fantasies has something to do with one day being King Consort of England. I wonder if he'll admit as much to me! He once said he wouldn't want Mary because he liked a safe pillow, but dangle a crown in front of him, and lo! He changes his mind."

"He may well change it back again. Cecil thinks so, certainly," I said.

"He will if I have any say in it! I shall leave shortly for my summer progress—through Hampshire this year. He will be one of my entourage. I shall make sure of that. He will be under my eye. We will talk," said Elizabeth, becoming dangerously silky.

We said nothing. Elizabeth's guesses were uncomfortably accurate.

"I wonder," she remarked, "that he doesn't offer to marry *me*! It would be a quicker route to the crown matrimonial. Yes, Ursula? I see that you are almost swallowing your tongue because you long to say something and fear it will displease me! What is it? Come along!"

"I don't think you'd say yes to the Duke of Norfolk, ma'am."

"No, I wouldn't! Who wants to marry a weathercock? And if I did," said Elizabeth—and suddenly the lioness was lolling in the sun, at ease, almost playful, *almost* a kitten, though not quite—"if I did, he'd lose his nerve at the altar. The priest would wait for him to say *I will* and he'd buckle at the knees and faint. And if he didn't and by some miracle he got the words out," she added, "Leicester would draw a sword and make some new slashings in the good duke's wedding doublet! Hah! Well, well. We shall ask the duke if he has anything to tell us—perhaps of marriage plans. Whatever is lurking in his mind, I fancy he will at least recognize the warning. You can tell Cecil that he need not skulk out of my sight any longer. I forgive him for his bad advice about that Spanish money. It's still useful money, anyway."

"Ma'am," I said, "there is one more thing . . ."

"Ursula," said Elizabeth, gently this time, very kindly, a sister speaking to a sister and a brother-in-law, all stateliness laid aside, "I may not do it. I may not imperiously interfere in the due working of the law. As a sovereign anointed, I am above the law, yes, but I must not trade on that. I must not countermand the verdicts of honest juries to please myself. Yes, Ursula? Once more, I give you permission to say what you are thinking."

"Gladys's accusers, Dean and Johnson, acted out of spite. Dean is already arraigned on a charge of treason and there is no question that it was he who murdered Gale and that Gladys was not concerned. Johnson can be brought into court and made to admit that he laid information against her for the sake of petty revenge. And surely any good lawyer can argue that the deaths of Mistress Fleet and the people at Hawkswood were ordinary things, part of the hazard of everyday life; that they happen in every community, and that Gladys is nothing but a foolish old woman. Ma'am," I said painfully, "you annuled my marriage to Matthew de la Roche. Was that not—taking command of the law?"

"And you know—Walsingham has told me—that I lied to you about his death. Yes, I did. But I do have the right to control the marriages of people who share the royal blood, even illicitly. I had my reasons for controlling yours, as well you know, my sister. Nor are you unhappy now because of it."

"That's true, ma'am. But Gladys . . ."

"Ursula, I am sorry. But in general, I am not above the law. It must take its course. If she is truly innocent, I trust she will be found so. If not . . . I can do nothing."

As we entered the boat that took us back to Cecil's house, I said furiously to Hugh: "*Cecil* can warp the law if he wants to! He arranged the outcome of Norfolk's lawsuit, I know he did! He made sure the verdict went Norfolk's way. But the queen won't do this one little thing."

"She won't do it *because* she's the queen," said Hugh sadly. His arm was round me, trying to give comfort. "And in the court that will try Gladys, Cecil has no power. We can only hope, and pray."

"I'm afraid for Gladys. Dr. Fleet will be a dangerous witness. He'll manage to make it sound as though she killed his wife!"

"Yes," Hugh said. "I'm frightened for Gladys, too."

"What can we do other than pray and I haven't much faith in that," I said bitterly. "I don't think even God can get past Elizabeth if she doesn't choose to let him!"

30

No Day for Dying

It was late October. The summer had ended in rain and gales, but on this day the skies had cleared, giving place to bright autumn weather. Touches of gold and russet had appeared among the green leaves of the trees along the three-mile road from London to Tyburn, glowing against the smooth blue of the sky. The sun still had some warmth. Those who had come to watch the spectacle were not in danger of catching a fatal congestion of the lungs. It was no day for dying.

Except for those unhappy souls who would travel that road today, on a journey from which they would not return.

Hugh and I were not on the road but had come early from Cecil's house, where we were still staying, and placed ourselves at the front of the crowd before the gallows at Tyburn. It was hard for me to look at the thing but, I said, "We must be where Gladys can see us."

Brockley and Dale were waiting at the Marshalsea Prison in London in order to walk beside the cart, so that Gladys could have friendly faces near her along the way. Many people would accompany the cart, some to jeer, but some, like the Brockleys, to give support to friends or relatives. We couldn't do that because Hugh couldn't walk so far. But we would be there for her at the end.

"I wonder if it helps," Hugh said, as we waited. "Can anything help, in such a case?"

"I don't know. I hope so, that's all. I think I'd like to see a friendly face at the last. I wouldn't want to die surrounded by avid strangers. Hugh . . . are you sure . . . ?"

"I saw the executioner yesterday. He will do what I paid him for. And we can take her body afterward, and have her decently buried. I've arranged it all. Don't worry."

There were soldiers around the scaffold to make sure that the crowd was kept under control and that prisoners with enough money or sufficiently violent friends would not be rescued. The executioner and his assistant, two black-clad figures, were waiting to begin work, standing side by side and talking to each other. I wondered what made anyone take up such a profession. It was hereditary, I supposed. This was what your father did, so you followed him. No doubt he instructed you from an early age, taking you for walks and explaining his work—later on, taking you along to watch. *You see, son, there are tricks to the trade. You can make it quick or you can make it slow. It's important, either way, to get the knot positioned just right . . . sometimes relatives pay you to make sure it's quick and that's one of your perks . . .*

The crowd was growing thick now, most of it in a holiday mood. Many had brought baskets of food, which they handed about to their companions. There were even family groups, with children. Close to us, a couple of small boys were enthusiastically acting out the last sufferings of the victims, dancing about with pop eyes and protruding tongues and then flopping their heads sideways, after which they collapsed on the grass, giggling. Hugh regarded them with distaste.

"We were right to send Meg home," he said.

"Yes. When she wrote pleading to be here, I wrote back telling her to spend the day in prayer. I wish I wasn't here myself, but . . ."

"I know. We have to be."

There was a murmur at the back of the crowd and heads began to turn. The cart was approaching. The sun was too bright, I thought angrily. It had no right to shine so tranquilly on such a scene.

A further squad of soldiers armed with pikes and staves were

264 • FIONA BUCKLEY

escorting the cart, beating back the crowd with the staves. There was only one vehicle, drawn by two patiently plodding draft horses. An impassive driver had their reins. At the back stood a priest, presumably reciting prayers though his voice couldn't be heard above the raucous shouts of the crowd. The rest of the passengers were frightened men and women with their hands already bound behind them. They had pale, dirty faces, many streaked with tears. Some stared blankly; others crouched and shivered as if with ague. They were all humble folk, convicted of commonplace offenses. Edmund Dean was not among them. His was a crime of greater stature and he was to die tomorrow. We would not be here for him.

We couldn't see Gladys at first and for one moment I had a wild hope that some last-minute mercy had been extended to her; that the queen had after all intervened and the news had not reached us yet. Then I saw Brockley and Dale, keeping pace with the cart, as near to one corner as the escort of pikemen would allow, and there, huddled in that same corner, was Gladys. Her gray hair, unwashed now for nearly three months, straggled over her face. She kept tossing her head, trying to throw the strands out of her eyes. She looked tiny, as though terror had made her whole body wither, and her eyes kept darting from side to side. Her mouth was twisted. She seemed hardly aware of the Brockleys, though they were within a couple of yards of her.

The cart came to the gallows' foot and stopped. The executioners moved forward to meet it.

"Steady," said Hugh. "Try not to faint!" I realized that I had sagged against him, and straightened myself. I had no business to give way. I must catch Gladys's eye if I could.

"I wish *she* could faint," I said. "Just faint and not know what's happening."

"Here are the Brockleys," said Hugh.

They had been finally pushed away by the escort and had found their way to us instead. Dale was tired from the long walk and her pockmarks were standing out. "Oh, ma'am, I feel so sorry for her! She was whimpering, all the way. We could hear her. Oh, ma'am."

"Master Hillman's here," said Brockley. "He joined us at the Marshalsea."

I realized that a man standing behind Brockley was indeed George Hillman. He greeted us soberly. "I felt I should come. I'd have been part of the prosecution if that man Johnson had had his way, testifying to the potion that gave me a bad night. I was at the trial. Master Stannard, Mistress Stannard, I was so impressed by the way you gave evidence in Gladys's favor. You tried so hard, and your lawyer reduced Johnson to powder. I really had hopes for your Gladys then. But two physicians and three vicars were too much for you. Especially Dr. Fleet. He did the worst damage."

"I'll never forgive him," I said. "Never. The others were bad enough, but Fleet . . . ! I can do nothing about Fleet," I said vindictively, "but the vicar of Withysham holds a living that is in my gift. I intend to rid myself of him."

At the gallows' foot, some brief formalities had been in progress. The captain in charge of the escort had handed a list to the captain of the guard already present, and they had been checking the list against the people in the cart. Distracted by Hillman, I had looked away. Now, a scream from the cart made me turn sharply. The executioner and his boy had climbed into it and were fastening nooses around the necks of the condemned. They were trying to put one on Gladys. She was twisting in their hands and shrieking in terror.

Surprisingly, her cries were echoed, from some distance away, behind us. The echo was followed by a horse's shrill whinny and the sound of hooves and shouts. Startled, we turned again and saw a rider forcing a way through the crowd, which had now spilled onto the road. He was laying about him with his whip, to get people out of his way, and the scream had come from someone who had either been knocked down or hit with the lash.

The head of the horse was visible above the hats and hoods of the throng. As it came nearer, we could see that the animal had been ridden hard. It was a chestnut but its neck was black with sweat. Its eyes were white-ringed, and there was foam around its bit. The rider, cloak flying and whip still flailing, was swearing at the crowd and shouting: *"Hold!"* at the soldiers and the executioners. The captain of the soldiers around the gallows raised a hand in acknowledgment and shouted a command at the executioners, who ceased their work. Gladys sank weeping onto the floor of the cart just as the rider reached it.

Without dismounting, he threw back his cloak, revealing that beneath it was the red and gold of a gentleman pensioner, one of Elizabeth's personal attendants. He pulled out a scroll, broke the seal, unrolled the parchment, and handed it to the captain of the guard, who looked at it for a few moments, bowed, and handed it back. The horseman asked a question and the captain consulted his list and replied. Puzzled, the crowd jostled and murmured. The captain shouted for silence and held the horse's bridle so that the horseman could have both hands free to keep the scroll open while he read its contents aloud.

"Her Royal Majesty, Queen Elizabeth, by God's grace the prince of this realm of England, being informed that the verdict on the prisoner Gladys Morgan is unsound, and unwilling that any subject of hers should be condemned unjustly, herewith commands that Gladys Morgan be pardoned and set free. Given under Her Majesty's Hand and seal, this twenty-eighth day of October 1569."

He let the scroll roll itself up again and looked down at the captain. "Release the prisoner Gladys Morgan," he said.

Gasping, I clutched at Hugh. "We must go to her," he said, and pulled me forward, calling to the captain and the messenger as he did so. Astonished faces in the crowd turned toward us but people gave way and we were there to receive her when the executioner lifted her over the side of the cart and into our hands. Hugh took hold of her firmly and then gave her to me. "Take her! I have something to do."

I put my arms around Gladys, feeling her terrible thinness. She had always been bony but now, after weeks of poor victuals, she was more bones than flesh. She smelt as bad as she had ever done and her hair was stiff with dirt, but I didn't care. I could only be glad to hold her close and safe while Hugh took a purse from his belt and murmured something to the captain, who beckoned the executioner down from the cart. As I drew Gladys away, I saw Hugh speaking to the man and taking money from his purse. Presently, he came after us, looking rueful but relieved.

"I've done what I can for the others, out of gratitude. Let's get away from here."

But getting away was impossible. The crowd was too thick and it was pressing forward, wanting its show. Lacking a sixteen-hand horse and a long whip, we could not force a path farther than Master Hillman and the Brockleys. Gladys, in any case, was hardly able to keep her feet. Sobbing helplessly, she sagged in my arms and I almost had to carry her. The Brockleys greeted us round-eyed, clutching at her and patting her shoulders, hardly able to believe what had happened. The red-and-gold-clad messenger was still nearby, watching the proceedings from his saddle, and at the gallows, the dreadful show was beginning anew.

Gladys slowly turned in my grasp, turned to look. And then, to my horror, she found her voice again and for one appalling moment, I thought she was going to destroy her own pardon.

"They were a-going to kill me and for what? For *what*? They kill folk for nothing. A loaf of bread stolen or a pocket picked when a family's so hungry the babes are all crying and their mother don't know which way to turn! Wicked it is, indeed to goodness. That man putting ropes round their throats ought to be ashamed. He ought to be accursed, that he ought. He . . ."

I think she had passed into such a state of fear and shock that she did not realize that what she was saying was dangerous, and mercifully, she was in any case mumbling rather than shouting. I don't think anyone in the crowd could make out the words. But I shook her, to silence her. "Gladys!" I said furiously. "Be quiet! Be quiet!"

It was Hugh who said: "Gladys! No curses now! Pray! *Pray!* You too, Ursula. Do as I do!"

I have never known what I believe about God or the afterlife. The priests seem sure, but where is the proof? On just one occasion, I had reason to think I had encountered a ghost but I've never been certain, and it had grieved me very much that after Gerald's death, I had never felt his presence, never had any kind of contact with his spirit. He had loved me. If he existed anywhere, surely, he would have tried to reach me, to impart a sense of that love, an attempt at comfort. He never had.

But all the same, I didn't know. No one does. Gladys's life had been saved, but if she were to spend the rest of it with curses on her lips instead of prayers, what would be her fate in the next world, if such a thing existed? At the top of his voice, ignoring laughter from people in the nearby crowd, Hugh had begun to recite the Lord's Prayer, and realizing what he wanted, I joined in, nodding to the Brockleys and nudging Gladys to do the same.

Hillman joined in too. Hugh went on with the prayer, finished it and began to repeat it, leading us on. A few of the more decent souls in the crowd also added their voices. The priest who had accompanied the prisoners sensibly took this invasion of his prerogative in good part, raised his own voice in unison with us, and helped us along. And, to my infinite thankfulness, Gladys at last joined in with us as well, lifting her cracked old voice in the cleansing and holy words that no witch would ever say, while on the cart, the executioner and his assistant were doing their work.

I watched. It was hard, so very hard. I wanted to shut my eyes, to run away, but I did neither. It seemed necessary, as an act of gratitude for Gladys's life, to send looks of compassion and well-wishing toward those desperate souls; to be—since Gladys no longer needed it—their friendly face at the last.

I stood holding Gladys in the crook of my arm and bore my part in the prayer for their sake as much as hers. The priest kept the prayer going, over and over, and somehow or other, it built up, overwhelming the jeers and laughter, until it had won almost the whole crowd over and nearly everyone was taking part.

The cart was already under the gallows. The executioners shinnied up their ladders and fastened the ropes. The expressionless driver chirruped to his horses. I wondered what they thought of it all, those obedient, good-natured animals. Did they marvel, in their uncomplicated equine minds, at the way the human beings around them were chanting; did they sense the fear of those in the cart or the tangle of emotions—avidity, pity, horror—emanating from the crowd? If so, they didn't show it.

They had been taught to trust the two-legged creatures in charge of them, and so, dutifully, they plodded forward, pulling the cart out from under its passengers. Who died.

In nearly all cases, quickly. Hugh had paid the executioner originally to see that Gladys's end was not prolonged; a few moments ago, he had paid for the same service for those she left behind. Executioner and aide earned their bribe, moving rapidly along the line of frenziedly kicking legs, seizing one pair of ankles after another and giving the downward jerk that broke the victims' necks.

Even so, what they endured in the few seconds before they were granted oblivion, I don't want to imagine.

Then it was over. The last prayer ended and silence fell. Dale and I were crying, but noiselessly. Gladys was crying again too, but these were healthier tears, of pity and sorrow, which are honest things.

But when the crowd, its death-lust assuaged, at last began to disperse and we could move away, my legs felt like lead. And Gladys was a problem, for she could hardly walk at all.

31

Landslide

We could not think how to transport Gladys the half mile to the inn where we had left our horses. If my legs were like lead, Gladys's legs appeared to be made of tissue paper. They gave way if she walked even a few steps. "Brockley and I will just have to carry her," Hugh said.

We were assisted, however, by the royal messenger, who rode up to speak to us, observed the difficulty, and although clearly filled with distaste at the sight and smell of Gladys, agreed when I asked him to help by taking her up in front of his saddle. I wouldn't have dared to suggest such a thing, except that I recognized the man. For Gladys's sake, we had decided not to go home until all was over, but—because I had a faint if only a faint hope of influencing the queen in her favor—I had joined the court and attended Elizabeth for a while during her Progress through Hampshire. I had never been given a chance to revive the question of Gladys and this last-minute reprieve had astounded me. But in Hampshire, I had come to know some of her gentlemen pensioners by name. I addressed this one by his. "Master John Haywood, isn't it?"

"It is, and for you, Mistress Stannard," he said, "I will perform this service, but as soon as you can get this retainer of yours, if that is what she is, into a soapy bath, the better!"

"Contacts at court are so useful," Hugh observed, grinning at me, trying to lighten the air.

Hillman was remarking that he knew the inn to which we were going, and that horses could be hired there. "I want to hire one," he said. "I have lodgings in the City. I came on foot through London, with the Brockleys, but it's a long walk back. May I come with you?"

We set off at last, glad to have Master Haywood with us, because the throng had some respect for his livery. We saw unfriendly glances aimed at Gladys and it was possible that we might have had trouble had he not been there. She did, alas, look so very much like a witch.

As we went, thankful to leave the gallows tree and its pitiful fruit behind us, Hillman remarked: "Tomorrow, when Dean dies, it will be all over. I hear that the Scottish lords refused even to consider Mary Stuart's reinstatement and that Leicester has confessed his part to the queen and had a good cry in her lap . . ."

"All that's true," Haywood said. "It seems that you have other contacts at court besides myself."

"Yes, Cecil told us about Leicester. I wish I'd seen it," Hugh remarked. "As for Norfolk . . . !"

"He had a chance to confess and be forgiven, during the Progress," I said. Having been in Hampshire, I knew this part of the story firsthand. "Did you know about that, Master Hillman? Norfolk lost his nerve and fled, first to London, then back to Kenninghall, in Norfolk. He'd already tried to encourage the northern earls—Westmorland and Northumberland mostly—to gather their followers and be ready to rise on behalf of Mary and the Catholic religion, and then sent them messages warning them not to, but he didn't know what they'd decided to do and he was frightened. He was summoned back to court to explain himself and in the end, he sent really desperate messages north, telling the earls to stay at home and take matters no further, and then he set out for court—but he'd dithered too long."

We were beginning to leave the horror of Tyburn behind us. We at least had Gladys safe. We hadn't had to leave her in that dreadful place. "Norfolk started out from Kenninghall," I said, "but as soon as he came within reach, he was seized and taken to the Tower."

"Signor Ridolfi's in the Tower, too," Hugh added. "I am sorry for his wife; it must be unpleasant for her, marooned in a foreign land with her husband in prison. I take it that you're not still in the Ridolfi household, Master Hillman?"

"No, I left it in July. That man Walsingham wanted me to stay at first—he was very anxious for me to take up where my cousin Julius left off—but after Ridolfi was arrested, there was nothing to spy on and besides, as I said that day in Cecil's study, I don't want to be a spy! I'd be a very bad one. I was looking for another post, but as it happened, just then, my circumstances changed. My late father had a manor house and some land in Buckinghamshire, which my elder brother, William, inherited. But at the beginning of August, William died—unmarried and childless. I've lost my brother, but I'm now the proprietor of the house and lands."

"I'm sorry about your brother," I said. "I suppose the inheritance is welcome, though."

"Yes, it is. Mistress Stannard . . ."

"Yes, Master Hillman?"

"That day in Cecil's study—your daughter Meg was there. Margaret Stannard, that will be her full name?"

"No. Her full name is Margaret Blanchard," Hugh said. "I'm not her father."

"Her father was my first husband, Gerald Blanchard," I explained.

"I see. Well, it doesn't matter. May I ask—what plans have you in mind now for her?"

"Not marriage," I said. "Another year or two of study at home; a year at court. Then she will be seventeen and we can consider marriage plans for her again."

"I thought," said Hillman sincerely, "that she was beautiful, and wise beyond her years. I have never been so impressed by a young girl. If, when she is seventeen, I come to you and ask permission to pay court to her, will you agree?"

I looked at him, thinking once more what a very likeable young man he was. "In three years, you will meet other marriageable ladies, and perhaps you'll decide on one of them, instead," I said.

"Perhaps. But if I don't?"

"I think we might look on you favorably," Hugh said gravely.

"Provided you continue to keep away from plots and spying," I added, equally gravely.

He smiled at me. "Do you know, I think I can promise that," he said.

I said: "We shall have to find out what Meg thinks," but there was a warm certainty within me that Meg would like young Master Hillman, and that he might well be her future, and a happy one.

We reached the inn and collected our horses. We were returning to Cecil's house. Hillman arranged his hireling, remarking that he was in London to see the lawyer who was untangling some of his brother's affairs, and was staying at the tavern owned by the father of Bessie, whom Walt was to have married.

"She's getting over it," he said. "Her father has his eye on another match for her, a nephew of the landlord of the Green Dragon, where you stayed for a while, I believe. It may work out well. From all I've heard, Walt wasn't any kind of paragon. Keeping quiet about a murder so as to wring money out of the murderer! Good God! I wouldn't want a daughter of mine to marry anyone who did that. Bessie herself realizes it, I think. Though Walt didn't merit the way he was treated after death. Dean is an abominable man. I am so thankful to know that Meg is well out of it!"

"There," I said, "you have our most heartfelt agreement!"

We parted courteously, exchanging details of Hillman's home, and our addresses at Hawkswood and Withysham, so that the households could correspond in future.

We would remain with the Cecils until Gladys was fit to travel. Then we would leave for Hawkswood. "I'll be glad to go," I said to Hugh as we helped Gladys into the house. "I'm homesick."

"Ma'am," I said, kneeling.

I had once more been passed through Elizabeth's array of guards and gentlemen pensioners, to be led into her presence, eventually, by Master Haywood.

"We have been expecting you," Elizabeth said, and glanced at Haywood and the ladies who had been with her. "Leave us with Mistress Stannard," she added.

They went out. Elizabeth had received me in a private room once more, though seated in dignified fashion in a thronelike chair and formally dressed in her favorite white and silver, all glittering embroidery and wide-open ruff. Now, however, she leaned forward to take my elbows and lift me to my feet.

"We are private together at this moment," she said. "We may call each other sister."

"I always feel that that's presumptuous."

"Not with my permission and when no one else can hear, and no one hides behind screens or tapestries in *my* apartments," Elizabeth said. "I was spied on when I was only a princess, but not since I became a queen, believe me. I think I know why you have come."

"To thank you. For saving the life of Gladys Morgan."

"I understand," said Elizabeth, in playful mood, "that she is a truly dreadful old woman. Haywood says you virtually compelled him to carry her in front of his saddle and that he has had to burn the suit of clothes he was wearing and ask an apothecary to sell him a preparation to get the nits out of his hair."

"He may be telling the truth," I said reluctantly. I too had had to resort to an apothecary, for the same purpose, and I had thrown away the cloak I had been wearing on the day that Gladys was rescued.

"But you care for her," Elizabeth said. "And when you came before, to plead for her, you reminded me that she had been the victim of spite, and that I had commanded the law in order to break your marriage to Matthew de la Roche. I myself am very doubtful that the curses of foolish aged women can kill. There are sicknesses and accidents enough in this world to account for most deaths. I was troubled, Ursula; troubled that your Gladys was going to her death unjustly; that you were defending her not just because you love her but also because she was not a witch. I hoped the law would find the truth, but the law—is not like that. It can make errors. I know what it is to live in fear of errors on the part of those who are in power. I learned that when I was a princess—and was spied upon."

She left her thronelike seat and drew me to the window, to share its wide, cushioned bench with her. "I kept saying to myself: I cannot interfere with the law. In Hampshire, I turned aside whenever I saw that you wished to speak of her again. But time went by and the day of the execution came near. I had insisted that I should know when it was to be carried out. The night before . . ."

I said gently: "You didn't sleep?"

"Not for one moment. I kept wondering whether your Gladys was asleep in her prison, or lying open-eyed in the darkness, as I was doing, waiting for her last dawn to break. By the time dawn did break, I was exhausted and I still did not know what to do. I broke my fast. I walked in the open air. An ambassador sought an audience and I talked with him. And then I could bear it no more. I called a clerk; I dictated the pardon; I cut through the law as though it were soft butter and I a heated knife blade. I ordered Master Haywood onto his horse and hoped, in God's name, that he would reach Tyburn in time. He was just, barely, in time, I understand. He told me about it on his return. Then I summoned Cecil and instructed him to see to what other documents were required; to inform the court so that its records could be amended."

"Ma'am, I am so grateful."

"Call me sister."

"Yes, Sister." I told her how it had been from our point of view.

"The rope was already on her, then?"

"Almost. She was resisting, crying out . . ."

"All right. Tell me no more of it. At least I—and Haywood—moved quickly enough, though by a very narrow margin. And now, Ursula, what do you wish to do? To go home?"

"If you will permit. As soon as Gladys is well enough, that is. She is still very weak and shaken. I think," I said, "that she will be better behaved in the future. She had a fever for two days after we brought her back to Cecil's house, but it went down and now she is different, much changed, in fact—gentler, more amenable. And," I added, "much more willing to wash."

Elizabeth laughed. "I will miss you, Ursula, but if you wish to go home, I will not keep you. Go, when you are ready. I may call on you to join me for my next Progress, but otherwise, you are free."

Gladys gained strength, but slowly. Meanwhile, the news from the north was uncertain. Norfolk's first response from the Earls of Westmorland and Northumberland had been poor but all the same, he had stirred up a degree of unrest, and his panicky letters calling the scheme off hadn't quite succeeded in doing so.

However, the Earl of Sussex, the Lord President of the North, was in negotiation with the earls and reported that he thought the situation would quieten down. Everyone hoped he was right.

The weather turned raw and foggy as November got under way. Gladys was by this time just about capable of sitting on a donkey and we began to think of setting out for home, but then Dale, as so often, caught a cold. It was nearly the middle of the month before she was better and we were really ready to ride for home. We had started to pack on the day that Haywood arrived, once more as a royal messenger.

It was a summons from Queen Elizabeth, to the Cecils and to me and to Hugh, not to leave for Hawkswood or Withysham but to join her immediately, in the well-defended castle of Windsor. There was a separate letter for me.

"*. . . as my half sister, I look on you as precious and I feel responsible for your safety and that of your husband. I have also sent for your daughter and her gentlewoman to leave Hawkswood and come to Windsor. You may bring your Gladys and the Brockleys too. I ask you to set out forthwith. Make no delay.*"

That was the closing paragraph. In the first one, the letter explained the nature of the emergency. Norfolk, before his plots and schemes dissolved around him, had roused the Earls of

Westmorland and Northumberland far more thoroughly than anyone could have supposed. They had begun lukewarm and then, apparently, heated up. When he tried to countermand his request to them, it was already too late. Probably, they felt he had betrayed them; perhaps, having summoned their tenants and armed them, they felt they had gone too far to retreat.

Like Gladys with her curses, Norfolk had started something that was going to take a great deal of stopping. It was moving, like a landslide. Lord President Sussex had tried to halt it but in vain.

The northern earls were in arms and on the march. The first reports said their combined armies were fifteen thousand strong.